PRAISE FOR TAG

"Carrabis writes another Hero's Journey, this time with a faithful dog, a blind bear, and a deformed, mute child."

"Riveting and captivating!"

"Carrabis' sense of humor shines throughout. You can almost see him dropping breadcrumbs for the reader to follow. He's playing a game of *Tag* with the reader and is a master of the game."

"Carrabis weaves another multi-character tapestry with interesting plot lines and dialogue you can hear."

"Carrabis brings the Middle Ages to life."

"Imagine your favorite professor telling you insider stories from Medieval Europe. That's Carrabis' *Tag*."

"I want to ask Carrabis if he time-travels. *Tag* reads like an episode of 'You Are There.' It's more like something you're living through than reading in a book."

"I saw everything, I tasted the bread, I drank the ale, I worked the fields, I heard the bells, I tasted the mustard. Incredible!"

"*Tag*'s Verduan and Patreo are the Middle Ages' Holmes and Watson. Cadfael watch out!"

TAG

JOSEPH CARRABIS

NORTHERN LIGHTS PUBLISHING

ISBN 979-8-9878048-8-9

Library of Congress Control Number

Characters, events, places, and things described, depicted, or referred to in this work are fictitious. Any similarity to actual persons, events, places, or things is purely coincidental.

Editing by Jennifer Day, Susan Carrabis

Cover by John Bernard Scullin

http://skolenimation.com/

Book formatting by Jennifer Day

Printed and bound in the United States of America First printing July 2024

Published by Northern Lights Publishing www.northernlightspublishing.com

For Susan
(because everything should be)

And AJ
(who said I could)

Thanks to Jennifer "The Editress" Day for once again making my writing readable.

Thanks to Bob Merry and Dr. Francesca Failla for reading an early draft and making suggestions.

ALSO BY JOSEPH CARRABIS

AUTHOR'S FOREWORD

Tag grew out of short story first written in March 1994. The original idea came from apple harvesting in a Pick-Your-Own orchard. A little girl laughed at her reflection in an apple. She became upset because whoever was in the apple laughed back at her. She bit into her reflection to "teach 'em a lesson" then spit out the piece in her mouth.

That short story went through almost yearly revisions until I rewrote it as *Blood Magic,* and it appeared in WordCrafter Press' *Midnight Roost* Anthology (Oct 2023).

Even though completed and published as a short story, I felt there was more to the story. This novel is the result.

Enjoy.

TAG

We must welcome the future, remembering that soon it will be the past; and we must respect the past, knowing that once it was all that was humanly possible.
  - George Santayana

To appreciate what has happened, you will have to abandon cherished notions and open your mind.
  - Matt Ridley, Nature vs Nurture

To surrender to ignorance and call it God has always been premature, and it remains premature today.
  - Isaac Asimov

Everything we value is valuable because of how we experienced it.

SECTION 1
THE HAND

CHAPTER 1

Eric pulled Julia to him and swung his axe.

The witch screamed. Cartilage and ligaments trailed from her wrist. Veins and sinews dripped blood where Eric's axe severed her hand from her arm. She pulled back into the massive black oak's bole where she hid.

Her severed hand released its grip on young Julia's arm and fell onto the oak's trunk. It climbed towards the witch's den like a strangely shaped, five-legged insect.

A lightning bolt struck the oak. Heavy rains followed. The witch shrieked as the rain's pure water flooded the bole.

The hand grayed and steamed where each raindrop struck. The hand slowed its ascent and stopped as its flesh turned to stone, forever frozen to the oak's trunk, forever separate from the witch's screams.

Julia ran to the top of the hollow encircling the oak and its copse of trees. Rain drenched her simple blouse and skirt. She slapped her sleeves as if walking into a spider's web, as if beating out burning embers. Her hand rested on her full chest to calm her breathing, and her dark green eyes stared back into the hollow, to the witch imprisoned in the oak by the rain.

The witch fell quiet and returned Julia's gaze.

Eric, farmwork starting to fill his equally young frame, came up beside Julia and spun her to face him. "Julia! We have to go. Now! Julia! The witch's blood has blackened my axe and sleeves." He dropped his axe to the ground. "My hands burn." He held them out. White patches shone against his tanned skin where the witch's blood withered his flesh. He cupped rain in his palms and rinsed his hands the best he could.

Julia turned back towards the copse and spit at the witch. "What can she do now? She's powerless in the rain."

Eric spun her again. "I've cursed us both, you fool. She'll not rest until that hand has killed us both and it will take more than my axe to finish her. We must get back before the sun clears the skies. This is for Father Baillot and the elders to deal with, not me. Not us."

He grabbed her rain-soaked arm and pulled her after him.

CHAPTER 2

Father Baillot stood like a sapling grown too tall at the copse's rim. His cassock hung on him as if fitted to another man and flapped in the light breeze to reveal boots too fancy for a clergyman. He focused on the oak at the copse's center. Thomas and Byell, Julia's older brother and father and both as broad and dark as she was thin and fair, stood beside him in clothes stained with sap and dirt from orchards and fields. Thomas reached over to his father, removed a tick working its way into Byell's heavy beard and crushed it in his teeth. Byell nodded a thanks.

Baillot held his saturno in front of him, both hands on the brim, and turned it slowly as if turning some great wheel, as if each turn lifted some great sluicegate another finger's breadth to control some water's flow.

Eric came up beside them with his father, Verduan. Eric started down into the copse and Verduan, so tall and broad his friends jokingly asked if they could stand in his shade to cool themselves, gently placed a hand on his son's arm. Eric glanced up and Verduan quietly shook his head, no. Eric stayed and waited.

The dry breeze shifted and both turned to see leanly muscular Galos, his looks more suited to a hunter or tracker than the village charcoal burner he was and always quick with a smile and helping hand, approached. "Smelled me coming, did you?"

Verduan patted his old friend's back. "You carry the scent of smoke wherever you go, Friend. You'll never sneak up on your prey."

Eric chuckled. "Or that pretty potter."

Galos blushed.

Round, melancholy Tardiff the Bellman joined them a moment later with The Baron's boss adorning his shirt.

Eric pointed. "That's the oak, Tardiff. She climbed into the bole when I chopped off her hand."

Tardiff gazed into the copse. "What made you travel so far from the village, lad?"

"We looked for apple grafts. Our fields and orchards weaken and we hoped to find grafts or strong saplings here."

The ground steamed as the hot sun lifted fresh rain heavenward and everyone sweated freely. All the men save Father Baillot and Tardiff took off their shirts, rolled them tight, and tucked them into their belts.

Something rustled off the path they walked. The brush moved against the wind.

The men drew what weapons they had.

Verduan lifted his shepherd's crook in two hands and held it quarterstaff-style. "Who goes there? Show yourself?"

Buco, Verduan's half-wild dog and as big as a year-old calf, barked and ran into the brush. "Buco, no!"

A young boy, golden haired, simple faced, with a bent spine and dressed in loose fitting rags, shyly emerged from the bush, Buco at his side, his nose deep in the boy's pockets.

Byell sighed. "Ah, Nory. Does Dire know you travel so far from home?"

Nory smiled and came forward, a dog wanting petting.

Thomas spat. "Why do you treat him so, father? He brings no one any good."

"He's good enough."

Nory smiled.

Baillot Crossed the hollow and Nory with one motion. "He's the bastard she raises for company?"

Verduan ignored the priest and put his arm around the lad. "Simple Nory. You followed us?"

The boy smiled at the men gathered. He bowed and made an exaggerated Cross towards Baillot.

Galos took Nory's hand in a gentle grip. "Here, Nory. Stay with me. We'll get you home safe."

Nory gently took the charcoal burner's hand and kissed it. A sooty smudge marked his face. Eric gathered some drool from Nory's chin and wiped the soot away. "What have you been up to, Nory? Did you find good berries to eat?"

Nory rolled his eyes, patted his stomach, smacked his lips, and pointed deeper into the woods.

Eric rubbed Nory's back, careful not to press on the lump there. "Perhaps you can show us sometime. But not today."

Nory stepped past the rim in a straight line for the witch's oak.

Verduan hurried forward and held him back. "No, Nory." He turned the mute's face to meet his and shook his head. "No, Nory. Danger. Bad. Understand?"

Nory frowned at him. He turned towards the bole a second time.

Verduan held him more firmly. "Nory, no. Bad." He gently slapped the boy's hand. "Bad, Nory. Bad."

Nory continued to frown. He slowly pulled back his hand, looked from the bole to Verduan and the others, and shook his head.

Galos took the boy out of the way. "Good, Nory. That's right. Stay away. Good lad."

Verduan looked at the priest. "Father Baillot?"

Baillot, still at the rim, donned his saturno, lifted his cross and rosary as if they were battle shields, and descended into the hollow. "Come then."

Tardiff inspected the oak. "If the witch was here, she's gone now."

Eric pointed a second time. "She was there." He raised his hand. "My axe handle rots from her blood and my flesh burns where it touched. See?"

Verduan lowered Eric's hand. "No one here doubts you, son."

Tardiff inhaled deeply with his face just outside the bole then snapped back and exhaled sharply. He shook his head and waved his hands about him as if stormed by a cloud of gnats. His nose ran and he wiped it on his sleeve. "Probably died in there, by the smell of it."

Galos followed the others into the hollow. "Your axe, Eric. May I see it?"

Eric looked to his father and Verduan nodded. He held it out handle first. Galos inspected it under the bright sun. "The handle rots but the iron isn't touched."

Tardiff looked at the axe in Galos' hand. "Witches fear water and iron. Isn't that why the church uses holy water and iron crosses to divine them, Father Baillot?"

Baillot grunted. His deep-set brown eyes darted from axe to oak and back but never lingered.

Galos handed the axe back to Eric. "We'll need to fix this when we get back."

Baillot opened the phial, lifted it towards the tree, and splashed the contents on the tree. The holy water sizzled and foamed as if it burned the tree's flesh. Light gray smoke, bitter on the nose, rose.

Byell stepped back. "Holy Water, Father?"

Baillot's eyes widened on the trunk. "The Blood of Christ destroys The Enemy's power." Baillot's cassock snapped about his boots like a pack of hungry dogs as he turned and went up the rise.

Nory mimicked the priest's gait halfway up the rise and smiled as he trotted back to the men still by the oak. Those who didn't chuckle openly hid a laugh behind a hand.

Thomas pointed to a dark patch on the tree. "What is this?"

Galos sniffed where Thomas pointed, pulled back, and spit on the ground.

Tardiff's eyes focused on the patch. "Something?"

"Eric spoke the truth. See?"

The men gathered. Galos fingers prescribed a dark, stone-like mold, his finger always hovering above, never touching. "The outline of a long-fingered hand as it clawed its way to the bole."

Tardiff pointed at vines running from it down the trunk and into the earth. "And these. The sinews and cartilage of the severed hand? The hand climbed the tree to return to the witch, to her hiding, but the rains turned it to stone before it succeeded? Looks like it died with fingers outstretched, clinging to the tree in the hope she'd return."

Nory nodded, his brow furrowed, as if listening intently to help decide what to do. Galos reached into his pocket, pulled out a piece of bread and offered it to the boy. Nory kissed his hand, put the bread in his mouth, and ran off up the rise.

Verduan watched Nory's escape. "If the witch's hand could live for a while without her, can she live without it?"

Galos spoke in almost a whisper, his eyes distant and lost in memory. "You've never seen a man lose a hand or foot in the field? Or an arm if he holds a wilding horse's reins too dear? They live, but not well."

Tardiff agreed. "She'll live." He faced Eric. "And if she's truly a witch she'll grow another in its place. She'll remember you, Master Eric. You and Julia both."

Byell looked up the rise, scratched his beard, and snorted. "Baillot's already gone. Do we tell him?"

Verduan shook his head. "Have you ever seen a priest so ignorant of church ways?"

Tardiff continued his study of the mark on the tree. "The last witch hunter I knew was a Galatian, one of the Warrior-Priests. Aldous? But that was long ago."

Verduan nodded towards the north. "Father Verrett talked of a priest some days journey that way, beyond the Coranth Mountains but this side of the River Kashel. I don't know his name. Rumor is he's a good man." He looked at the ground, at the oak, and finally the men around him. "I leave tomorrow."

SECTION 11
VERDUAN OF NANT

CHAPTER 3

Father Patreo looked up from his workbench. Well-soled boots crunched dry earth as someone with a long stride made their way to his small cottage. A book lay opened at Patreo's side, the pages illuminated with strange beasts. He used a leather strip to mark his place and closed it. Gray, yellow, and ocher powders lay in separate, small piles on his workbench. He covered them with a white, muslin cloth.

He closed his eyes and focused on the footsteps.

Male. Heavy. Healthy heavy, not sickly heavy.

Patreo frowned. Most visitors to his cottage came sickly.

A horse clomped and cart wheels squeaked from the opposite direction. The footsteps, horse clomps, and squeaking cart wheels combined into a strange rhythm, music from an unknown land; step step clomp clomp squeak, step step clomp clomp squeak, step step clomp clomp squeak. It made an interesting contrast to the birds singing in his gardens.

Patreo glanced at the sunlight coming in his far window. He received word Baron Bassys' mistress would arrive soon. Rumors fly when others ride and run when others walk, and the rumor was she carried The Baron's child. Bassys wanted no bastards in his court hence she fled north, out of his holdings, to keep the child.

If she didn't reach him, The Baron would slaughter her before the child quickened.

He shuffled his stool to a clear space on his workbench. The stool's three legs screeched on the hard wood floor and he winced at the sound. Patreo's index finger tapped his lips as he considered what best to give the girl.

She couldn't show. If she did, Bassys would have slain her already. So three months? Four maybe?

And there were wisewomen and herbalists closer to the castle than he, so she meant to escape and keep the child. She didn't go east or south into Muslim lands, and to the west she'd be known, seen, so she heads north where she's not known but where Patreo the Tomekan will find a convent in which to hide her and the child.

A few taps later he pulled over his mortar and pestle and reached for red raspberry leaf. He crushed the herb by hand into a mortar then pestled it into a fine powder for a tea to prevent miscarriage. Satisfied, he next took ginger, sweet basil, and mint and did the same in a second mortar, this time mixed to prevent nausea should she need to travel hard and fast.

In all these, the cupping of the mortars and the turning of the pestles familiar, comforting motions, like the stars and planets, the sun and moon in their orbits. He would also teach her how to massage her hands, an old technique for quieting the stomach.

She and others came to him. Most for oils. Or ointments. An unguent. A balm. Something to ease a muscle or a joint, start a cycle too late in coming or end one gone on too long, relieve a cramp, ease a headache or sore. Some to stop a bleed or set a bone from some accident in the fields.

He checked the mortars and considered a sprig of spearmint

mixed with the red raspberry. No. A few more grinds and it would make a fine tea mixed with honey.

He frowned and raised his head. Step. Step. Clomp. No squeak. The music - the boots and horse and cart - stopped outside his gate. The birds quieted. The horse shied.

The boots' owner spoke softly. The horse quieted.

Voices. Low, careful greetings. One, the boots' owner, spoke with an accent from where? The south? Definitely from the other side of the Coranth.

The accented voice rose at the end, a question. Both voices, louder, each speaker's purpose understood and accepted by the other. The horse and cart clomped and squeaked on, the boots' owner spoke a quiet word as the boots turned towards Patreo's cottage.

Patreo rose to look out his near window. A tall, broad-shouldered, deep-chested man. Thick, black beard and unruly hair falling out from under a light brown, broad-brimmed hat. Good protection from the sun on roads and in fields. The man had bright specks of gray in his beard and hair like the twinkling of stars on a moonless night.

He looked back the way he came and nodded at each house he passed on his way.

Patreo cocked his head. He's counting the houses he's passed? He has numbers? Must be a herdsman. Has to keep track of his sheep or goats. And why count now when his question's been answered?

To remember. He plans to come again. Or in case he has to.

The man wore clean, well-stitched brown pants, and a rough cheesemaker's shirt, also clean and open at the neck revealing skin darkened by the sun. He carried a pack on his back and kept a good, stout shepherd's crook in his hand.

Patreo considered.

He works in the fields? Outside, in any case. And the crook carried like a staff? He doesn't limp. For protection, then?

The man wore black boots over his calves. The boots were scooped in back so his legs wouldn't catch.

Definitely someone who works. Someone used to bending his knees and doesn't want them pinched from behind. And who has money. Some anyway; his boots are well made. Perhaps a cattle-man? A dairyman?

The man pushed the gate open and walked the well-worn path through vegetable, flower, and herb gardens from lane to Patreo's door.

Patreo opened it as the man's knuckles came down to knock. The man's fist was clean and carried the scent of cattle, pigs, sheep, and dog, the latter strongest of them all. The scent of cattle, pigs, and dog would be gone with a good scouring. The smell of sheep stayed always.

The man held his fist motionless above Patreo's face.

"Do you mean to strike me or say hello?"

CHAPTER 4

The man lowered his fist. "Forgive me. I'm Verduan of Nant, and I have a story to tell you."

Patreo motioned Verduan inside. Verduan's eyes grew wide as he scanned Patreo's workbench with its balms and salves and powders, a cloth with something underneath, and distilling vessels all placed within easy reach, his shelves of open and stoppered flasks, drying herbs, books; Patreo's cottage held more of study than of sleep. His nose twitched at the pungent airs coming from Patreo's mortar and pestle and he focused his attention there.

"Nant. That's the most eastern town in the kingdom, isn't it?"

"Yes. You know of it? We are governed by Baron Bassys and through him by King Gaumand. But we are on the outskirts of the kingdom and little bothered by the royals or foreigners. We have little to offer either."

"What can I do for you, Verduan of Nant?"

"You are Father Patreo?"

"Patreo of Tomeka, yes. And anointed in the Scholastica Order, yes."

Verduan studied Patreo's workbench. "I'm sorry, Father. I don't know of it."

"One of the Benedictines." Patreo waved a hand over his workbench. "Does this disturb you?"

"I expected an older man. This is your rectory?"

"This is my home. Where I study."

"Where is your church?"

"I'm in disfavor with the bishopric." Patreo kept his eyes on Verduan's face. "At present."

Verduan glanced at him and went back to the jars and flasks and mortars and pestles on Patreo's workbench.

"Too much studying, they say."

Verduan looked up and met Patreo's gaze. He smiled weakly and swallowed.

"Perhaps some wine after your long journey." Patreo motioned to a stool in front of his workbench. "It must have taken you, what, seven days to get here?"

Verduan sat mechanically. "Five."

Patreo lifted a pitcher and poured wine into a goblet. He uncorked a flask on a shelf and dribbled some liquid into the goblet before handing it to Verduan.

The big man sipped. "Thank you." He swallowed a mouthful. "Your wine is good. Sweet. Flowery. Its taste is unfamiliar. What fruit bears this wine?" He downed a second mouthful.

"Poppy juice. To help you relax after your trip." Patreo held the uncorked flask under Verduan's nose. "What story hurries you from Nant to Tomeka in five days' time?"

Verduan let his pack slide from his shoulders and lowered his staff to the hard planked floor. "My son and a girl, his wife soon-to-be. They are cursed for chopping off a witch's hand."

Patreo reached for Verduan's goblet. "Tell me more." He refilled the goblet and handed it back.

Verduan continued, and Patreo looked up from his herbs and mortar when Verduan finished his story. "Why come to me?"

Verduan peeked into Patreo's mortar. He stared at the tools, medicines, powders, herbs, stones, phials, flasks, and decanters cluttering Patreo's workbench. "Are you an herbalist, Father?"

Patreo chuckled. "Do you know Greek? *Apothēkē*? Storehouse? More storehouse than anything else."

Verduan pointed to the three small mounds under the muslin. "What are those?"

"Are you always so inquisitive when seeking help, Verduan of Nant?"

"A little knowledge avoids much trouble, don't you think?"

Patreo smiled. "I do." He nodded towards the cloth. "Have you ever heard of Greek Fire?"

Verduan shook his head.

Patreo removed the cloth, took a pinch from the bluest pile, and placed it in front of Verduan. He took a smoldering ember from under one of the vessels on his workbench and touched the pinch. The pinch disappeared with a *shshsh*ing sound as a cloud of bluish smoke rose rapidly from where it lay. He took a pinch from the yellow pile, dabbed some water on it, and touched the ember to it.

It crackled and popped like fat-soaked tinder. A darker smoke rose and smelled of rotten eggs. Finally, the yellow pinch burned and floated. The water didn't put it out.

Patreo returned the muslin cloth to its place.

"What about the gray pile?"

"It's not ready yet. It may never be." He opened the book on his workbench and pointed at the leather strip marking a passage there. "This book is a translation of a translation, the original language lost or forgotten. So I experiment and go slowly. No errors that way." Patreo closed the book. "Any other questions, Verduan of Nant?"

Verduan sat back and shook his head.

"Then my question remains: why come to me?"

Verduan sipped his wine. "Our priest is new to us. We...some of us...we..."

"Nant has a new priest? I thought Father Verrett served Nant and the villages around."

"Father Verrett served our village and others for more than fifty years. You knew him?"

"How long has the new priest been with you?"

"Less than a year. He came to us with the bishopric's seal. The new priest is Father Baillot. Do you know him?"

Patreo squinted into the distance. "Knowledgeable on doctrine? Ecclesiastics? That him?"

Verduan shrugged. "It is not difficult to be more knowledgeable than simple farmers."

"Even the inquisitive ones?"

Verduan spoke over his cup. "I'm sure Father Baillot wishes I asked fewer questions." He sipped. The wine made it easier to tell his story. "We sought someone...with a broader knowledge." Verduan waited until Patreo looked him eye-to-eye. "A knowledge of oak and ash as well as line and verse."

"You traveled alone five hard days through woods and mountains, come to my door, and now wonder if my knowledge is greater than you care to know?"

"I traveled five hard days from Nant to Tomeka because in Nant I heard of a priest with knowledge of The Old Ways on this side of the Kashel. In each village along the way I asked if any knew of such a priest. That eventually got me to Catiorec where they mentioned a Father Patreo in Tomeka. Here I asked about you and they said you knew the ways of herbs and roots, metals and waters. Outside, the Burger on the cart said yes, this was Father Patreo's cottage, and that you cured his son."

"You are a tracker, Verduan of Nant?"

"A herdsman. With fields and orchards."

"You are wise."

"I am old."

"Not so old to travel here alone in five days' time!"

"I did not travel alone." Verduan let go a piercing whistle and Patreo covered his ears at the sound. A great white and black shape leapt his gate and cleared the window in two bounds.

Patreo laughed. "A horse? No, a dog." The dog lumbered over, lapped Patreo's offered hand, and rested its head on Patreo's lap. Patreo patted its head and scratched the heavily furred ears. "And who is this - " he leaned over and looked between the dog's legs " - handsome fellow? Your familiar?"

Verduan patted his thigh. "Buco, here."

The big dog sat licking Patreo hand.

"If he's a familiar you're the witch. He never takes to people like that. He's still wary of Father Baillot and has known him a year at least. How did you get him to take to you so?"

"I heard you talk quietly outside. Once when you stilled the shying horse, the other before you entered. I guessed you had a companion and not a child. No one leaves a child unguarded in a new village and you don't seem the type to take a child on the trek from Nant to here. Only a fool would drive a herd that far, so a dog, and its scent is fresh on your clothes, so it was close by. As for why it favors me..." Patreo chuckled. "I greased the back of my hand with pig tallow when you tipped back your wine."

Verduan's hand slapped the workbench and he bellowed with laughter. He drained his cup and rose. "Tell me, Father, have I come to the wrong man?"

Patreo motioned Verduan back onto the stool. He lifted a roped bucket. "Water from my own well. Boiled and cooled. May Buco drink?"

"Why boiled and cooled?"

"Something learned in my travels in Muslim lands. An easy precaution against dark spirits in the water."

Verduan's brow rose as he looked at the water in the bucket. "Thirsty, Buco?"

The dog wagged its tail. Patreo placed the water beside Verduan and the dog lapped. They both watched the dog drink its fill.

Patreo took his stool on the far side of his workbench. "Tell me, does this witch have a name?"

"We know her as Sullya. Sullya the Witch."

Patreo frowned. "Sullya? My mother told stories of Sullya the Witch when I was a child, something to keep me quiet at night. This can't be the same Sullya. She'd be ancient now."

"Do witches truly die?"

"Is there more to your story?"

Verduan stared into his empty cup. "Is there more wine on your shelf?"

Patreo placed the pitcher on the workbench in front of Verduan who refilled his goblet. Buco pawed some straw together, circled, lay down, closed his eyes and slept.

Verduan smiled at his dog and continued his tale.

Patreo listened and nodded, hands together, fingers loosely intertwined and steepled, his nose hidden, eyes slightly obscured and closed as if he slept while Verduan told his tale.

When the big man finished, Patreo looked up and tapped his lips lightly. "Do you know the bishopric wishes me transitioned to a far western parish? Preferably one of the church capitals. He worries about the influence of these small townships on me."

Verduan hesitated. "I can see you have much on your mind, Father." He reached down for his staff. "I thank you for your time."

Patreo looked down, his eyes roved from one experiment to another over the surface of his workbench. "I'm not in favor of the transition. The bishopric wishes me away from his churches and to be someone else's problem."

Verduan shrugged. "Holy Mother Church knows what's best."

"*D'accord.*"

"Latin?"

"French. 'But of course'. I suspect he worries more about my influence on his churches than of their influence on me. Too forward thinking, perhaps. Or not forward thinking enough."

Verduan rose and gently nudged Buco with his boot. The big dog opened and eye, yawned, rolled on its back, lolled its tongue, and offered belly. Verduan frowned. "You're an educated man, Father, and I can see you're busy with other matters. Sorry to have troubled you with this."

Patreo motioned him back down. "Sit. You and Buco have travelled hard and deserve a decent meal and a warm bed. Besides, it's because I'm educated I must stay and help the townships." He waved at his cluttered workbench. "I'm learned in both the old ways and holy doctrine. That's too good a combination to waste on politics, especially church politics where the Old will forever war with the New."

SECTION III
FORGERON THE TINKER

CHAPTER 5

Forgeron pulled his two wheeled handcart behind him. Pots, pans, knives, kitchen utensils, and tools swung on cords on the inner and outer walls of the cart's shed-like compartment and made a jingling clatter as he walked. His green felt hat's broad brim was pulled low, covered his ears and flopped over his eyes with each step like a puppy dog's ears. He turned his cart's pull-shafts and legs swung down. He lowered the shafts until the legs touched the ground. After stretching and rubbing his shoulders and arms, he pushed his hat back a bit to unshadow his eyes, frowned, and scratched his unruly beard.

Breakfast smells came on the wind. He wiped sweat from his brow and his frown turned into a smile.

"Metal working!" he called out as he neared some cottages.

No doors opened, no shutters moved. "Smithing, Repairs to any and all." He passed one house with chickens roosting in its thatched roof and shook his head. "They'll lose their eggs that way." He raised his voice in song, "Blades sharpened, knives and axes all, test them on some good sausage to prove their edge."

Laughter and a deep throated dog's bark came from the next cottage.

He sang out, "Eggs taste better when fired on iron."

The door opened and a tall, broad-shouldered man with a thick black beard came out. "You've not had breakfast?" A huge dog barrelled past the man and ran out to the tinker. The man called, "Buco, come!"

The dog paid no mind. It approached the tinker, tail down, ears back, sniffed but didn't growl.

The tinker lowered himself to one knee and held out a hand, palm up.

The dog wagged its tail slightly and lifted its ears.

The tinker laughed. "So far so good. You're Buco, eh? Let's seal our friendship with a gift." He reached into a pocket and pulled out a small, thin, strip of dried beef. Buco's ears came up, his tongue came out, and he snatched the beef from the tinker's hand.

The man nodded. "He'll come back for more if you treat him like that."

"Well, at least he didn't piss on me. So far, we're equals." Forgeron patted the dog's massive head. Buco swallowed and looked up at him. "That's it, Buco. That's all I have."

Buco nuzzled the tinker's pocket and the tinker pulled out another strip.

The man shook his head. "Told you."

The tinker gave the strip to Buco. "That's it. I swear, Dog. Or my mother take me for a liar."

Buco trotted towards Verduan's barn.

The tinker pulled a rag from his pocket and took a moment wiping the dog's drool off his hand. "I suppose I needed a wash after my journey." The tinker smiled at the man. "I am a traveler, a peddler, a worker in metals and ores am I, your Lordship, with no one to feed me - "

The man laughed deep in his chest and finished the tinker's lament. "Except these two arms and legs. Yes, I've heard it before."

"Do you need something repaired? Something made? Perhaps something to amuse good Buco here?"

"Buco favors you and he doesn't favor many, so there might be work for you." The man's tone turned serious. "My son's axe. The shaft rotted and the head won't accept another. If you can't mend it, can you make him another?"

"The head won't accept another shaft?"

The man scratched his beard before answering. "Do you believe in witches?"

"I've known some women..." The tinker let the statement hang.

Verduan laughed again. "Breakfast for a new shaft?"

"For a new shaft. Hickory or ash. If that won't take, we can talk some more."

Buco returned from the barn, barked, lolled his tongue out of his mouth, and pranced in front of Forgeron.

"And something for Buco because he favors me."

Verduan offered his hand. "I am Verduan. You'll find both a'plenty in a copse the other side of town. They say a witch, Sullya by name, lives there."

"I am Forgeron, and if she's got firm breasts and a round bottom, she's bewitched me already."

Verduan repeated the Tinker's name as if savoring a strange spice on his tongue. "Forgeron? You're not from these regions?"

Forgeron opened the back of his cart and laid out some tools. "Aye, Brother. Not from these regions. Do you still have the head and shaft?"

Verduan came back with a well-handled shaft ending in an odd, brownish rot, and an iron axe head, dull colored but otherwise unmarked.

"What happened to these? You mentioned a witch?"

"My son cut off a witch's hand to save his girl from her fate. The witch's blood stained the blade and rotted the shaft."

Forgeron sniffed them, spit on them, sniffed each again and held first the shaft then the head up to the morning sun.

Verduan watched. "A tinker's incantation against evil?"

Forgeron shook his head. "Curious what kind of witch's blood rots wood and tarnishes iron."

CHAPTER 6

Forgeron stood at the rim of the hollow, adjusted a small axe in his belt, and watched Father Baillot. The priest, oblivious of his approach, held his face close to the hand-shaped growth on the witch's oak. Forgeron couldn't tell if Baillot kissed it, sniffed it, or cursed it. Baillot's words came to him when the slight breeze stopped rustling leaves and vines, and he turned an ear towards the priest to hear better.

Baillot murmured something Forgeron couldn't make out. He took a phial from his belt and sprinkled its contents on the oak.

Holy Water? But he's not making the Sign of the Cross?

Forgeron remained silent as Baillot stood back from the tree. The priest murmured something, touched where the water fell upon the tree, and pulled his hand back quickly. He waved his fingers in the air as if cooling them from a sudden burn then wiped them on his cassock. Forgeron moved back into the under-brush and lowered himself to the ground. He picked up a dried twig and cracked it.

Baillot spun and his eyes searched the entirety of the hollow's rim. They moved past Forgeron without stopping. He smoothed the folds of his cassock, straightened his Crucifix and saturno, and walked up the rim past Forgeron without noticing him.

Forgeron remained hidden until he no longer heard Baillot's steps or voice then ventured into the hollow. At the oak, he turned and scanned the rim roundabout. Satisfied he was alone, he focused on the patch of oak bark which held Baillot's attention so intently. "What is it you hold so dear, Good Father?"

The breeze shifted slightly and Forgeron's eyes opened wide when he caught a sniff of the bole. He loosened a cord keeping a wineskin close to his side. A small pocket lay flush on the side of the wineskin which rested against him. He opened it.

Eric entered his home to see his father frowning as he made ledger marks in his book, a prized possession. "Is everything alright, Father?"

Verduan looked up. He hoped to give his son a good start in life. A piece of land, a small herd, enough acreage to feed the animals and provide for the home. He planned on working with him, making sure Eric would do well. Eventually to give him everything, this cottage and its outbuildings even, and spend his days bouncing grandchildren on his knee.

Now?

Now.

"Everything's fine, Eric. Just fine."

"I saw a tinker's cart outside."

"Yes, a foreigner, I think. Forgeron by name. A metalsmith. I gave him breakfast and he's off to find some good stock for your axe."

"He leaves his cart unattended?"

"Buco's sleeping in the back of it."

"Buco sleeps in a stranger's cart? He makes friends faster than I do."

Verduan smiled at his son's joke. "Yes." He closed his ledger and rubbed his eyes.

"Is something troubling you, Father?"

Verduan blinked, focused on his son, and forced a smile. "No, nothing. Just hoping that Tomekan priest will show up and help us deal with..."

"I've brought us trouble, haven't I?"

Verduan placed his ledger on his shelf. "No, and I won't hear such talk."

"Admit I've been a vexation since my birth, Father. Mother died having me."

Verduan turned slowly to face his son. He placed his hands on Eric's shoulders. "Look at me, Eric."

The boy kept his eyes upon the floor.

"Eric, look at your father."

The boy raised his gaze. Verduan wiped Eric's cheeks with his thumbs. "You are my son. And you bring me honor by being my son. Your mother died so I could have you, and the love I have for her I have for you. Have I ever done anything to make you believe differently?"

Eric shook his head then looked up at his father. "I'll make you proud of me, father."

"I am proud of you already."

"You paid Father Verrett to teach me letters and numbers. What has that learning got me? Thomas doesn't know how to read or write, he has no numbers, and he already has his own fields."

"Thomas is five years older than you and grew up harder than you."

Eric looked down again. "Because of Byell?"

"Because of many things."

"You don't like Byell, Father?"

"I like him well enough."

"Thomas isn't like Byell."

"Thomas hasn't yet become a man and I doubt he'll become one. No Nant girl stays long with him."

"Would you rather I court another?"

"Julia's a fine girl, Eric. Have I ever led you to think otherwise?"

"She doesn't..."

"And proof she's a fine girl, that." Verduan gently turned his son towards their door. "Come, let's wake Buco and see to our fields. I gave the Tinker your axe head and he'll fix it if he can." He guided his son out. "Go get Buco. I'll be out in a minute."

Verduan waited until he heard Eric play with the big dog. He took his ledger down from the shelf, opened it, tore out the last page he entered and stuffed it in his pocket. "Something for Galos' fire, this."

Forgeron lay down his wineskin, reached into his shirt and pulled out a pig's gut tube stitched on one end and tied on the other. He untied it and squeezed. A waxy white substance came forth. He dabbed his finger in it and smeared it on his upper lip.

He leaned towards the bole and wafted some air out of it towards his face and sniffed experimentally. Satisfied, he pulled a tinderbox from a pocket, gathered some dead twigs, lit them, and stuck them in the bole.

He peered in and stood with his head in the bole for a few moments. He doubled the twigs over and let them catch until the flames closed on his hand. The burning twigs went into the bole and he peered in as they started to fall.

They burnt out before they stopped falling but he got a good look at what they passed on their way down. "A ladder? Sullya, you clever witch. You planned your escape well."

His attention returned to the oak's bark and he focused on what held Baillot's gaze. The witch's hand caught his eye. He lifted his wineskin and pulled a small mirror and a curved piece of glass from the pocket.

The mirror he used to aim the sun's light on the hand, the glass he held slightly above until the magnified image shone clearly. He pulled back and frowned. He touched the hand lightly and it left a gray powder on the tip of his fingers. "Could it be?"

He opened a pocket on the bottom of his wineskin, pulled out a smaller skin full of water, and sprinkled a few drops onto the witch's hand. It steamed and dissolved. He touched the moist surface gingerly and quickly pulled his hand back, poured water over his fingertips, and shook the moisture from it.

"Quicklime? To dissolve the flesh? You are a strange witch, Sullya. If witch you are."

CHAPTER 7

Julia watched her mother shape two loaves of bread. "Take these to Zevke. Here's a copper for his ovens."

Julia put the two loaves on a handled, wooden tray, placed a cloth over them, and walked to her family's gate. She stopped, her hand on the latch, at the sounds of rich baritone singing and metal jangling.

Forgeron came around the corner. Tools hung from the sides of his cart and bumped and jostled each other like busy neighbors on a fairground. "Hello, Good Woman of the House."

Julia blushed. "I am not the Woman of the House."

"Don't fool an old man, Good Woman. Someone of your beauty, your wisdom, your delicious loaves of bread."

"They're not baked yet."

"Two loaves of soon to be delicious bread."

"You're funny."

"So if you're not the Woman of the House, may a humble Traveler know your name?"

"Julia. My mother's inside. Do you want me to fetch her?"

"Oh, please. But first, you're Eric's friend?"

Julia blushed again. "Yes."

"Oh, I think there's more than friendship there. No hope for a lonesome Traveler, then?"

"You're funny."

Julia's mother opened the door. "Who are you? What do you want?"

"He knows Eric, Mother."

"I breakfasted with Verduan and did some work for him. You would be Idee? He said you might have some pots needed mending."

Idee moved between Julia and the gate and crossed her arms over an ample bosom. "And what's your price?"

Forgeron laughed. "Good Mother, I'm too old to care about such things."

"No man is that old."

Forgeron raised his hand in protest. "Madam, I mean no harm. Work comes easier when I make people smile and laugh, that's all. My price is a meal and some coppers. If not both, a silver will do. If I trouble, you, I'll walk on and we'll both be the wiser."

"Bring those loaves to the baker, girl."

Julia hurried past Forgeron, her eyes focused on the road before her. She didn't hide a smile as she walked past him.

Forgeron watched her go. "So Zevke's the village baker? Might he need some metalsmithing? Perhaps a bellows for his ovens? Maybe - "

"Eyes forward, Master Tinker."

Forgeron's head turned slowly until his eyes rested on Idee. He smiled. "Only following her path so I'll know where the baker lies."

"I have two pots that've seen better days. There's leeks and garlic for cooking. One copper."

"Can you spare some conversation while I work as well? Surely there's no charge for conversation?"

Idee went back into her house and came out with two pots needing hammering and rebrazing. "I have work to do, but I'll talk a bit to suit you."

~

Julia strolled through Nant and flirted with the few men she met who weren't in their fields. Galos the charcoal burner cocked his head and smiled but only on one side of his mouth. "Young lady, shame on you for teasing an old man's heart. Aren't you spoken for? Isn't Eric to be your husband?"

She pouted coquettishly. "Eric's a boy." Her smile returned. She swayed the loaves and tray on her hip from side to side. "And Master Eric hasn't asked me yet." Her free hand adjusted her barbette so her hair caught the sun.

Galos laughed. "Don't advertise what's not for sale, girl."

She frowned, her coquettish nature quickly replaced by confusion. "What do you mean?"

He held sooty hands up, palms out, and laughed again as he walked on. "Ask your mother, Julia, ask your mother."

Julia harrumphed and continued on her way, her lips clamped shut against her thoughts, her jaw thrust forward like the vane of a windmill.

A few streets later she stood before Zevke's ovens. "Julia! Loaves for me to bake?"

She handed him the tray and held the copper out to him.

"Is all well with you, Julia? You seem..."

"Do you think I'm pretty?"

Zevke blinked. His jaw worked but his lips kept shut. "Well, of course. You're a beautiful young lady, Julia. What makes you ask such things?"

"What does it mean to advertise what you don't sell?"

Zevke bowed his head and cocked it, his eyes on Julia's frown and darting eyes. "Julia, I - ?"

Saida, Zevke's wife, middle-aged and matronly with comely homespun blouse and skirt covered in an old miller's apron, came out of their house with a moist towel in her hand. She brushed back long, black hair and wiped the surface of the loaves so they'd develop a hard crust and shiny surface while they baked. "It means don't flirt unless you plan on making good your offer."

Julia's face reddened. She turned and walked away so quickly her skirts rose dust devils in her wake.

Saida's darkly brown eyes watched Julia move off, her arms swinging in small arcs at her sides and her fists tightly clenched. "Trouble, that one."

Zevke shrugged and put the loaves in an oven. "Confused, more likely."

Saida shook her head. "No, trouble."

Forgeron burnished one of Idee's pots in a bellows-fed fire off the back of his cart, then held it up to the morning light. "What do you think, Woman of the House?"

She reached out for it and he pulled it back. "Not yet, Good Mother. This needs to cool first."

"Why not dip it in water? I can get you a bucket from our well, and we have ducts bringing water from the Vell. We are not in short supply." She turned towards her cottage.

"You have ducts? To bring water from the river? How is it pumped?"

She smiled coyly. "Not pumped. Our charcoal burner, Galos, showed us how to build a series of water steps. The river pushes the water up so far, it fills a trough, when the trough fills enough it spills into another duct and so on until it waters our fields."

"Galos?"

"You'll meet him if you stay in town long enough."

"I wish I could. My work calls me elsewhere sooner than I'd like."

"You're a tinker. You go where there's work to be had, don't you?"

"I passed some fields outside Nant's center on my way into town. Do the ducts feed those fields as well?"

Idee nodded and held out a second pot.

"But those fields don't look well fed."

"It is the witch, Sullya. She cursed us with a summer of heat. The last rain we had drove her into her lair."

"The oak in the hollow off the south road out of town?"

"You've been there?"

"Only to fetch some hickory to repair Master Eric's axe."

"So you know the evil he's brought down on us."

He tested the temperature of the pot he held, nodded, and swapped with her. "I know successful tinkers listen more than they talk."

"Oh, you can tell me what you know. Eric's to marry my Julia, you know. The one your eyes followed as she walked away with bread for the baking."

Forgeron made no attempt to hide his admiration of Idee. "She takes after her mother."

Idee inspected the freshly burnished pot while Forgeron turned the other over in his hand. "You may have a woman in every town, tinker, but you'll not have one here."

"Ah, Good Woman, the only woman I have in every town is Mother Church."

Idee laughed.

"Oh, 'tis true, Lady Idee. I had a love long ago but the church called me away, never to return."

"You're a tinker. You go where you want."

He smiled, his eyes on the pot as he took a firm brush to it. "Aye. I go where I'm needed."

"Needed?"

"My nose tells me where there's pots needing mending, metalwork wanting to be done."

"Smart nose."

"And when to keep out of other's business."

"A tinker without gossip?"

"Oh, no. Everyone's secrets are safe with me." He looked up, caught her eye and winked. "Of course, if you have secrets for the telling, as I said, a successful tinker listens more than he talks."

She laughed.

"So tell me about your priest, then. Baillot? He's not been here long, has he?"

Forgeron worked while she talked. When she asked a question, he answered with a question leading to another. He talked freely of the weather - too hot for too long and no rain since the witch fell - villages he'd traveled through - there's not much work in the east and this cart's too heavy to bring over the mountains. He travels a circuit starting at King Gaumand's castle and eventually working his way back to replenish his supplies in the city - and who else might need metal-work.

The conversation stilled for a moment and she asked, "What can you tell me of Eric's axe. It is cursed, isn't it? With witch's blood?"

He pumped his forge and turned her pot in his hand. "Master Eric's axe. There was an evil upon it, that is true. Witch's blood? That I don't know. Metalsmithing is both science and art, old and new. I used both to mend it."

She stepped forward, rearing over him as he worked, and wrinkled her nose.

"Forgive me, mother. I've worked a hot forge today and grown use to my own richness."

"Richness, is it?"

He laughed, took a rag from his cart, dipped it in the water used to cool his firings, and wiped it up and under his shirt, across his neck, and over his face.

"Eric's axe. It was a challenge to mend?"

He handed her the finished pot. "If I say yes, I confess I'm not a good tinker. If I say no, I admit too much pride in my work. Would you have me an idiot or a fool?"

She clapped her hands and laughed. "Nant already has one of each, a dumb, misshapen boy the former and an undersheriff who's only use is to ring a bell the latter."

He laughed with her. "I hope to meet both. Now, good woman, I'll take that copper you offered and be off."

CHAPTER 8

Forgeron pulled his cart down a lane. He followed a sweet voice singing until he stood outside a cottage needing thatching. A pile of wood stood to the left of the door, to the right, on a crude bench, pots, plates, and mugs, each beautifully painted, waited to be picked up.

The singing paused and Forgeron called out. "Hello to Haasel the Potter."

A svelte young woman, her eyes white with cataracts, her sleeves rolled up revealing muscular forearms and her hands reddened with mason's clay, opened the door. She held a cane in her left hand and reached out with her right. "That's a new voice. Who calls me?"

"Forgeron, Lady of the Clays. A tinker, a metalworker. Perhaps the wheels of your stone need smoothing? Perhaps an axe for your wood needs sharpening? Your roof's letting light through. Perhaps rain and soon snow? I can thatch if there's no metalwork to be done. I - "

"Enough, Tinker Forgeron. What is your price?"

"A copper for each deed done and something to drink or eat. A

"

silver if there's no food or drink to be had. Good conversation always brings the price down. A tinker often walks alone. Pleasant talk with a pretty lady is valued highly."

She moved towards his voice and held her right hand out. "Come here. Let me see you."

"M'lady?"

"I want to see your face. With my hands. You can tell a lot from a man's breath on your palm, the width and straightness of the nose tells you if they've lived a life of pain. A cut in the ear, perhaps covered by a hat, tells you they're someone's servant run away, or a soldier no longer under oath. The creases of the face tell if the person laughs more than cries, and often why. A strong smile, good health. A weak smile, illness, perhaps someone to keep at a distance. The - "

"Enough, M'lady. Enough. You see well for one without eyes."

"Will you let me see your face?"

Forgeron lifted his cart handles. "I'd rather not, M'lady. I bear too many scars. My features would wound your delicate hands."

She held her cane in both hands, diagonally crossing her body, and planted her feet firmly. She moved her head slightly to let each ear hear the sounds he made. "Then move on, please."

Forgeron turned his cart back down the lane. "As you wish, M'lady Potter."

When he reached the corner where the Potter's lane met Nant's main road, he stopped to consider his next direction.

Haasel the Potter called out. "Move on, Tinker. Either direction, I don't care. But don't tarry here, not near me."

Forgeron turned his cart south and whispered, "Yes, M'lady. Yes."

The Potter stood still, her body tense, her ears focused on the retreating Tinker. A light breeze rolled down the street and rustled her skirts.

She spun. "Galos?"

He came around a corner of the lane and her blind eyes stared straight at him. "Speak, Charcoal Burner. Your fires stay on your clothes. I know you're there." She held her cane in both hands, opposing grips, in front of her.

Galos walked up and held his hand out, close to her face, as if letting a dog pick up his scent. "Aye, Haasel, it's Galos."

She pushed his hand away. "No need for that. You need to walk downwind of me or wash the soot from your hands and clothes. And even then I'd know your voice, your laugh."

Suddenly he grabbed her cane by one end. Her free hand claimed the other end. She let him keep his grip and whapped his knees. She trapped his hand, turned, and twisted the cane over her head. He flipped over her, landed flat on his back in front of her, and laughed. "Ow! You hold your cane well. Good girl."

She relaxed and let her cane touch the ground. "I had a good teacher." She offered him her hand. He rose and dusted himself off. "Have you met the tinker, Forgeron, making his way through the village?"

"What did the Tinker want?"

"Work, he said."

"You think he wanted more?"

She swayed slightly, a pendulum swinging between answers like hours on a clock. Seconds passed before she spoke. "You do not trust him, Master Charcoal Burner?"

"I do not know him. There's a difference."

"Are you following him?"

"Should I be? Me thinks you know me too well, Mistress Potter." He gently took her hand and guided it to his face so she could feel his smile. "You know me too well."

"I would know you better, if you're willing."

"The scent of charcoal doesn't offend you, Mistress Potter?"

"You do not offend me, Master Charcoal Burner." She stroked his rough beard, her fingers brushing over the scars hidden underneath.

He gently pulled her hand away. "I would not have you suffer such ugliness, Mistress Potter."

"I would gladly caress such beauty, Master Charcoal Burner."

Galos took her hand, kissed the palm, and returned it to her. "I know, Mistress Potter. I know."

CHAPTER 9

Finding Zevke the Baker required little effort. The smell of fresh loaves and rising smoke made the path obvious through the village streets.

Forgeron pulled his cart up to a clay house with ovens like large honey hives on either side and facing the street. A heavy man in dark boots, dark blue linen pants, shirtless but with an apron running from hair-covered chest and shoulders to the top of his boots and tied in back, moved back and forth between the ovens.

Nory came out of the house with a piece of fresh bread in his hand. Zevke handed him a dried block of wood and pointed to a fire at the bottom of an oven. "Careful, Nory. Place the wood, be gentle and quick."

Nory shoved the bread into his mouth, did as he was told, then wandered off down the lane.

Saida came out of the Baker's house carrying a basket of loaves fresh from the ovens. She smiled at Zevke then noticed Forgeron and quickly covered her head. She bowed and walked hurriedly away. Forgeron's eyes followed. He turned back to the Baker and smiled.

Zevke scowled at him. "My wife, Saida."

"A noble woman."

"A taken woman."

"Friend Baker, I admire beauty. I do not covet it nor am I jealous of those who have it."

"You're the Tinker's making his way through Nant?"

Forgeron walked over to the house's door, his eyes fixed on some small marks, unique but hidden among many scratches on the lintel. He kissed his fingers then touched them to the scratch.

Zevke's eyes narrowed. "You are not a common tinker."

"I have traveled some. Do you need any metalworking done? A bellows repaired, perhaps? An axe sharpened to better cut wood? A maul reshaped? Some wedges cleaved?"

"And what's your price for such work?"

"The lad thinks highly of your bread. Perhaps a loaf and some coppers? And conversation, if you're willing."

Zevke gazed in the direction Nory went. "He's a good lad, that one. Simple. Some say cursed, a halfling for those who believe such things."

"He has no family?"

"An old woman, Nant's midwife and herbalist, Dire by name, cares for him. He is often with her, running errands, gathering herbs and roots, beside her when she cares for someone, bringing her what she needs."

"A midwife and herbalist. I doubt she'd need my wheel or hammer. Where does the Good Woman Dire live?"

"No one knows. She comes and goes as she's needed. How she knows when someone's in need, we can guess. Perhaps she's a witch herself? She can be gone days at a time and no one knows where she travels. Gathering herbs for her nostrums, probably."

"And what of Nory when she's not to be found?"

Zevke considered the tinker. "You ask a lot of questions for a tinker."

"Just making conversation until I either find a need for my skills or know it's time to move on. Is it time for me to move on?"

Zevke shook his head, no. "It is part of the tinker's craft to talk, I know. Bakers do much the same until townsfolk know their bread goes down well with a stew or wine. Set your wheel turning, tinker, and we can talk some more."

Forgeron lifted a heavy grinding wheel and its brace from his cart. He sat on the edge of his cart, turned the wheel and kept the motion going with a foot pedal. "Good Woman Dire doesn't believe Nory cursed?"

"Dire's too old to care about curses. One day she carried Nory bundled in her arms. Idee was suckling her own and had milk to spare, Dire was to get two baskets of vegetables from her garden but hadn't yet collected, so a deal was struck." His eyes turned back to Forgeron. "But that was years ago. Dire was old then and is older now. Her ears betray her and her eyes sometimes dim, but she's still quick when there's a need, and what she cannot do the good people of Nant do for her, as far as Nory goes."

"You gave him bread for throwing some wood on your fire. You see to his needs?"

"A helpful lad, but you have to watch him. He can't remember fire burns." The baker shrugged massive shoulders and pulled a hand axe from his belt. "We can start with this. Let me test the edge when you're done and we'll see if there's more."

Tardiff the Bellman shadowed his eyes and gazed out over Nant's common fields. Verduan kept a small patch here as well as his own fields, the latter harvested for sale and these he harvested for the hungry. Byell also had his own fields but often spent his days at the common as the Red Fox, the village inn, made a handy stop in either direction.

He spotted Verduan and Byell standing at the shadowed edge of the field, waved, and headed towards them.

Nearing them, he realized neither looked happy. Byell leaned against his spade. Verduan picked up a handful of dirt and rubbed it between his palms.

Tardiff watched the two men's dour faces as he approached. "Is all right with you?"

Byell nodded at the dirt in Verduan's hand. "The crops are wasting. Something burns our fields without fire."

Verduan dropped the earth, brisked his hands on his pants, pulled a withered stalk from the ground and showed it to Tardiff. "They sprout then turn brown in a matter of days. No fire and it's hot to the touch." He dropped the stalk and put his fingers in his mouth, wetting them to cool them and removing them quickly. "Ugh. Bitter."

Tardiff took a pinch of the dropped earth, touched it to his tongue and spit it out quickly. "Like the Vell. No fish swim there. This earth has the same bitterness as the Vell."

Verduan kept his eyes on the rows of withering grains. "I wouldn't know. My fields are watered from my own well. Byell?"

"My animals drink from my well, as do Idee, Thomas, and Julia. But my crops are fed by a duct cut from the Vell and they wither."

Tardiff's eyebrows lifted. "Nant's well is fed by a duct from the Vell. I've heard no complaints, though."

Byell spit on the ground between the three men. "The witch cursed us, Verduan. Your boy cut off her hand and she cursed the village. Crops wither and livestock falters. More each day. People say the village is cursed. Two families have left that I know of. Perhaps more."

"My boy cut off her hand saving your daughter's life. And this isn't the first time the summer's been hot and crops have withered, or have you forgotten?"

The hairs rose on Tardiff's arms. Byell's lips tightened and he stared up into Verduan's eyes. His hand went to the knife in his belt.

Tardiff put a hand on his arm. "Byell, hasn't your family had enough misery? Don't make me put you in jail again."

Byell turned his gaze to the Bellman. He wrenched his arm free of Tardiff's hand, turned, and headed towards the Red Fox.

Tardiff and Verduan watched him walk off. Verduan shook his head and said quietly, "If there's anything here that's cursed, it's him and his stupid ways."

Tardiff looked away. "The man lost a child, Verduan."

"Years ago."

"Some people never escape their loss."

Verduan grunted and turned back to his withering crops.

"Where is the Tomekan priest you contacted? You returned three weeks ago and no one's seen him yet."

Verduan knelt and gathered another handful of dirt. "I don't know. Church matters weighed heavily on him. He's probably forgotten us."

"Have you dealt with the tinker come through town?"

Verduan let the dry earth trickle from his palm. "Forgeron, a metalsmith." He glanced up at the sound of the Red Fox's door as Byell entered. "He fixed Eric's axe in exchange for some breakfast. What of him?"

Tardiff shook his head. "Nothing. I like to know of any strangers in Nant. Should anything happen. Part of my job."

"Buco likes him."

Tardiff smiled. "Ah. He must be okay, then."

"I've been busy in my own fields. Is what Byell said true, people are leaving Nant?"

"Some have left, yes, but for many reasons."

"If enough people leave, there won't be enough taxes for The Baron to keep our lands safe. He'll come and claim them and station his own men here."

Tardiff looked at the dying earth. "The Baron is well satisfied with his taxes at present. Let's deal with today's trouble today, tomorrow's trouble tomorrow."

Verduan nodded and gazed over the fields. "Aye."

CHAPTER 10

The sun capped the western mountains as Forgeron pulled his cart down Nant's main thoroughfare. Loud voices, the tinkling of mugs, laughter, and bright lights came through windows a ways up. Above them a wooden sign showed a running red fox, beneath them a tilted flagon dripped ale and a browned leg of lamb dripped gravy.

Forgeron parked his cart in the lane beside the inn and entered.

Eyes rose and took him in. Talk paused but only long enough for people to identify the stranger in their midst. He smiled and nodded in return. Talk, laughter, and the clanging of mugs returned. Lamps and candles lit much of the Inn's interior but dark paths and places remained. The scent of braised lamb and beef, ale and wine, mixed with light smoke from the lamps, candles, and a few men with pipes as Forgeron closed the door.

Two young men, their arms bare, shirts open, and aprons around their waists moved from darkness to light and back with pitchers and platters as patrons raised their hands or lifted their heads or cocked an eye in the their direction. Someone stood in the dark near the door, cup in hand, their oil-stained coat pulled loosely around them and their hood pulled low, perhaps just come in from the cool night air.

A few tables stood free but Forgeron chose a table with two free chairs. Two men he hadn't met during the day occupied seats across from each other. One said something and the other laughed.

Forgeron put his hand on a free chair's backrest. "May a thirsty, hungry, tinker join you, Good Sirs?"

One man smiled. "We wait for Galos, the charcoal burner, but that leaves one seat free and you smell better than he. Sit and be welcome." He pushed a chair out for him.

A moment later the Inn's door swung open and several patrons lifted a mug towards the newcomer.

Forgeron nodded. "A well-liked fellow, he."

"That is Galos."

Galos took the remaining seat without asking. "You're the Forgeron the Tinker? That is your cart parked outside?"

Forgeron nodded. "You need some metalworking done? I thought I'd already exhausted Nant's needs but can rearrange my schedule if - "

"You have strange markings on its sides."

Forgeron hesitated. "Merely nicks, dents, and scratches made plying my trade."

"Are you the original owner of the cart?"

Forgeron's eyes narrowed. "No, I inherited it."

"Metalsmithing is your father's trade?"

"My master's. The one I learned the craft from. Many years ago."

Galos nodded and waved at Slewe the Innkeeper. "I knew a metalworker but that was years ago."

"I hope my brother metalsmith served you well."

"Quite well, yes."

Forgeron rose from the table, his smile returned. "I've had a good day. Save me the seat while I buy a round for the table." He weaved through the people, smiles and nods as he went, and stopped by a large cask the Innkeeper drew from. Forgeron and Slewe talked. The bald Innkeeper's hands rested on his big belly, his normally quick, active fingers intertwined and stilled between each pint's pouring. He nodded towards individuals and his index fingers quickly singled them out from other customers, and whispered something only the Tinker could hear. Forgeron glanced where Slewe nodded and pointed, smiled, laughed, and each time his eyes focused long where Slewe drew his attention.

A final, last, deep laugh and Forgeron brought two fistfuls of pints back to the table.

Galos snickered. "Know all the town's gossip now?"

Forgeron placed a mug in front of the charcoal burner. "Quite the talker, that one."

"What brings you to our out of the way Nant? Is there enough here to keep a tinker in coppers?"

"I metalsmith. Not blacksmithing, although I can if required, nor whitesmithing. I work in betwixt and between."

Galos made introductions all around. "This fine fellow is Byell, farmer and herdsman, and the gent across from you with the curious eye is Tardiff, The Baron's man in Nant."

Forgeron placed mugs in front of the others and nodded a greeting to each. "Tardiff The Baron's man. I'm sure you have many questions for me. Happy to answer as I can."

Tardiff sat back and lifted the offered mug. "None have complained so far and all have praised your work."

Byell looked at the person standing by the wall. "And Buco likes you."

The four laughed.

Byell nudged Tardiff. "Who is that one? Keeps silent and doesn't show their face. A worry, there."

Tardiff followed Byell's gaze and shook his head. "No idea and as long as they stand there and do no harm, nor do I care."

More laughs around the table.

Two rounds later Forgeron still sipped his first pint and noticed Galos also nursed his. "Red Fox's ale doesn't suit you?"

"Suits me fine. It's not good for a man works with fire to befriend too much drink."

Forgeron listened to the others' tongues wag. He mentioned Eric's axe and Byell nodded. "Witch's blood on that."

"I searched for hickory to make a new handle. Found some in the copse about an hour's walk on the east road."

"Aye, you chose no wood there, I hope."

"A good Father directed me elsewhere. I gather that wood is haunted?"

"Baillot, that be. A witch, Sullya, hides there."

Others heard the discussion and brought their mugs over. Most listened and nodded. Some offered comment.

The one with oil-stained clothes and hood stayed by the wall, neither spoke nor lifted their head to watch who talked, only turned their head to follow conversations.

Forgeron jangled his purse. "Let me buy one for the house for all this good conversation." He nodded at the one by the wall. "Come join us before I leave for the night?"

A thin, gloved hand rose from the dark woolen clothing's heavy folds, waved a pass.

Forgeron sipped his drink and let everyone finish their stories. "Thank you for your tales, good friends, and now I go on to the next village."

Someone commented on the lateness of the hour and darkness of the night.

"No worries to me, my friend, although your concern is appreciated. I've always enjoyed the stars and heavens as my blanket and forests for my bedside."

He downed the last of his cup in one great swallow and left, unsteady on his feet, accidentally bumping into the hooded one still in the darkness by the door. "Sorry. Too much in my cups, me."

He turned his ear up to hear the voice but nothing was said. Instead he caught the scent of barn and hay, herd animals and fodder. The hooded one simply moved away, but not before Forgeron's hand felt the curve of hips, the fullness of breasts, and his nose caught the scent of fear-laced sweat masking a faint perfume.

SECTION IV
THE BODY

CHAPTER II

Nory kept his distance. He walked slowly, carefully, so the hooded figure wouldn't know Nory followed.

Grandmother Dire taught Nory how to walk in the woods unseen, to walk when bees flitted from flower to flower, when beetles hummed and crickets chirped, when martins and bulbuls and warblers sang and flew, to use natural sounds to mask his movements.

Who is this who walks in Nory's woods? They walk the silent way, but not as silent as Nory.

Nory is proud. Nobody walks as silent as he. Grandmother Dire taught Nory good.

Nory sniffed the air in the figure's wake. Nory knows that smell but it is masked, hidden.

Nobody hides smells from Nory.

Nory always finds the hidden bread, the scrap of meat, the last sip in a cup.

Chickadees flitted back and forth as Nory followed.

The figure, head to toe in a flowing black robe, not a priest's cassock, tight at the waist, with a shining, white sword carefully hidden in the folds of the robe itself.

Ha.

Nory knows. Nory sees. Can't hide things from Nory.

But who is this?

They move so quietly. Like Nory. Like Grandmother Dire.

Is this someone else Grandmother Dire teaches? There's never been any others in Grandmother's cellar, in the dark of the earth where she works.

She lets Nory there, she shows him her magics, what she does, and talks to him because Nory is good, Nory listens.

And Grandmother Dire always has something to eat.

But who is the black hooded, black robed figure? Even their face is covered.

With a mask?

Grandmother Dire made Nory a mask once. To ward off evil. If he saw someone sick, saw someone fall, take out your mask, Nory, put it on your face, breath through here, you'll be safe.

Good Grandmother Dire.

The figure walked the River Vell upstream from the village and kept along its bank, hidden from the road except where the Vell and road met to water horses and travelers. The robed one stopped now and again to peer into the flowing water and some-times raised a hand to block the morning sun's reflection as it came through the trees and struck the water.

At one point the figure stopped, turned, and backtracked slowly, careful with each stop, and their gloved hands moved aside brush and undergrowth by the Vell's side.

Whoever it was focused on the water's edge. They knelt and took a small, clear phial from inside their robe, unstoppered it, and scooped something from the Vell's bank into it.

They held the phial up to the sun and turned it slightly from side to side.

Satisfied, they stoppered it, hid it back in their robe, stood, clapped their gloves together to clean dirt and dust from them, and followed the river's edge back towards Nant.

Nory wanted to follow but they might have found something good to eat by the Vell and Nory investigated.

No, nothing. Nothing but shiny dirt.

Strange.

He reached out to it. Perhaps it was good to eat? A spice, maybe? The robed one gathered some into his flask, yes?

A black hand descended on this shoulder and pulled him back before his fingers touched the shiny dirt.

The robed figure spun Nory until they faced each other.

The figure placed a finger over the mask's lips then pointed at the shiny dirt. Nory looked at the dirt and the figure lifted Nory's face back so they faced each other again.

The figure wagged its finger and shook its head, no.

Nory looked at the shiny dirt again.

The figure pulled his head forward again, wagged its finger and shook its head, no. It moved Nory gently aside and kicked the shiny dirt into the Vell. Nory watched it foam in the swirling water and then it was gone.

Nory didn't like the robed figure taking Nory's food away like that.

The figure turned Nory so he faced further upstream and into the woods, and pointed.

Something shined in the sunlight.

The figure patted its stomach and pointed again.

Nory headed towards the shine.

Halfway there his nose twitched. Dried beef. Mutton. And bread? And wine?

The robed figure knows where food is hidden in the forest?

The hidden one is a friend?

Nory must thank his friend. He turned.

But the hooded figure was gone.

Nory hadn't heard a thing.

Nory's nose twitched again.

He walked quickly, not always moving as Grandmother Dire instructed, and stopped.

The shine came from knives and pots and pans and *oh!* a bright, shiny hammer hanging on a two wheeled cart.

Nory had no use for pots and pans or knives but a bright shiny hammer? Everybody had pots and pans and knives, but nobody he knew had a bright shiny hammer!

Nory lifted it from its hook. He had to use two hands. It was heavy. He struck some rocks with it and they cracked.

Bonk Bonk On the head!

The woods fell quiet and Nory laughed. He liked the hammer.

Nory looked back at the cart. He knew this cart. He'd seen it in the village. At Zevke the Baker's and other places.

This was the Tinker's cart!

But the Tinker had been gone a day, perhaps more.

Why did he leave his cart here?

Nory followed his nose around the cart and dragged the hammer after him.

Yes!

Beef and mutton and wine and bread inside the cart.

Oh, lucky Nory!

A bright shiny hammer and food!

Nory gathered fallen limbs and branches. Those too big to lift he pulled over the tops of bushes and vines so as not to leave any drag marks, each one placed carefully to conceal the cart.

He would come back later. This might be a magic cart. More food might be here another day.

Nory gathered the foodstuffs to him. Bread and meats went into pockets and, if necessary, up sleeves and inside his shirt where there were no holes for things to fall out. He uncorked the wineskin and tipped it into his mouth, then just as quickly gagged and spit it out.

Pugh!

Sour. Bitter.

He hung the wineskin back up on its peg inside the cart.

What to do about the hammer?

He hid the cart well but surely the Tinker knew where he left it. He might return.

Especially if it was a magic cart. Dire showed Nory magic but said real magic was rare and only existed in people's hearts.

Nory didn't understand but Dire gave him food and patted his head when she said it so it must be a good thing.

The hammer.

It was too heavy for Nory to carry back to the village.

He would hide it.

A short way off stood an elm with a lower branch split from the trunk. He dragged the hammer there. Twigs flipped and snapped as the hammer passed over them. He hid the hammer in the crack so he could find it again and crack more rocks.

Bonk! Bonk!

Nory giggled.

Something fluttered on the other side of the elm. Crows cawed and Wasps buzzed.

Maybe more food there?

A woman's body, her face swollen and beaten, her barbette shading her eyes which seemed to gaze towards the Vell, her right arm extended, her fingers pointing. Her left arm lay behind her, under her body, and the ground beneath her damp from a pool of drying blood.

~

Eric and Thomas watched Nory break out of birch, elm, and ash trees where the Vell met the road. He leapt over vines and creepers and continued in the undergrowth on the other side without slowing.

Eric called out but Nory didn't slow. "I didn't know Nory traveled this far from the village."

Thomas shadowed his eyes and measured the sun's height in the sky. "Know what time it is?"

Eric watched the fleeing halfling. "I'm sure Nory does. Have you ever known him to move so quickly?"

Thomas snorted. "Nory knows when Zevke takes fresh bread from his ovens, when someone has a meal ready who'll have a little extra for him. He always knows where and when there'll be food for him."

"Do you think he's alright?"

Thomas continued on the road out of town without considering Nory's path. "I think Nory will fare this witch better than most of us. Best follow his path north, though, by the river. We'll find fresh saplings there we can harvest."

CHAPTER 12

Patreo rode a lope-eared donkey into the village. He passed Verduan's cottage and Verduan ran out to him. "Father Patreo!"

"Verduan. Sorry not to come sooner. Church politics. Had to get permission to enter another parish." Patreo looked around. "Buco guarding your herds today?"

"That or with my son. Or playing with the other dogs. Or the creatures in the forest. I found him as a pup, you know. Nursing at a bear sow beside her cubs. No idea what happened to his bitch mother. But he followed me when I backed away, more attentive to me than the sow's snarls, so I kept him. He knows no fear and knows friend from foe with nothing more than a sniff."

"Good dog, that."

"Aye. Father Baillot doesn't know you're here?"

"He's my first stop. Unless you have some water for Geselda here." He patted the donkey's neck with a gloved hand.

"What happened to your hand?"

Patreo held it up and laughed. "Oh, nothing. A slight burn. My experiments with Greek Fire, remember? I wear the glove to keep some ointment on it while it heals."

A woman walked hurriedly to the center of the road, shaded her eyes from the sun and scanned in both directions.

"Looks like the woman has a concern."

Verduan nodded. "Idee, Julia's mother. I mentioned her when we talked."

Idee marched up to them. She spoke as quickly as she walked without acknowledging Patreo's presence. "Is Julia with Eric?"

Patreo scratched Geselda's ears. "Should she be?"

She ignored him and shook Verduan's arm. "Is Julia with Eric?"

"No, Idee, and I haven't seen her."

Idee ran down the road, her skirts lifted in her hands.

"You have an interesting village."

"I wish it weren't so."

"I should go tell Father Baillot I'm visiting. A short respite from my parish duties. I'll offer the bishopric suggested I council with an older, wiser priest."

"Give me a moment to tend your noble steed and I'll walk with you."

They saw Idee conferring with Baillot as he left the rectory. He stood looking down at her, shaking his head and adjusting his cassock. She threw up her arms and ran off as they approached.

Verduan waved. "Father Baillot, we have a guest in our village."

Patreo bowed. "I'm Patreo from Tomeka. The bishopric suggested you as first among many regarding counsel on parish matters. You've gained much respect at the Holy See."

Baillot's eyes flared wide when Patreo faced him and offered his hand. He placed a hand over his heart.

Patreo lowered his hand slowly. "Are you ill, Father?"

"The bishopric sent you?"

"The bishopric suggested I consult with an older, wiser priest. I come of my own accord to you." He nodded towards the fleeing Idee. "Have I come at an inconvenient time?"

"Patreo." Baillot stared down at him. "That's not a common name."

"I am from the west and named in my mother's tongue. My father left before I was born to fight in the Holy Land and never returned."

"You do not know your father?"

"I seek him when Mother Church and time allow. Beyond that..." Patreo shrugged.

"Are you a bastard, then? Unfit to do holy work?"

"The church thinks otherwise. If my presence offends you..."

Baillot turned and waved him away. "I have no space for you at the church. You'll be gone in a day?"

Verduan answered with a question. "Perhaps Father Patreo can stay with me while he's here?"

Patreo nodded as Idee raced up to Baillot with Eric close behind, both panting. "Thomas and Eric found Julia."

Baillot glanced at the nodding Eric. "Dead, Father. Beaten and left for dead."

Patreo made the Sign of the Cross and whispered a prayer.

Eric's eyes focused on his father and Patreo as if unaware of their presence, as if they appeared suddenly from some mist.

Verduan took his son's arm in a gentle but firm grasp. "This is Father Patreo, Eric. He's come to help us with Sullya, if he can."

Tears filled the young man's eyes and he yelled at Patreo. "Why couldn't you come sooner? This is the witch's doing, punishment for cutting off her hand. You could have stopped her and my Julia would be alive still."

Baillot's eyes also watered and his face flushed. "It is Julia? And she is dead, you're sure?"

Eric sobbed openly. "Yes, Father."

"Beaten?"

Eric nodded through his tears. "Yes, Father."

Baillot turned towards his church, hesitated, opened his mouth as if to speak, hesitated.

Patreo cocked his head as he watched. "Father?"

Baillot nodded at Eric. "Show me. Us. Verduan, get Tardiff and follow us." He took Idee's arm in his. "Have comfort, good woman. Nothing is sure yet."

Patreo stood as the others moved. "Is there something I can do?"

Baillot's eyes widened on him for a moment. "Yes. Perhaps. Come. I may need your help."

CHAPTER 13

Zevke and Saida sat in their kitchen. A candle flickered in the middle of their table and they watched it burn down. Daylight came in the east facing window and Saida poured weak wine into her cup.

Zevke pushed his cup across the table towards her.

She ignored his cup and nodded at the candle. "Time to turn the breads, husband."

He reached across the table to her and she pulled her hands back, out of his reach. A moment later she lifted her cup and sipped. She kept the cup at her lips and rolled it across them so she would not speak.

Zevke stared at her then at the candle. He brushed flour from his apron. "Soon. Yes."

Saida put her cup on the table and turned it slowly. Her eyes and fingers inspected the small striations where the potter failed to smooth its surface before placing the cup in its final fire. She did not look up and a single tear fell from her eye. "I told you she would be trouble."

"But not for us."

"Are you sure no one saw you?"

"What would they see? Zevke the Baker gathering herbs for his breads?"

She shook her head and smiled into her cup. "You always travel so far south of Nant to gather herbs?"

"Nobody goes near those ruins. They believe they're haunted."

Another tear followed the first. "What made you go inside? Did you think herbs grow on dark stone walls?"

Zevke rolled his eyes and they stopped to watch the gathering shadows. "You are worse than a nest of hornets, woman."

"She was broken?"

"God, woman. Do you think I did the breaking?"

"Is that where you planned to meet?"

Zevke's eyes fell on her. "One mistake years ago. Will you ever leave me free of it?"

Saida lifted her cup as if toasting her head. "Years ago you sought comfort in another. The woman saw you cleaned and told others, and they came for us in the night." She sipped. "'Prince of the Synagogue! The Devil's lieutenant,' they shouted.

"Gentiles hear "synagogue" and assume all jews are evil."

She continued, unhearing, and recited from memory the lies told about her. Them! "The Princess of the Synagogue is at his right hand. The Devil sits on a throne in the Synagogue. Around them are sorcerers and Sorceresses. Magicians are people of rank and status who come next. On the edge are Hags and witches who must bow to the Devil, Prince, and Princess."

Zevke slammed his fist on the table. The candle fell from its holder and went out, drowned in its own wax. "I went in search of Sullya the Witch."

She gasped.

"Are you happy now, hag that you are yourself? Does it make you glad to know?"

"Why did you seek her out."

"I thought...I hoped..."

"No, Zevke."

"Is it wrong to want my daughter back?"

"Our daughter?"

"Is it wrong?"

"You sought to reverse Byell's curse?"

He shook his head. "What does Byell have to do with this?"

"Julia had a sister. Remember? A twin. We met them when we first came to Nant."

"She was lost in the Vell. What of it?"

"That was a too hot summer, too, and the Vell didn't flow at all. Byell offered a daughter to Sullya in exchange for plentiful harvests for as long as his land remained his. How could she be lost in a river that barely flowed?" She sat back, arms folded across her chest, triumphant.

Zevke's eyes popped. "No. How do you know this?"

"Idee and I talk. She tells me her troubles. I tell her mine."

"Does she know - "

"I talk, I'm not a fool."

He shook his head, his eyes still wide. "I just sought her to learn if she could tell us where our daughter might be."

"She is dead, Zevke. She is dead, you killed her. I remember gathering things in our arms, fleeing in the night. I asked if you had our daughter but you didn't answer, only ordered me to hurry."

Zevke's focused on dust devils dancing in the light. He whispered, "There wasn't time."

"You left her. You killed her."

"The villagers wouldn't kill a child."

Saida ignored him and her face filled with an ancient rage. "To save yourself you lost her to us. I remember. Do you?"

"Will you never let me forget?"

Saida watched the candle. "Julia, she was dead? You're sure?"

"So she seemed to me."

"You did nothing to her?"

"I carried her body to where I thought she'd be found."

"But nothing more?"

"Do you think so little of me you believe I would lie with the dead?" He slammed his palm on the table. "One mistake - "

"Our daughter."

"Which I'll never forget."

"You couldn't leave her? No one would know or suspect."

Zevke's memories turned his face into a battleground. "And leave her people wondering? Cursed like us to never know what happened to their daughter? Better to know she's dead than know nothing at all. Or do you think our curse should be visited on others? None should know what's become of their child?"

Saida paid no attention. Her eyes darted back and forth. "There's been no gossip. No rumors. No one running through the village saying they found her body. You say she was dead. But when you went back she was gone. And your shirt was bloodied. Do the dead walk? No. You think someone moved the body after you left it?"

Zevke reached for the flask. "Her basket was nowhere to be found. And she wore fine clothes. Finer than one could find in Nant. Perhaps to meet someone? Perhaps they found her and took her somewhere to heal?"

Saida grabbed the flask by its neck. Her hand whitened with the grip. "Someone will find her basket. Someone will know what you did, you fool."

"I did nothing."

"Nothing." Saida spit on the floor. "Ha. You moved a dead girl's body, you old fool!"

"Silence, woman. Pour me wine and be silent."

She nodded at the dead candle. "Time to turn the bread, husband."

He left her at the table and went to the door. "Yes. Time to turn the bread."

CHAPTER 14

Grasshoppers chirped and took flight. Bees buzzed from flower to flower. Wrens and blackbirds flitted from limb to limb. A bushtit danced on the dead girl's barbette tugging at a loose thread, another made a hole in a stocking.

The woods grew silent as Baillot, Tardiff, Eric, Thomas, Verduan, and Patreo gathered in a semi-circle around the body.

Idee pushed through them. Thomas moved to hold her back but not quick enough. She looked at the young woman's body and collapsed against her son.

Patreo pointed to a sprout of turf back aways from the body. "Lay her down over there." He reached into his cassock and pulled out a small phial. One quick shake and he uncorked it under her nose. "Breathe slowly, Mother. Deep and slow."

Her eyes fluttered then focused. She pushed him away and scrambled across the hard earth to the body.

Baillot frowned at the phial still in Patreo's hand.

"Crushed Buckthorn with cayenne and some other herbs, Father."

Idee gently adjusted the dead girl's blouse and skirt. "I taught Julia needlework and weaving. She made these as I watched."

Tardiff squatted beside her and gently took her hands in his. "Are you sure this is your daughter, Idee?"

Idee pulled her hands free and hugged the body to her. The blood on the face and neck turned her blouse into a patchwork of ruddy shapes.

"Forgive me, Idee, but the face. It would be hard to tell by the face - "

"You don't think I know my own daughter?"

Baillot made the Cross over the body and turned away. "Prepare her for burial. Father Patreo, you'll attend."

Patreo stared at him. "Father, I'm not her confessor, I shouldn't - "

Baillot glared back. "You'll attend." He stepped away, his rosary raised to his lips, and turned before Patreo could respond.

Patreo looked to Verduan. The huge farmer shrugged. Patreo's gaze went back to the girl's body. He cocked his head to the side for a moment then he focused on Idee as she picked fallen debris from the body.

He knelt beside Idee and the body. "There are some questions, Idee." He reached for the barbette. "May I?"

Idee stopped his hand. "You think my daughter a harlot? Her head to be uncovered?"

Patreo held his hand where she stopped it, neither moving it forward nor returning it to his side. "No, mother. I merely note this barbette fits poorly and I know you would not let your daughter out so. Also, if she follows you, her hair should be light. The strand I see is dark."

Idee's eyes focused where Patreo stared and opened wide. She let go his hand.

Patreo lifted the barbette enough to let some hair fall free. "Is this your daughter's hair?"

Idee's eyes remained wide. She said nothing.

Patreo's fingers brushed aside the hair. He looked at his fingers a moment and brushed his thumb over them.

"What? What is it?"

"Her hair is powdered to be this color." He spit on his fingers, pulled on the lock of hair, and showed everyone the residue left on them. "See?"

Eric paid no attention, his eyes on the lock. "Her hair. It is Julia's color."

Idee wailed.

Patreo spoke compassionately but sharply. "Mother, did your daughter have access to such?"

Idee sobbed and shook her head, no.

Patreo continued. "I note you wear a mild perfume. Sweet rose and lavender, correct? From flowers gathered in Nant's fields, yes? This body bears the scent of tonka, rosewood, and cinnamon. Not applied recently. She's not had access to them in quite a while. Faint and still there. Quite expensive, these, in any form, and it seems used generously here. Did your daughter have access to these oils and you did not?"

Idee pulled back, opened her eyes wide, sniffed, and frowned. "No."

Eric hovered close by, inhaled, and frowned as well.

"Your daughter worked, did she not? On the farm and in the home? Her hands should be callused, should they not?"

The body's right arm lay away from it, its index finger extended beyond the others as if pointing or showing the way. He lifted the hand and smoothed his hand over it, palm to palm. "I neither feel nor see calluses here. This feels more the hand of someone manor born."

Idee sat back abruptly. One hand went behind her to brace her fall and the other felt the frown on her brow.

Patreo focused on the fingers themselves for a moment, then

lowered the hand to its original position and focused on Idee's face. "Understanding this may or may not be your child, may I continue?"

Idee nodded, her eyes locked on the dead woman's features, beaten to the point identification wasn't possible.

The left arm lay under the body, hidden. Patreo scooched around to that side and pulled it gently. The sleeve grew darker and darker as he did.

He stopped and looked up at Thomas, standing behind Idee. "Thomas, pick up your mother and have her walk, get some air in her lungs."

Thomas frowned at him.

"To clear her mind. Please."

Thomas guided his mother up and took her to Father Baillot, still in prayer.

Verduan knelt beside him. "What is it?"

Patreo pulled the arm free of the body. The arm had no hand, only a cleanly severed stump.

Verduan whispered, "No animal did this."

Tardiff leaned over and examined. Checking to see Idee's position, he also whispered, "A doctor cut that arm. Not a sword or a knife wielded by a military man or a thief. Whoever made that cut knew how to slice through bone, how to cut muscle without tearing. Who in Nant knows such things?"

Eric cursed himself. "It is the witch. I took her hand, now she takes Julia's."

Patreo inspected the severed wrist and addressed Eric. "You still believe this is Julia?"

Verduan shook his head. "If the witch did this then she's a doctor, and we have no physicians in Nant, certainly no surgeons. Each house does their own butchering. Sometimes they help each other with larger animals."

Patreo lifted the wrist into direct sunlight coming through the trees and shook his head. "If a witch then one with a strong arm and a sharp blade. This cut is clean." Patreo gently touched the cheeks and mouth. "And who so cleanly cuts a hand from an arm then brutalizes the face?" He rested back on his heels. "What color were Julia's eyes?"

Eric leaned over them. "A clear, dark green like no other. It would remind you of rain on young ash leaves. Why?"

Patreo spread his cassock like wings to hide his manipulations of the face. "Verduan?"

The big man peered over Patreo's shoulder and made the sign of the Cross.

Idee pulled herself free of Thomas' grasp. "What? What is it?"

Patreo blocked her view. "Someone take Idee, please."

Verduan and Thomas each took an arm and pulled her back. Verduan whispered, "She has no eyes."

Idee fell against Thomas.

Baillot spoke from behind them, his back still turned. "She saw who did this. They took her eyes so we could not gaze into them and see his image there?"

Patreo spoke without looking up. "*His* image, Father?"

"You think a woman did this?"

"The eyes, if they were as distinct as Eric tells us, may have been removed to hinder identification. But if such is the case, why take the eyes and leave such easily recognized clothes?"

Idee wailed.

Patreo covered the face and stood. "No one has skill such as this? You're sure?"

Eric's nostrils flared. "Is she..." He cleared his throat. "Disturbed?"

Idee struck him across the face.

Baillot coughed then hissed, "Eric."

"I merely offer, if someone did this. I mean, not an animal..."

Tardiff stood. "We have no one fit to examine her."

Verduan looked at Patreo. "You've studied much. Could you examine her?"

Idee shrieked. "She's dead. What is there to examine?"

Patreo wiped his hands together. "Whether your daughter or not, mother, we examine to learn. The dead speak if we know how to listen. Whoever did this may have revealed themselves without realizing."

Baillot stepped back among them. "Revealed themselves how? Do you speak to the dead?"

"Not as you might think, no." He lifted her handed arm. "Notice how loose this shoulder is compared to the other? Her arm was wrenched at the shoulder and forced up behind her so she would not struggle. So she was brought here under force, not of her own free will." He lay the arm back in its original position.

He moved her head slightly from side to side. "And these bruises. Do you not note their shape and size? They tell us a hammer struck her. A mallet of some kind. And the blows crush the bone down, not up. Someone tall delivered these. Taller than this girl, anyway. See also, they're all on the face, neither crown nor back of the head are touched, but the bones of the face are broken. That tells us both the weight of the hammer, the force of the strike..." he paused. "And that their purpose was to obscure the girl's identity. Her face would be known. If not by those in Nant, someone traveling in search of her."

He stood and gazed down at the body. "Did you see the nails of the remaining hand? Well cared for but broken to the quick. This girl gave her life dearly. Unless her assailant wore a mask, they'll be scarred. My guess is the first blow felled her, the rest done when she could no longer resist."

Tardiff crossed his arms. "All well for the dead. What can you tell us about the person who did this?"

"A strong woman, although not likely. A woman's violence is slow, methodical. This wasn't planned. It happened spontaneously. A servant, one used to labor. If she's manored or royal born, perhaps a servant, but strong? Or a lover - a cavalry lord? - spurned at the last? She resisted and horror followed? But most likely a man."

Baillot sneered. "Ha. *His* image."

Tardiff looked into the body's eyeless sockets. "What of the eyes?"

Patreo looked around. "They were taken after the body lay dead for a while. There is no blood about the brow or cheeks. Either the assailant returned for them or someone found the body and harvested them from the corpse."

Idee fell back against Thomas again.

Tardiff took off his coat and handed it to Verduan. "Cover the body."

Idee seized the coat and laid it over the body. She tucked it under the remains as if tucking a child in for the night.

Eric looked around the wood. "This is the witch's work. She's come back to haunt us."

A nudge from Verduan directed Patreo's gaze to Baillot who leveled full, red eyes on him.

"Yes, Father?"

"You know a great many things. Far more than is necessary to become a cleric."

Eric focused their attention on a haphazard piling of pine, elm, and oak boughs deeper in the woods. "Thomas, did you stack those there for shelter? I didn't notice when we first came by."

Thomas shook his head. "We hadn't gone that far." He motioned to Eric. "Come."

The cleared brush revealed Forgeron's cart.

Idee's eyes widened. "I know that cart. It's the Tinker's cart. The one who came through our village yesterday. You know it, Eric. He mended your axe."

Tardiff inspected the Tinker's wagon. "Where is Forgeron?

Eric, Thomas, see if there's a body." He pointed to the side of the cart where Forgeron's hammer normally rested on its cradle. "A tool is missing. What goes here, do you think?"

Verduan came over. "His hammer. A heavy sledge for the first shapings. He had several but he hung his sledge there when he was working."

Tardiff looked underneath and around the cart. "Eric, Thomas, look first inside, then in increasing circles on the ground. Find me that hammer."

Patreo joined Eric and Thomas in their search, glanced at the cart and ran his hand along its nicks and cuts.

Thomas returned and took Idee's hand in his. "I don't believe this is Julia, mother. Look at the remaining hand. I worked with Julia in our fields and orchards. This child's hand is smooth, as Father Patreo said, the hand of the child of some manor. She wears Julia's clothes but she's not from Nant. We can go, ask. I'll wager no one's daughter is missing today."

Idee looked down at the body and nodded.

Thomas spoke decisively. "I say let the Tomekan priest examine her."

Patreo continued glancing around the wagon in search of the hammer and spoke absently. "None are missing except Julia."

Thomas grabbed Patreo's arm. "What?"

Patreo pointed at Idee. "Julia's missing. Didn't you say so, Idee?"

"She did not return from her village rounds and her chores aren't done."

Tardiff pulled his hat back and scratched his bald spot. "But didn't you say you saw your daughter this morning? Forgive me, Idee, but this child's blood puddles and by its look is at not that old. The ground is not thrashed around her. If she struggled we would see signs on her clothes and in the foliage. Perhaps this girl intended to be here. She met the killer - "

Idee hissed, "Forgeron."

" - he committed his crime and covered his cart so none could be curious and draw near."

Verduan shook his head. "What tinker do you know leaves their cart and wanders off with only a hammer so heavy it could crush stone with one strike?"

Eric kicked aside some fallen leaves. "Like these?"

Verduan stood beside him and moved the shattered stones with his boot. "No, that's more the work of a child or someone testing the hammer's strength. Those stones would be gravel if it was meant to be done."

Eric and Thomas looked at each other. Eric nodded and Thomas spoke. "We saw Nory running towards town on our way out here."

Tardiff cleared his throat. "No. Nory is guilty of some things, I'm sure, but not this. And I'll accept the Tinker covered his cart so none would be curious, but why kill the girl? He covered it because he means to return and didn't want to pull it to his destination and back?"

Patreo listened quietly. He stepped away from the cart, away from where they gathered, and studied the ground level vegetation.

Baillot walked over and followed his gaze. "What is it? What do you see?"

"Nothing, just the path of some mouse or vole."

Baillot threw up his hands. "We have a dead child at our feet and you trouble us with animal tracks?"

"I wonder at the child's remaining hand. Did she regain consciousness long enough to point at her killer escaping?"

Idee's nostrils flared. "She points at the Tinker's cart. Lift Tardiff's coat and you'll see."

The Bellman knelt on one knee and lifted his coat enough to

expose the hand. Verduan, Thomas, Tardiff, and Eric followed the finger.

Verduan shook his head. "Nothing. She doesn't point at the cart or anything else."

Eric added. "Only the Vell on the other side of that rise."

Tardiff looked at Patreo. "Can you examine the body, Tomekan?"

"An examination will tell us much but I doubt we'll find a clear answer regarding who murdered her."

Idee threw her hands up. "Forgeron! The Tinker!"

Tardiff grabbed her arms and turned her away from the body. "Thomas, take your mother home. Tomekan?"

"I doubt the Tinker had a part in the girl's murder and admit we can't be sure."

"So despite the missing hammer you will swear to a murder here?"

"Have you ever heard of someone who stumbled to the ground, cut off their own hand and used it to bludgeon their own face?" Patreo kept glancing at the elm at the end of the path. "No, she knew her attacker. And whoever did this didn't flee. There's no sign of hurry here. They walked away."

Tardiff shook his head. "There is too much for me to understand here and now. Tomekan, can you examine her here or must the body go somewhere else?"

CHAPTER 15

Dire entered her cellar from a bulkhead concealed in a thicket of stranglebushes. She wore thick clothing even on the warmest days. They protected her so the stranglebush thorns didn't slow her - sometimes she needed to hide in a hurry - and they allowed her to hide her preparations in their many folds.

She lit candles then a lantern, trimming wicks so there'd be heat and light but no smoke. A wall held animal parts, a workbench several tools. Beakers and bowls and corked jars covered shelves far back into the dark. A lectern held several books.

A pigskin glove, the fingers spread and held open with pins, rested palm up in the center of the workbench. Pig ligaments and sinews ran up through the fingers. The woman picked up a magnifier and studied the glove, sometimes pulling the sinews to see if the fingers fought the pins. They did.

She smiled.

"What have you there, Grandmother?"

She spun and lifted a fine edged knife from the bench in a single move so swift it belied her age.

A form clothed head to toe in black, barely discernible in the dark corners of the old woman's workshop, came forward just enough for its shape to be recognized in the gloom. A mask, equally black and showing only the eyes, covered the face and muffled the voice. "Easy, Grandmother. I mean you no harm."

"How did you get in here?"

"The same way you did, I imagine. Fine workmanship on that glove, by the way. How many have you made?"

"How long have you been sitting here in the dark?"

"Is it for sale?"

Dire placed a protective hand on the glove. "Do you have coppers?"

Coins jingled in a pouch.

"By the sounds they make not enough."

"May I see the glove? To know what I'm missing?"

"Pull back that hood and remove your mask. To know who I'm talking to?"

"I saw one just like it withered into an oak in a wooded hollow. Do you know the one I speak of?"

The old woman squinted. "Go away before I call Tardiff the Bellman. He'll know who you are soon enough."

The purse jingled. "There's gold amongst the coppers, Grandmother."

"Then what is your business? What do you want with me?"

A gold coin flipped through the air and fell heavily on Dire's workbench. She held it up to the light and bit with her two remaining teeth.

"Who else knows the secret of making these, Grandmother?"

"Those schooled in the East. The Arab Mehtars. Anatomy is not favored by the Church."

Another coin sailed and struck the bench. She gathered it to her bosom with its twin.

"I saw no instructions for its making while I waited."

The old woman snickered and tapped her head. "All here. If

you leave words someone will find them, read them, and the Church speaks many tongues."

"You made them for someone outside the Church then?"

"Go away. You ask too many questions."

"Or some officer of the Church?"

Dire cocked her head. "Your voice. I know that voice. Or one quite like it. Pull back your hood and mask. Let me see who questions me."

A hand extended from the dark folds of the robe and tossed a yellow powder into the air. The mask lifted just enough for the wearer to blow sharply. The falling powder flew on to Dire's face.

She fell forward. Her hands reached out to the intruder's shoulders to break her fall and brushed against the hood.

Her head wagged back as her eyes glazed over. She mumbled, "You have no ear..." and spoke no more.

The intruder lowered her to the floor and covered her with a blanket. "Sleep, Grandmother, and when you awake, I will have been but a dream."

CHAPTER 16

Byell stood on the edge of his field. In front of him lima and tomato rows alternated, a thirsty crop with a ditch so water would disperse throughout the field evenly. Behind him his orchard started, apple and pear trees, another thirsty crop running dry. A mallet hung loosely in his right hand, slipped through his palm, and landed with a dull thud on the dry earth by his boots. He wiped sweat from his brow and looked down as if confused by the sound, then slowly raised his head and scanned the horizons. "No rain." He clenched his fists. "No clouds, no rain."

His thirsty crops pulled what water they could from the ditch, lima and tomatoes paired as the ox yoked with the ass, and both suffered for it.

A duct ran from the Vell to his fields and he spent the last hour damming it so no Vell water would reach them. Tardiff stated it correctly; the Vell's water quenched like poison and none knew why.

He sobbed and pulled a leather pouch from his pocket. "You promised." A knotted cord held the pouch's top closed. Sweat ran down Byell's cheeks and mixed with tears. "I gave you my daughter. You promised."

He pulled the cord and the pouch opened. He bit his lip until it bled, tasted the blood on his tongue, spit into the pouch, and mixed the contents with his finger.

"You promised."

He walked his fields. Every few steps he took some grains out of the pouch and sprinkled them on the ground.

"You promised."

At the end of his transit movement caught his eye. The trees around his fields had once been loud with wildlife. Birds followed him when he furrowed and he talked with them. "Are those grubs to your liking, Mr. Grouse? Does that worm serve, Mrs. Tanager? And you, Mr. Grosbeak? Are you getting your fill?" Swifts flew over him as flies and grasshoppers took flight. Opossum and stoat waddled at a safe distance behind him to catch any gleanings.

Now the trees were silent. He prayed to gods old and new to bring the wildlife back and kept his eyes alert for any signs of life in his fields, so the dark movement, the fluttering of black against the withering green of the trees, caught his eye and he looked.

A figure stood there. It was head to toe in black and Byell couldn't tell if it watched him or not.

"Hello? Who goes there? What business do you have at my fields?"

No response.

Byell shoved the empty pouch back in his pocket, walked back to his mallet and picked it up, but when he turned the figure was gone.

Not even a hint of movement in the trees.

"Laying down? Hoping I won't see? To dig up my fields because your own are fallow and you know I've used blood magic on mine?"

He strode to where the figure'd been.

Nothing.

No movement in the trees, no path roughly made through the brush, not even footprints.

Byell scratched his head.

A drop of sweat tippled over his upper lip onto the still dribbling blood, mixed with it in the wound, and burned.

Byell shook his head.

Far off, through the trees, the figure in black stared at him.

Byell raised his mallet. "Who are you?" He drew the back of his hand over his brow to keep the sweat from his eyes.

The figure was gone.

CHAPTER 17

Verduan and Patreo pulled the Tinker's cart into the village. The body lay on the cart bed and beneath its top, Idee and Patreo covered the body with cloths found in the cart, all to keep it from village eyes.

Tardiff walked in front and shooed people out of their way. Idee walked behind and wept, not fully accepting Father Patreo's verdict the child was not hers. One hand rested on the body or made minor adjustments to the covering cloths when the cart jumped over a rock or bounced over a rut. Eric stayed at her side, his steps shortened to match hers, and comforted as he could. Father Baillot walked a few solemn steps behind mumbling prayers. Thomas remained in the wood where the body and cart were found, hidden lest anyone return.

Baillot guided them to the sacristy. He moved vestments and wine goblets from a table and lit candles all around. Verduan, Patreo, and Eric lifted the body and lay it there.

Tardiff pointed to the door. "Verduan, stand outside and make sure no one bothers us."

Verduan nodded and closed the door as he left.

Patreo carefully pulled back the cloth covering her and began to remove the clothes.

Idee stopped him. "What are you doing?"

"Learning how much and what kind of evil was done, Mother."

She pushed him back. "Then let me. I'll do that."

Patreo bowed but held his ground. "We must be careful how we remove what is worn. I will assist you."

Baillot nodded and Idee stepped back. She turned Eric to face her. "Go, bring my husband."

Eric looked past her and caught Patreo's eye. "I'd rather stay."

Patreo nodded slightly. He wet a cloth and dabbed matted blood from the dead girl's hair. "Let him stay. You, mother, will know best where your husband is this time of day. It is best you bring him, please."

Baillot motioned her away with a wave of his hand, his eyes fixed on Patreo's ministrations. Idee snorted and left.

Patreo leaned over the body slightly. He turned the head and quickly directed Tardiff's eyes. "See this? Touch it gently. It yields. The skull is cracked. Eric, wash away the rest of this blood until the wound is visible."

Patreo's fingers massaged behind the ears then the neck. "And the blow was fierce enough to snap the neck."

Tardiff inspected the wound. "The blow to her head killed her then?"

"Surely."

"So the violence done to her. It was after death?"

"Yes, but not long after. Or while dying. These marks on her face, either her heart still beat enough to send blood there or it was moments after she died and blood still ran through her veins."

Patreo continued exploring. "Her eyes were removed by

someone who knew what they were doing. Someone skilled in torture."

Tardiff crossed his arms over his chest. "So not because she saw something?"

"There could be many reasons. Someone thought she saw something - her killer - and feared the eyes would retain the image, perhaps, but whoever did it was skilled in the doing."

"Why cut off the hand?"

"A Gourdin punishment. For theft. Brought here from the Crusades. Or because that hand would identify her and the other wouldn't. In any case, someone who's served, knows those who served and knows them dearly, or a Gourdin themself."

Eric stood back, his eyes closed. "Not punishment for taking the hand off the witch?" He crossed himself.

Patreo frowned down upon the body. "The witch's retribution would be so clean? She would want to cause pain as well as damage. The bones would be shattered before the hand was taken." He lifted the arm with the missing hand. "See? The arm itself is whole."

He held the arm up in one hand and felt along its length with the other, then opened her blouse and exposed her chest.

Tardiff watched. "What are you doing now?"

"Sometimes Black Muslims will torture a woman, remove one or both breasts, as punishment for some sin."

Tardiff shook his head. "You could not tell her whole clothed?"

Patreo continued his examination. "Eric, you and Julia were to wed, yes?"

"Yes."

"Would you know if...?"

Eric glanced, blushed, turned away. "Those are not...similar, yes. Julia's are not as full."

"Yes. Quite."

Eric hovered, near the body then not, near the body then not, watching then not, watching then not, keeping an eye on Patreo's ministrations then turning away to adjust candles, adjust drapes, to dab the face, to dab his own.

Tardiff put a hand out and stopped him. "You flutter like a bee seeking sweet flowers, boy. Does being this near the dead bother you?"

Patreo considered. "Is there some other test of identity you'd like us to perform?"

Eric's face reddened and he looked away. "Is she whole?"

Patreo gently felt under her skirt. "No." He felt along the base of her stomach up to her navel and down the sides. "And pregnant."

Eric released a slow, steady breath. "Then she is not Julia."

Tardiff reached across and held the boy's shoulder. "That is not the test you might think it be, Eric."

"Do you doubt her love for me?"

Baillot coughed and turned away from the body. He took a long, slow breath. When he turned back, he lifted his cross and waved it as Eric. "Let us be satisfied with Eric's test."

Patreo washed his hands in the sacristy basin and dried them on the cloth Eric used. "Father Baillot, I don't think - "

"Do not tell me how to deal with those in my own parish."

Patreo continued drying his hands. "If we are convinced this is not Julia, then where is she, who is this child, and why is she wearing Julia's clothes?"

CHAPTER 18

Bonk! Bonk!

Nory kept his eyes on Thomas.

Bonk! Bonk!

Thomas sat under the elm holding Nory's hammer. He pulled a piece of bread from his pocket, crumbled some and tossed it to some wrens who watched him carefully. He lifted the hammer as they neared but ventured close enough.

Bonk! Bonk!

Nory ran to Byell's orchard after seeing the body and ate the Tinker's food.

As much as he could, anyway.

He ate so much his belly rebelled and brought it back up.

Plenty more, though. Plenty more. Eat slowly, Grandmother Dire told him. That way the food stays down.

Bonk! Bonk!

Nory returned for his hammer and found Thomas sitting there. He stayed behind a broad oak with a split trunk covered with red, flowering persian pea vines. Nory quietly entwined himself in the loose ones and didn't move.

Chickadees chirped and fluttered around him. He was too near the peas for them and they told him so.

Nory put a finger to his lips and frowned at them.

They found another vine and grew quiet, only when a new one arrived did they chirp their displeasure.

Nory waited.

Nory wanted his bright, shiny hammer.

If Thomas found it, he'd tell. He knew Nory was here earlier in the day.

Thomas would tell people Nory hurt the girl with his hammer.

Grandmother Dire would be angry at him.

Grandmother doesn't get upset often, only when Nory makes trouble or doesn't know what he's doing. She gets upset to protect him. She is Nory's friend.

Footsteps on the road.

Nory pulled back even more, not to be seen.

It was the new priest, the one Nory didn't know.

Was he coming for Nory's hammer?

He made a ruckus as he left the road for the wood. He moved as if wanting someone to follow, to know he was there.

"Thomas?"

Thomas turned from stump and brushed dirt from the seat of his trousers. "Here."

Nory leaned forward slightly. The wrens and chickadees quieted. A vine snapped. The priest stopped for a moment then continued.

"The girl is not your sister, Julia."

Thomas sagged against the elm with the news. "You're sure of this?"

Patreo looked at the elm. "Yes, quite sure. You can return home now, if you wish."

"Walk with me, Father?"

"Thank you. I'd rather stay and pray here, where the horror took place. I'll be back shortly."

Thomas shook Patreo's hand and headed for the road. Patreo bowed his head, made the Sign of the Cross, and prayed silently.

His head came up when Thomas' footsteps were out of hearing.

He bent over and parted the vegetation covering the track he found earlier. "What animal leaves so square a track as this?"

He gathered some small stones, stood before the elm, and tossed them into the deep center of the split where a small well formed.

A soft *chink!*

He waited until he was sure no bees or wasps or snakes rested there then reached in.

He pulled out the hammer, unbloodied, bright and shiny in the sun.

Nory hated this new priest.

He was going to steal Nory's hammer!

Nory forgot where he was and stood.

Vines pulled on him and snapped.

The priest stopped inspecting the hammer and looked where Nory hid.

Nory pulled himself back down quickly.

The priest returned the hammer deep where the elm split, turned to Nory, put a finger over his lips, and winked.

Nory didn't move. Chickadees and wrens and warblers bustled around him as fresh peas fell. Bees and hummingbirds flew into flowers freshly turned towards them.

The priest left.

Nory hated this priest but he didn't steal Nory's hammer.

Could this new priest be a good man?

The question was too much for Nory right now. But the priest didn't take Nory's hammer so Nory was glad.

CHAPTER 19

Tardiff gazed at the proclamation nicely framed upon his cottage wall. Someone told him the frame was *ornate*. "That is ornately carved," they said.

He didn't remember who said it. Probably one of the gentlemen who brought it to him. He remembered wanting to ask, "Who is Ornate?" and realized before making a fool of himself that *ornate* was *how* it was carved, the intricacy of the design, not *who* carved it.

The frame remained nicely carved after many years on his cottage wall, the vellum it framed not so. Baron Bassys made him UnderSheriff of Nant, a reward for faithful service in The Baron's guard, but so little happened - and perhaps that was Bassys's reasoning? Give the title to Tardiff the Fool because nothing happens there and no one cares if it does? - none called him UnderSheriff any more.

No, now it was Tardiff the Bellman. What had been patrolling the road and questioning travelers unknown to him became walking through Nant ringing the bell announcing the canonical hours of worship, making sure people were about their business and nobody else's, and finally walking through every six hours, same bell in hand, or to summon help if a fire burned unattended or a sheep or goat wandered from its flock.

Tardiff the Bellman. The job paid for his cottage, wood for his fire, food for his table, and the cup or two at the Red Fox now and again.

Ha.

Tardiff the Fool? All this for walking around ringing a bell?

Ha!

Oh, but let there be a body found and everyone runs to get Tardiff because he'll know what to do.

Ha. Tardiff knew he was given this office because he knew how to keep his mouth shut when he overheard The Baron's business, knew it's better to have a full belly in The Baron's guard than to be a body loosed through The Baron's privies to the cesspit's outside the castle walls.

Now Tardiff collects The Baron's taxes and sends them once a year to Melia, to The Baron's coffers, and with my regards, Lord Baron, all is well in Nant and its surrounds.

But a body?

Of an unknown girl? Not of the village?

Where did she come from?

What was she doing?

Why was she wearing Julia's clothes?

Tardiff knew three words and he wrote them as precisely as he could, first making sure his ink flowed and his scroll rolled and unrolled without cracking. He wasted one whole scroll practicing the words until they looked as he remembered.

Satisfied, he put on his boots, hat, scarf, slung a wineskin over his shoulder and shoved a piece of pig rib rich with meat into his pocket.

It would be a day's journey to Turo and back, the next town, to where he could pass his message on and be sure it reached The Baron's hand.

It is how each year's taxes went. It must be safe.

He stood inside his door and unrolled the scroll one more time to make sure his message was written clear.

"Lord Baron, Help."

He'd attached the seal he used to send taxes so The Baron would know from whence it came.

He opened the door.

Father Baillot stood there.

Baillot glanced at the open scroll as Tardiff absently rolled it up.

"Father Baillot. Is there something you need? Whatever it is, can it wait? I have something I must do."

Baillot stood silent, his dark eyes darting about under his saturno's rim.

"Well?"

Baillot kept his eyes steady on Tardiff's face. "I have business in Turo."

Tardiff's eyebrows rose and Baillot smiled.

"I'll be gone...not long. Only a day."

"Oh?"

"I was wondering...if you could watch my parishioners for me. While I'm away."

Tardiff became magnanimous. He walked Baillot into the street without closing his door. "Of course, of course, Good Father. And perhaps there's something you can do for me, as well. It will take you no time. You know the Sergeant there? Good, good, good. Perhaps you'll hand this to him for me? Nothing to be concerned with. One of my regular messages to The Baron, to let him know all is well. Yes, yes, yes. Thank you, Good Father, thank you."

Baillot set off towards Turo. Tardiff reached into his pocket, pulled out the pig's rib, put it between his teeth, went inside his cottage and closed his door, satisfied his obligation to The Baron and The Baron's taxes done.

~

Idee found Byell pouring some of the witch's dust into his palm before scattering it over some green shoots in the field. Her voice startled him and he quickly hid the pouch in his shirt. "Byell, is Julia helping you?"

"You sent her to deliver peppers and tomatoes, didn't you?"

"But you've not seen her since?"

"Is there a problem?"

She huffed over the rows of vegetables and looked at his hand, still inside his shirt. She shook her head. "You are a fool, Byell. Your foolishness cost us one daughter and now we've lost another."

He pulled his hand free of his shirt and made as if only picking a tick off his aging frame. "What are you talking about, woman?"

"Thomas and Eric found a dead girl's body in the woods north of Nant, along the Vell."

Byell swallowed. "Julia?"

"She wears Julia's clothes but the Tomekan priest thinks not."

"The Tomekan priest? The witch-hunter Verduan found for us?"

Idee snorted, her eyes still on the hidden pouch beside Byell's belly. "All he need do to find the witch is find that pouch on you." Her hand snapped out. She snatched the pouch and pulled his shirt at the same time.

The pouch she held aloft, between them, like a prize. "You thought this worth the price? You betrayed us for a sack of dust? You sacrificed our daughter for a witch's promise?"

She threw the pouch on the ground. It opened slightly and a

small cloud of dust, much like a frightened mouse, came out and hurried back inside.

"You are a fool, Byell. You lost us one daughter, now we've lost another."

She turned away from him, her hands clenched in fists, and kicked her way through rows of dying greenery.

He called out after her. "But the Tomekan says the body is not Julia."

Idee didn't slow, only yelled over her shoulder. "And our one remaining daughter is gone, her basket empty and left beside the South Road out of Nant."

She spun back to face him, fists on hips and face red as if from too strong a wind. "You cost us two daughters. Our daughters. My daughters. And I'll bear another man's child before I'll carry yours again, you fool!"

She turned back and tromped off through the barely greening rows.

Byell picked up the pouch of magic dust and murmured to it. "You promised." He put the pouch back in his pocket and looked across his dying fields. "You promised."

CHAPTER 20

Dire rolled over onto her knees in silent darkness. She'd been asleep? In her workshop? For so long the candles and lamps burned out?

Something whimpered close by her side as a hand nudged her shoulder.

"Nory? It's okay. Grandmother's here."

A hand stroked her hair. The whimpering turned into joyful crying.

"Help grandmother up, lad. There's a good boy."

Gentle hands guided her to her feet and steadied her. Once standing, she was embraced. Her hands searched for and found Nory's familiar features. "Can you help grandmother outside, lad? Is it day or night outside?"

Nory put his fist into her palm and made the sign she taught him for "day late."

She felt herself tugged in one direction. "Afternoon? How long did I sleep?"

Nory's hand made a circling motion. "A full day? Oh, you must have worried so much. I'm sorry, my boy. Have you eaten, Nory? Are you hungry?"

He took her hand and patted his stomach, then ran it over the remainder of the food tucked in his clothes.

"Where did you get so much food, Nory?" She hugged him. "Doesn't matter. Let's get outside then. Help grandmother, there's a good lad."

Nory's hand shaped "Show you."

"Show me? Show me what?"

Nory stepped to Dire's workbench. He sprinkled powder from her tinderbox into a shallow pot then dribbled a few drops from one of her phials. A moment later the mixture sparked and a flame grew. He brought over several candles and lit them.

Before he finished, Dire gasped.

Julia lay on some hides, unconscious. One of Dire's heavy woven blankets covered her neck to foot.

"Nory, what have you done?"

Nory shook his head and wrung his hands together. He moaned and his eyes went from Julia to Dire and back, then focused on Dire's shawl. He tapped it and Dire saw dust-like particles bounce and sparkle in the candlelight.

She gathered some in her palm as they floated to the ground. Carefully, she brought the grains to her nose. "Wormwood?" She touched the tip of her tongue to the grains. "Lettuce oil and lime tree root. That one meant me to sleep, soundly and quickly, but not to harm or hurt." She took Nory's hand so he looked straight at her. "Think now, boy. Have you seen any strangers, any newcomers, in our village?"

Nory nodded vigorously and held up three fingers first, then one.

He puffed up his chest and flexed his arms then motioned as if setting a grinding wheel in motion followed by working a blade on it, testing the blade, and working it again.

"A tradesman? A tinker? A metal-worker? Come through the village looking for work?"

Nory nodded and held up a second finger. He motioned throwing a cloak over himself and pulled his already tiny frame in. He lifted an imaginary cup to his mouth and looked back and forth as he did so.

"Someone small? At the Red Fox? Smaller than you?"

No. Same size.

"Man or woman?"

Nory shrugged and drew the imaginary cloak tighter around his face.

"Who's the third one?"

Nory imitated Father Baillot shaking holy water on everything around him followed by the sign for "other."

"Another priest? From another village?"

Nory nodded.

"The first too big to be my caller. The second too small. And no priest I know knows how to mix sleeping dusts."

She frowned, remembering. "Are any of them missing this ear?" She pointed to her right ear.

No.

Julia moaned and began to move.

"Did you do this to her, Nory? Did you hurt Julia?"

No.

"Did you find her? Bring her here?"

No.

"How long has she been here?"

Nory cowered and shrugged.

"That's okay, Nory. Is anyone outside? Does anybody know we're here?"

Nory straightened up. He put a hand to his brow as if shielding his eyes from the sun, shifted his eyes back and forth, then shook his head, no.

"You checked before waking me. Good boy." She knelt. Her fingers moved gently through Julia's hair and came up bloodied. She shuffled to get a better look and turned Julia's head slightly. "It's bad and you'll live."

"But where did you get such finery?" Her hands moved under the blanket and her eyebrows lifted. She pulled the blanket back.

Julia wore a finely made black robe, albeit poorly fitted to her, sewn too loose, made more for someone believing their body would ripen.

Dire's hands moved quickly but gently over Julia's body.

Julia moaned.

Dire spoke knowing Julia couldn't hear her. "Be still, girl. You've got no wounds, nothing's broken. You're bruised, but if there's other damage inside, I haven't learned it yet." Her hands stopped below Julia's navel. She undid some buttons and checked again. "You're with child." Her hands went further. "But not harmed. Not this time, at least."

Dire dipped her bloodied hand in a bucket of water by her bench and dried them on her skirt. "Who bashes in a girl's head then leaves her here in royal clothes under one of my blankets?" More dust floated from her and she snorted. "Did you do both, my one-eared friend? Either? Neither? Are you an avenging angel or a demon?"

Dire lifted Julia's head, bunched the hide to form a pillow, and gently lowered Julia's head back down.

Julia winced. Her eyes fluttered briefly and her head rolled to the side, away from Dire's manipulations.

"If you can feel, you're not dead. Not yet."

Dire pulled a small bottle from her shelf, uncorked it, opened Julia's mouth, poured in half the bottle, and massaged Julia's throat so she'd swallow and not choke.

Julia's breathing evened out and her face relaxed. "Yes, child. Sleep." She tapped Nory to get his attention. "Bring me some water for this child. From the old bucket over there, not from the bucket by my bench, that's from the Vell. Don't drink there anymore. Nory. Understand?"

Yes.

"And a cloth, lad."

Nory threw a rag over his shoulder, lifted the bucket in two hands, waddled over, and watched as Dire washed Julia's bruise.

Satisfied, Dire sat back and looked at the herbs drying on strings strung from rafters, the animal parts pinned against the dirt walls, the phials and bottles on her shelves. "Nory, will you go into Nant for Grandmother? I must stay here and keep Julia safe. There are things I need, some in the field, some the Baker keeps handy and one or two I've seen at the Red Fox. Julia will sleep for a while and I can take care of my needs from the field. Do you promise to remember what I tell you and bring them here, come back only yourself? Make sure you're not followed?"

Nory nodded vigorously, relieved to know Dire still loved him, fool that he was.

Dire gathered some things into a sack and slung it over her shoulder. "Nory, make sure no one's near when we leave."

Nory silently stepped through the brambles, barely moving a one. A moment later Nory's hand came back through the brambles, its index finger crooked up and inviting her to follow.

"Make us a path to the road to Nant, Nory. Make sure our way is clear."

A moment later the lad vanished into the wood.

Dire was in sight of the road when Nory appeared in front of her and slowly lowered himself to the ground. Dire drew herself down flat to the earth and she watched Nory close his eyes and low to focus with his ears.

Two voices, both male. One deep and resonant like an orator's, the other more from the chest, a singer's or showman's, heading south.

The singer spoke first. "You left her at the ruins?"

The orator, confronting, defending. "You question me now? She is gone, isn't that enough?"

Nory shook his head, closed his eyes and lowed again.

The singer again, his voice tight, frustrated. "You left her alive? You didn't bash in her brains as you did the other one?"

"My mother showed me what was done to her and described the two who maimed her. I found a woman as my mother described and avenged her."

The singer hissed. "You found the wrong woman, you fool."

"Yes, but then I found the woman my mother described, and so much alike you couldn't tell the difference."

The singer laughed without humor. "How lucky we are you didn't avenge your mother twice."

"Fattening our purses and serving Our Lord supersedes avenging my mother's folly. Besides, you told me to find a substitute and I found one. My work is done."

"You didn't think to bind her? To put her in a cell?"

"To be honest, I thought it unlikely she'd wake. Live, yes, wake, no."

The singer picked up his pace. His voice held a tone of disgust. "I'm surrounded by fools."

The orator didn't move. "And I am surrounded by clowns and whores." He stood there until the singer had moved some distance ahead then slowly followed.

Soon their voices were beyond hearing. Nory stayed low to the ground, his head lowed, one ear up then the other, until he was sure.

He stood and signaled Dire it was safe.

CHAPTER 21

Galos poked two opposing holes in his pile and watched thick, gray smoke rise. He poked two more holes, also opposite each other, and the smoke thinned and turned blue.

Galos nodded and smiled. He reached into a leather pouch on a woodpile, pulled out a thin strip of dried venison, and gnawed on until it softened enough to tear a piece off. Its juice glistened down his chin.

A bark came through the wood. The mice and chipmunks, their cheeping and squeaking serving as soprano accompaniment to his deep tenor as he worked, grew silent and burrowed deep in his wood stacks for protection. Galos reached for a solid piece of oak. It didn't sound like a wolf but game had become as scarce as harvest and he didn't want to be caught unawares.

A moment later Verduan's dog, Buco, trotted up and sat beside him. Galos rubbed the big dog's head. "Buco, does your master know where you are?"

He heard Verduan call from down the road. "Buco! Leave Galos be. He has no food for you."

Galos winked. Half the venison remained in his hand. He took his axe and carved off a thumb-wide piece.

The dog kept his eyes on the venison while Galos worked.

"Buco!"

The dog whined. Galos tossed the venison. Buco caught it in midair and took it behind the woodpile.

Verduan walked up with Patreo by his side. "Galos, have you seen my dog?"

Galos stared at Patreo and frowned for a moment. He looked down and shook his head before smiling at his friend. "Verduan, a dog? When did you get a dog?"

Patreo looked to the ground and walked behind the woodpile. He leaned over, momentarily hidden, and returned with Buco trotting beside him. The dog's flues globbed mucousy saliva as he walked.

Galos put a hand over his chest and pulled back, eyes wide with alarm. "By all the saints! A dog! I'll bet he's a good dog, isn't he?"

Buco snuffled Galos' hand holding the venison.

Verduan put his fists on his hips and glowered at Galos. "Is that your smoked venison? Did you give him your smoked venison? Do you know the smells that dog makes when he eats your smoked venison? He sleeps in the barn and still we're not safe in the house. Even the goats and cows leave their stalls when you give him your smoked venison."

"Who's your friend?"

Verduan made introductions. "Galos came to Nant years ago with Father Verrett. He went on his yearly pilgrimage and returned with a charcoal burner. Nant has prospered thanks to them both."

Galos offered his hand. "Welcome Father Patreo from Tomeka. Verduan says much about you."

Patreo shook Galos's hand. Done shaking, Patreo held his hand open at his side and looked about him.

Galos laughed and tossed him a rag. "Smoked venison and charcoal black. Sorry, Father. I don't think of such things anymore."

Patreo nodded a thanks and wiped his hands.

"Nant has kept you busy, Father?"

Patreo nodded a second time. Verduan rolled his eyes. "A small village has few secrets."

Galos chuckled. "What made you walk behind the woodpile?"

Patreo pointed. "The ground still bears the dog's drool. An easy path if one looks." He patted Buco's side. "He'll be needing water soon. Your venison's dry work."

Verduan smiled and nodded towards Patreo. "I told you. A wise one, he." He walked his dog towards a wood and called over his shoulder. "There's a rivulet not far into these trees. Buco can drink himself full there."

Galos ran to them and pulled on the thick fur around Buco's neck. "No. Not there."

Verduan chuckled. "Don't worry, we won't bother your tree taps."

Patreo looked around. "Tree taps?"

Galos's face reddened as Verduan explained. "Oh, Brother Galos mixes cedar and spruce, pine and birch...what else do you put in there?"

Galos shrugged. "Nothing."

Patreo stared at him. "Perhaps holly? Maybe some juniper when in season?"

Galos's eyes narrowed on Patreo. "It is nothing. To take the scent of the woodpiles from me. For special days."

Patreo said nothing and nodded.

Galos led Buco back to his woodpiles. "I have plenty of water here."

Patreo's eyes went to a half-empty bucket on the ground.

Galos pointed at his piles. "To temper the fire. He's welcome to drink. I can go to the rivulet when I need more."

SECTION V
THE CIRCUS

CHAPTER 22

chapter

Haasel stilled her wheel to better hear the tinkling of harness bells moving down the street. The bells kept time to the steady clomp clomp clomp of horses' hooves. Wagon wheels creaked. Another wagon followed with smaller horses, each with a single bell, each bell roughly palm size and bronze-cast from the sound. They jingled quietly until the wagon wheels clapped through a rut or over a rill in the road. Two more followed. Haasel picked up the mingled scents of bear and pony. "Not quite the lion and the lamb, and close."

She grabbed her cane and opened her door. Bright sunlight warmed her face and arms. The jingling and tinkling stopped. The draft horse's foreleg stomped a definitive clomp and shook itself of flies. Its rein and harness jingle came from quite high off the ground as if held in the hands of a musical giant. The second wagon's bells sounded as its horses stopped but the sound was from someone deliberately plucking it, not from a movement of the wagon or horse.

"Hello, Good Lady!" A deep, bellowing voice called to her from the first wagon's driver's seat. It carried a slight echo from the cabin mounted on the wagon's frame. The door between the cabin and the driver's seat opened and Haasel heard a woman's voice, old, harsh, gibbering as if in a delirium. The driver closed the door with a thud and the woman's voice was gone.

The driver continued. "A circus, Good Lady! Acrobats! Jugglers! Strange tasties from distant lands made while you watch. The poetry of Homer read by none other than myself! And other plays of the ancient Greeks and Persians! Storytellers sharing our ancestors' lore!"

Someone shifted on the second wagon's driver's seat but made no other noise. A servant, perhaps a slave.

"And news of the Mongol." The voice tightened slightly, the words slightly rushed, the speaker's tone betraying a hidden excitement. "They do brutal things to beautiful women."

Haasel smiled but her hands shifted on her cane, an involuntary motion of defense, a preparation to swat whatever came near. "Where will you set your stage?"

"In the village center if the...sheriff?"

Haasel shook her head. "Nant has no sheriff."

She pressed her lips together. Best not to answer too much. She did not like this one. Of the others, she knew not, but this one...this one she feared.

"What? No sheriff? Nant has no sheriff? Who guards this metropolis?"

A chuckle sounded from the last, third wagon where two women hummed softly.

Haasel kept her smile and counted sounds, determined the number of players in this troupe.

The first wagon's driver spoke again. "The village center. It's not far?"

She nodded down the road. "You'll find what you want that way. I must check my kilns, be sure my pots carry their glaze."

"Thank you, Good Lady. Our first performance is tomorrow eve, God willing."

Haasel nodded. "God willing."

The reins snapped, the bells jingled, the horses' hooves clomped, the wagon wheels creaked.

Haasel went back inside. She bolted her door, closed and locked her shutters. Her rooms were dark except when she opened one of her kilns to place or remove a pot or plate or cup.

CHAPTER 23

Patreo brushed Geselda's flanks outside the barn while Verduan cleaned the stalls. He removed his glove, washed his hands in the animal's trough, and dried them on his cassock before he tucked the glove between two buttons.

Verduan stared at the healed but still red blistering of the revealed hand. "That burn. What caused that?"

Patreo held his hand up as if to inspect it. "Oh, I got sloppy making an unguent. Nothing to be concerned about. All better."

"It looks like the burn I got, but from neither fire nor remedy. Mine came from working in my fields. And Byell's, among others. Worse in their fields than mine, though. Where the fields were wet from the last rain, the one that drove Sullya into the tree."

"May I see?"

Verduan lifted his hand. "It's all gone now, although for a day my palm blistered so much I thought my fingers would fall off."

Patreo turned Verduan's palm directly into the sun. The palm and fingers were healed but some pocks remained. "It bothers you no more?"

"When wet, sometimes."

Patreo nodded. "I have an ointment back in my saddlebags that may help."

Verduan stared into his palm wondering what Patreo saw there. "You carry the world in your saddlebags, Father?"

"The world I leave to Mother Church. My saddlebags carry what I may need in my travels."

The donkey brayed and nuzzled Patreo's cassock. He pushed her head forward. "Quit begging, girl. You're plump enough as it is."

Geselda snorted and bowed her head to the trough. Verduan came out with a barrel of used bedding slung over his shoulder. Nightjars and waxwings flew from the barn's dark interior into daylight to snatch insects following Verduan's bounty. The nightjars squawked and flew back into the dark. The waxwings created a softly plumed, red-wing tipped halo about Verduan's head as he walked.

Patreo pulled Geselda's head from the trough before she could drink. She stamped a hoof in protest and snorted again.

"Verduan, where does your water come from?"

Verduan emptied the barrel on a compost heap and dropped it to the ground. "From my well behind the barn."

"Where does Nant get its water?"

"Some have wells. Others rely on the Vell. Why?"

"Your animals all drink from your well?"

"From the trough out here or their buckets inside. But all are fed by the well."

"And Buco?"

"That one would drink a cow's piss if it suited him." Verduan came up beside the trough and ran his hand through the water to clear the surface. He cupped a handful of water, lifted it to his nose and inhaled deeply. "Is there a problem with the water?"

"Those with wells, their animals are healthy and well, yes? Those who draw water from the Vell, their animals founder?"

The water fell through Verduan's fingers to lush green grass surrounding the trough. Verduan stared at Patreo. "Yes. I never thought of it, and yes. A duct brings water from the Vell to the town well and those who take their water there also suffer."

"But the Vell." Patreo looked to the mountains between Nant and Tomeka. "It feeds two villages I know of before coming here. Maybe more. Have any other villages's animals grown weak? Have any other cows or goats gone dry?"

Verduan shook his head. "I don't know. Traders would know, those who come through. They always bring gossip." He snorted and shook his head. "Except the metalsmith. He had no gossip to share. He asked a lot of questions and was gracious enough, but that's part of a tinker's trade." He patted Geselda's side. "But tales from other villages upstream on the Vell, he had none."

Patreo let his donkey drink from the trough and kept his eyes on the mountains.

Verduan considered priest's gaze north. "You think the tinker a concern? He left his cart unguarded in the middle of a wood. What tinker does that?"

Patreo patted Geselda and watched her drink. "No, I don't think the tinker a concern."

"How can you be so sure?"

"Did you notice the marks on the side of his cart?"

CHAPTER 24

Nory repeated Grandmother Dire's list every few steps. He scuffed his bare feet now and again to see the sunlight sparkle in the little dust devils mimicking his steps.

Jingling bells and the clomp clomp clomp of heavy hooves caught his ear.

A troupe of circus wagons, each with a brightly colored cover, shuffled past. The biggest man Nory had ever seen, a giant with dark skin like someone who worked the fields daily, drove the first

A man dressed like a jester drove the second wagon. The bells on his three-lobed hat - each lobe tapering to a point, one lobe red, one green, the last gold - tinkled as the wagon bumped along the road. Two chestnut mares, both healthy and bright, pulled it.

A circus pony and a huge muzzled bear walked behind the second on leads. The pony wore bright colors and pranced even though no one was looking. The bear ambled. It occasionally turned to the pony and stopped only to be tugged forward by the lead from its muzzle to the wagon.

A third wagon followed. Two horses similar to those pulling

the second wagon pulled this one. Two women dressed in bright, multicolored clothes, their faces thinly veiled, sat in the driver's seat. Their voices harmonized as they sang, and it reminded Nory of beautiful birds sitting on a nest. They smiled at Nory as they passed.

Two horses also pulled the last wagon, but this last wagon had two more horses, much like the other four, following on leads. A dark-skinned man in forest greens held the reins. His clothing so contrasted with his skin color Nory thought the man some kind of wood god risen from the earth.

Nory waved.

The man in front smiled, waved, and called out something.

Nory frowned. He knew that voice.

The man waved and called again. The jester kept his eyes ahead of him on the first wagon.

Nory moved his fingers over his throat, a sign Grandmother Dire gave him to let all know he's mute, cannot speak.

The man in the lead stopped his wagon. He drew a blade from his boot and glared at Nory. The man drew the blade over his own throat and a thin red line appeared.

The jester jangled his horses' harness. "He's mute, Dobrogost. Let him be."

That voice. The jester's voice. Nory knew that voice, too!

The giant jumped down from his wagon, his knife still in his hand.

Nory stepped back. He looked between the cottages to find the quickest escape.

The jester snapped his reins. "Don't be a fool, Dobrogost. He's dumb. Mute. And look at the size of him. He wouldn't even feed your bear on a good day."

The giant laughed, regained his seat, snapped the reins, urged his wagon forward.

Nory crouched in the shadow beside a cottage, his head cocked to the side and his body slightly inclined like a dog guarding a mole hill.

The wagon hit a rut and the giant rocked in his seat. He put his knife back in his boot and dabbed his neck with his sleeve.

Nory knew. These are the men he heard when he and Dire left for supplies. These are bad men. They frightened Nory. He didn't like these men. These men would hurt Nory or hurt those who cared for Nory.

Nory's chest swelled and he stood tall.

Nory would not let these men hurt the people of Nant.

Nory would get his hammer and hurt these men if they tried to hurt the people of Nant.

Nory stayed behind the cottages, far from the street, and followed the circus wagons into Nant's center. They stopped in front of the church. The giant tied the reins to the brake, jumped down, and walked across to Tardiff's office.

Tardiff's office had a jail cell.

That would be a good place for these men. The jail cell.

Nory looked up and down to see if Tardiff was near. Nory would tell Tardiff these were bad men and should be in the jail cell.

The big bad man knocked on Tardiff's door. Tardiff didn't answer.

He knocked again. Nory saw the door rattle under the giant's fist.

Tardiff still didn't answer.

Who would help put the bad man in Tardiff's jail?

Verduan!

And Galos!

And Zevke. Zevke was a good man. He always gave Nory bread.

What about the new priest?

All of them! They would put these bad men in Tardiff's jail cell.

But first he would tell Grandmother Dire to stay away from the circus and these bad, bad men.

CHAPTER 25

S lewe watched Nant's happenings from behind the Red Fox's side door. He kept a pail of swill handy, ready to throw into his pigs' trough, in case anybody saw him and asked his business.

The circus wagons came into town from the East Road, the border, circled the center once, stopped at the head of the same road, and like an emptying clown cart, people began stepping down.

Was one wagon for the men, another for the women, a third for their costumes and paraphernalia, the fourth for...what?

Not their food stuffs, he hoped.

He wanted them to spend their earnings at the Red Fox! He wanted them to encourage townsfolk and other travelers to spend their coppers here, as well.

The witch business had not helped Nant's merchants. Local still bought from local, yes, but trade waned within days. Tradesmen went and carried the story with them in all directions, most left Nant as quickly as they entered lest the curse drag with them.

A steady trade route became a trickling trade route then dried completely. Few traveled the North-South Road. One tinker, the metalsmith Forgeron, and he'd gone days past.

And the rumors going round about him!

Verduan's friend, the Tomekan priest Patreo came from the north.

But another priest? Baillot touched nothing but sacramental wine and holy water. Would this Tomekan priest be any better?

At least Father Verrett downed a glass or mug or two with those in his care. He knew how to enjoy, he did. A good holy man who knew when a sin meant nothing or much, who read a heart as easily as he read the Scripture.

Many was the night Father Verrett and Slewe talked long after the doors closed, each with a single drink in front of them that lasted until the early morning hours, more important to listen and care than slosh and waddle.

Both knew their place in Nant society; what people shared in the confessional was often a boast in one's cups and what was a secret in one's cups was often an admission in the confessional.

Aye, Father Verrett knew Inn and church served much the same purpose. From different ends, perhaps, and still much the same purpose.

He confided much to Slewe. Who else in Nant knew Father Verrett served as confessor to an abbey, one of the few men the abbess allowed inside? Oh, the stories Father Verrett told.

It shocked Slewe to learn holy sisters felt the same needs other women felt.

And then there were the stories of the orphans - male and female - who came there and ended up in his care. Horrible things done to children in the name of the church.

Slewe was the first to know of Galos and how Verrett, returning from a pilgrimage, found Galos wounded in mind and body and left for dead along the road. He dragged Galos into the wood and made a shelter for them, brought fruit and small game, and stayed with Galos, tending and healing him as well he could, until Galos woke to confess some sin Verrett wouldn't share. Father Verrett gave him unction and his strength returned.

Galos asked what he could do to repay the Father and Verrett mentioned Nant needed a charcoal burner, did Galos know the art?

Galos said he some similar training and became Nant's coal-burner. Of more than that, Verrett would not say and Slewe, respecting the priest to know what to share and what not, asked no more, but wondered now and again, what was Galos' story that such troubles would befall him on a road between Nant and the Holy Land?

Slewe was also the first to know Verrett planned a pilgrimage to the Holy City, to seek release from his holy orders, a priest he'd remain but now in a monastery cell, some books to transcribe and illuminate to end his days.

He showed Slewe the herbs Dire gave him to ease the pain. Wonderful creations God put on this earth. Pity Mother Church did not see such learnings so.

So a final pilgrimage. He would return, he hoped, with a new cleric, spend a few months introducing him and getting him settled, then be on his way.

Except he never came back.

And Baillot, in Slewe's eyes, was not much of a replacement.

A shadow moved out from behind one of the wagons.

Two bears ambled forth.

No, one a huge brown bear, the other a man as big as the bear, perhaps bigger with skin near the color of the bear's fur, the man's only other coloring being billowing bright white pants, an equally billowing purple shirt open to the waist, and a red fez.

Strangely, the bear dressed much the same.

Oh, how much such a man must drink and eat! The Inn would swell to bursting with others come just to see him consume!

The driver of the fourth wagon pulled up beside the giant. A clown in jester's garb save a red scarf covering his head came up to them. They spoke quietly. The giant pointed to the south road and the wagon moved on.

Slewe cursed. Fewer mouths to feed. There go his profits.

Father Baillot came out of his rectory. He took a step towards the wagons and froze.

The giant bearman and jester turned and smiled at him.

Baillot went back into his rectory. Slewe heard the door slam and bolt from across the town square.

The jester went back behind the wagons. The giant bearman kept smiling. He unhooked the bear's lead from the wagon and walked with it towards the rectory.

He didn't see Father Baillot emerge from the south transept, run past the cottages, his cassock held high so as not to impede movement, and hurry up the North Road out of town.

CHAPTER 26

Patreo and Verduan walked south on the main road into Nant. Verduan held a dead sturgeon in either hand. "Belly up. Held in the eddies and belly up. All of them. You said we can't eat them, why do you want me to bring them home?"

Before Patreo could answer, a soft music, the plinking of an oud and the call of a zurna, filtered towards them. Verduan stopped, focused then smiled. "A circus, Father Patreo! We had one come through two years back. They had a dancing bear and jugglers. And their puppet show. I laughed so hard. Then there was that girl, her voice. You would cry to hear it, so beautiful."

Fast footsteps overcame the music. Father Baillot raced down the road towards them, his head bowed. He waved his hands as if summoning a great North wind and bellowed as if to give that wind a voice.

Patreo mumbled, "Hide the fish."

Verduan slid them up his sleeves and grabbed his cuffs in his hands.

Patreo called to Baillot. "Good Father, what's wrong? What troubles you so?"

Baillot stopped, his face flushed and his cross swinging back and forth as if it continued walking down the road without him. He stared without speaking.

"Father Baillot?"

Baillot's eyes opened wide. They darted to both sides of road, into the woods, into cover, and came back to them. "Verduan. Father Patreo." He paused. His mouth opened and closed a few times as he licked his lips. "A circus. A carnival."

Verduan laughed. "I told Father Patreo we had one two years back. Before your time, Father Baillot. They - "

Patreo cleared his throat. "Is there a problem with the circus?"

Baillot blinked. His nostrils flared briefly and he inhaled sharply. "They are heathens, these circus people. They bring fortunetellers and soothsayers with them, not to mention what diseases they may bring. The Death, you know - "

"We can ask where they've last been, send someone to see how those villages fare."

Baillot didn't slow. "They sell potions. Elixirs made from the things of the field. They - "

Patreo nodded at each phrase and interrupted at the last. "You mean like what I used to revive Mother Idee?"

Baillot's eyes roved over Patreo's cassock as if to see what medicants were hidden there.

Patreo continued. "Let's talk to the circus people, learn what their purpose is before they set up their stage and booths." Patreo bowed. "Father Baillot, if you would lead the way?"

Baillot stared at him as if unsure of his meaning. "I have business elsewhere. I must be on my way." He pushed past them.

Patreo gently placed a hand on Baillot's passing sleeve. "But Father, if this circus is the threat you claim, aren't your parishioners your immediate concern?"

Baillot's eyes widened. His nostrils flared. He exhaled as if his breath was a sulphurous blast from hell. He turned. His cassock whirled about him, his cross swung in a great arc, and he hurried back towards Nant.

Patreo leaned into Verduan. "Did you tell anybody where we were going?"

"No. Why?"

"Then how did the Good Father Baillot know where to find us?"

"Maybe he wasn't looking for us?"

"Then why was he hurrying on the road out of the village if the circus threatens Nant?"

CHAPTER 27

Z evke left Saida to work the ovens. After the day's events, he needed something stronger than the communion wine Father Baillot gave him in exchange for communion bread.

Did he know Zevke gave him matzo?

Did he think Zevke smiled and nodded because he was so grateful for weak wine?

Didn't matter.

More than a drink, he wanted gossip. Had anyone found the girl?

People coming with loaves for him to bake said a circus was in town. Perhaps something to give him and Saida a little laughter at the end of the day?

The ovens were Zevke's pride and joy. He built them himself with guidance from both Galos and Haasel, two good people in the village. He knew more baking could be done by keeping the ovens hot even when not in use. Most bakers let their ovens cool overnight and then spent a few hours the next morning stoking them to get back to temperature.

Galos explained how to curve an oven's walls so heat was

directed back to some point at its center. Zevke shrugged, raised his eyebrows and hands wide and palms up, not understanding.

"Here, let me draw it for you." The two kneeled in the dirt in front of Zevke's cottage as Galos sketched out the size and shape of the ovens based on how many loaves Zevke would bake each time, and explained where in the ovens it would be cooler and warmer so different types of breads could be baked and baking would occur for longer and shorter periods of time depending on placement. Beside the sketches, Galos drew symbols and numbers.

Zevke put a hand on Galos' sleeve. "What is that? Some magic? An incantation?"

"Don't worry, old friend. It's a kind of magic, true, but its name is mathematics." Galos went on to explain how each number described some part of the oven's architecture, how each symbol related one part to another.

"Where did you learn this mathematics?"

Galos shrugged followed by a shiver. "In the Crusades."

"Defending Holy Jerusalem?"

"As a prisoner of the Gourdin."

Zevke watched Galos work through his calculations. "I know little of them."

Galos leaned back, his eyes still on his numbers and symbols. "They are a good people. Some better, some worse, like any you'll meet in the world. They know arts and sciences we do not. Their belief encourages learning."

"Doesn't Holy Mother Church?"

"Holy Mother Church only encourages what learning benefits Holy Mother Church. And Holy Mother Church would rather kill you than convert you. And even after you're converted they might kill you anyway just to be sure." Galos stood up, satisfied with his drawing, and brushed dirt from his knees. "The Gourdin will teach you and most will let you decide which path you'll follow."

"You they taught?"

"Because I respected them. They were my adversary, not my enemy. I would not kill one already wounded. Battle them, yes, but slaughter them, no. I let them gather their dead and retrieve their wounded for treatment. One got the better of me on the field outside Jerusalem and, realizing who I was, brought me still bleeding into their camp. I may have been their prisoner, but they never put me in prison."

Zevke watched the charcoal burner, how at times his eyes flashed when he spoke, how at other times they grew distant and saw things Zevke guessed at: his Gourdin captors? His Gourdin friends? Battles fought and won? Battles fought and lost?

"You escaped?"

Galos snorted and smiled. "They let me go if I promised to battle no more."

"But you were a knight!"

Galos laughed and patted Zevke's shoulder. "Some would say I still am. Come, let us ask Haasel what type of clays and bricks best build the oven we have in mind."

"You are being very kind, Brother Galos."

Galos waved his hand dismissively. "I am a businessman, Friend Zevke. Build the proper ovens with the proper clays and design, and you'll be buying my charcoal until I teach my skills to another. You are an investment to me, nothing more."

Zevke frowned. "Nothing more?"

The marks on Zevke's lintel caught Galos's eye. He stared at Zevke then back at the marks, walked over to them, stared at Zevke again and stopped.

Zevke straightened his back, his eyes on Galos.

Galos kissed his fingers, touched them to one mark, then looked at Zevke and nodded. "A Brother and a Friend."

Haasel listened attentively when Zevke and Galos explained the oven's purpose and design to her. Her hands never left the clay becoming a pot on her wheel as it turned and turned and turned, her ears attentive while her eyes were not.

Finally she cut the pot free of her wheel and placed it behind her on a shelf along similar shaped pieces. "You'll need a frame first, then mold to that frame, and glazed on the inside to reflect the heat, and ..."

Both Galos and Zevke scratched their heads as Haasel listed the construction details.

Zevke cleared his throat. "Sister Haasel, a fresh loaf every day as long as the ovens last for you to supervise their construction?"

Haasel cocked her head towards Galos' voice. "And charcoal for my kilns?"

Zevke looked at Galos pleadingly.

"And charcoal for your kilns."

She clapped her hands and laughed. "Ha. Done and done. When shall we start?"

The deal struck and decisions made, Galos and Zevke left Haasel to her wares. Galos glanced at Zevke out of the corner of his eye as they walked. "You know, of course, I'll also get a loaf every day for making all this happen."

"Every other day."

Galos sighed. "Very well. Every other day."

What started as business evolved into camaraderie and strong friendship ever since. The three usually met in the Red Fox and drank a pint or two. Saida joined them sometimes. She claimed it was only to make sure Zevke made it home, but she often laughed hardest and caught her breath as she wiped tears from her eyes.

Now Zevke looked for signs of the circus. Somewhere, usually in the town center, a stage would be going up. A ring would be marked out where a muzzled bear would dance. A horse pony would show its good steps, not knowing someday it would be slaughtered, too old and too tired to show any steps and now pulled behind a wagon, not pulling it forward.

Zevke understood. Such was the way of all things. Sometimes things got too old, too tired, and had to be put away.

He smiled as he entered The Red Fox. Slewe poured a cup and had it ready for him before he sat down.

The Innkeeper leaned into him. "Have you heard?"

Zevke's stomach churned. The ale soured as he sipped it. "Heard what?"

"A dead girl, a young woman, found in the forest."

Zevke kept his cup up to his face, his eyes peered over the rim as if in hiding. "Oh?"

Slewe shared what he knew.

Zevke cocked his head and frowned. Slewe's news didn't make sense.

Her face bashed in?

A hand chopped off?

Zevke spoke from behind his cup. "You haven't said who it was. Does anyone know the child?"

Now Slewe pulled back. It was his turn to frown and cock his head. "Julia. You should have heard Idee wail. Her face was so battered they identified her by her clothing."

Zevke's head came up from his cup and he stared at Slewe. "By her clothing?"

"It was the only way they could tell. Idee saw it was Julia's blouse and skirt. She helped the girl make them herself. Can you can believe it?"

"They are sure it was Julia?"

"Brother Baker, what kind of game do you play?"

Zevke shrugged and once again hid behind his cup.

CHAPTER 28

Patreo and Verduan heard the musical sounds replaced by heated discussion as they neared the center of Nant. They rounded a corner to find two wagons on either side of a growing stage. A leanly muscular middle-aged man, his face half made up in jester makeup and wearing a red sash and a jester's red, green, and gold three-belled hat, stood in animated conversation with Tardiff.

A bear bellowed from Baillot's rectory. Verduan and Patreo turned as one. A muzzled brown bear with a bright red fez and a chain around its neck waddled atop a barrel rolling towards the wagons. Behind him walked a mountain of a man a head or more taller and broader than Verduan. Except for his posture the man could be mistaken for a bear himself; from the eyes down the man's face was covered in thick reddish-brown hair. He held the other end of the chain and carried another barrel on his shoulder. Even the back of his hands carried his reddish-brown pelt.

He pulled lightly on the chain and the bear dropped down. The man spoke quietly and evenly from across the town center yet his voice seemed to come from shops and alleys and yards and even the ground itself. Everyone clearly heard him as everyone turned to face him. "Hello and welcome to Dobrogost's Traveling Delights. Beasts and bewilderings. Music and mysteries. Stories and songs. Wonders and wishes. How may we serve you today, good people of Nant?"

The man smiled a strong set of clean white teeth at everyone and finally focused on Tardiff and the half-jester. He shrugged the barrel off his shoulder and lowered it to the ground with his free hand.

Patreo leaned into Verduan. "Is this the circus you remembered?"

The smiling man-mountain bowed low from the waist, his free hand coming across his stomach and concealed by his flowing, patchwork shirt. He raised back up with the same smile. "I, of course, am Dobrogost, a Persian by birth, a traveler of the world by choice. My troupe and I hope for a few days rest in your fine city. In return we offer many wonderful enchantments and entertainments. What is your pleasure?"

The half-jester broke free of Tardiff, came over, took the bear's chain, and whispered something to the giant.

The giant's eyes fixed on Tardiff a second time. He nodded and motioned the half-jester away.

His smile remained as he walked towards him, eyes bright above his flame-colored face, arms spread wide in greeting. He acknowledged Verduan and Patreo with a courteous nod as he closed on Tardiff.

Tardiff noticed them and motioned them over.

The giant smiled down at Verduan and Patreo. "Hello, Good Father. But you are not the priest I saw earlier today. Nant is blessed to have two priests serving it?"

Patreo bowed. "I am visiting. A traveler, like yourself and your troupe."

Tardiff interrupted. "As I told your jester, I have received no word of performers heading towards Nant."

The giant smiled and pointed at the man in makeup. "Ah, Korol is not my jester. He's on loan to us for the time being. Isn't that right, Korol, Master Jester?"

Korol the Jester bowed.

The giant continued. "We are happy to pay whatever fee your Lordship deems necessary for the privilege."

Tardiff looked around. "There are several of you. Where will you stay? And where will you house your animals?"

"We are used to the stars as our blanket. Our animals stay with us. There is no need to quarter any here."

"How are you provisioned?"

"I see an inn with food and drink. What we don't have in our wagons we can get there, I'm sure."

Tardiff held up a hand, palm out, ready to raise another objection. Before he could, the giant took it and shook it gently, as if in greeting. "And I'm sure we will bring business to Nant with our presence. Word will go to the surrounds. Should we send business away, we will recompense as our pockets allow." The giant cocked his head and smiled. "Fair?"

Tardiff looked across at Patreo and Verduan. "What do you say, Father Patreo?"

Something caught Patreo's eye. He pulled back and made a swatting motion. "Let them stay. Nant could use some merrymaking."

The giant turned his head and smiled down on Patreo. "Thank you, Gracious Father. Perhaps you'll join us in our merrymaking on opening night?" He giant's lips curled back in more of a snarl than a smile. "We put on a show few can forget, I promise you."

The giant turned back to Tardiff. "Settled, then?"

Patreo continued swatting something. "You have several

animals: your drafts, your bear, your circus pony. Do you carry water for them?"

The giant turned to gaze at him and nodded towards the rectory. "I took from the church's well." He reached into his pocket and took out two gold pieces. "As you are a churchman, will you accept our offering for these two barrels I filled?"

Patreo swatted one more time then brought his hands down as if done with whatever vexed him. "I'll see Father Baillot's parish gets them. I look forward to your first night's performance. By the way, I have some herbals if these gnats bother your animals. It'll keep them free of them and help preserve their coats."

The giant laughed like thunder. "Perhaps you should use some yourself."

Patreo joined in the laughter. He nodded at Verduan and they left Tardiff to haggle fees.

Once down the street Verduan let the sturgeon slip back into his hands. "What became of Father Baillot? Surely he would be back before us. And what are we to do with these fish?"

Patreo nodded. "To the second, I wish to examine them. Their internals may tell us why they died. To the first, does the rectory have its own well or is it filled from the Vell?"

Nory knew they were all talking to the bad man.

Nory couldn't hear what they said but everyone smiled.

No, no, no, no, no.

Don't smile. He's a bad man.

Verduan, Tardiff, and the new priest kept talking with the giant.

Nory picked up a stone and whacked the side of the cottage where he stood.

Everybody kept talking but the new priest's eyes flickered from Tardiff and the giant to follow the sound. He looked at Nory and nodded slightly.

Nory shook his head, no no no no no.

The new priest looked back at Verduan and the bad man but signed "Bad man?"

How did the priest know Grandmother Dire's signs?

He must be Grandmother Dire's friend.

So he would be Nory's friend.

Nory's hands flew. YesBadMan.

What?

Nory slowed his words. Sometimes Dire had trouble understanding him.

Him. Bad. Man.

Thank you, Nory. Go be safe now. Thank you.

The new priest knew! He understood! The new man is a bad man!

Nory liked the new priest. Nory smiled. He nodded quickly and hurried away to Dire's cellar.

Nory would tell Grandmother Dire: the new priest is a good man.

SECTION VI
THE GALATIAN

CHAPTER 29

Byell stood, hoe in hand, on the eastern boundary of his fields. He faced his fields with his apple orchards behind him. They rustled in a slight wind. He sheltered his eyes from the sun and scanned the horizon.

No rain. Not even a cloud. For days.

He turned and considered his trees. Not as full as they should be this time of year. "It'll be a poor harvest. If any."

And his bees were silent. He frowned at his hives. His bees should be out and about their business, but they were silent. Everyone knew his hives produced the best honey, his bees kept Nant's fields and orchards green and flowered. He planned to give one hive as Julia's dowry when her time came, and that would be to Eric, he was sure. Then his and Verduan's fields would join and both families would prosper.

But today no bees flew. He tapped a hive.

Nothing.

He stooped, cupped some earth in his palm, picked up and touched his tongue to it and just as quickly spit it out. "Ugh. Bitter."

He walked into his field and tested the soil with his hoe, shook his head, spat, and spoke low, quietly, speaking to himself as if defending himself to another. "I did what was asked. Why haven't you done what you promised? Why haven't you opened my fields and nourished my trees? Where are the blessings you said would be mine?"

Movement at the far end of the field caught his eye.

The figure in black. Were they sifting dirt in their gloved hand? From Byell's field? Some dirt went into a pouch at the figure's side.

"Is it you brought this curse on me?"

The figure moved off into the wood, seemingly unaware.

"Are you a demon sent to witness my end?"

He sat and dug his heels into a furrow as tears filled his eyes. "I am a fool." He slammed his palm into the ground and dug his fingers into the unyielding earth. "A fool." He slammed his palm into the earth a second time. He opened his eyes wide and stared into the heavens. "A fool," he shouted. "A fool, a fool, a fool!" Each repetition louder than the last and each accompanied with his palm slamming the earth.

He dug his fingers into his eyes. "I did what you asked. I gave you of my own blood, and now every time I look upon one daughter I see the shadow of the other, a ghost who haunts everything I do! I am cursed. Cursed! How do I atone for what I've done?"

Idee called from the far end of his fields.

Byell took his knife from his belt and ran the blade across his throat.

He heard Idee call out then heard nothing at all.

CHAPTER 30

Eric marched towards Tardiff's cottage and slowed as he approached. One of Baron Bassys's soldiers, a sheriff's deputy according to the standard on his mantle, stood outside the door, his sword out, his hand on the hilt, and the tip a finger's breadth into the ground.

The deputy spread his feet slightly when Eric neared.

"I have business with UnderSheriff Tardiff."

The deputy smiled dismissively through his rough beard. "Tardiff the Bellman? Master Donam, the Lord Sheriff, talks with Tardiff the Bellman."

"I'll wait."

The deputy shook his head, no, but said, "If you must." He didn't move but gripped his sword more firmly.

Verduan taught Eric to always seek allies, make friends whenever possible, because friends help you achieve your goals, enemies move you towards destruction.

But how to make this man a friend?

Eric noticed a bright yellow patch, the figure of a man walking, under the standard. "What is that in honor of, friend? I've never seen its like."

The deputy stood tall. His hand relaxed its grip and smiled down on the younger man. "I served King Gaumand as a tracker, one of his best and the right to wear this shield is my reward. I helped find the hidden camps and the stragglers when the Turks crossed our borders. I now serve Baron Bassys as a deputy to Sheriff Donam."

Eric raised his eyebrows. "You're a hero, then."

The deputy looked down at the earth and shook his head, but his smile remained. "No, just doing what I could for the King's and in The Baron's service."

Eric looked around. There was only this one man and he stood at this one door. Did he know all the ins and outs of Nant? Eric doubted it. "Good day to you, then."

"Another time then."

Eric went around Tardiff's cottage to its rear door. Here Tardiff kept a small garden and a stable for his goat and horse. The tinker's cart waited on the other side of the garden wall, where Verduan and Patreo placed it should further investigative need arise.

Eric lifted the latch slowly, tiptoed into Tardiff's back room, and listened.

A strong, male voice, one used to giving orders and being in authority. "For the last time, Tardiff, I'm not here because of some message you sent The Baron. What message? Neither I nor The Baron received any message from you about the doings in Nant. Ask me again and your title of Bellman will be the official one, understand?"

"My apologies, Lord Sheriff."

The sheriff - Eric assumed Donam by name - calmed slightly. "But I will grant you, a dead body and a missing child on the same day. It is odd. You know nothing of this?"

"I told you, Lord Sheriff, Nant is a quiet place. Two lads found the body and it is being prepared for burial as we speak."

"But it was a young woman's body?"

"Aye, but not a woman known to Nant."

"How can you know this when you say her face was destroyed?"

"All the children of Nant are accounted for save one - "

"The girl whose clothes the body wore?"

"Yes, Lord Sheriff. And - "

"And none have seen her since this other girl's body was found?"

"Aye, Lord Sheriff, but how can the two be related?"

"How much of a fool are you, Tardiff? One woman dead, the other missing, the dead wearing the clothes of the missing, and evidently the dead mistaken for the missing by your own town folk?"

Tardiff said nothing.

Donam erupted. "Well?"

Shuddering silence.

"Was the dead woman whole?"

Tardiff cleared his throat. "Not according to the priest - "

"A priest examined the body? Since when does a priest know if a woman's pure?"

"This is a Tomekan priest, schooled and knowledgeable in many things. He is the closest we have to a physician - "

"And do you know what Baron Bassys' physician would say to that? 'I do not offer sacrament,' he would say, 'Why is a priest performing mortems?'"

"Perhaps in Tomeka?"

"Tomeka? On the other side of the Coranth? What brought him to Nant?"

"Our town is bewitched."

Donam's voice rose in question. "You have a witch in Nant?"

"Sullya. From long ago come back to haunt us. Some say she lives in an oak in a forested hollow south of Nant. Others claim she haunts The Cloisters, the old ruins southeast of Nant. All say she's cursed our fields and orchards. Our last parish priest, Father Verrett, knew how to handle such things. Our new parish priest, Father Baillot, doesn't seem knowledgeable in such things. We sought the aide of someone well versed in these matters."

Donam frowned. "Baillot? I know no Father Baillot. The Bishopric always lets The Baron know when changes occur in the villages under his protection."

"Father Baillot's been with us a little over a year now. Father Verrett went on his yearly pilgrimage and Father Baillot returned in his place. The Good Father received his reward on his journey, it seems, and the bishopric graced us with Father Baillot as his replacement."

"He came with the bishopric's seal?"

Tardiff cleared his throat. "I can't read, my Lord Sheriff."

Silence. Tardiff cleared his throat again. Eric heard the shuffling of feat.

Donam spoke again. "I'll see this Father Patreo first, then I'll speak with Father Baillot. My deputy and I will be at the Red Fox. Bring them to us there. First Patreo, then Baillot. See to it." A chair scraped across a floor. "Understood?"

"Yes, my Lord Sheriff."

Patreo stood at a workbench in Verduan's barn. The barn's dark interior offered a reprieve from the day's heat. He ran a hand over the workbench's surface and brushed away mouse droppings, scatterings of hay and grain, a few small feathers, and the like. "This will do."

Verduan stood on the border of sun's light and barn's dark at his barn's door. "This will do for what?"

"Do you still have those fish we took from the Vell?"

Verduan held up a sturgeon in each hand.

Patreo patted Geselda's rump and he reached around her to his saddlebags hung over her stall's gate. "Treating you well, girl? Giving you enough sweet oats to keep you happy? Put the fish on the workbench, Verduan, would you?"

Verduan did as asked. "All my livestock are in the fields or paddock, she is treated better than most."

"As well she should be. She's a special beast."

Verduan hesitated. "Your familiar?"

"A gift from the bishopric."

"I thought you weren't in favor with the bishopric."

"They thought she'd help me leave their diocese quicker."

Verduan laughed.

Patreo pulled a thick, dual wicked candle, two round pieces of palm-sized glass, and a small, sharp knife from one of the saddlebag pockets.

"Do you have your tinderbox handy? Light both wicks on this candle, please."

Verduan blinked at the resulting brightness. "How is one candle so bright?"

Patreo took the candle and put it on the other side of the fish from him. "Two wicks, close together, give off more light than two wicks standing apart. The closer they are, the more light they give off."

"You're a witch."

Patreo chuckled. "So the bishopric thinks more often than not." He sliced one sturgeon open along its belly and let the intestines fall out.

Geselda snorted and moved to the far side of her stall.

"Your donkey is wise. I've never known the Vell's sturgeon to smell so. How long were they dead to smell so strong?"

Patreo picked up one of the discarded feathers and used its quill to separate the sturgeon's intestines from each other. "Not dead long. The blood hasn't thickened. The fish still bleeds."

He picked up one of the glasses. It caught the dual-wicked candle's light and Verduan shielded his eyes. "More things the bishopric doesn't like?"

Patreo held one out to Verduan. "A *dioptres*, a reading stone, from the teachings of a wise Arab, Ibn al-Haytham. I often journey into their lands on church business."

"What business would the church have with the Arab?"

"Sometimes to serve the church I must learn what the church does not teach. It's what kept me from Nant. The Arab have a broader understanding of witches than the Christian. Among other things." He lifted the *dioptres*. "This allows you to see what is too small to be seen otherwise, things you might miss without it." He held it so the candle's light shown intently on the gutted sturgeon. "Hold this here, just this way."

Verduan held the reading stone tenderly, as if it would bite.

"Hold it securely, Verduan. It's science, not magic."

"With you the two are one in the same."

Patreo held the other stone over the sturgeon's splayed intestines. "Hmm." He took the second fish and repeated his surgery. "Put the light on this one, please."

Verduan leaned over to see what captured Patreo's fascination and his motion unfocused the candle's light.

Patreo steadied Verduan's hand without looking up. "Steady, please." He used the quill to spread the intestines. "Yes." He took the stone from Verduan and held it so the light fell on the second fish while keeping the other stone the correct height over the fish's guts. "Look. See the kidneys and heart? They are swelled. These fish are poisoned."

"The Vell's water is poisonous now? It's been fresh since I was a boy."

"It is poisonous now because someone is poisoning it. These swellings come from ingesting white lead. Plants will die of it; humans will suffer horribly then die. Livestock, too. We have to stop Nant from drinking from the Vell. Any wells, any ducts, will be dangerous to the touch, death if drunk, and more so the closer they are to the Vell. We must tell Tardiff. He'll know what to do."

CHAPTER 31

Thomas walked north along the Vell, his head bowed and his eyes focused on the ground. A walking staff swung from his right hand and fluttered through grasses and shrubs along the side of the road. Forest smells of sweet rose and sage scents rose up to greet him. Occasionally he flushed ground nesting nightjars and bustards. Once a flock of ground jays rose at his approach and the air crackled with their squas and wingbeats. Some flew into tree trunks in their panic and fell back to the ground, startled. Grub seeking warblers and grassbirds darted past him where his staff opened spaces for them to feed. Insects stopped their chirping and buzzing as he walked past. It seemed as if the Vell itself quieted at his approach.

He came to where they found the girl's body and tinker's cart.

Someone moved in the brush up ahead. Quietly.

Thomas stopped, dropped to the ground, and gently moved the tangle of leaves and undergrowth aside.

Nory stood beside an elm. He reached in with both hands. Something glinted in the sunlight filtering through the trees.

Whatever it was, it was heavy. Nory gripped it tightly in both hands. When he turned it, it sometimes caught the sun dully, sometimes not at all, sometimes as if Nory held a mirror up to the sun.

Thomas stood to get a better view.

A hammer?

Not far from where they found the girl's body and the tinker's cart?

"Nory!"

Nory cringed. He fumbled putting the hammer back in the tree and lost his grip. The hammer thudded to the ground at his feet.

"What do you have there, Nory?"

Nory backed away from the elm, his eyes darting from Thomas to paths through the trees. He shook his head and shrugged his shoulders.

Thomas kept his eyes on Nory as he approached. "What did you do, Nory?"

Nory's eyes widened. The hooded, black figure moved silently through the woods not far behind Thomas.

Thomas stopped by the elm, his eyes on Nory. He took them off only long enough to be sure his hand grasped the hammer. He lifted it.

One side shone of metalwork in the sun. He turned the hammer in his grip. Blood tainted the other side.

Thomas's eyes widened and focused on Nory. His nostrils flared. "You killed that girl, Nory?" He lifted the hammer and shook it in Nory's face. "You killed her? And what did you do with my sister? How did you get her clothes?"

He grabbed Nory's rags and pulled him close. "Tell me, Nory! Tell me or I'll kill you!"

Thomas' eyes flared as he raised the hammer over his head.

A bone-numbing thwack hit his forearm. He pulled his hand back as the hammer fell behind him.

He kept his hand on Nory's rags and turned.

Something flashed in the sun, struck the side of his head.

He fell.

Nory looked at Thomas, crumpled on the ground. Polished black leather boots stepped into his field of vision. He raised his eyes slowly. Billowing black robes flowed from the top of the black boots up a strong body to a black hood-covered head with an equally black scarf covering all the face save the eyes. The wearer sheathed a sword, its eyes on guiding its sword into its scabbard, its arms turning the billowing sleeves into great feathered wings.

Nory fell back against the elm and whimpered.

The black robed stranger looked up. "I'm sorry, Nory. I didn't mean to frighten you." The wearer pulled on a knot securing their scarf to their hood. "I worried Thomas would hurt you. I had to stop him but I didn't want him to know who I am."

The stranger pulled the scarf free.

"I know you didn't hurt that girl."

Nory's eyes opened wide. A smile burst through the fear on his face and he leapt into the other's arms and began kissing his savior's hands and face.

The other chuckled. "Yes, Nory. You're safe now." They pushed Nory back slightly. "But promise me, you won't tell anybody who I am. It'll be our secret, right? If you must give them a name, tell them my name is Simon. Alright? Will you do that for me, Nory?"

Nory kept hugging and kissing Simon's hands and face.

Verduan and Patreo stood beside the town center's well and peered inside. "Is there a test for the well, Patreo?"

"There is but I'm not able to make it. You may think I carry the world in my saddlebags but I didn't anticipate this."

Baillot ran down the far end of the street. He turned, glanced back the way he came, and snapped his head around, its motion stopped only for a second when a wall or doorway or gate or alley met his eyes.

Verduan scratched his beard. "What troubles our noble churchman so?"

Baillot ran out of sight around a corner. A moment later they heard "Holy Mother, no!" followed by a cry of pain.

They ran. Dust rose with their steps as their boots clacked down the street.

They turned the corner. Patreo, his cassock lifted to keep his legs free, skidded to a stop. Verduan ran into him and knocked him down.

Father Baillot lay on the ground, curled on his side at the far end of the lane, his saturno lay tilted on its crown an arm's length away. Someone dressed head to toe in black robes knelt beside him. A hood, seemingly part of the clothing, covered the person's head and hid their features, like a mask. Despite the heat, the kneeling person kept the hood tied closely.

The person stood at the sound of Patreo and Verduan colliding, saw them, ran between the nearby cottages and into the woods.

Patreo and Verduan hurried to Baillot.

He shook and gasped. They rolled him onto his back. He stared at them, his eyes glazed, unable to focus. He gasped again and inhaled deeply. Patreo massaged his stomach. "Easy, Father. Lie still until we know what happened."

Verduan lifted Baillot's crucifix and held it out to Patreo. "This is what happened."

A crossbow bolt dropped from where its arrowhead pierced the surface of Baillot's heavy gold crucifix.

Verduan looked into the woods and around villager's homes. "Can we move him?"

Patreo followed his gaze. "Yes, we can move him. He'll stand in another minute. Did you recognize who stood beside him when we entered the lane?"

Verduan watched for movement around them and shook his head. "No, but someone quick and used to movement. A hunter? A soldier, perhaps?"

Patreo helped Baillot to his feet and handed him his saturno. "Come, Father."

Baillot wobbled and Verduan steadied him with a strong arm. "Where are we going?"

Patreo considered. "Do you have ale, wine, spirits of any kind at home?"

"For purely medicinal purposes, yes, some tonics and - "

"Good. My saddlebags are still with Geselda. We'll take him there."

CHAPTER 32

Dire carefully spooned Julia a soup made from the things she'd gathered, some of Nory's cache from the Tinker's wagon, and what he brought back from his rounds in the village.

Julia's eyes fluttered open. She lay in the dark. Hay tickled her back and the blanket covering her smelled of mare sweat. She remained silent, except her eyes darted about, fixed and focused on first one dark shape then another.

Dire lit a candle and Julia squinched her eyes tight against the sudden brightness.

"It's okay, Julia. You're safe. No one will hurt you here."

Julia opened her eyes at Dire's voice. "Grandmother?"

"Do you know what happened to you?"

Julia raised herself up on her elbows. "Where am I?"

Dire sighed. "In my secret place. It grows less secret by the day it seems."

"Are you a witch?"

Dire cackled. "Not in the way you mean, child."

"Are you going to hurt me?"

"Do I have reason to hurt you?"

"May I have something to drink, Grandmother?"

Dire lifted a ladle from a pail and offered it to her. "Here. Drink slowly."

Julia sat up. The horse blanket fell from her and she quickly covered her chest. Dire handed her a kirtle and smiled. "It's sized for me, girl, to wear when I'm working. But it'll cover you fine until we find something better."

Julia fitted the kirtle over her head and shoulders, worked her arms up through the sleeves, pulled it under her bottom and down her legs. "What happened to me?"

"Nory found you, clothed in finery with a bad bump on your head and in the woods outside of Nant. He thought you dead and came to me for help. How did you get in such a state?"

Julia reached behind her head. Dire caught her hand and brought it down. "Are your brains scrambled, child, or do you choose not to answer me?"

"I don't remember." Julia shook her head slightly and blinked. "It hurts to move my head."

"Well it should, I imagine. Someone meant to do you harm and lots of it."

Julia hand moved slowly under the folds of the fallen blanket.

Dire shook her head. "The child's safe."

Julia stared at the old woman.

"And so are you. No harm's been done to you."

Julia closed her eyes and shook slightly. A moment later a tear slid down her face. "I - "

"Didn't want Eric to know he had a child? Or is it someone else's child and you didn't want Eric to know he wasn't the father?"

"It is Eric's child.

"Yes, a daughter. Does Eric know?"

Julia grabbed Dire's hand. "No, Grandmother Dire. Please don't tell him. He's not - "

"The father?"

"I tell you he is. I've not been with any others."

"'Any others'? Not 'another'? Be wary with your words, daughter. They tell others much without our realizing what we say."

Julia reached out to Dire and sobbed.

"But what of Eric? He's not ready? Old enough? Has nothing to offer? Neither do you, as far as I know. And many's a happy couple who started with the same, or less."

Julia looked away.

"What is it? Do you not want the child?"

Julia pulled back and crossed herself.

Dire laughed. "The art of helping mothers lose unwanted children is ancient knowledge. Didn't you know I helped your mother with her births?"

Julia frowned.

"Yes, births. You had a twin."

Julia stood, her eyes wide. "No."

"Yes. Sit."

"Where is she?"

"Dead. Lost to the Vell when the two of you were barely walking. But first answer me. Do you want the child or not?"

Julia's tears welled up. "I do not." She reached out and clung to Dire as the old woman hugged her and patted her back.

"Do you wish to let the father know?"

Julia's face tightened. "Eric is the father."

"Of course."

Julia pushed Dire away. "What do you know? I should go to Sullya the Witch. Ask her forgiveness and to lift her curse."

"There is no Sullya the Witch."

"Ha. I saw her. Eric and I fought her in Ash Hollow. Eric chopped off her hand. She cursed us. And Nant. All of us. Because we fought her and won."

Dire reached behind her to her workbench and lifted the pigskin glove. "You cut off something like this?"

Julia pushed herself back from the old woman, her eyes wide, her voice a whisper. "You're Sullya the Witch."

Dire cackled. "No. Maybe. Once. Long ago. And only a witch because the church said it so. But never black arts or black magic. Nor white, for that matter. No, only schooled in things the church didn't want taught. To all, anyway. To those they selected, and those mostly men, yes, of course, sure, line them up. But to women? To the ones who held the lore through generations long past? No, never." She spat on the ground and stamped the wetness into the earth.

"But the hand..."

"To see if I could. To learn how it might be done. To get an idea of who would want to do it and why."

"You won't hurt me?"

Dire and Julia turned at a scraping sound. Slivers of daylight danced through Dire's cellar as Nory worked his way through the heavily vined bulkhead.

A figure head-to-toe in black came in behind him. "No. Dire won't hurt you."

CHAPTER 33

Verduan supported Baillot as Patreo opened the cottage door.

Baillot raised his head and looked about. "This isn't my church."

Verduan's voice boomed through the cottage. "Eric?"

No answer.

Patreo led them to the cot Verduan gave him. "Just as well. The fewer who know he's here, the better."

"Why *is* he here?"

"I have to get my saddlebags." A moment later he returned, his saddlebags draped over one arm and an unstoppered blue jar in the other. "He's here because whoever shot him will look to his church first to finish their task. From there they'll look in Nant proper. They won't know to come here unless they know us, and I know no one who dresses as the assailant did. Do you?"

Patreo sat Father Baillot on his bed and dusted off his saturno.

Verduan took it and watched Patreo's ministrations. "He's very quiet."

"His wits are addled. He'll be fine with some rest. Get him a cup of your tonics. Make sure there's more wine than anything else in it." Patreo eased Baillot's arms out of his sleeves, lifted him slightly to free his cassock, and handed it to Verduan.

Verduan stood back while Patreo started on Baillot's white undershirt and pants. "I didn't know priests wore so many garments."

Patreo answered without looking up. "Neither did I."

Baillot blinked and looked at him. "Where am I?"

Patreo spoke softly. "You're safe. No one will harm you here. Do you know who stood over you in the street? Someone dressed completely in black?"

Baillot looked around as if seeing for the first time.

"Is he in pain? Perhaps some of that poppy juice you gave me in Tomeka?"

Patreo rested an ear on Baillot's chest, his face close to Baillot's, inhaled deeply and shook his head. "He doesn't need any."

"Not for him, do you have any for me?"

Patreo rubbed the sides of Baillot's neck. "Sleep, Father Baillot."

Baillot's eyes lost focus and closed. A moment later the priest snored.

Verduan frowned. "Are you sure you're not a witch?"

"A healer's trick. To put someone to sleep so you can examine them unhindered."

Verduan dusted off Baillot's cassock. "I don't know priestly ways, Patreo. Is there something special I should do with these?"

Patreo applied salve to a deepening blue bruise where the bolt struck Baillot. "We'll get him fresh clothes from his rectory."

~

Patreo stood at the rectory door. "Did you notice anyone following us? Hear anything?"

Verduan shook his head. "Not that I could tell." He carried Baillot's rolled up clothes under one arm and waved at the circus jester watering the wagon horses with his other. The jester smiled and waved back.

Verduan looked around upon entering. He stepped up to a cupboard, turned, looked at a wardrobe and took Baillot's clothes from under his arm. "What do I do with these?"

Patreo nodded towards the wardrobe. "Sacred clothes can not be hung with others."

Verduan opened the wardrobe and stopped, Baillot's cassock draped over an arm.

Patreo glanced at him. "What is it?"

Verduan nodded into the wardrobe. "What does a priest do with these?"

A strange blade the length of a man's forearm lay on a shelf on a soft but thick black cloth. Two twisted cloth braids, the same fabric as the cloth itself, formed a loose knot supporting the guard, itself two thin blades curving away from the user's hand and towards the thrust. The entire design allowed the blade to be quickly removed without disturbing the cloth. More spike than blade, it was triangular, the base thickest at the hilt and moving to a flanged point. The blade could be easily thrust in but would rip open and disembowel when pulled back out.

Patreo lifted the blade and held it up for inspection. "Surprisingly light for such a device." He ran a finger over one of the edges and a thin line of blood formed on it. "And sharp for such a strange edge." He sniffed the tip of his finger. "And poisoned? Strange priests you have here in Nant."

Verduan looked at him. "Said the priest with knowledge of healing and poisons and all things magical and mystical."

"Ha."

Verduan moved aside a hanging Lenten cape to find a place for Baillot's cassock and stopped. "And this?" He lifted a beautifully crafted arbalest and held it out for inspection.

Patreo's eyes widened. "Are there bolts?"

Verduan reached back in the closet and came out with a full quiver of shafts, some with differently colored quills. He stared at them.

Patreo nodded. "Different weights for different ranges, and none are the bolts that knocked him down."

"This is how you're prepared for the priesthood?"

"Not I."

Verduan hung up Baillot's cassock, brushed the priest's saturno, and placed it on a peg in the wardrobe. He closed the doors and joined Patreo. "If not you then how do you know so much about them?"

"Who can we trust to guard Baillot?"

"You think whoever shot Baillot will try again?"

"Anything we say is speculation. There are too many questions and not enough answers at present: Who stood over him? Were they the archer or were they going to help him? They ran off as we approached. That points to the former over the latter. Perhaps we caught them by surprise?"

Verduan walked to the door and stared outside. "Someone to guard." He scratched his beard. "Thomas, Julia's brother? Or Byell, her father. Eric is my son and still a youth." The big man frowned.

"Something?"

Verduan's head wagged back and forth. His mouth opened and closed again.

"Come now, out with it."

"I have a question for you regarding Eric."

Patreo waved his hand dismissively. "He's too young for this purpose except to raise an alarm."

Verduan inhaled deeply. "Any of the others I mentioned?"

Patreo joined him at the door. "A witch sundered from her hand, a young woman murdered, probably beaten to death and definitely mutilated, another missing. An attempt on Father Baillot's life and his wardrobe contains weaponry. Whatever ails Nant is neither obvious nor intuitive. Is there someone who has no stake in the events of the past few weeks? Someone who's only tie is that they live in Nant? Preferably for many years so they're known? And trusted?"

Verduan snorted. "Galos."

Something creaked behind them followed by a thud.

Patreo fell to the floor.

Verduan turned as a gold communion goblet cracked against his skull.

His eyes blurred. He fell to the floor and rolled into his attacker.

The other person toppled.

Verduan scurried onto the attacker's back, instinct working as he fought to maintain his senses. One arm around his attacker's throat.

The man stood and lifted the full weight of Verduan with him.

Verduan drove his knees into the attacker's back. The man staggered forward slightly and knocked the wardrobe over.

He spun to throw Verduan from him.

Verduan's legs stretched as if caught in a demon wind. Tables and chairs scattered as his legs knocked into them. Plates and cups shattered on the floor.

The attacker backed into a wall. He pinned Verduan against it as he drove his elbows into Verduan's sides.

Verduan gasped as his breath escaped him. His eyes watered and his grip on the man's neck weakened. He braced his feet against the wall and kicked back to knock the attacker forward.

The attacker fell, Verduan still on top of him.

The attacker shrugged Verduan off and stood. Verduan followed but kept his arms in close to protect his ribs.

His eyes cleared enough to see the goblet rise again. It came at him a second time and the world went dark.

CHAPTER 34

Saida walked through Nant much like a bee busying itself among flowers: she stood at one cottage's door, basket on her arm, heavy cloth over the top; voices rose like bees buzzing as Saida and the lady of the house exchanged greetings and gossiped; bread was offered, coin exchanged; goodbyes were said, and off Saida flew to another cottage flower.

She knocked on the Bellman's door. No answer. "Tardiff? It's Saida with your bread."

He answered from out back, "Here in my garden."

She came behind his cottage, bread in hand. The Bellman stared at the ground on the other side of the garden wall.

"Is all well?"

"The tinker's cart was here. Now it's gone. There are wheel ruts and boot prints, but I've never seen their tread before, and whoever it was moved the cart without sounds."

"Would you like one loaf or two?"

He took the loaves, gave her two coppers, and she was on his way.

A loaf on the bottom Saida saved for Father Baillot. His loaves she made special. The finest yeasts, the finest flours, sweetened with the finest honeys.

Father Baillot's loaves, the ones he had at his meals to sop up the last of his vegetable-rich soups, his mutton and beef-rich stews and gravies, those loaves Saida made with special ingredients and with just enough clove honey to mask any tastes she cared to add, should there be a need.

One day a poison.

She prepared.

She learned the way of herb and root, bark and mold, learned in their craft from other bakers of the faith, others who learned to protect themselves, to prepare should the worst come, one to kill, the other to save.

She knew what to use when.

Twice Zevke and Saida fled villages because the church found them for who they were and burned them out. Zevke and Saida hurrying, hiding, their hearts bursting from their chests, tucking their heads against blows imagined and real.

They lost a child. Her child.

She vowed to her god and to herself, her hand on the mantle signs, never again.

Never again.

She kept a cart ready. Sheltered and ready. Anything needed for the day would come off the cart, be used in the moment, then cleaned and restored to its place, always ready, always prepared, for escape in the night.

Nant, she believed, was different. Galos and Haasel helped generously when Zevke and Saida arrived and bartered forward: goods and services now for fresh loaves of bread and dainty morsels later.

Verrett was a good man. He saw the signs on the baker's lintel, smiled, and nodded with understanding.

Baillot, though.

Baillot saw the signs. Saida smiled and nodded as he gazed over her and Zevke's head, negotiating the price of his daily bread. He said nothing but she told Zevke later, "He knows. He knows what we are. Best be ready. Prepare, husband."

Zevke shook his head and dismissed her warning, too tired to care who knew what or what they did any more. He answered, "Let them come. I no longer care who knows. I'll pray as I pray and the rest of the world be damned."

Let her fool of a husband pray. Little use his god had been to him. Did his prayers return his daughter to him? No!

Ha!

And now he seeks out a witch?

Bah!

Maybe Saida would taint her husband's bread.

Saida knocked on the rectory door. "Father Baillot, I have your bread ready for you."

Nothing.

Perhaps he was in the church preparing for a service?

No.

Perhaps in the sacristy donning his garments or in private conversation? Once, making her deliveries, Saida saw Julia leave the rectory by its rear door, her eyes darting back and forth as she adjusted her skirts and hurried through the afternoon shadows of village cottages.

She entered.

Nothing.

But wasn't there talk about a young woman's body being here?

No body lay there. "Who knows what papists do with the dead?" she muttered.

She went back to the rectory and knocked harder.

The door rocked open slightly.

"Father Baillot?"

She pushed the door open. Just enough to stick her head in.

"Father - "

She pulled back and her eyes opened wide.

Table and chairs overturned? The wardrobe toppled? Plates and cups smashed? Holy goblets on the floor?

And that stain on the one. A bloodied handprint?

She knew things were changing. She told Zevke as much.

But she was the one who watched the priests. It always started with the priests.

Saida hurried away with her bread.

Galos, Nory by his side, walked towards the Red Fox and waved.

She lifted all the loaves save Father Baillot's from her basket. "Here. More bread than Father Baillot needs. Fill your bellies. A gift from Zevke the Baker."

Galos took a loaf and handed it to Nory, took a loaf for himself, tore off a piece of bread and chewed. "Thank you, Saida."

Saida lifted skirts and hurried to the bakery.

Zevke held his peel like a staff at the sound of Saida's hurried steps. She came beside him, placed one hand over his shoulders for support, and caught her breath.

"What ails you, woman?"

"Have you been to the church? Something's happened to Baillot. The rectory is ruined."

He pulled a towel from a rising loaf and punched it down. "What are you talking about, woman? How do the priest's misadventures concern us?"

Tears filled Saida's eyes. "They will come. They will come and drive us out."

"I worked my ovens all day and you delivered bread. We did nothing and people came and went seeing what we did. Who will come for us?"

"You think they need an excuse? They will know us for what we are and this will be their excuse."

He recovered the rising loaf and stood, palms on the table, his arms supporting his massive frame, his head hung between thick shoulders. "I am tired of running, woman. I'm tired of running and being afraid. We are known and liked. Who will come? Who?"

"Someone. Someone new to the village. The sheriff and his deputy are here."

He raised his head to look at her. "They are?"

"I told you trouble would follow us."

CHAPTER 35

Eric entered the Red Fox some minutes after Sheriff Donam and his deputy took station in a dark corner opposite the door and in clear view of the window. Donam sat with an empty mug and full pitcher of ale in front of him, his left hand caressing his mug and his right caressing his sword's hilt. He scanned the Red Fox from door to kitchen to make sure none entered without his knowledge.

His deputy had a mug in front of him from which he occasionally sipped. His eyes stayed on the window and measured those who walked past. His right hand also stayed on his sword's hilt.

Slewe came now and again to see to their needs. He learned after one such visit to announce his approach and remain out of their line of sight.

Eric entered from the Inn's side door and caught Slewe in the kitchen. "What can you tell me about them, Slewe?"

"Donam and Taitano? Sheriff and deputy, they talk little except to themselves, drink less, and eat nothing, hence worthless to me. I should charge them rent for the space they take up at my tables. They are The Baron's men, and where The Baron's men go, trouble follows."

"They say nothing about the body?"

"They wait for the Tomekan priest and Baillot, that's all I know, and that from Tardiff who not long ago stood where you do."

"Where is Tardiff now?"

Slewe rolled his eyes as he dried his hands on a kitchen rag. "Do you not listen, boy? Didn't I just say these two wait for the priests? Tardiff is off to get them."

"Have you seen my father?"

"First Julia gone missing and now your father?"

"Learn what you can from them. You are right. Trouble follows them. I can feel it."

"I am an innkeeper. Not a spy."

Eric snorted. "Yes, and whenever anyone wants to learn the town's gossip they come to the Red Fox first." He left by the same door he entered so not to be seen. At Nant's center he stopped and leaned against the town well. Verduan wasn't in town, wasn't in his fields, not home, not in his barn, not with Buco hunting. Where might his father be that wasn't part of his normal routine?

He remembered one of Father Verrett's teachings for when numbers don't sum or subtract as they should: start at the top and work your way back.

～

Thomas wobbled as he stood. He reached to the elm for support and tenderly felt the side of his head. No blood but his head ached as if his brains'd spilled out.

His walking stick lay on the ground. He bent over to pick it up and sprawled on his hands and knees. A moment later his stomach emptied itself.

"Hello?"

Thomas recognized the voice. "Eric?" He stood again with the help of the elm and his staff. "Over here."

He felt himself falling again and strong hands caught him. "Thomas, what happened to you?"

"Nory."

Eric turned Thomas' head gently to see the bruising. "Nory did this?"

Thomas opened his eyes wide, blinked once, twice, and worked his jaw as if coming out of a brawl. "What day is it?"

"Come, Dire should look at this. If not her, I'm told the Tomekan is good with cures."

Thomas used his staff to move debris aside. "The Tinker's hammer. Nory pulled it from this tree. It's what he used to kill the girl."

Eric reached in and pulled back an empty hand. "How big a hammer?"

"Do you see the side of my face? That's how big a hammer."

He touched Thomas' face. Thomas twinged. "Did Nory take you by surprise? And swing a hammer large enough to leave that much a mark with enough force to level you so?"

"He's bewitched. He called familiars from the wood to help him."

"Before we thought he'd be the only one untouched by the witch, now he's her ally?"

Thomas pushed Eric out of his way. "You're little concerned since Father Patreo declared the girl wasn't your angel."

"Nor your sister." Eric put a hand on Thomas' arm. "Have you seen my father? Or the Tomekan, for that matter?"

Thomas glared at him, pushed his hand away, and walked out to the road. "I was attacked and rose as you approached. I've seen neither. Or do you think your father and the Tomekan are Nory's allies who battered in my skull?"

Thomas took two steps and fell again.

Eric helped him stand and took Thomas' free arm across his shoulders. "The Sheriff is in Nant at the Red Fox. He may want to know of this."

~

I dee stood hands-on-hips in their fields as a figure head-to-toe in black raced into the woods. She called out but the figure neither slowed nor acknowledged her. Instead, it moved into the shadows between the trees and disappeared.

Who, she wondered, would be so rude?

And who lived in Nant dressed like that except Father Baillot?

The Tomekan, maybe?

Then what was a priest doing in Byell's field?

The day was only two-thirds done and held enough excitement and misery for any three. She watched her step among the bean and squash furrows, gazed up looking for her husband, gazed down again to be sure of her steps.

She shook her head and headed across the field. "Byell! Byell?"

The Tomekan priest put too many questions in her head. Either the dead child was her Julia or it was not. The dead girl wore Julia's clothes but appeared to be of royal or at least manored blood.

"Byell!"

She soon saw him face down in the dirt by the orchard's edge.

What a fool! Drunk again, she was sure.

He often drank alone when none were around to see. Especially since...she felt her face flush anew.

He could bury himself in the barrel. What solace did she have? None.

None!

Not even worth anything to her as a man any longer.

He lost their daughter and his manhood in one fell swoop.

Wonderful magic you got, wasn't it, Byell?

Many nights she woke after he came to bed, his snoring louder than Tardiff's bell ringing, and she woke to watch him in the darkness, his back to her, and saw his belt hanging on its peg, and knew the knife he kept so sharp was there, a few steps away, waiting for her to decide, to act, to run it into his back, through his lungs or across his neck 'till his blood spurted to the beats of his dying heart, so much like a pig or cow or goat or lamb being slaughtered.

Oh, so many nights she had considered such.

He lost their daughter to the Vell, he said. They went to fill their buckets, another season so dry nothing would grow and before Galos taught them the way of ductwork.

Byell claimed he plunged in after her but when they found him on the bank his clothes were dry and his hair unmussed. Fell asleep in anguish, he claimed, and the sun dried him.

Father Verrett frowned and made the Sign of the Cross but said nothing more. People searched the length of the Vell but no trace was ever found.

Since then, she found flasks hidden where he thought she would not look, and everyone thought he mourned for their loss and couldn't be consoled.

Little did they know he mourned for his stupidity and consoled himself in drink.

And when he told her?

She thought she dreamed his story.

The sheer horror of it had to be a dream.

Certainly no father could do such a thing.

But so drunk one night, his tears mixing with his wine until he drank his sorrow by the cup, he told her what really happened, the weight of it more than he could bear.

The witch, he said, had watched him.

What would he give for his lands and swine to flourish, to prosper, to grow wild beyond his dreams?

No fool, he told Idee, he asked the witch, "What do you require of me?"

But the witch knew before she spoke the deal was struck because she chose wisely; Byell was jealous of any man who prospered. In his mind he kept a ledger of who had what, where they got it and how, and always asked why them and not he?

Even her, he told her on their wedding night, chosen because no other man would want her and so she could be his and his alone.

Up until that night, she thought she was chosen because he loved.

She was chosen so he could have for his own what no one else wanted.

And the witch, he told her, said the daughter at his side was needed to make the magic work.

"How so?"

"So powerful a working requires blood magic. Your daughter will give her life, your fields and pigs and all that you touch will grow wild and free."

Byell took Sarah and hid her behind him. "Go away, witch. What man gives up a child for so wild a promise?"

The witch shrugged and moved back into the woods by the Vell. "Then let everything about you wither: your children, your fields, your herd, and you. You won't accept my barter, then accept my curse!"

She spat on the ground and made the Devil sign at him three times.

The blood in his veins flowed cold. His heart tightened in his chest. His parents told him many stories of the power of the witch when he was a child, how she would come for him if he didn't live a decent life, sleep when he should, do what he was told, act like a man, and here she was, keeping their threat, their promise.

My life or the child's? he wondered.

I can have more children, can't it?

Ha! Idee laughed. Not by her could he, and no other woman in Nant would go near him, the smell of his swine always so strong about him.

Ha!

He had to court her and always downwind of her. Even when he bathed in Dire's salts, the scent remained. Weakened, and it remained.

The witch took their child, their Sarah, and deep in the woods burned her alive, so she told him, and their sweet daughter's screams he heard, and that is what haunted him so.

Every time a pig squealed, it spoke Sarah's suffering at the last.

And the witch returned. "Here, her ashes and my words bound in this pouch. Use the dust inside sparingly. It is magic. Powerful magic. *Blood Magic.* Do you understand?"

Idee approached Byell, still face down in their field. She spat on the ground and made the Devil sign herself the best she could with each step.

"See how powerful my magic is, husband? Maybe I'm the witch you should have consulted?"

He didn't move.

"Byell!"

Crows and ravens harassed pigeons and mourning doves from the trees. Their squawking and calling made her look up.

The figure in black stood there at the edge of their field, watching.

"Byell, who is that? Someone helping you with your cups? More likely someone bringing you cups in exchange for our roots and herbs."

Byell remained motionless.

She kept her eyes on the stranger as she walked over to her husband.

The ground was wet and an ugly brownish-red under his face and neck.

She nudged him with her boot. "Get up, drunkard."
Nothing.
The stranger watched. The birds returned to the trees.
Idee bent over and rolled her husband on to his back.
She screamed.
The stranger was gone.

SECTION VII
THE CLOISTERS

CHAPTER 36

Dire rose, spun to her workbench, and grabbed a knife in one smooth movement. Her free hand took Julia's arm and drew the girl behind her. "Nory, come to me. Quickly now."

Nory frowned and signed, What?

She barked as if ordering a dog. "Here! Now!"

Nory looked at the cloaked figure beside him and back at Dire. He quickly signed Friend! Friend!

Dire held her ground and kept herself between the Julia and the intruder. "Who are you? What have you done to my Nory?"

The robed figure held its hands palms out in front of them. "Easy, Grandmother. What makes you think I mean you harm?"

"The last time you called me Grandmother I slept for a day, maybe more. Will you do that now?"

The figure cocked its head slightly but otherwise stood still. "Will you lower your knife?"

Her eyes flashed to Nory. "Who is this, Nory? Are you alright?"

The robed one's sword flashed from its scabbard. The knife flew from Dire's hand and buried itself in a far earthen wall. The sword returned to its sheath.

"Grandmother, if I wished you harm, I would do so. Please, be at ease with me."

Dire's eyes fell on Nory a second time. "Do you know who this is, Nory?"

Nory grabbed the robed one's gloved hand and kissed it.

"Tell her who I am Nory. Go ahead. It's alright."

Nory's face beamed.

"I trust you, Nory. You're a good lad."

Nory signed Simon. Friend.

The robed one patted Nory's shoulder. "Thank you, Nory. Good lad."

"Why do you disguise yourself?"

"Why do you work in a cave cellar hidden in the side of a hill? Because you don't want people to know what work you do. Allow me the same courtesy, Wise Woman."

"I sent Nory for herbs and elements. To help Julia. He brought some and had to travel to find others."

"And he's brought them." The robed one reached into a fold and pulled out two packets. "I added some things which may be useful. Later if not now."

"You know the old ways?"

"I respect the old ways. And the learnings of others. Don't you?"

Dire reached out and the robed one placed the packets gently in her hand. Her eyes never left the masked face.

"Do you know the alchemicals for melting iron? Cold smelting, it's called."

Dire's eyes narrowed. "You've traveled with the Gourdin? In Arab lands?"

The robed one laughed, deep and bellowy. "Let's say I've travelled. Do you know the process, yes or no?"

She nodded.

"Good, you'll find the uncommon elements in the smaller

packet. Mix it up for me, but leave it in its powder form."

"When do you need it?"

Another laugh. "The way things are going in Nant, yesterday would have been about right. Tomorrow will do."

"Will you come for it?"

The robed one patted Nory's back again. "Give it to Nory, quickly sealed so it touches no air. He knows how to get it to me." He gently turned Nory to face him. "You understand, Nory? You know what to do?"

Nory kissed the gloved hand again and again and again.

"Thank you, Nory. You're a good lad." The figure bowed. "Now I must be off."

"Put us to sleep again, will you?"

The robed figure retrieved Dire's knife from the wall and handed it to her hilt first. "Is there a need?"

"What is happening in Nant that draws you forth?"

"Bad things. Evil things. From long ago. You will make me the cold smelting powder?"

Dire nodded.

The gloved hand stroked Nory's face. "You'll bring it to me, Nory? You know where to leave it?"

Nory held the glove against his face and nodded.

"Good lad. I bid you all adieu."

Dire held up her hand. "Wait. Where are you from? Can you at least tell me that?"

The robed figure hesitated. "Galatia. I am from Galatia."

Dire pulled back slowly. "May I see your sword?"

A deep laugh. "You are wise, indeed." He drew it, turned it so the tip pointed at his heart, and offered it to her hilt first.

Dire didn't take it, instead ran her hands along the blade. Satisfied, she nodded and stood back. "A black robed figure, masked, who carries a white Damascus steel blade? From Galatia? No." She shook her head. "A Galatian Warrior-Priest? Of the Old

Order? Impossible. The Galatians died in the last battle of Jerusalem, overwhelmed by the Jannenites and betrayed by the Mehtars. Who are you, really?"

The figure laughed but with no mirth. "You are correct, Grandmother, except most, not all, died defending Jerusalem. Some of us remained, only to be hunted by our own people because - "

"Because you were priests of The Old Ways. The church needed you to defeat the Muslim, and once defeated the church had no more use for you so they stripped you and handed you over to your enemies."

The figure bowed. "Holy Mother Church did not count on our enemies being more merciful than She herself. Since then, I and those of my brothers who remained scattered. But we continue to do our work as we are able. There are many who still honor us. And we know who we are. We leave our signs for our brothers to see." The figure chuckled. "The years, you know. They can change how one looks and moves." He sighed. "But the signs remain."

"Nant needs a Galatian now?"

"You'll have my cold smelting powder ready when you say?"

Dire nodded.

The Galatian crouched by the briary door and listened, looked back and nodded, parted the vines without disturbing their array and left.

Dire focused on the curve of his hood and mask as they eclipsed the day's fading light. She placed her blade slowly on her workbench. "Who is that, Nory? Will you tell me who that is?"

Nory frowned, looked to the hidden door and back, and deepened his frown.

"It's okay, Nory. I'll keep The Galatian's secret and Julia can't understand. Who is it?"

Nory held up his hands and signed slowly. Simon. Friend.

Dire cackled. "Aye, Nory. You're a good lad. But your friend

Simon has both his ears. There's not one Warrior-Priest, Knight of the Old Ways, there's two. Are both our friends? What do you say, Nory? Do you know them both?"

Nory cocked his head, shrugged, shook it.

Dire chuckled. "Aye, Nory. Aye."

CHAPTER 37

Tardiff adjusted The Baron's sash. It fit well originally, when his chest stood out more than his stomach. Now it was a bit tight and not in the chest. Perhaps Idee could adjust it? Or one of the other village women. He would ask at the Red Fox when he returned with news of the priests.

He made sure The Baron's insignia rested across his chest, over his heart. Should he put on his sword?

No, the insignia would be enough. People would know he came on official business.

In Nant, people probably already knew Sheriff Donam and his deputy waited for him at the Red Fox, which table they sat at, what they drank and ate, what they said to Slewe and his people, and how their patience waned waiting for him to bring them news.

He opened his door as Dobrogost approached. The giant carried staves taller than a man and a long-handled sledge-hammer over one shoulder. Between his arm and side several wooden signs rattled with his steps. His free arm and hand held the leash of the muzzled bear.

"Master Tardiff, I hoped to find you." Dobrogost put the leash between his teeth and offered Tardiff a sign upside down. Reclaiming the leash, he asked, "May I post these on the roads in and out of Nant? Let travelers know we're here and providing merriment? Might bring business into town that otherwise would detour away."

Tardiff held the sign upside down and scanned as if reading. "Yes, these are fine. Post them as you will. Be sure to remove them when you leave."

Dobrogost's slight smile grew wide as Tardiff's eyes returned to him. "Of course, of course."

"Before you go, have you seen the priests, Baillot or Patreo?"

Dobrogost shrugged. "Sorry, Master Tardiff. I've seen neither in quite a while."

The bear reared up and grunted.

Dobrogost pulled lightly on the leash. "Down, Bron." He smiled at Tardiff and glanced at Tardiff's hand on his empty scabbard. "Oh, don't mind him. He's hoping we'll find something tasty in the woods. Honey, perhaps."

Tardiff stared at the bear's face.

"Your bear is blind?"

"Yes. A precaution. So he causes no mischief. So he knows to obey."

Tardiff eyed the bear as it waved its paws in the air. "I have business to attend. Be on your way."

Dobrogost stood back and pulled on the bear's leash to move it out of the way. Tardiff hurried off.

Dobrogost smiled broadly at the Bellman's retreating figure. "Of course, Master Tardiff. Of course." He pulled more fiercely on the bear's leash. "Good job, Bron. Good job."

The bear bellowed through its muzzle.

"Is it time to check on our guests? Are they hungry, do you think?"

The bear snuffed the air through its muzzle and bellowed.

"Yes, yes. Let us go, let us play. Time to feed whom we may." He snapped the bear's leash.

Bron fell back to all fours and then to the ground. It tucked itself into a ball, placed its front paws over its face, and whimpered.

"What troubles you, foolish beast? That was the sound of the leash, not the knife. Are you deaf as well as blind?" He tugged gently on the leash. "Come along."

The bear, shaking, rose on all fours.

They strode off.

CHAPTER 38

Donam watched Slewe wash tables at the far end of the inn. He tapped Taitano's sleeve and nodded at Slewe across the room.

Taitano read his master's face, nodded, and kept his eyes on Slewe.

Donam said in a normal voice, "Innkeeper."

Slewe kept washing tables.

Donam raised his voice slightly. "Innkeeper."

Slewe wet his rag in a pail and went to the next table.

Taitano nodded each time Donam spoke.

Donam's voice grew loud. "Innkeeper."

Still nothing.

"Innkeeper!"

Slewe looked up, dropped his rag on the table, and hurried over as he dried his hands on his apron. "My apologies, Sheriff. I did not hear you across the room. How may I serve?"

Taitano glanced at Donam and rolled his eyes.

"Two more ales."

Taitano's knuckles wrapped the table. "And some bread, if you have it."

Slewe reached for their mugs. "Yours is still half full, Lord Sheriff. Shall I wait or - "

Donam barked. "Two more ales. And bread for my deputy. And be quick about it. Then leave us in peace."

Slewe bumped into some chairs as he bowed and backed his way to the kitchen. "Certainly, my Lord, certainly." He returned a moment later with a tray carrying two ales in fresh mugs, a loaf of Zevke's best rye, a crock of spiced mustard, and a knife. He placed everything in front of them. "Anything else, my Lord?"

Taitano lifted the bread in a roughened hand. "No. Back to your tables."

"Should you require anything else, it is best to stamp your foot or bang the table. Many years in a noisy inn, my ears don't hear as well as they use to. My apologies, Lord Sheriff."

Taitano rose, his hand on his hilt. "Back to your tables!"

Slewe stumbled over chairs and tables hurrying away.

Donam placed a hand on Taitano's arm. "Sit, Deputy."

Taitano grunted and sat. They watched Slewe pick up his pail and rag and wash tables at the far end of the inn.

Taitano sawed off a heel and placed it jagged edge up in front of himself. He glanced with knife up at Donam who frowned and shook his head, no. Taitano dipped his heel in the mustard. "A deaf innkeeper. Do you think his profits suffer much?"

"Has Dobrogost found the other girl?"

"No, not yet. His people are finding villagers who will talk."

"Find villagers who will whore, you mean?"

Taitano thrust the knife into the bread as if thrusting a dagger into someone's heart. "Celibacy doesn't suit us all, Lord Sheriff."

Donam pulled the knife from the bread. He tested its weight and motioned as if to throw it into the wall slightly above Slewe's head. Suddenly he sat up and aimed between Taitano's eyes. "Of all the kitchen maids, of all the nurses, of all the bastard-bitches and royal governesses, of all the help, of all those running to and fro at The Baron's command and under his roof, you choose to fuck the one he commands none but he may touch?"

Taitano stared down the knife.

"I should slit your throat myself and deliver you to his Lordship The Baron."

"Lord Sheriff - "

"Don't speak. Every time you open your mouth I question my stupidity at keeping your secret. Slip your wick into a willing cunny of course, but did it have to be hers? When all know His Lordship likes them whole to bleed on his first taking?"

Taitano sat motionless, his eyes on the sheriff. He neither drank nor chewed.

Donam relaxed in his seat, adjusted his cape around him and lowered the knife. "Do you know why she traveled this far north of Melia? Why here?"

"I loved her, Lord Sheriff."

"You and how many others?"

Taitano's nostrils flared. "Lord Sheriff - "

Donam took the knife up again. "Either answer my questions or fall silent until you need speak."

Taitano opened his mouth and Donam interrupted. "One more word that's not an answer and I'll cut off your other ear, Deputy." He ran the blade gently up Taitano's chin to his left ear. "Understood?"

Taitano nodded without pulling away.

"Ah, good, good." Donam sat back but kept his hand on the blade. "Why did she come this way?"

"Sarah."

"What?"

"Her name is Sarah."

Donam smiled and lifted the blade in Taitano's direction. "That's not an answer to my question, Deputy."

"She wanted to get beyond the Coranth to where The Baron has no influence?"

"That's better." Donam lowered the knife again. "Dobrogost killed her?"

"He claimed it a personal matter and a mistake. He asks your indulgence."

"Better to ask The Baron. The kitchen maid was his to offer, not mine."

"He found another girl to take her place."

"And she's whole?"

Taitano shrugged. "He claimed she fit Sarah's description perfectly." He glanced out the window. "He thought to take her, remembered The Baron's likings, and chose not."

"I asked if she's whole."

"He didn't venture, lest his lust overtake him." He fell silent.

"Is there more?"

"Korol, the one who dresses like a clown, disagreed on some particulars."

Donam cut off the other heel, dipped it in the mustard and offered it to Taitano. "Eat your bread. What particulars?"

"The girl had no burn mark on her hand. Sarah burnt the back of her hand as a child working in the kitchen. It scarred her, not badly but recognizably, for life. How this Korol knew about the burn I don't know."

"Did you see this other girl?"

Taitano chewed the bread and shook his head, no.

Donam taunted his deputy. "Pity Dobrogost could not fulfill his desires on her. Could you imagine if she saw his manhood swell? She would've thought a horse wanted to mount her, don't you think?"

Taitano's chewing slowed. His eyes narrowed.

"But The Baron's mistress, what of her? Did Dobrogost know she wasn't pure, do you think? He knew The Baron would not want her and so she was safe for the having? Better to use her up before The Baron parted her left from her right?"

Taitano's jaw tightened.

"Is that why he bashed her face in, do you think? She said no to him and he decided she'd never say no to anyone ever again? Was that the giant's personal matter?" Donam made a show of sipping his ale. He lowered his cup and wiped draught from his upper lip. "Do we know if she said no to anyone? Aside from you, the first few times you asked, anyway?"

Taitano's hands drew slowly under the table. Donam picked the knife up again. "Eat your bread, deputy. Drink your ale. Place a hand on each, if you value them. You'll have opportunity enough to draw your sword before this tale is through."

Taitano placed his hands on the table.

"Even this innkeeper says their forms were much the same, and he never saw the body. The gossip is strong to carry such conviction."

Taitano nodded and chewed.

"Korol took the kitchen maid's hand?"

"Dobrogost. Part of his personal matter, it seems. Evidently his mother lost her hand in some mishap and he wished to return one to her."

"Take a young woman's hand and graft it onto an old woman's body? Do you think Sarah would know who she stroked then?"

Taitano looked out the inn's main window.

"This is the local story about a witch's hand, then?"

Taitano grunted.

"The giant's mother is a witch." Donam shrugged. "Let this be the strangest news in my day and I'm happy. Whose idea was it to switch their clothes?"

"Korol felt someone finding a well-dressed, perfumed, woman dead in a wood would come to us. Find a village girl and it goes no further than the Bellman."

"Did he plan to scar her, as well?"

Taitano nodded.

"Let us hope this village lass is whole, then. For your sake if no one else's, eh, Deputy?"

Taitano watched Donam and said nothing.

"And let us hope she is soon found." Donam's eyes dropped from Taitano's to the bread and mustard. "Finish your meal. Then bring Korol to me. He may be better suited to me than others in The Baron's employ." He cut off a thick slice of bread and used the knife to push it across the table to his deputy. "Don't you think?"

CHAPTER 39

Patreo woke in the dark to a damp feel coursing his face and brow. He opened his eyes. Torchlight came through bars on a heavy door from a hallway and he blinked. "How long?"

Verduan wiped the Tomekan's brow with a cloth wetted from a bucket beside him. "Not quite a day."

Patreo pushed Verduan's hand away and sat up. His motion continued into a forward roll.

Verduan caught and steadied him. "Easy."

Patreo raised his hand to feel his head and stopped as metal clanged against metal. "Manacled?"

"Your powers of observation are not diminished."

Patreo gathered the links and pulled. They held firm to a brick and wood wall. "This is no barn. There're no animal smells here. This is a jail cell?"

Verduan squeezed out the cloth over the bucket and draped it over the side. "The blow has not worsened your wits."

"Has someone called the sheriff? What am I accused of?"

Verduan raised his fist and rattled a similar chain. "Us. We."

Patreo took a second look at their surroundings. "You're in here with me? What is your crime?"

"I befriended you on a dark day." Verduan ran his hand against his chain's wall anchor. "This is not as I remember it."

"You've been in jail before?"

Verduan chuckled. "I was a mischievous youth. My father decided a night in a cell would wisen me." He pulled sharply on his own chain. "This is not the Sheriff's workings. Tardiff does a good job keeping the Sheriff and Baron far away from us. Besides, The Baron and his men want you to know who you've sinned against."

"You know this place? Where are we?"

"If we're where I think we are, it is known as The Cloisters, an ancient place southeast of Nant. It is said strangers came and built this place long, long ago, before even our ancestors founded Nant by the Vell."

Patreo ran his hands over the brickwork and foundational wall. "Indeed. This is Roman Concrete. Not many know its secret."

"Another mystery in the church catacombs?"

Patreo shook his head. "No, but it does tell us how long these walls stood. Close to a thousand years, perhaps. Is it still inhabited?"

"Some say they've seen half-human creatures come and go and use these places as a gateway to hell."

"Are there others like it near Nant?"

"I only know of the one, approached on a dare as a child. It is haunted." Verduan tugged on his chain. "But this chain work is new. Recent."

"And anchored in Roman concrete. We'll not be tearing these out of the wall soon."

Patreo ran his own hand over the base of the stonework. "It's wet?"

"It's blood."

"Yours?"

Verduan shook his head. "Nor yours. I came to as our captors locked the door and left. In the moment before the door swung shut, I saw it was blood."

"The last I remember we put Father Baillot down to rest."

"Aye."

"Was there someone in his sacristy when we entered?"

"You directed me to the wardrobe. If I'd opened the closet, we would be toasting ourselves at the Red Fox now."

Patreo shook his head in disbelief. "Forgive me, Verduan. Who could overpower you?"

Verduan chuckled. "From the way he handled us, someone more bear than man. At least as big. And whether bear or man, well trained. And strong. He put me over his shoulder and carried you under an arm."

"The Persian circus giant?"

"You know of another capable?"

"You said 'our captors'. There was more than one? Did they speak? Did you get a name? Recognize a voice?"

Verduan snorted. "Yes. As I came to once, slept, and when next I awoke I recognized a voice. Just the one, there were no others, and the speech was spoken more to keep things in memory than anything else. I don't know if he was one of our captors. He seemed surprised when he looked in and saw us here."

"Did you see a face?"

"I chose not to move until I knew your fate, so feigned sleep as he passed."

"He who? Whose voice was it?"

Someone threw back the door's bolt. A wavering shaft of light entered their prison as the door opened. A newcomer stood there. "He recognized my voice, Father Patreo."

Patreo raised his hand to shield his eyes from the torch.

They heard a bear bellowing close by, it's angry voice echoing throughout the depths.

The newcomer pulled the door shut, reset the bolt, and disappeared in the darkness.

Patreo's chain clanked as his hand fell. "Wait! Father Baillot!"

CHAPTER 40

Eric opened the door to the cottage he shared with his father. "Thomas?"

He half-carried, half-walked his friend back to Nant the previous night and, too tired to continue, decided they could rest here. He gave Thomas his own bed and took the floor, wrapped in some heavy blankets. A low moan and small scratchings came from the door in the middle of the night. He rose to let Buco in and the dog promptly trotted to the blankets, still warm from Eric's slumber, circled twice to make a nest and lay down. He looked up at Eric and, as much as a dog could, grinned.

Eric wrestled some of the blankets from under the dog and cuddled up beside him. "If you've been eating Galos' venison, it's out with you. Understand?"

The dog licked Eric's face and was asleep before Eric finished arranging himself to rest.

In the morning, Eric woke hearing Thomas' snoring. Thomas' bruise had purpled during the night and Eric knew this meant it was healing. No doubt still tender, but mending, and he let his friend rest.

He let Buco out, released the animals to their corral and fields, and cleaned out their stalls. He took a moment to brush Geselda, the Tomekan priest's donkey, before sending her out after the other animals. "Do you know where your master is, girl?"

The donkey brayed.

Her gave her some sweet oats. She gobbled them up and licked his hand for more.

"Don't be greedy, girl."

She nosed some saddlebags hanging over her stall's gate and brayed again. "Does the priest keep special food for you in there? Does he spoil you as you carry him about?"

He opened the bags. Corked bottles and flasks, herbs tied in small bundles, a tinder box, tightly wrapped things he didn't recognize.

And books.

No bible. Nothing with the church's seal.

Books.

Eric opened one. Strange writings. Not words or signs or symbols he knew. Father Verrett taught him much, but Eric knew none of these languages if languages they be.

But he understood the pictures.

People dancing around fires under the crescent moon. Stars bright above them. Strange animals with what must be their names under them.

And that. That was a witch's symbol. He recognized that from one of Father Verrett's books, one the old priest quickly snatched away, said it was for later, said was not for young minds such as his, said it gave instructions on how to protect the church.

Eric carefully placed the books back in Patreo's saddlebags. Geselda snorted. Eric felt through the bags and pulled out a small brown brick of grains. It smelled bitter but Geselda came forward. He held it out and she gobbled it from his hand. He licked the few small brown tainted grains from his palm and smiled. "Sweet feed. For you on the trail." He patted her neck as she chewed. "You're spoiled." She swallowed and he let her out into the paddock with the other animals.

~

Dobrogost fed and watered his drafts then closed the gaps in the semicircle of the three stage wagons to work on a platform erected at their center.

Galos walked past and stopped. "Need any help?"

The giant stopped his work and smiled. "Very kind of you, good sir. You are a citizen of this fine city?"

Galos chuckled. "Nant's a city now? Yes. I'm Galos, a charcoal burner."

The giant offered his hand. It engulfed Galos' halfway up his forearm. "Dobrogost, the circus giant, strongman, animal tamer, carpenter, ironsmith, ..." He looked down and shook his head. "I'm sure I'm forgetting something." He glanced under his brows at Galos and his face broke into a broad smile.

Galos laughed. "And clown? You have a good sense of humor."

"Our circus already has a clown. Besides, at my size, it is easier to laugh than take offense."

"Who would battle you?"

"Go behind these wagons and you'll see a bear, Bron, blinded at birth. I suspect he would challenge me if I let my guard down."

Galos walked behind the wagons and came back. "Seems tame enough. Considering there's no bear there."

Dobrogost reached into a tray in the left-most wagon's driver's seat and pulled out a hammer. He stopped in mid-move. "No bear? A leash?"

"Not that I saw. Has your bear escaped?"

"He's muzzled. He'll starve or come back before long."

Galos' stared at the hammer in the giant's hand. "Your hammer looks worn."

The giant looked at it. "Ah, yes. I had an accident and never washed it. I should know to take better care of my tools." He lifted the hammer over his head and brought it down on a stake. The blow drove it halfway into the ground.

Galos shook his head. "Blood on a hammer. I hope that's not an omen for your opening night."

"We'll know soon enough. We plan on performing our first show as the sun sets tomorrow eve. Now if you'll forgive me, I must make sure our stage stands well and fast. Must rehearse at least once before we open, you know."

"Sure you need no help? I have time if - "

Dobrogost drove a second stake deep into the ground. "I thank you, Charcoal Burner Galos, and I am sure. Please forgive me. I work quickest when I work alone."

Galos waved as he continued on his way. "I look forward to your show."

Dobrogost muttered without looking up from his work. "You do now, Charcoal Burner. You do now."

Eric began his search at the Red Fox. The sheriff and his deputy had taken rooms there for their stay in Nant and if not already up, he would wake them. His father and the Tomekan priest missing, Thomas attacked, his beloved Julia missing, a dead girl in Julia's clothing.

He would report these things and the sheriff and deputy would help him discern their meanings.

Slewe opened the door to him. "Master Eric. A little something to start the day? Some fine bacon to see you on your way?"

"Are Donam and his man up?"

"Donam and his man left in the middle of the night without paying their bills. If they don't return by the morrow, whatever they've left is mine by right of law."

Eric stopped at Zevke's for a fresh loaf, and now he stood back in his own doorway with only the echo of his own voice in answer.

"Thomas?"

He checked his bed. Not made, the sheets scattered and half on the floor as if Thomas stumbled getting out, and chairs pushed out of the way in a line to the door. He went to the cupboards. Nothing taken, nothing eaten.

He went into the barn. "Thomas?"

Nothing.

He stood at the edge of the fields he worked with his father, cupped his hands around his mouth and called out. "Thomas."

No reply except the cackling of hens, the snuffling of pigs, the bleating of lambs and goats. Their cows raised their heads but continued chewing. Their draft shook herself then dropped and rolled on the ground.

He turned, stepped, stopped, and turned back.

"Geselda?"

Several of the animals looked at him as if to shrug.

"Geselda! I have some sweet feed for you."

Their draft got up and trotted over. "Have you seen the Tomekan's donkey, girl?"

A shake of the head and a nuzzling of his hand. Eric went into the barn and came back with a handful of oats. She licked them in, snorted, and returned to her dirt bath.

Buco came trotting up to him and sniffed the bread still in his hand. "Donam and Taitano, and now Thomas. Is anyone in this village where they're supposed to be?"

He broke off a chunk of the bread and tossed it to the dog.

"Let's have some breakfast, Buco, then perhaps we can find father."

Inside, he opened the cupboard to get some honey for his bread. Looking up, he saw his father's ledger. He lifted it from the shelf and saw several other tomes stacked behind it. "I didn't realize he was so prolific. How much can be written about the daily activities on a farm?"

He gathered them under one arm, grabbed the honey, sat at the table, and read.

~

Thomas rode Geselda to the church to view the body. "Not my sister? The Tomekan doesn't know my sister. Who's he to decide?"

Every few steps he leaned forward, put his arms around her neck and buried his face in her mane. Dizziness moved through his skull in waves. Shaking his head made things worse. His head ached as if after a night of too strong drink. Only the steady smell of the donkey's hair soothed him.

He heard a soft jingle as he neared the town center. A stage stood between three circus wagons. Two women practiced some kind of dance behind the wagons. The jingling came from zills on their fingers.

They watched Thomas approach. Their dancing changed. No longer practicing steps, they directed the moves to Thomas as if he were an audience of one.

Thomas got off Geselda and blinked.

The bruise on his head throbbed. One woman lifted a bottle and cup from the back wagon's sideboard, danced over to him and poured wine, all while shaking her breasts and thrusting her hips.

Thomas took the cup and smiled. "Thank you."

She blew him a kiss and joined her partner. The two women caressed each other as they danced. The one who offered wine bent over and the other came up behind her, grabbed her hips and thrust into her. Both continued to gaze into his eyes. They smiled and licked their lips, their breaths came heavy, their lips slightly parted.

Thomas sipped the wine. He stepped back to steady himself and bumped into Geselda. She brayed and stepped aside. Thomas watched the women dance and blinked.

Dobrogost's bright clothing fluttered and Thomas turned to see the giant smiling down at him. "They are beautiful, aren't they?"

Thomas nodded. His eyes returned to the dancers.

They continued thrusting and caressing, grabbing and smiling. The rear dancer reached around and grabbed the breasts of the other. She pulled her upright so they stood front to back, both facing him. The one in behind massaged and lifted the other's breasts to Thomas' watering eyes.

He wiped a hand over them to clear them, to get a better look. His eyes focused on the roundness of their breasts, the fullness of their hips.

The giant chuckled. "They are wonderful, aren't they? Imagine being between them. Imagine the pleasure a grown man might have locked in their embrace."

Thomas gulped his wine.

"Are you a grown man?" The jester slapped Thomas back, slightly knocking him towards the dancing women, and laughed "You certainly are growing. One might think you're dowsing."

The women continued dancing and laughed.

"Or perhaps you're enchanted?"

The dancers continued their moves, now with arms reaching out to him as they took small steps back towards the rear wagon.

Thomas' head throbbed. He ran a hand over the front of his pants and the throbbing grew.

"Would you like to be enchanted?"

Thomas took a step towards the dancers, a smile on his face.

The giant put a hand on his back and guided him another step. "Go on. A big, young fellow such as yourself? You can handle the two of them as easily as one, I'm sure."

Thomas dropped the cup. It shattered on the ground. He paid no attention. The dancers climbed the stairs into the back of their wagon, all the time pawing and mauling and grabbing each other, all the time writhing, their dance as intoxicating as the wine in his cup.

Thomas, wobbling and with the giant's guidance, followed.

Eric's stomach growled and he realized he hungered. His father's ledgers kept him busy through most of the day. Many of the pages now carried his tears.

The axe he carried, the axe given to him by his father, the axe his father promised him since he first learned to walk and greedily followed his father to the fields, to the orchards, to the barn, to the town. The axe which swung on his father's hip as he lifted Eric to his shoulders so he needn't run to keep up with his father's long stride.

The axe his father taught him to hold, to use, to throw.

The axe with which he chopped off the witch's hand.

The axe ruined by her blood, its handle rotted and the head tarnished.

His father had placed it under his and his wife's wedding bed and each night thereafter. Each night before they drew the covers over themselves they took out the axe and kissed and cradled it as if it were their son.

226

Because an old belief, a belief carried by their Hutsul people deep in the Carpathians, said making love over a *molfar*'s axe assured them of a son.

And Verduan and his wife dearly wanted a son.

A son they had.

Eric. Him.

And he grew straight and strong and tall.

But now Nant suffered.

As did his axe.

Had the witch's curse worked back through time? Is that why his mother died giving him life?

Dire had been called, but she was busy saving Julia and her twin.

Who was also lost.

He knew the story well.

Perhaps the witch's curse worked back through time but killed the wrong child?

It didn't matter.

Now he knew, he understood.

"I am the product of devilment."

He lifted the axe from his belt. The metalsmith had done good work repairing it. It shone even in dim light. And the handle tapered perfectly for hands big like his father's.

Did the metalsmith's work change him, though? The tinker healed the axe, did it heal him? Make him whole? Change him from witchling to human?

Eric shook his head. "No wonder all I touch is cursed. I entered this life already the child of some spell."

He closed his father's books, stood, and replaced them in the cupboard.

"Buco."

The big dog raised its head from the floor where it lay.

"Come. We must find father."

The big dog woofed and stood by the door.

CHAPTER 41

Tardiff sat in the church, his hands clasped in prayer, his eyes closed, his lips working holy words into supplications for forgiveness. It had been years and now the weight of his...

He looked up at the Cross, at Jesus hanging there, holding himself there, welcoming the nails and the sword to absolve Tardiff...

But I did not sin, Father.

Jesus' downcast face condemned him, the silence of the altar deafened him.

No, nor did you stop someone else from sinning.

What could I do?

You did nothing.

It was not my problem to solve, Father!

He wept at the Cross' silent judgement.

It is your problem now, Bellman Tardiff.

A sound came from the rectory next door. A scraping. Something dragged across the floor?

Had Father Baillot returned? Donam ordered Tardiff to bring Fathers Baillot and Patreo to him and Tardiff found neither.

Donam would not be pleased.

Tardiff stood in front of the altar, crossed himself, and went outside.

The rectory's door was ajar. Sounds came from within.

He knocked. "Father Baillot?"

Baillot opened the door with sweat on his brow and his cassock tied around his waist, his upper body covered only by a white muslin shirt. He stepped outside and pulled the door shut but not before Tardiff saw the front room in disarray, half the furniture where it should be, the other half scattered about.

"What battle happened here? Father Baillot, are you alright?"

Baillot shook his head as if caught in a chill. "Yes, fine. Nothing happened. I'm busy. What can I do for you?"

"I'm to bring you and Father Patreo to Sheriff Donam." He nodded towards the inn. "He's staying at the Red Fox."

Baillot's eyes widened on the inn's front door. "Perhaps later. I must prepare for communion service."

Baillot opened the door enough for himself to enter and Tardiff put a hand on his arm. Baillot's nostrils flared. His face tightened and he glared at the Bellman. "Take your hands off me."

Tardiff frowned. Baillot was not the best churchman but his attitude today did nothing for his reputation. Tardiff's crisis emboldened him. "I have need of confession."

Baillot backed into the opening between door and street. "Perhaps later. I told you, I'm busy."

Tardiff grabbed Baillot's arm. "No. Now. I've held this sin long enough."

Baillot rolled his eyes, inhaled deeply, and shrugged himself free of Tardiff's hand. "Very well. As you wish, then. Meet me inside the church, in the confessional. I'll be in momentarily."

Back in the church, Tardiff took a moment to stand before the Cross. He knew what he had to confess, not how to confess it. He was not a party to the crime, only a bystander who overheard the crime plotted, not even committed. He thought it idle chatter among the royalty: The Baron and his men planning to take one daughter from each village, an homage to the Passover of the Jews; take the first-born daughter instead of the son.

He thought it a joke until he saw the children ushered in the front gate.

Wanting to be accurate and guiltless, he practiced his words. Some came out in a stutter as the memory of his inaction shook him like a strong north wind.

He stood before the altar, Jesus' downcast eyes full on him. His words grew from a whisper to a storm as the past flowed from him.

"It was The Baron's doing, Lord. I...I was just a palace guard. I took no part. No part. Everyone knew his taste for the flesh, for the young, untainted, unbroken."

He shivered. "But I manned the gate. I opened it in the night when the coachman's bell rang in the darkness. One ring, one sound for each child brought to him. From all over the province. Not just Nant.

"No, his workers gathered them from the Coranthians to Beckland, from the eastern borders west to Rappo. And every time I'm in the Red Fox and the bell rings when someone enters I flinch and curse my birth, every time the church calls me to worship, I weep." He stretched his arms and wailed as if Christ's nails pierced his own flesh. "And now to be Tardiff the Bellman, each hour I scream in silent rage that I opened that gate."

He heard doors banging in the rectory. He upset Father Baillot, he knew, but today he didn't care. He heard the rectory door closed and locked. Tardiff finished his practice quickly to be sure he'd say everything as planned.

"I did not hire women to find young girls, too young to be broken, to be put into service in The Baron's castle until they grew under his attentive eye, until he could pick the one among the many, so he could choose them at will."

Baillot would be walking in the door any moment.

Tardiff reached up, his hands spread wide to share Christ's crucifixion. "I did not hire Sullya to barter for Byell's daughters, to take the one and leave the other, to offer dust - *worthless dust!* - in exchange for his child's life."

The church door opened. Light came in and bounced off the altar's regalia.

Tardiff shouted. "I only knew what they'd done. I only opened the gate when their note sounded. I am not to blame."

Buco trotted up to him and nudged his side.

Tardiff shook his head. "What?"

Eric came in from the street and stood in the doorway, a silhouette against the setting sun. "Buco, come."

Tardiff turned and faced him.

Eric held the big dog's collar and scratched his head. "Tardiff, have you seen my father or Patreo, the Tomekan priest?"

CHAPTER 42

Forgeron, his hat pulled low and his steps careful, walked the back alleys of Turo in the darkness of night. He followed the Vell's course as much as he could and carried a missal tied with a knotted red cord. A strange script, one only a few could read or write, covered the missal's pages. Symbols intertwined with the script. Here and there figures appeared, each marked by the strange script.

A large building on the water's edge revealed itself after he walked a curve. The Miller's shop. He tapped on a window; three by a moment's silence, three by a moment's silence, then one-one-one and silence. He glanced around, saw no one, and continued to the Miller's door. It opened a crack. Forgeron passed the missal to the Miller's waiting hand.

A thumb passed over the cord, counted the knots, dipped the missal as if nodding a head.

The door closed.

~

H aasel smiled and stilled her wheel when she heard Galos singing down her lane. She called out, "Enter, Master Charcoal Burner, O' he who can't sing a note. What brings you to my door today?"

"All hail, Mistress Potter. I need to borrow your kilns."

"You are a charcoal burner. What need have you of my kilns?"

"I need a hot fire. Hotter than I can make in a short period of time. Hotter than Zevke's ovens."

"Pity you didn't learn more of the Tinker. He had a forge that would serve your purpose."

His voice lowered and she could tell his face turned down, as if he spoke more to the earth than to her. "His cart is behind Tardiff's cottage and can be seen. I need a cookery hidden from public view."

She placed a hand on his chest. "What troubles you, Galos?"

He took her hand and kissed it. "Nothing troubles me. Yet. I wish to prepare. If Nant had a glassblower, I'd be talking to them."

Her breath quickened at the feel of his lips on her fingers. She clasped his hand in hers and her voice softened. "You always announce your presence."

He smiled and lifted her hand to his cheek so she could feel him smile. "It seems a simple courtesy."

"I can hear your smile in your voice. Do you know that?"

"I know your hearing is better than mine."

"Most others don't go to the trouble of announcing them- selves. Some attempt to sneak up on my door. I suppose they wish to startle me. They don't realize I can hear them approaching on the lane."

"Do you think they're cruel?"

"Not necessarily cruel, unless it's the cruelty of the young and ignorant. People rarely view others as equals, peers. They always seek the upper hand in one way or another. The sighted world thinks their sight gives them an advantage." She lowered her hand from his face. "But few people know how to listen."

"Do I take advantage of you, sneak up on you?"

She laughed. "You smell too strongly of ash and smoke, Master Charcoal Burner. If you're moving quietly, it's to sneak up on another. You've never given me cause to fear."

"But do you fear me? Perhaps without cause? Tell me true, Mistress Potter."

She didn't like the melancholy in his voice. "I've never feared you."

He pulled his hand back and she held it tighter, refused to release it. "Tell me, Master Charcoal Burner, what troubles you?"

He kissed her hand and freed his hand from hers. "Do I get the use of your kilns?"

She yielded. "Do I get to know what you're making?"

Galos chuckled. "I hope not."

"I could help you."

"Still, I'd rather not."

She nodded. "Will this harm my kilns? Will I still be able to fire them?"

"I would not let harm come to you or your kilns, Mistress Potter. Know that before you know all else."

She raised his hand to her face so he could feel her smile.

"I do."

CHAPTER 43

Dire entered her cellar slowly. No candles burned, no lamps lit. Granted, she'd been gone most of the day gathering necessities, visited her own separate stores making sure all was well and good, but Nory was a good lad. She asked him to stay and keep watch over Julia and that he would do.

But not in the dark. Dark or light meant little to him. He navigated day and night equally well. He may be simple, but whatever gods watched over him gave him other skills, the ability to know the natural rhythms of the land, to feel oncoming storms. Sometimes she thought him more animal than man, not that it mattered. He was gifted to her and she thanked whatever gods might be that she heard his infant cries, his tiny, malformed body dying from lack of milk, and followed the ancient secret paths, the underground labyrinth underlying much of Nant, from the far back of her cellar to the ruins, the ancient Cloisters, and found him wrapped up in a blanket covered with ancient symbols, someone's unwilling sacrifice to a misunderstood god.

She knew the caves' system. Over the years she'd explored as much as she could and much remained hidden, creating guides so she could find her way light or dark. The caves surfaced all over Nant, on all sides, several places along the Vell and north, and long ago knowing their flow meant escaping those who considered her knowledge dangerous, who thought her wisdom witchcraft.

Nory, she knew, also explored, although not with her blessing. She worried after him, if he got injured or if something else lived in some cave, a wolf den or bear waking, snakes or centipedes.

But of those things Nory knew more than she. Creatures who should see him as food saw him as friend. They would sniff where he hid food in his clothing and he gave to them freely, chuckling, a child playing with its peers.

Her hands found her tinderbox on her workbench. She opened it and blew on the still glowing ember inside. A moment later she walked through her cellar lighting candles and lamps.

Except this one, the one to the rear of her cellar, near the opening to the underground riot of caves, the area where she often brought things needing to cool or needed to be kept cool, the one in back and in the deepest part of her cellar, was missing.

Where was Nory?

And was Julia with him?

Nory didn't need a torch to navigate the tunnels. Julia would.

Had she gone exploring and Nory followed? Or had they travelled together and Nory, not caring either way, left her to carry a torch? Had Nory gone off for some purpose and Julia grabbed the torch to follow, frightened to be alone in the dark?

Nant, it seemed, became unsafe overnight. She sometimes heard noises far off, far away in the labyrinths, and took guard lest the noises, unnatural, get too close.

She went to her apothecary. The things she needed her hands found quickly. At her bench she took mortar and pestle and created powders, mixed them, then wrapped them in twine to form them into balls with the starting threads hanging free.

She took the loosely twined balls and put them in her satchel. That she slung over her shoulder, lit a long, full candle, and walked into the tunnel at the back of her cellar, each step her candle pushing back the edge of darkness.

SECTION VIII
CAVERNA MAGICA

CHAPTER 44

Patreo dipped his bread in his weak beef broth. "I wonder if all prisoners dine so well."

Verduan said nothing.

"You could sit over here, enjoy what little light the torch affords us."

Verduan tore off a piece of his bread and chewed.

"What bothers you, Verduan. What have I done so horrible to offend you?"

Verduan looked at the priest. His chewing slowed and he swallowed. "Did Baillot speak the truth?"

Patreo paused in his dipping. "Could you be more specific?"

Verduan inhaled as if rising from too deep water. "Anything. Everything. He knew quite a bit about your family. Was I a fool to seek you out?"

Patreo shoved his remaining bread in his mouth. He placed the bowl with its remaining broth carefully on the floor against the wall, so as not to step or trip on it.

Verduan shook his head. "You are careful for a condemned man."

Patreo rose and tested the bars of his cell door for the third or fourth time that hour. "Half of what Baillot said is true."

"Which half? Are you a witch, the child of witches or not? What was it he called you and your father and uncle? Acceptors? Devilworkers? He spoke a foreign tongue." Verduan searched for the word. "An idiot man? What was it he said?"

"From the Greek, an *iatromantis*. A healer. One schooled in the Old Ways. Yes, like my father and uncle before me."

"I thought you didn't know your father."

"He and my uncle left on the Crusades before I was born."

"How could you know what they did? How could they teach you?"

"They left their books. My mother hid them, should anyone come looking."

"So you were trained as a witch."

"A healer-prophet, translating from Greek."

"A magician."

"A student of Empedocles, but more along the lines of Melchizedek, the prophet-priest-king of the Old Testament. You have your letters. Have you read his story? The church has banned it."

Verduan rose and threw his bowl down in disgust. "I know none of these things. You read what the church has banned? Then Baillot is correct and I've tied my cart to a witch? How did Baillot know these things? Tell me plainly, are you a witch, a devilworker, or not?"

Patreo knelt and used the hem of his cassock to sop up Verduan's spilt broth. He wrung it out over his own bowl. All the while he chuckled softly. "If I am, I would lie. If I'm not, what proof could I offer? In either case, your heart must tell you if I am to be trusted, if I am working to rid Nant of its vexations, or not."

Verduan lifted him up from the floor. "Are you so hungry you'll swallow swill?"

"Do you think Baillot will return soon?"

"Do you plan on enlisting him in our escape?"

"You heard his words, not his tone. Did he accuse or question my family history?"

Verduan's fingers curled into tightened fists. "Half his words were in some other tongue. How should I know how he spoke?"

"Consider, Verduan. You have time to clear your mind and think, don't you? It doesn't appear to you we're leaving soon, does it? Then you might as well rest, clear your mind, and think."

Verduan harrumphed, closed his eyes, then frowned. "You're right. He talked more like a soldier or counselor, not a priest or inquisitor."

"Good. Now, how long since food was left under our door?"

Verduan threw up his hands. "Lord God has put me in prison with a fool. A moment's sanity and we're back to the day's lunacy."

Patreo pulled on the door's bars. "This place is built of Roman concrete. No point in attacking that. These bars seem equally ancient. Not recently forged. This is older iron, don't you think?"

"What do I know of ages and irons. You want to know the age of the bars? Ask Forgeron if you can find him."

"Perhaps I shall." Patreo unbuttoned his cassock so it opened above his groin. He spread his legs slightly, reached between them, and pulled out a small pouch.

Verduan shook his head, stepped back, and crossed himself. "You are a witch. You can separate yourself from what men hold most dear? Does your manhood grow feet or wings? What man so easily does that?"

"I still have what men hold most dear, as you term it, Brother Verduan. I keep this under it in case I am searched. They will feel it and assume I'm quite the man and nothing more. Shall I show you and prove it to you?"

"My god, what other blasphemies are you capable of?"

"Ah. Well. Watch." Patreo poured the contents of the pouch into his bowl of weak broth. "Let us hope this broth is as weak as it tastes."

Verduan watched, shook his head, and turned away.

A moment later a sizzling turned him back. The broth steamed.

"What is that?"

"Come closer. I need to remove your chains."

Verduan hesitated.

Patreo pulled the big man's manacles forward and dripped the steaming broth into their locks. "Be careful. Hold your hands so the broth stays on the iron. Be sure it doesn't drip onto your flesh."

He did the same for his own manacles.

Both men's locks gave off a greenish mist. Verduan held his manacles up to inspect the broth's workings. Patreo moved his hands down. "Don't breathe the vapor. It'll do to you what it's doing to the iron."

Verduan kept his eyes on his manacles. A moment later they opened and fell from him. His eyes opened wide, He rubbed his wrist and stared at the Tomekan priests. "Magic?"

"Old knowledge. Learned in my father's and uncle's books. And studied on my own. Remember I said I'm from the Occitan order?"

Verduan shrugged. "So?"

"They are recognized by Mother Church, but exist slightly outside its Order. Like the Templars and Hospitaliers."

Verduan held up his chains. "Do you have any of whatever it is left to open our cell door?"

Patreo lifted the still steaming bowl. "Now that we're more mobile, let's find out."

CHAPTER 45

Zevke ran to Nant's center bathed in a cold sweat that fixed his shirt to him and trickled in little rivulets down his legs. A big man, he did not take to running. His size and build befitted a baker, one used to the slow frothing of the yeast in the flour, the steady kneading, the feel of freshly risen dough under his palms so like a woman's full breasts, the long hours at hot ovens, the thumping of loaves and listening to the echoes inside their crusts indicating this one done, that one not.

Running he knew from fleeing villages. From seeing Crosses marching up to his home. From gathering what he could and running, not caring what was dropped, what fell from his hands, what fell from his cart, finally unhitching his old horse and pulling the cart himself because he moved faster and she would block his escape.

Oh, he sacrificed much to keep his skin safe. He did not want unwelcome hands kneading his back or face or thighs. He'd seen what happened to his parents long, long ago and it left its mark, much like a baker's sign to let others know this loaf was wheat, that one rye, that one marbled, this one whole.

The sweat was the same. The fear-scented sweat twisted his gut so tight his belly brushed against his spine, and the fear was the same running into this village as running out of others, others not even Saida knew of.

He stopped before entering the town center proper, bent over and hands on knees, his breath in rasps.

Slow, Zevke. Let others see you as they know you, the quiet baker quick to smile, always with a loaf for the orphan and widow.

The sweat dried on him. The sun came through an apple tree and threw his shadow against the cottage beside him. He leaned against the cottage and sought some shade while his breathing slowed.

A door slammed. Zevke peeked around the cottage's corner.

Baillot ran down the South Road, his cassock held up over his knees so he wouldn't trip and fall.

Zevke'd never seen the Father move so fast. He stood and stretched his back. His breath escaped him slowly and he relaxed. "At least the good Father is alive and well."

He brought an apple blossom to his nose and inhaled deeply, his eyes closed and a smile warming his face.

Someone started yelling inside the church.

The blossom and the branch holding it snapped back, suddenly free of Zevke's hand.

He flattened himself against the cottage wall.

Laughter came from across the town center.

Zevke peered through some lower branches. Nant was busy today. Far busier than it should be this time of day.

Across the town center, three circus wagons formed a semicircle. A stage grew out from the wagons into the circle's center. A bright red rope went from the left-most wagon to the right-most, supported high above the stage by rods like flagpoles leading troops into battle. A multi-colored curtain patched like Joseph's coat dropped from the right end of the rope, a bright red cord kept it gathered against the right-most wagon.

A cacophony of colors which flowed well together.

Like the laughter. Women's laughter. From behind the circus wagons.

A dark-skinned giant garbed in brightly colored clothing appeared, his back to Zevke, an arm around someone's waist and lifting them off the ground as he walked. The latter flopped in his arms like a child's straw-stuffed doll, someone unable to handle their drink or recovering from his first time drunk.

The giant turned and the person's feet dragged in a small arc with him.

Zevke saw their face. Master Thomas? Drunk? Ill?

More laughter. The giant spoke to someone. Two women appeared, laughing, their clothing thin and revealing even in the distance. One grabbed Thomas' hair and lifted his head. She kissed him long and hard, their mouths open, and Zevke imagined her tongue searching, a serpent seeking scurrying creatures among Thomas' teeth as if they were stones along a path.

She dropped his head and all three laughed again. The giant kicked a wagon.

A tall, lithe man in jester's clothing dropped from it. They talked but Zevke couldn't hear what was said. The giant nodded and threw Thomas over his shoulder as if he were a bag of grain. Zevke doubted Thomas knew or understood what was happening to him.

The giant spoke in a deep, penetrating voice.

Zevke heard one word above all others: Sullya.

Sullya the Witch?

The giant shifted Thomas on his shoulder, nodded to the jester, bowed to the women, grabbed some leathers and a donkey appeared at their end. Donkey, giant, and Thomas went off as if following Baillot on the south road out of town.

The jester and women walked back behind the circus wagons, out of sight.

Something brushed against Zevke's thigh and his heart banged in his chest.

Buco sat beside him.

Zevke blinked. "You are Verduan's dog? You are worse than Nory, always wanting something to eat. I have nothing for you today. Go away."

More yelling from the church.

The dog trotted towards the church doors.

Verduan's son, Eric, walked down a side street. "Buco, come! We have work to do."

The church door creaked and Eric turned to it. The dog's flanks disappeared inside.

Eric strode to the church. "Buco! Here!" He opened the church doors wide and stood there. "Buco, come."

Zevke's sweat caught his shirt against his broad back and shoulders once again. He kept his back to the cottage wall until it met a back lane.

He hurried away.

CHAPTER 46

Donam and Taitano stood outside the main entrance to The Cloisters. Towering oak, elm, and ash, their limbs reaching out to each other as if caught in a dance, their green leaves swelling and turning like billowing sleeves from some forest spirit's blouse, blocked the sun but not the heat. The heat drew moisture up from the soil, from exposed roots and rocks, and gave it sprite-like shapes that walked among the trees, along the paths, that ducked here and there, playing a bizarre hide-and-seek without sharing the rules of their game.

Taitano pulled his crossbow off from his shoulder, mounted a bolt and held it at the ready.

Donam unsheathed his sword and scanned the woods. "What is it?"

Taitano kept the stock tucked in his shoulder. His fingers gripped the tiller with white knuckles. He spoke quietly. "I do not like this place."

Donam laughed at his deputy. Taitano's attention climbed the trees, leapt to The Cloisters' walls, walked along their tops, jumped down to the massive entrance, to the fallen gates, and began again.

Donam sheathed his sword. "It is good to know you are so vigilant when there's nothing to fear."

"You do not fear this place?"

"Why should I? I serve the Master here."

Taitano kept his crossbow at the ready and glanced as Donam. "What master?"

Donam twirled in the mists like a drunk dancing his way home. "I serve the Master here and in all places, always."

"What master, damn you?"

"Ahura Maternus. The First One, the First Principle."

Taitano glanced beyond Donam into The Cloisters' courtyard. "Who? The what? Does The Baron know you serve another master?"

"I serve Ahura Maternus at The Baron's side."

Taitano lowered his crossbow slightly. "Ahura Maternus? The King's name is Gaumand. What do you play at?"

Donam proceeded through the gateway. "Come. I will show you."

Taitano stayed at the entrance's portico. "You've been here before?"

"This is a holy place."

Taitano's crossbow lowered. His eyes ran along the rotted timbers, the fallen stones, the mildew-covered gates. His voice came out as a whisper, as if in Vespers at church. "This is a holy place?"

"Come. I will show you the altar."

"The Baron worships here?"

"How long could you have been in The Baron's service yet know so little of his ways?"

"I am not privy to his thoughts."

Donam laughed. "No, only his mistress."

Taitano kept his crossbow lowered and turned to face the Sheriff, one hand still on the tiller, the other at the trigger. "What are The Baron's ways?"

Sheriff Donam's hand slid along the entrance's moisture-dampened wall as they walked into The Cloisters' main court. Across from them, one building, its stonework mostly held in gnarled and twisted roots like unnatural fingers, showed stairs leading to an ancient altar, the building's fallen roof scattered around it. An enclosed archway led from the fallen altar to what once served as either monastery or jail. Taitano couldn't determine which or if brothers or prisoners would be housed there.

Donam licked moisture from his fingertips. "You know our Lord The Baron gives liberally to Mother Church?"

"What royal doesn't?"

"And in return, Mother Church lets him know about her priests and monks and sisters entering and leaving his domain, and as much of the history, the strengths and weaknesses, of each as church records allow?"

"And he sends word when troubles arise, when a parish is in need of another shepherd. What of it?"

"Nant's priest was a Father Verrett. Very knowledgeable in both church matters and ways not favored by Mother Church. He'd served Nant since The Baron's father's was a child."

"What are we doing here, Lord Sheriff?"

"Verrett served Nant well, but not The Baron. The Baron traveled in his youth and learned much..."

"Does this tale have an ending?"

"...much of the Old Ways, ways not favored by Mother Church. He knew the history of this place. It served Ahura Maternus whom some knew as Cernunnos. In all names, The Horned One."

"Satan?"

Donam laughed. "A myth the church propagates so people

will fear." He stood at the altar and waved at an engraving in the altar's flanking stonework. "See this?"

Years had eaten away much but Taitano could still see enough to wonder what god the Sheriff and Baron served: a human body clothed like an old Roman guard. Its right hand threatened with a battle-axe, its left held an elliptical shield. Two words, Iao and Sabaoth, were written upon it, but Taitano knew not what they meant. The creature's head was a grand cock, its beak open, its legs were coiled serpents standing on a thunderbolt.

Taitano refused to near the figure. "I've never seen the like of this."

"Of course you haven't. You're an ignorant man of wood and field." Donam pointed to the altar itself. "Look."

Taitano kept his crossbow in a firm grip. "What is that?"

"Blood."

"The Baron sacrifices animals here?"

Donam ran his hands over the altar as if caressing a lover's rump. "The Baron made his first offering years ago. A bastard son."

"The Baron offered a human sacrifice?" His face whitened. "His own son?"

Donam ignored his deputy's disgust. "Twisted and deformed. The Baron's physicians didn't think the child would live."

A light flickered briefly in the archway where it met the monastery-like building. Taitano kept his eyes on Donam. "You took part?"

"I brought the child. Left it on this altar."

"You?"

Donam stood before the altar, spread his arms and turned slowly. "Do this three times and He reveals Himself to devout and honest seekers. Did you know that?"

The light flickered again, closer this time, a spark driving back the misting demons rising in the choking heat.

Donam's eyes rolled up in his head as he spun in ecstasy. "I returned and the child was gone. Accepted. Taken."

Taitano raised his crossbow until it pointed at Donam's chest. "You're coming with me. To the King. This is too beyond for me to fathom. He'll know how to deal with your crime."

Donam ignored him. "The Baron thinks well ahead of most men. A gift from The Horned One for good service. Baillot was half The Baron's age but followed The Baron devoutly. The Baron sent him into the church's service with the promise he'd come back to The Baron's domain when the time came."

"Draw out your sword and lay it on the ground. Kick it to me."

The light flickered closer still. Taitano's eyes remained on Donam.

"Baillot was to return to take Verrett's place. The old priest never returned. That, too, I know."

Behind Donam, along the top of the thick stone wall, someone in white robes like a bishop, with a red cap and girdle bound the waist, ran silently and without stopping.

"Baillot was supposed to report to The Baron upon his arrival. He never did. The Baron waited. Now this mispleasure comes to Nant, to this holy place."

The flickering moved again. A shadowed figure moved with it.

"The Baillot serving Nant is not The Baron's priest. I am here to learn why."

Some stones fell as they rolled beneath running feet. The light flickered again.

Taitano turned, his crossbow at his shoulder, his eyes along the site, his back to Sheriff Donam.

"The Baron planned long and well. He sent his people to bring him virgin children. Better to sacrifice. More acceptable gifts to The Horned One. A demonstration of good service." Donam drew his sword.

Taitano turned to meet him.

"Sarah was not to be his mistress." Donam chuckled. "Well, not The Baron's mistress."

"What?"

"You killed her when you slept with her. Her blood is on your hands."

Taitano stepped back and put a hand to his head. The dancing mists made breathing difficult. He blinked.

"You, Taitano, you spoiled the virgin before she could be offered, before our next sacrifice. Sadly, she learned her purpose - no idea how, not that it matters - and had to be destroyed before she alerted others of The Baron's good deeds."

Taitano's mind cleared. He gripped the crossbow in sure hands. His nostrils flared over its tiller and bolt. "You killed my Sarah?"

"You, foolish Taitano, have ruined my Lord The Baron's plans. Another had to be found. A local girl, and it seems a twin to your lovely kitchen maid. Except now she, too, is lost. And all of it on your hands." Donam moved in quickly, knocked the crossbow from Taitano's hands, swung his sword.

Taitano heard a *whoosh* pass his head. Donam bellowed. His sword clattered to The Cloisters' courtyard stonework.

A crossbow bolt pierced the Sheriff's hand. His sword rattled slightly towards Taitano as the momentum of Donam's swing died.

A second *whoosh* followed and Donam grunted as if startled. A second bolt pierced his brow and buried itself until only its feathers showed above his eyes. He fell.

Taitano dropped, rolled, gained his crossbow, rose and spun, raised it to his shoulder, held it ready.

A figure dressed in black but not like the first, this one's face smeared with fatted dirt to hide its features and a crossbow slung over his back, ran to the end of the wall and jumped. Taitano heard the person land, roll, rise and run beyond The Cloisters' wall.

More stones grated from the archway. Hurried steps moved away. The light disappeared into the darkness, the figure with it.

Taitano spun, his crossbow up, a second bolt at the ready. He shifted back and forth, not knowing where the attack would come from.

CHAPTER 47

Julia sat on the cold, damp ground. She pulled Dire's kirtle and blanket tight around her and tucked it under her feet. The torch she carried when Nory beckoned her to follow flickered weakly. It would go out soon and it would be dark.

She looked up hoping to see the moon and stars.

Roots. Dirt and roots. She asked Nory who built these tunnels, who found these caves. She might as well have asked a rock. He smiled and nodded and scurried along, his short bowed legs moving faster than her straight supple legs could follow.

She shivered and pulled a hand inside the kirtle and blanket to run it down her legs, to beat some heat back into them.

Not many had seen her legs.

Now she was sure not many would.

She wrapped them around Baillot more than once, at first unsure, then each time more and more sure until her body shivered but not with any cold.

She asked him once, how does a priest know how to do such things?

I am no priest, he told her.

She chuckled and he licked her breasts until her nipples hardened and she welcomed him again.

The child was his.

She had not told him but there were no others. The child was his.

If not a priest then who are you?

He got up from their bed, reached into his wardrobe and pulled out a strangely shaped blade.

She sat up and pulled the covers about her.

He laughed and put it away. "I was a soldier once. In training to be a knight. I served a knight. Fought by his side and learned from him."

She did not think it of him. He had a lean musculature, yes, but certainly not one fit for battle.

"It was years ago. I gave up my Cross and Mantle, sold each tool of my craft whenever my pockets emptied and my belly wanted filling, until only a few tools of the soldier's trade were left, this pike's head being one and that, even, shorn from the pike it once graced." He laughed. "Much like me."

"Where did you fight?"

"In the Holy Lands, the last Crusade. It was a noble cause. I and my brothers fought the followers of ibn Mukidh."

"Did you prevail?"

"We killed most, not all. Some of us were captured, tortured. I..." He turned the pike's head in his hand, thrusting into and parrying an unseen foe. "I escaped. Fled. Ibn Munkidh's followers, the Jannenites, vowed to see the last of us dead. I've been fleeing ever since."

She protested. "But you know the orders, the stations."

"I was raised in the faith much like you." He returned the pike's head to the wardrobe. "Have you ever seen me do anything other than the common services, perform anything other than the common offerings, offer anything other than the best known stations? No. I do what anyone raised in the faith would know how to do, something seen so many times it can be done without thinking, without even knowing what the words mean."

"But your robes, your Cross, your - "

"Found on a dead priest on the road I traveled. He had papers of transit and I could read."

"Killed?"

"Not by my hand. I've done much but I've not murdered except on order of my King."

"Do you know who killed him?"

"I know they were fools raised in the faith, otherwise they would have taken his Cross, his Rosary, his vestments, the few coins in his purse. The only thing they took was the one thing I wanted: his food. They took his food and drink and left everything else where it fell."

"If not Father Baillot, what is your name, then?"

"Ioan. From a land not far north of the kingdom."

He stood before her naked and she took his hand. "Why are you telling me this now?"

"Because..." he sat down on the bed next to her and stroked her face. "Because I care for you."

She dropped the covers and helped him back into her.

The memory warmed her but not enough.

She came to these ruins she had no idea how long ago. To meet him. They were to flee together, to escape Nant to some other town, perhaps some other kingdom. But then she heard a sound, something hit her head, and she woke in Dire's hiding place.

The torch flickered.

She bowed her head and wept.

ory reached up and tugged on an exposed root until it
snapped. He tilted his head back and let the sweet juice
drizzle down his throat. Soon his hands found pea roots and
beets. He imagined the flowers growing above them, remembered
where he'd seen them growing, and knew where he was under
Nant.

He snapped off carrots and ate them.

Dire taught him what to eat and when, what to not eat and
when not to eat it.

She led him through these caves with a torch.

Nory didn't need a torch. He listened to the sounds from
above, to the echoes of his own steps. He smelt what grew down
below and knew what echoed its growth above. He felt the sides
of the earthen walls, felt where trickles began and ended, where
tunnels branched and where caverns led, and kept count in his
head.

He often brought things he found above down below.

He wanted to bring his pretty hammer here, to keep it safe,
but it was heavy. Too heavy for Nory to carry.

Perhaps Simon would bring it here for him?

Julia was somewhere far behind him. Too far behind for him
to hear. The moaning up ahead, though. He heard the moaning
clearly.

Something sad. Something tired. Something hurt.

Nory knew these things.

It bothered Nory to hear such things.

Nory knew!

Nory would bring food!

Food always made Nory happy.

Nory broke off roots, tubers, pulled beets and carrots down
from above.

He filled his arms.

He followed the moaning. It grew softer as he neared.

Nory moaned.

A moan in answer.

Nory moaned again.

Another moan in answer.

Nory hurried.

He stopped at the smell.

Something sick. Dying?

Nory wasn't sure.

Definitely sick.

Nory kept moaning, walked quickly.

That's when he found the bear.

It lay on its side and breathed slowly.

It growled as Nory approached.

Nory reached out and felt its breath. He bit off part of a carrot, took it from his mouth, and put it under the bear's nose.

The bear's tongue came out of its mouth and pulled the carrot back in.

Crunch.

The bear moaned.

Nory kept feeding it carrots. When there were no more carrots Nory fed it beets.

The bear was hungry.

Sometimes it licked Nory's hand and moaned.

A stream rippled through a nearby cavern. Nory knew. Nory would get the bear some water. Nory knew thirst. Perhaps the bear did, too?

He petted the bear's muzzle to let it know he would come back soon.

He felt blood, scratches. Leather straps. One of the bear's paws was caught tight in the straps.

The straps went behind, over, and under the bear's head.

What was that on its head?

The bear wore a hat?

Bears don't wear hats.

Silly Nory.

No! Circus bears wear hats!

This was the circus bear!

Nory found the circus bear!

Oh, Nory was so happy.

The bear moaned when Nory touched its paw.

Nory's fingers felt along the straps.

A mask? The bear wore a hat and a mask? Simon wore a mask. Maybe the bear and Simon were friends?

The bear's face bleeds.

Nory felt one of the bear's paws trapped in the straps of the mask and hat. Its claws gouged and regouged its muzzle, some of the blood dried and clotted.

Poor bear!

How did it get in Nory's caves?

Bears liked caves. Dire told him so, therefore it was true.

Ha! Nory understood. The bear walked into Nory's caves.

But the dried, clotted blood?

The bear came on three legs?

It limped!

Nory knows what it is to limp. Sometimes Thomas threw things at Nory. They hurt and made Nory limp until he was far, far away.

And now the Bear rests so Nory can feed it, to make it strong, so it will not limp!

Nory pulled its paw free, undid the straps and pulled the mask and hat from the bear's head.

The bear nuzzled Nory's hand.

Nory understood.

Sometimes people in Nant - Thomas most often - made Nory put on hats and clothes that didn't fit when no one was around and they laughed at Nory.

Nory would make sure the bear wouldn't have to wear hats and masks again.

He leaned over and kissed the bear's face.

There was something else wrong with the bear's face.

The bear had no eyes.

It gently brushed Nory's hand away when he felt along its brow.

Nory would see for the bear.

Nory would help the bear because he understood the bear and the bear understood him.

Nory scratched behind the bear's ears.

The bear pulled Nory's hand down to its muzzle, licked it, and let it go.

Nory kept pottery shards he found behind Haasel's workshop by the stream. He would fill one with water and bring it back to the bear.

He and the bear would be friends.

CHAPTER 48

Verduan and Patreo stood in the moss-covered, arched roof hallway outside their cell. Patreo rubbed his wrists and lifted a dwindling torch from the wall. "Which way?"

Verduan cautiously extended a finger to the still steaming door bolt as if he expected it to snap out and strike him. "Which way what?"

"You've been here. Which way out?"

"I came here on a dare as a child and pissed myself when I got lost because I heard voices."

"But you got out."

"Someone got me out. I don't know who. A woman's voice, though. Sullya? She inhabits such places. But why free me and not eat me. Witches do such things to children. I fell asleep in a huddled ball in a corner somewhere. I woke up on the South Road to Nant."

Patreo handed Verduan the dying torch and went back into their cell.

"You plan on locking yourself in again?"

He gathered some dried brush and came back out. "Bring over that torch. We're going to make a fire."

Verduan handed him the torch. "You hoping to lure people with buckets?"

Patreo stuck the torch into the brush. It caught and blazed. Once it got going full he stamped it out.

Verduan looked up and down the hall. "I don't think anyone saw your signal."

"Watch where the smoke travels."

Verduan shook his head and mumbled something but did as he was told.

A plume of thick smoke rose from the embers and wafted down the hallway in one direction.

Patreo pointed. "That way. The smoke travels that way because there's a draft in that direction. Follow the smoke and eventually we'll be out."

"Out where?"

"That I don't know. Out under the sky eventually. If the smoke didn't vent outdoors at some point we'd be dead by now."

"You learned all this reading your father's and uncle's books?"

"We'll need to carry the embers. I don't see any other light in either direction. Someone carried a torch here and mounted it on the wall to let others know where to find us." Patreo gathered more brush and leaves. He dried out one of the bowls and placed the brush and leaves in it. "Put the embers on top. Breathe on them enough to keep them lit, enough to create smoke we can follow."

Galos came to Idee's gate and called out, "Hello the house."
No answer.

He held an empty sack in his left arm and jingled coins in his pocket with his right. "I've come to buy from your garden. Idee? Byell?"

Still no answer.

He opened the gate and knocked on the door.

Nothing.

He heard a woman's sobs in the distance and followed the sound.

In the middle of their field, Idee patted the ground with a shovel.

"Idee?"

She didn't respond, instead she knelt on the ground, her feet under her and the toes of her leather boots and pattens pressing into the earth. She wet her hands with tears and smoothed the dirt with callused hands. Sometimes wails interrupted her tears. She raised open hands over her head, made fists, and brought them down with enough force to bowl the freshly turned earth.

Galos walked slowly and carefully. Byell's fields were not producing well, certainly not enough for a worthwhile harvest. Here and there white powder blotched the dark earth. Nothing grew where it touched.

He stopped when he realized she sat beside a grave. Around the grave, the earth was tainted with blood.

"Idee, what happened? Who's buried here?"

"Byell consorted with the Devil. Did you know? The figure of a man, head-to-toe in black. Cassocked like a monk or priest with blackened face and wearing a hood and flowing cape."

Galos looked into the woods surrounding the field then knelt beside her. "Here? Do you see this figure now?"

"He was here. He made Byell slice his own throat with his own blade."

"This figure, did it move like a man?"

She patted the ground and nodded. "It watched while I found Byell, his throat cut, right here. This very spot."

"You've never seen this figure before?"

"Did you know Byell drank? Too much, I said. I told him often but he never listened. He said our daughter's screams deafened him."

"Julia screamed?"

"Byell'd seen the figure before. At least once. He told me when he'd been too long in his cups. He said it did something to his fields. Cursed them so his magic wouldn't work."

Galos reached down and scooped up a palmful of dark earth and white powder. "This?" He lifted it to his nose and sniffed carefully.

"He carried a pouch of her ashes. Blood magic, he said. To make our fields prosper. Did you ever see it? Tucked in a pocket, only revealed when our crops faltered." She laughed. "They faltered more with than without."

"What pouch? What magic?"

"His pouch and the magic grew thinner each year. Some years we prospered, others not, but neither more nor less than any others in Nant or its surrounds."

Galos shook his head. "Julia's ashes? That's impossible. I saw her alive and well just a few days ago. Make sense, woman."

"He told me the whole story once. I'm sure he forgot he did. He thought I turned cold because we lost our child, but no, I welcomed him until I found him sobbing into his cups, the smell of the threshers heavy on him. From then on I would not have him. I would cook and clean and do what I could for my children, but him I kept a stranger to me."

"What did he tell you?"

Idee's head wavered as she spoke, her eyes fluttered. "Sullya the Witch has come and gone through Nant for as long as any can remember. Whenever she grows old she takes a child, takes the life from it, and grows young again."

"Sullya took Julia to grow young again?"

"Sarah screamed. Her voice haunted Byell every day of his life."

A movement on the far edge of the field caught Galos' eye. Crows and blackbirds rousted but nothing more. Is that what Byell and Idee saw?

"Sullya said she must be burned alive for the magic to work. Half the ashes she gave to Byell and taught him their use. The other half she used on herself to make a bath, a paste, and when she washed it off, she was young again."

"How do you know this?"

Her head fell forward for an instant. It came up slowly. "Oh, I know. My mother told me how my father was lost to her because he slept with the witch." Her body shook and she continued. "The witch bade Byell enter her. He said he could not resist, although hideous she was, her face the color of the sky with streaks of sunshine coming through, her eyes red and with snakes writhing in her hair. She wore a collar of skulls so low she revealed her breasts, young and full again, she forced him to suck, held his face against her, and when her breasts were empty she forced him to kiss her purple lips even though fangs and tusks stuck out."

She patted the mound beside her. "He claimed he feared too much to resist."

"Idee, why did he not tell us? We could have hunted her down, been done with her, ..."

"Her powder never worked. And when he told me what he'd done, I never worked for him either."

Galos put a hand on the burial mound. It yielded slightly to his touch. "How long has he been dead?"

"A good day now. Perhaps more. I don't know."

"But I smell fresh blood. Where is his blade?"

Idee rose up on her knees. She reached under her hem and between her legs. Her hand came back dripping with blood, the knife bloodied from tip to handle.

"Idee!"

The crows called. He looked up. The figure. Just as Idee described him.

"Who are you?" Galos ran towards the figure, his eyes never leaving the figure, always keeping it in sight.

The figure drew a white steel sword from inside the folds of its cape and struck an elm. Robins and wrens and blackbirds and warblers took to the air, blocking him from Galos' view.

"Wait! Stop!"

The birds settled and the figure was gone.

Galos returned to Idee and Byell's dead bodies.

Patreo walked and breathed on the embers to create enough light to see where the smoke wisped.

Verduan walked slightly behind and to his right, a hand on Patreo's shoulder so he wouldn't get lost. "Do you have a fondness for prison walls? You run your hands over them as if you're caressing a lover."

"Have you noticed the walls are both brickwork and earthen?"

"You find the strangest times to be fascinated by things."

"Both brick and earth are cool, the earth slightly damp, as if sweating."

"Wonderful. We walk beside a feverish giant. There are stories of such in the north."

Patreo stopped and tapped the wall until a root showed itself. "Yes. That's where I'm from. I know them well."

"Excellent. You stay here and commune with your northern giants. I'll take the embers, make a real fire from them, and speak highly of you when I find daylight."

"We're near the surface. These roots don't grow deep. The length of a young man's leg, not more."

Two steps further Patreo's hand stopped at a doorjamb. "There's a door here."

"A way out?"

Patreo raised the glowing embers. An unlit torch leaned out from the wall and he lit it.

The door was unlocked and had no bars, no way to see in or out.

Patreo gave Verduan the embers.

"I'd rather have the torch."

Patreo opened the door and both men reeled back against the far wall.

Verduan screamed, "The stench of the dead! We're in hell!"

Patreo held a fold of his cassock over his nose and peered into the cell. "Don't be an old woman, Verduan. It's the stench of the dead, yes, but it's from those two bodies, not hell."

Verduan peered over Patreo's shoulder and whispered. "Isn't that the girl we found by the Tinker's cart?"

Patreo handed the torch to Verduan and kept his cassock tight against his face. "Stay back here. Some creatures feast on the dead. They aren't pleasant to behold."

Verduan nodded but said nothing.

He lifted the body's arm and inspected the face. "Bring that light closer, would you? Stand outside the door and hold it arm's length in."

Patreo checked the face, the eyes, the marks he remembered from his previous inspection. "Yes. It is." He shifted to the other body and inspected. "From the face and skin, from the swelling of the hips and flattening of the breasts, an old woman, but one who nursed often and well. Is Nant missing any ancients who were wet-nurses in their day?"

Verduan shook his head.

Patreo lifted the arms. "The fingers are cut from this hand. Gangrene set in, but look: she or someone else knew to let the flies have her. They would have sealed the wounds given enough time."

Verduan took a tentative step in. "Those are huge maggots beside her. They must have feasted well."

Patreo followed Verduan's gaze.

"Not maggots. Her fingers." Patreo made the Sign of the Cross over the bodies, let his cassock fall and dusted his hands on it. "We'll return if we're able. To bury them properly."

Verduan smothered the torch and stepped inside the cell. He whispered, "Someone's coming."

A faint light grew in the direction they travelled.

They pressed themselves up against the cell wall and swung the door closed as quietly as possible.

The light continued its approach. Its motion betrayed the strong, steady gait of whomever held it as they walked.

Booted footsteps stopped outside the door. Light flickered underneath it.

Verduan lifted his dead torch like a club. The door swung open.

Verduan struck.

The other person's torch met the arc of Verduan's and guided it away. They turned into Verduan's momentum and threw him against a wall. "Stop."

The person held their lit torch up to their face.

Patreo pulled back. "Father Baillot?"

CHAPTER 49

Dire walked slowly through the tunnels, one hand feeling a knotted cord waist-height along the wall, the other holding an unlit candle. She had a satchel over her shoulder, and she carried bread, some dried beef, and a full wineskin. Nory had been gone for a while. She was quite sure the lad would be fine. He knew this cave system better than she did. She showed him the paths she knew once and that was all it took. He'd remember them forever.

Strange how that lad's mind worked.

But she knew he wasn't as simple as everyone said.

He knew which tunnels led to vegetable fields, which tunnels came out to orchards, which tunnels opened near the road north of Nant, which tunnels surfaced not far from the Red Fox.

No. Not as simple as everyone said.

This tunnel opened to The Cloisters, the ancient ruin south-east of Nant. She came here often. Voices, screams, sometimes came from here. On the darkest nights. Earlier she believed the stories, that this place was haunted.

But she found Nory here. Wonderful Nory who was her joy in

her old age. He wasn't quick enough for her to teach all her ways, but he was a good lad and she cared for him. She had no family and Nory was family enough.

She heard voices now, but strong and sure voices. Arguing voices.

She made her way through the cellar rooms, the dungeons, of The Cloisters until she reached the archway leading from temple to altar. Few knew this was a holy place in its time.

Dire knew. She'd explored. Looking for old books, old inscriptions on walls, anything to add to her knowledge of healing ways.

But it became obvious The Cloisters weren't for healing. What evidence she found pointed to darker ways.

She'd seen this before, when she traveled in her youth. The new religion came through and pushed the old religion out, except the old religion never left, only went underground, and here quite literally it went underground. Nant had been a crossroads, a nexus, before the Mongols came and were finally driven back. Old religion, strange religions, battled new, and The Cloisters remained. The Old Ways perverted to battle the New, the purpose of this place had changed hands but not changed ways.

What could have been the feelings, she wondered, of those workers of the Old Ways, when presented with the vaunted God of Love, the Prince of Peace, whose emissaries condemned them to torture and death? What wonder they clung to their old faith and died in agony unspeakable rather than deny their gods.

She crept into the archway and lit the candle as the satchel grew heavy on her back. Two men stood before the altar: their clothing bore The Baron's mark.

One held a crossbow and crouched and glanced around him, his eyes wide, his head spinning at each creaking branch. The other stood tall, spoke loudly, his arms wide and supplicatory, quite at home in this place.

And talked of Nory.

Dire's hands tightened into claws.

She knew. She suspected. No one leaves a babe on an altar, no matter how deformed his body may be.

This was Donam? The Baron's man? Lord High Sheriff of The Baron's surrounds? Acting on The Baron's orders? To kill his own son? No matter a bastard or how twisted its body be!

Who does that to a child?

Someone just as deformed and twisted. Someone preaching the Old Ways and not knowing what they preached.

Dire moved still closer, to the next opening in the archway.

The one with the crossbow glanced in her direction.

She ducked down and hid her candle.

Their voices turned away from her. She raised so her head peeked above the stonework, her ear up, and listened.

This was a place of sacrifice? Not since before her mother and grandmother's time.

They came here, Dire in her mother's arms, fleeing the Church, moving under moonless nights from town to town, seeking refuge.

They refused to teach Dire the Old Ways, the ways of field and forest, fearing she would be hunted in her own time.

But the memories. Her father and grandfather killed giving them time to flee.

She watched and learned at her mother's and grandmother's knee. She asked and asked and asked.

And finally they yielded.

She learned the Old Ways. Even as they moved, as they gathered their things before they could be found out.

Until they came here and remained. Their bodies buried somewhere deep inside, not even Dire remembered where anymore, a place so hidden they could finally rest.

And when they passed she traveled to learn more, to learn different, to learn enough to always be safe.

That's how she found Zevke and Saida, one day in her travels, beaten and left to die, their cart overturned, their belongings burned, a cross carved into their backs and their faces equally scarred, no doubt victims of the so-called "People's Crusade."

Dire brought them here and nursed them back to health, healed their wounds, used Old Way so no marks remained. Zevke and Saida were of another Old Religion, the one from which the New One sprang, but few of the New counted it as such.

Zevke remembered this place. She saw him here more than once and remained hidden, wanting to observe and allowing him to act as he would so long as no harm came to others.

But the Sheriff? The Baron's man? And what of this other, standing in fear of him, of this place?

The Sheriff and The Baron abandoned her beloved Nory. Did they also beat and torture poor Zevke and Saida?

Dire remembered the Old Ways. She had not practiced them to their fullness in years, but the knowledge remained.

The sheriff drew his sword.

Dire stood, made the Sign of The Old Ones, and focused her gaze on the sheriff. Her hands moved as if shaping a ball and tossed the emptiness in the sheriff's direction. "A pox. Take it."

A crossbow bolt pierced the Sheriff's hand, knocked his sword free. It clattered on the stones about the altar.

Dire opened her eyes wide. The Old Ways worked? This quickly?

She formed another ball, tossed it, and spoke again. "A pox. Take it."

Another bolt pierced the Sheriff's skull. He fell.

The other looked around. Where had the bolt come from?

Dire knew. She ducked and ran back into the tunnels, back to her cave.

She would work the Old Ways on The Baron and his kind.

CHAPTER 50

Queen Danika's attention stayed on her youngest daughter, Ouive's, hands. The child insisted on learning embroidery because her two older sisters, Solas and Marianne, were learning it and Ouive, who thought herself already a queen, would not hear "No" as an answer.

To anything.

Marianne, the eldest and already entertaining princes from the north and west, decided Ouive would be good training for when she, herself, sat on a throne and provided heirs to her sovereign.

Solas, the middle child, quiet and pensive, the deep thinker of the three, watched and wondered at both her sisters, always attentive to how Queen Danika behaved publicly and privately towards her children, and otherwise was silent except for the one, unoften spoken but never-the-less penetrating and exacting question.

She is the one who vexed her tutors the most. They would assign readings and she would read past them, turning her lessons into interrogations, seeking her tutors' weaknesses and ignorances. Not to threaten, merely to understand.

Danika knew Solas, of the three, would be the most formidable queen. She would find a strong future king for this daughter as no others would rule beside her, she would puppet them and rule in their stead.

A chamberlain cleared his throat at the entrance to the Queen's council room. She responded without looking up. "Yes, what is it?"

The chamberlain bowed. "A message from one of your heralds, Queen Danika."

Ouive dropped her embroidery and ran on short, pudgy legs to the chamberlain. "Let me see it. I can read now."

The chamberlain held the letter just high enough so Ouive couldn't reach it even when she jumped.

Marianne chided her youngest sister. "Queens never run."

Danika hid a smile. Just yesterday Marianne played hide-and-seek with Prince Reguld, laughing and panting as she stepped through his questing arms.

"Daughter, bring it to me. I will read it first, then, perhaps, you may read it."

The chamberlain looked at the Queen. She nodded. He lowered the letter to Ouive's clasping hands.

She walked back to her mother and turned the envelope over and over in her tiny hands. "I can't open it."

"Bring it here, child. It's not for you to open until you're a queen."

Solas smiled as Ouive immediately obeyed but only for the promise of reading the message later. She looked at Danika and the Queen winked conspiratorially to her.

Solas, like her mother a moment earlier, hid her smile.

Ouive held the message up and snatched it back when Queen Danika reached for it.

The Queen cocked her head, raised her eyebrows and glared at her youngest child.

"Remember you promised."

Queen Danika held her hand out and Ouive placed the letter in her palm. "Daughter, I did not promise. I said I would read it first and perhaps you could read it."

Ouive pouted. She crossed her arms over her chest. Her mouth worked back and forth but she said nothing.

Queen Danika lifted Ouive to her lap. Their dresses' fine needlework crinkled against each other. "You must learn to listen exactly if you wish to be queen, Daughter."

"Yes, Mother."

"Promise?"

Ouive buried her face in the Queen's bosom. The Queen eased her back and turned Ouive's face until they met. "Promise?"

Ouive nodded.

"Say it."

"Yes, Mother."

The Queen let her child nestle against her. "Good. And as a reward, you shall read it after I'm done. See what being an obedient and noble child gets you? Rewards you did not dream of."

The Queen reached into her knitting chest and removed a small knife. Ouive's eyes opened wide.

"To cut errant threads, child. And occasionally to open letters and reveal what's within. Never to be used on errant children."

Marianne and Ouive laughed. Solas smiled.

The Queen turned the envelope over to cut the seal.

A single letter in a dob of red wax: A.

She took a deep breath, cut the seal and read. Her hand quivered slightly.

Solas, glancing up from her embroidery, lowered it to her lap, her eyes now only seeing her mother's face, perfumed and rouged with the finest powders and oils, going white.

Queen Danika folded the envelope back up and slowly placed it on the table they all shared. Her eyes stayed locked on it during its entire motion.

Ouive's hands reached.

The Queen pulled her daughter tight against her.

"Chamberlain, tell the King I would see him."

Solas' hand hovered over the envelope. Queen Danika nodded and lowered Ouive off her lap. "Read it with your sister, child. She can help you if you don't know the words."

Solas opened it as Ouive danced beside her.

Solas frowned. Ouive clapped her hands. "I know all the words! I know all the words."

Solas looked at the Queen, her face a question mark.

Marianne, her fingers still busy with needle and thread, asked without looking up. "Well, what does it say, Sister? If you know all the words, tell us what it says."

Ouive tucked her tiny fists into her tiny hips and rocked her head as she spoke. "'They are found.' That's what it says. 'They are found.' See? I can read and I know all the words."

CHAPTER 51

Haasel's hands guided her clays into the shapes Galos specified. They were not easy shapes to make. Cylinders with walls so thin they'd break simply by falling to the ground? Yet able to withstand pressure applied along their length? Fitted with wax stoppers and bound with threads?

And all in ovens so hot she could barely put the cylinders in or take them out?

Madness.

Sheer madness.

The current cylinder cracked. Another test failed. Her nostrils flared and she snorted. "Oh, Brother Galos. If I knew the need I could fashion these faster." Several successful attempts hung out back, cooling. Still, she experimented. It gladdened her to make Master Charcoal Burner happy.

She pushed back from her table. The Red Fox had a standing order and she would be late filling it if she spent more time experimenting on Galos' behalf.

Enough.

She dabbed her hands in a water pail and dried them on her

apron. A moment later she stood outside in her garden, oblivious to the dark night. A vague orange scent came on the wind and she heard moths flutter. Reaching out, she felt the mock orange bush's blossoms expand to her touch. A moth landed on her hand and used it as a support to dine.

"Tell me, little moth, is the moon out? Does it shine bright?"

A rustle on the other side of her garden wall. Clothing brushed against grasses.

She sniffed gently. Neither animal nor human smell.

"Who goes there?"

More rustling.

She didn't have her staff handy.

She backed cautiously towards her door.

Something leapt over her wall, landed softly on booted feet, behind her. Strong arms came around her, pinned her arms to her sides. A slightly muffled voice. Male. Whispered. "Relax, Lady Potter."

She knew that voice. No, not that voice, a similar voice.

Whose voice?

Heavy feet came up the lane on the other side of her cottage. Long strides. Someone tall and powerful. Her front door banged open.

Why was there no scent to this stranger holding her? There was a scent, none matched to anyone she knew of. Juniper? Holly? Amongst other woodland smells?

She spun, grabbed. Long robes. Strong arms. Gloved hands. A sword on one side, a knife on the other. She reached for the face. A mask covered it, the mask held on by a finely made scarf. That and the robe. Excellent workmanship. Made to be both strong and soft, supple.

Who weaves a cloth like that?

Her blind eyes blinked in confusion.

The long-strided, tall and powerful one, now inside her house. A deep voice. From the circus?

"Potter! Come out come out wherever you are. My master has need of another virgin. And if you're not one, we'll make you one. Come, come now. Show yourself."

Pottery crashed. Her worktable upended. The door to her bedchamber crashed against a wall.

The muffled voice. "Up you go."

Her savior lifted her as if she were a feather, placed her on the wall, landed beside her.

A gloved hand tapped her thigh. "Swing your legs over the wall."

She did.

The well-made boots landed as quietly as they came. "Jump. I'll catch you."

She did.

"We must quickly away." Strong arms lifted her. "Allow me to carry you."

She tucked into the robe, her head underneath her savior's chin, and remembered her father lifting and carrying her as a child, taking her when he delivered his earthenware to customers.

"Who are you?" she whispered.

"Simon. A friend."

SECTION IX
THE JANNENITE

CHAPTER 52

Korol removed a thick leather glove. The red and black butterfly seemed hesitant to land on his glove-covered fingers. With the glove removed, the gentle creature lighted. It moved gracefully on the back of his hand, one little step followed by the next, its legs working in tandem pairs. More than once it shifted its wings slightly like a circus tightrope walker shifting her pole to maintain balance.

Korol whispered to it and the long antennae turned in the direction of his breath. Its whole body followed. Its wings opened and closed in rhythm to Korol's words and he wondered if it warmed itself against his breath. The day was young. It hinted of being another warm day but as yet the air still held a morning coolness, a dampness.

River waters, in the morning, tended to be slow and sluggish, not gaining strength and current until late in the day. Then the evening brought some relief and the waters and life in them slowed once again.

Sunlight came through the woods and lit leaves and petals.

Wrens and bluebirds sang. The air was heavy with the morning's musk of earth and suckle and vine.

The butterfly turned to face the sun, flexed its wings and fluttered off.

Korol waited until he was sure it would not return and pulled a clear, stoppered flask containing a whitish-gray powder from an inner pocket.

He wouldn't want the butterfly to suffer.

The flask had thirty marks on its side. Each mark represented a day. Each day Korol sprinkled enough of the white lead into the Vell to almost empty the flask to the next mark.

Each day he marked his spot with a dash of the deadly powder, the next day he walked ten paces further upstream, each day he dropped not quite a marksful into the swirling waters, grabbed a fallen branch still stocked with leaves, and stirred the waters until the powder dissolved and couldn't be seen.

Often he waited until he saw a frog or a fish stop moving, get carried by the current, so he'd know the poison had taken hold and would work its way downstream to Nant.

He worked in the mornings, in the quiet, when most simple farmers and herdsmen were busy with their crops and animals, wearing simple clothing so none would recognize him, neither his Jannenite robes nor his jester garb.

The former, too easy to be seen in the gloom of the woods, too bright when he came out to the river's banks, head-to-toe in white with red girdle, boots, and cap. The latter would associate him with the circus and trouble would ensue.

Instead he borrowed from actors' trunks, clothes and fragments gathered in their travels, sometimes with padding here or there, or powders and wigs from the women's stores. Today he wore colors of earth and forest, the gray of bark, the green of leaf, the brownish black of earth.

And still a knife, should he need it.

This chore, poisoning the Vell just north of Nant, given him by The Baron via Dobrogost. "Do it so no other towns are affected. Nant's lands are enough."

The white lead and other poisons his own making, as was the glove fashioned for Sullya so she could play witch, again at The Baron's command.

But these things he did so he could travel. The circus allowed him passage where a Jannenite could not go. Ibn Munkidh gave him a task: one had escaped. No one knew how. Even tortured unto death, the jail keeper proselytes claimed to know nothing of it.

"He will tell the world we exist, who we are. We will no longer work and worship in silence if others know."

Korol kept his head bowed, his eyes down, fearing to look into the Master's face. "Aye, my Lord."

"I commission you, Korol. Go find this one. Hunt him down. Kill him before he tells others of us."

"Aye, my Lord."

"And if you find him dead, kill all who know him at his moment of passing lest he share his knowledge before he gave up his ghost."

"Aye, my Lord."

The Master held out his left hand. The pigeon-blood ruby on white gold ring blazed on his finger in the tabernacle's thousand candlelights.

"Swear it."

Korol gently brought his lips to the fingers. He thought to caress the Master's hand, merely to hold it still and steady for his kiss.

But the Master's eunuch guards clasped the hilts of their Saracen blades even as he formed the thought.

He leaned forward to the point he felt off balance and kissed the Master's ring. "I so swear, my Lord and Master."

He drew back, head still bowed, eyes still down.

The guards' blades rested in their scabbards. The Master waved him go. The Master himself turned and exited the tabernacle's main hall.

After he'd left, after his guards had gone with him, Korol backed out to the main doors, head still bowed, eyes still down, and when the doors closed behind him, he turned to face the sun.

~

Taitano held his crossbow up, a second shaft held in his trigger hand, ready for loading once the first shaft flew, one for the black robed who jumped from The Cloisters' wall into the dense forest beyond, the other for the shadowed one who hurried through the archway into the ruin's dark interior. Taitano shifted his attention back and forth, his weight going from one foot to the other, his legs moving like a court dancer to keep him balanced when his target came into view and he loosed his bolt. "Show yourselves, damn you!"

No challenge came.

He felt the tension in his body, the sourness in his gut, and chided himself. "You were trained in the King's Guard, Taitano, and each year you softened saw you shuffled like an old dog, first to The Baron then to his Sheriff." He looked down at Donam's body and lowered his crossbow. "Shall I think of this as a step up in the world, my Lord Sheriff? Perhaps I'll be sheriff now?"

He sat on the steps in front of the altar. Donam lay in front of him, his blood puddling the front of the altar. Taitano smiled. "What an honor for you, Lord Sheriff. You are sacrificed to your Horned God. I hope both he and you are pleased."

Donam, his body crumpled back over his legs and his eyes looking up as if to see the shaft that did him in, said nothing.

"What, my Lord Sheriff? No comment? No witticism? No

tasteful word to add insult to my injury? I've never seen any marks of heraldry on your coat. You never served The King? Then how came you by your position in The Baron's holdings?"

He pulled the two bolts from Donam's body and held them close for inspection. "These are finely made but not by any fletchers or arrowsmiths I know. The King's Guard use no fletching such as these."

He held the bolts towards Donam. "See these markings? They indicate the bolt's manufacture. Good fletchers, those who know their trade and practice it well, sign their work in some way. These markings are unknown to me, but they bespeak someone proud of their work."

He tested the sharpness of the head against his thumb, then quickly pulled it away and nodded. "And these heads. They are designed to penetrate armor." He held the head up close to his eyes. "Forged. The arrowsmith's signature." He held the bolt towards Donam a second time and pointed to the head. "See? These were made by someone who supplies armies for a living, not by someone teaching their children how to hunt."

He looked at Donam's bloody wounds. "And used by someone who appreciates the level of workmanship necessary to prevail in warrior-craft."

He leaned over, cleaned the bolts on Donam's coat, then twirled one between his fingers to test the weight and smiled at its balance. "These are foreign made." He looked down at Donam's body. "But you'd know nothing about that, would you, Lord Sheriff?"

He placed the bolts in his own quiver and knelt beside Donam's body. "I am not a spiritual man, my Lord Sheriff. Raised in the church, but who isn't these days? What I mean is, your Horned God or Mother Church make little difference to me. Threatening the woman I love made all the difference to me. You asked if I knew why she came this way. I do, from her own lips: to find her parents, to know the people from which she came."

"And you took that away from her, not I." He removed his knife from his belt and slit the dead sheriff's neck. "Forgive me, my Lord Sheriff. Only to make sure we are done with you, to make sure you do not rise again." He wiped his blade on Donam's coat. "Now, if you'll excuse me, I'm off to find her family and let them know what became of their daughter, what you and your god planned for her. I hope, for you, that will be enough."

He stepped down from the altar and stopped. Cloven hoof-prints leading up and away. He knelt and examined them. "Your god's, Lord Sheriff?" He brushed away leaves and twigs and took a long look, then stood. "Only if your god is really a man. Only men leave prints heel first, and a heavy man to leave marks as deep as that. Let's see where they lead."

Korol returned to Nant's center and walked in back of the semicircle of circus wagons and stage at their center, glanced at his wagon, and stopped. The hair rose on his arms and the back of his neck. It pushed gently against the rough wool of his clothing and made him itch. His hand involuntarily went for the knife hidden in the folds of his clothing.

He breathed slowly and deeply, one of the exercises taught him in his order.

Calmed, he walked around the wagons to where Dobrogost completed setting up the stage. The giant looked up from his labors as Korol approached. "Where have you been so early in the day?"

"Praying."

Dobrogost grunted.

"Has anyone been behind the wagons?"

"Yes, I know. Bron is gone. I don't know where he is. Someone let him loose or took him as a pet. In any case, we'll have to rely on the pony alone." Dobrogost shook his head. "Poor thing. Slipped his leash but not his muzzle or fez. And blind. I've no idea how he'll eat. Probably find him starved somewhere deep in the woods." He stopped working, shook his head again, and shrugged. "Poor thing."

Korol's face tightened with each word Dobrogost spoke. "I don't care about your bear, Dobrogost. Answer me, has anyone been behind the wagons?"

Dobrogost stood at his full height, turned, and faced Korol. He sat on the front of the stage as if it were a chair, his feet still flat on the ground, and stared down at the jester.

Korol's hand rested over his knife.

Dobrogost continued staring. "You are brave for a clown. Or foolish. Which is it, do you think?"

Korol lowered his hand slowly and breathed deeply. "Sorry."

Dobrogost stood and continued his work. "A townsman. Galos. A charcoal burner, although by his look more forest mason than charcoal burner. His eyes are quick and there's a strength about him clothing doesn't hide. Why?" The giant laughed. "Did he steal something of yours?"

"Did he carry a knife?"

"Bron was missing when he came. He didn't free him."

Korol stroked his beard.

"See you're ready for our first performance. We should not keep the good people of Nant waiting."

Korol returned to his wagon.

On a back guard, clearly marked but not where most would look to see, a series of marks. He ran his hand over them to make sure they were intentional, not some accident while he was away.

The priest escaped his first attempt and now was gone.

Or he returned and no one knew of it.

CHAPTER 53

Tardiff nodded at Slewe as he entered the Red Fox. "Donam and his deputy haven't returned?"

Slewe shook his head, no, without looking up from mopping the floor. Tardiff thought the simple tool should receive compensation for the Innkeeper's rough handling.

Tardiff sat and placed a copper on the table. "A pint of ale, Slewe?" Paying customers always put Slewe in a good mood.

Slewe leaned his mop against a chair, poured a pint, and grabbed up the copper.

"Does something trouble you, Slewe?"

Slewe lifted his mop and renewed with calmer strokes. "The sheriff and his deputy. Bah! Their bill grows by the hour. I'll petition The Baron if I must. Or sell their goods, I will."

Tardiff sipped his ale. "May I see their rooms?"

"Will you pay their bill?"

Tardiff shook his head. "No, probably not. But I will swear before The Baron they cheated you."

Slewe evaluated Tardiff. He glanced at the Bellman's side and frowned. "You carry a sword today? What ails Nant that you carry a sword?"

"Just about the Lord Sheriff's business. Thought it would look more official if I carried a sword instead of a bell."

Slewe grunted and grabbed a ring of keys from behind the bar. "Done. Let's go."

"Do you have any other guests?"

Slewe stopped at the hallway's entrance. "No, why?"

"May I have the keys? This may take a while and I best work alone."

"If you find any coin, it goes in my pocket first."

"Agreed."

Slewe handed him the keys and went back to his mop. Tardiff finished his ale and entered the inn's hallway.

The deputy's room was sparse. Taitano seemed a military man so that didn't surprise him. Only the necessities for quick travel. A table holding a whetstone, half a loaf of bread, and an empty mug sat opposite the bed which had been slept on and not in.

Tardiff closed and locked the door.

Donam's room bore ornamentation but was disheveled. Not searched, simply not ordered, except for the table. Unlike his deputy, Donam's table sported no food, only a candle and an opened book, black covers with red binding. Tardiff had seen maybe two books in his life. This would be his third. He stood over it.

One page had words - he knew they were words even if he couldn't read them. The other page had a drawing. Tardiff studied it.

"The ruins south of Nant?"

The artist drew stars over the ruins.

"Stars but no moon. Tonight and the next three nights then?"

Tardiff carefully turned the page.

The artist drew disemboweled creatures: men, women, goats,

sheep, cattle. And children. There were different words next to each. The facing page showed some kind of stonework.

"An altar? Not one from Holy Mother Church, I'd swear."

Tardiff walked to the room's door and called down the hallway. "Slewe, can you read?"

E ric let Buco run free. Holding the big dog back was pointless. Buco only responded to Verduan and the point of Eric's taking Buco out was to let the dog find his father.

Buco kept on wanting to go south. Eric's father only traveled the road south out of Nant on market days, and then he'd load his wagon with fruit and vegetables, perhaps he'd tow a pig or two for slaughter, and then he'd have the draft pulling the wagon and Buco either beside him or trotting along beside the horse.

He told Eric Buco and the mare talked back and forth but he didn't know what they talked about.

Eric always laughed because Verduan whinnied like a horse and barked like a dog when he told Eric about his trip, Eric always safe with Idee and Byell.

And Julia. He grew up loving Julia. Loving her before he knew what love was. First as a brother, then as a friend, then as a husband-to-be. She always teased him, never saying yes and never saying no.

Now no one knew what had become of her. It mattered little about all the other troubles come to Nant, Julia's loss weakened him like strong drink in an old man.

And he may have caused it. He cut off the witch's hand. He caused her to curse them.

He lifted his axe from his belt and readied to hurl it into the wood, then shoved it back in his belt.

He had learned much from Father Verrett. Sullya the Witch

terrified him as a child, now as a man about to start his own family witches and magics didn't make sense.

He stopped walking and listened. He couldn't hear Buco. Unless the dog traveled far, Eric could always hear his bark, hear him trampling through the brush, hear him rousting ground-nesting birds.

Now nothing.

"Buco, come!"

Nothing.

"Buco! Come!"

Nothing.

Eric cupped his hands around his mouth and lifted his head so his voice would bounce off the dense foliage above, a trick his father taught him. "Buco! Come!"

Rustling. Routing. Charging.

Buco stuck his head into the road from a barrage of vines and berry bushes about a hundred paces ahead. He looked at Eric as if to say, "What?"

"Good dog. Come."

Eric couldn't see it but knew the big dog wagged its tail by the way its head moved back and forth.

But Buco didn't come. He barked.

Eric reached into his pocket and took out some dried beef. "Buco. Are you hungry?"

The dog whined, but instead of racing to the food it turned back into the brush. Eric heard it hurrying off.

"Buco! Come! Now!"

Eric ran to where Buco's head came into the road. The big dog left a clear trail into the wood. Eric followed. He heard the dog trotting on ahead. Twice he passed a spot Buco marked.

Then the forest cleared. Buco sat facing Eric's approach.

When Eric made his way through the trees, Buco stood up and

walked in a circle, stopping to stare at Eric as each circuit completed. Eric slowed. He knew this place. Every Nantian child knew this place. They were told stories about it, told never to go near it, told monsters lived here, told to stay away. Naughty children were threatened with being brought here and left to stay overnight.

Buco stopped circling and met Eric halfway. He nuzzled Eric's pocket and Eric absentmindedly gave him a whole stick of dried beef.

Buco turned and chewed as he walked through The Cloisters' main entrance to the courtyard, past the altar and into the archway, into the gloom.

Eric swallowed.

Buco thought Verduan was here?

What would Verduan be doing here?

Verduan told him never to come here, told him it was dangerous to be here.

Had the Tomekan brought his father here?

Didn't witches gather here?

Eric took a deep breath, shook off a chill, lifted his axe from his belt, and followed.

Z evke pulled the rope over the cap of their cart tight and muttered. "You've killed us, woman." He heard Saida enter their cottage. No doubt she'd have sold or given away all the bread in her basket. They had done so well here, had grown comfortable here.

Too comfortable?

He doubted it.

Since coming to Nant his eye invited him to wander only once, and he knew he couldn't go through with it, only wanted to prove to himself that he wasn't the man he used to be.

But Saida had taken that and all other options away with her foolishness.

Stupid woman.

She called to him from inside their home.

"Out here."

She came out without noticing his efforts to tighten the rope. "The ovens are cooling, husband, and we can bake another set before noon."

He grunted with the effort.

"What are you doing?"

He stopped tying down their belongings. His hands flattened against the blanket-covered mound on the cart as if pushing a rock uphill. "We are through here. Understand? A witch returned to Nant, no rain for at least a month, a dead woman found in the woods, Julia missing, water from the town's well that tastes like poison and kills all it touches? The sheriff and his deputy walking about, asking questions. Why do they come now to a village at the crossroads of nowhere? I thought us safe here. The priest ran out of town. Did I tell you that? I don't know where he went but we're soon to follow."

Saida pulled back and stood in the doorway. "The sheriff...perhaps the dead - "

"Bah! The dead you always have with you. What brings him to Nant now? We were safe. Unknown. Hidden. But the sheriff and deputy? You said so yourself. Don't think others are soon to follow? This is a start. This is always how it starts. A reason is found and then we are made to blame."

"The Tinker, he knew - "

"Knew? Knew, did he? I told you, something he picked up from some other tinker in his travels. He knew nothing. Besides, he's long gone, probably dead, as well, and his cart is behind Tardiff's jail."

Saida shook her head. "No, it's not. I just came from there. The Tinker's cart is gone."

"Perhaps Tardiff moved it."

"No, Tardiff didn't know. He was surprised it was gone. Besides, he has other things to concern him."

"The Tinker's cart is missing?"

"Yes. It was behind the jail for a number of days and now is gone."

"Add thievery to the list of new activities in Nant."

"The circus people, they may have stolen it to see if there's anything in it they can use. Their first performance is tonight."

"We won't be here to see it."

A voice pulled their attention to the other side of their cart. "Please don't go."

Saida stepped back into their home. Zevke raised on tiptoe to look over the cart. "Show yourself!"

A figure, head-to-toe in black with a flowing cape, a hood over their head and a mask covering their face, stepped around the cart, a beautiful, gleaming sword in its hand.

"Do you mean to kill us? Force us to stay?"

The stranger sheathed their sword. "Sorry, no. Merely to ask. I would prefer you to stay."

"Who are you?"

The figure hesitated. "A Galatian."

Zevke pulled back. "Impossible. They were lost to history years ago."

The mask nodded. "I hear a lot of that, and still I stand here asking you to remain in Nant."

"What is your name?"

Another hesitation. "Simon."

"Why should we stay?"

They heard a chuckle under the mask. "Because Nant needs a good baker? Because you're good people in fear and good people should never fear?" The Galatian sighed. "Because it's time for me to put my cowl away and hang up my sword? Because I like the smell and taste of melted butter on fresh, still warm bread and would learn from you, become your apprentice?" The Galatian shrugged. "So I could take care of Nory?"

Zevke stepped forward. "What have you done with Nory?"

The Galatian held his gloved hands up, palms out. "Nothing, I assure you. I'm not sure where he is, and I'm sure he's safe."

Saida came forward and stood behind and to the side of her husband, ready to jump behind him and back into their home should this stranger move too quickly. "Do you know what we are?"

"You are a baker and his wife. You provide one of the three things necessary for life; air, water, bread. Anything else is not my concern."

"But it would be the church's concern. Did the priest send you?"

"Baillot? He's not a priest."

Zevke glared. "What?"

"You wouldn't know. He does the services poorly nor does he know all the stations. His prayers are sometimes mumbled. I doubt he knows all the words."

"You've been in his church?"

"I've talked with him."

"He knows who you are?"

The Galatian laughed. "I hope not. If he did, he'd run from Nant as fast as he could."

Zevke's eyes narrowed. "He did run from Nant. I saw him. He took the south road as if Hell nibbled his backside."

The Galatian's gloved hand came up to his masked chin. "Really? When did this happen?"

"Just yesterday. There was much happening in town. Father...I mean, Baillot...running down the south road I don't know where, the circus people seemed to be caring for Thomas, Byell and Idee's son, I don't know why. The giant carried him somewhere."

"Which direction?"

Zevke pointed. "South also."

"Anything else?"

"Eric and his dog, Buco, hot on the trail of something. I hear his father, Verduan, and the Tomekan priest haven't been seen for a few days."

The Galatian looked down and put his fists on his hips. "And the circus plans its first performance either tonight or tomorrow night."

"What makes them wait so long? Surely there's slim tidings to be had in Nant with all that's happened. Wouldn't it be better if they moved on?"

"Not for the performance they've planned."

Saida stood beside her husband. "What will happen to us if we stay?"

"Stay and you will receive my thanks. Perhaps the thanks of others. And if the thanks of others, a promise never having to fear again. Is that enough?"

"Can you guarantee the last?"

The Galatian shook his head. "I'm sorry, Good Woman. There are few guarantees in life. What I offer is this: do what I ask and I will use all my power to make it happen."

Saida placed a hand on Zevke's arm. "Accept, husband."

Zevke turned to his wife. "Before you feared for our lives every moment of every day no matter how well we were received and now, on this stranger's word, you wish to stay?"

Her eyes stayed on the unflinching black mask, on the steadiness of the Galatian's voice and the ease of his movements, almost as if he danced rather than walked or ran. She looked up into Zevke's face and brushed flour from his beard with her hand. "Please, yes."

Zevke took her hand in his and looked into her eyes. He nodded, kissed her hand, and spoke as he turned to face the Galatian. "Very...where did he go?"

CHAPTER 54

Queen Danika gathered her daughters to her in her royal chamber. Ouive, as always, danced for attention. Marianne checked herself in her mother's great mirror. Only Solas sat quietly and watched her mother weave a tapestry of celestial colors from red, gold, and blue yarns died from sheep's wool. She could hear the sheep bleating if she listened carefully as she sat by the chamber's glass windows. The Queen's chamber had two glass windows, two of the few actual glass windows in the King's castle. She couldn't imagine their cost, especially as these windows could be opened or closed via supporting hinges and rods, something Father's artisans brought back from their time in different lands.

The Queen's fingers nimbly worked shuttle and yarns, her slippered feet moved pedals and shifted back and forth as if learning to dance on this great loom's feet.

The Queen caught Solas' eye and smiled. She continued weaving and didn't slow. "You wish to learn?"

Solas answered quietly, her voice almost blending with the steady *shoosh shoosh shoosh* of the machine. "Yes, Mother."

Ouive stopped dancing and stood beside her mother. "Me, too! I want to learn, too!"

"I will teach your sister first, for she is older. When she knows well enough, perhaps she will teach you."

Ouive stamped her foot and crossed her arms over her tiny chest. "I want to learn now."

Queen Danika, without stopping her weaving, turned only her head and looked down at the young child. She lowered her head such that her face, under her white makeup, red lips, rouged cheekbones, manicured eyebrows and thick curls, presented a flat, wide-eyed, flared-nostrilled goblin's countenance, and said nothing.

Ouive's arms fell down to her sides. She quickly bowed her head and whispered. "Sorry, Mother."

She spoke to all her daughters but her eyes fell on Solas, her middle child. "I have a task for all of you."

Each became attentive in their own way. Marianne stopped primping but kept looking at her reflection in the mirror. Ouive looked up at her mother with hopeful eyes. Solas raised her chin so her eyes fully met her mother's. She, of the three, answered. "Yes, mother?"

"I will be gone for a bit." She met Solas' full on gaze. "I want you to take care of your father for me. Men are such children and he, especially, will fret while I'm gone. Make sure he smiles every day. Play games with him." Her eyes remained on Solas but she addressed her youngest child. "You, Ouive, you should dance for him at least once a day."

Ouive curtsied. "Yes, mother."

"Guide him in the kingdom's affairs. Give him counsel even when he doesn't ask for it, because he rarely will and needs it most often when he doesn't ask."

Solas nodded.

A steward knocked on her door.

"Enter."

"The King would see you, my Queen."

Queen Danika stopped weaving and rose. "Tell him I - "

King Gaumand came into her chamber. Cries of "Father" broke out from his daughters. "Aren't I pretty, Father?" "Watch me dance, Father!" "How may I serve you, Father?"

The King kissed his daughters on their heads before embracing his wife, Queen Danika. He held her close and she reveled in his encircling arms. She whispered into his ear. "How may I serve you, My King?"

He kissed her and winked. "I will honor your request on one condition."

She cocked her head slightly.

"A hundred of my Guard must accompany you. Fifty of them will be archers, the rest lancers and swordsmen."

"My King worries so for my safety?"

"Your Lord the King loves his Queen and wishes her safe return."

Ouive weaseled her way between the two of them. "Where's mother going, Father? She'll come home safe, won't she?"

Gaumand lifted his youngest daughter. She sat in his arms but his eyes remained on Danika. "Your Lady the Queen won't tell me where she travels, only that she must."

"Where are you going, Mother?"

"Not far. Not outside the Kingdom." She noticed a Commander of the Lancers standing in the hallway outside the door and nodded towards him. "Who is that fine fellow, Husband?"

"Adi, come."

Adi clicked his heels and entered. He clicked his heels again when he stopped in front of the King then turned and bowed to the Queen. "This is Adi."

The Queen offered her hand.

The Lancer Commander kissed it. "My Queen."

"Commander Adi is the first of my lancers and perhaps the finest soldier in my service. I've placed him in charge of your journey and is the guarantor of your safe return."

The Queen nodded. "Will your troops be ready at morning light?"

"If that is your wish."

"It is, if the King agrees."

The King nodded.

Adi saluted. "It shall be so."

The King kissed Ouive and let her slide to the floor, kissed Danika, and went to the door. He motioned for Adi to follow.

Outside, beyond the Queen's hearing, he leaned into the Royal Lancer and whispered. "See My Queen returns safely to me and you will receive your own title and lands."

"Yes, My Lord."

"If, on the other hand, she doesn't return to me, neither should you."

"Yes, My Lord."

Haasel sat on a stool, her elbows resting on a workbench, her chin cupped in one hand and the other feeling along the workbench's surface hoping to discern where she was. Simon allowed her to walk only the last twenty or so paces and then guided her hands to feel the bramble-covered entrance and this stool. She knew they were inside something because the echoes of their footfalls were plain, as was the slight change in his voice. This place was special, almost holy, because he spoke quietly, reverently, when they entered.

She knew he stood beside her for a moment and shuffled something on the workbench her hand now felt along. He stepped away and came back with something flapping hollowly, empty skins perhaps? He lifted what sounded like two mortars and she heard soft grains, sand-like, sifting out and into the possible skins. She heard him pull cords tight and assumed he tied them.

Then he said, "If I come looking for these, tell me I already have them."

She wasn't sure she heard him correctly but he moved through the bramble-covered opening before she could ask for an explanation.

The place smelled of medicants and electuaries. She felt for sources of heat - lamps, fires, a stove, a hearth - and found none. At one point she got up and stepped in small arcs, her feet tracing half-moons as she walked. The dirt under her boots skittered and she knew she walked on hard earth, earth stepped on several times over a long period. The half-moon walk was a trick of the blind who lost their cane: move the feet in small arcs, one in front of the other, with some part of the foot always touching the ground, and more weight on the rear foot than on the front. Move the feet slowly. Your feet will tell you where you should and shouldn't walk.

Wherever she was, it was moderately large. She walked its width - she assumed it was its width - in thirty steps. In thirty steps, her hands in front and waving like tree limbs in a light breeze, she felt other stools, a pallet on the floor with blankets, two water cans, jars of oil, jars of herbs, jars of balms. Her hands found the far wall and there she felt leathery things, some with stiff rods in them. Animal parts, dried and with the bones intact.

Finding one wall, she kept the fingers of one hand lightly touching it and followed it around. At all times she felt dried, hard packed earth.

She came to what amounted to a door - brush and reeds, vines and bramble - blocking a hole. Cool air came through them and she heard owls answered by wolves, feral cats fighting, and the scurrying feet of smaller forest denizens. Her hand made it across the doorway and started a rod swinging on a hook. She lifted it. Just the right height for someone slightly smaller than her to use for walking. But the grip wasn't one used by the blind to find their way, so an older person used this. Its length was smooth so its use had been long.

She used the cane and kept her steps to small half-moons, just in case, until her feet touched other pails, empty. Wooden shelves were built into the dirt walls.

Simon carried her here. He moved well and swiftly and did not seem troubled by her weight. He either moved the brambles aside or brought her in another way, but which other way she didn't know.

He said, "I must leave you for a while, Lady Potter. I thought someone would be here to care for you but they are away."

"Who would you have left me with?"

"A friend."

"I suddenly have many friends."

"More than you know."

She reached out to him and felt again the functional, well made clothing. "I am afraid."

"You are safe here."

"My pots? My works? My kilns?"

"Are also safe. What may be destroyed or taken will be returned, repaired, or otherwise made new."

"How can I trust you?"

Her savior gently lifted her hand from his cloak. "Because I, too, am a friend."

The brambles rustled when he left so she knew he didn't fear being seen or heard when he did so.

Haasel's head turned, her ears seeing in the dark for her. "Whimpering? Someone hurt?"

She waited until she could be sure. She stood and took the

cane in her hand. "I know how wide you are, friend Cave, but not how deep. Let us find out."

She swung the cane in front of her as if it were her staff. Her feet half-mooned. Her free hand found the dirt wall and she kept her fingers lightly upon it as she walked into its echoing night.

~

Baillot helped Verduan to his feet. "Yes, Baillot. No, not a priest." He stepped into the hall and walked back the way he came. "Come. There's not much time."

Verduan massaged the back of his head and held his torch high, the better to see. "I'm too old for this."

"I apologize. It was my head or yours. How would you choose?"

Patreo kept pace with Baillot's hurried steps. Verduan stayed close behind. "When you asked me about my training and background, you weren't asking as a priest?"

"I believe I knew your uncle. Perhaps your father, although briefly."

"You are young to have served in the Crusades."

Baillot spoke without stopping, sure of his direction. "Older than you, younger than them."

"You were a knight?"

"First an attendant, then a soldier under your uncle's tutelage."

"What became of them? I don't know their history beyond what my mother told me."

"Beyond the last battle of Jerusalem, neither do I. Aldous, your uncle, woke me in the middle of the night and had me mount his charger. I was barely awake when he handed me a message. I heard batterings on the city gates and moved to dismount. He threw me back in the saddle. 'Ride, you fool. Deliver that message to our people in the north. There is a new enemy in our midst.' He slapped the charger's rump with the flat of his sword and I barely held on trusting the horse to know where to go."

"You don't know what became of them?"

"Captured by the Mehtars, I believe."

"So they are dead?"

Baillot shook his head. "I doubt such. The Mehtars were far more civilized than our own. An enemy who lowered his sword was made a prisoner but barely so. More often they were given succor and asked to promise no more violence. If they did, they were allowed to become citizens or go on their way. If they did not agree..."

"So my uncle and father are traitors if they still live?"

"No, they are wise beyond their peers. Your father and uncle were Galatians, Knights of the Old Order. They were trained in head and heart as well as sword and staff. They would lower their arms to understand and parley. If they didn't like what they heard, they would give warning and raise their arms again." Baillot stopped and turned to face Patreo. "But I doubt such happened. The Galatians were wise beyond counsel, Warrior-Priests. Few could match them in battle of mind or body."

"Then why didn't you stay?"

"Because of the new enemy in our midst: white robed, red hooded devils, the Jannenites, the greatest *Furūsiyya* - Knights - of the Arab empires. The Galatian opposite and, I fear, a Galatian's equal."

"You were a Galatian, then?"

Baillot began moving again. "Not yet, only training to be one. Now I fear the order is gone."

"Then why your subterfuge?"

"Fleeing with my lord's message, another horseman pursued me, a Jannenite. My mount was the faster, but as I lost him he screamed an oath to hunt me down and fulfill his vow to end our order once and for all."

"Surely that was years ago."

"It would not be to a Galatian, nor to a Jannenite. To them it was yesterday."

"Is that who attacked you in Nant?"

"I don't know."

Baillot stopped, fell silent, and frowned.

A faint light appeared ahead of them in the tunnel. Verduan pushed past them. "You two continue your conversation. I see daylight and wish to embrace it. I miss it dearly."

Baillot grabbed his shoulder, held him back, and motioned the two of them to silence. "Cover the torch."

Several voices but none distinct, no words clear. Some laughter. Young voices. Children? Crying?

The three leaned towards the sounds as if the slight motion would reveal all.

The voices moved away and the light faded.

Baillot whispered, "I appreciate your need, Verduan, but that light may not be what you think, and if it is what I think, it's best we approach cautiously."

CHAPTER 55

Baron Bassys sat on his throne and listened to the soft cooing of pigeons in a cage on a golden legged table beside him. The tabletop was a mirror and the pigeons took a disliking to their reflections. The Baron sometimes answered their coos with coos of his own, dropped crumbs into their cage, and smiled when they pecked each other over his offerings.

His steward came in. Before he could announce the visitor, The Baron said, "Soka?"

A man in the browns and grays of freeman's garb came in past the steward who bowed, closed the doors and waited outside to be summoned.

Soka kneeled before the throne.

"What does my spy have to tell me?"

Bassys listened to his spy's report. He slid an arbalest bolt top to bottom through his fingers as the spy talked. When Bassys' fingers reached the feathered bottom, he lifted his hand and let the bolt swing until the head pointed down, secured it against the armrest of his throne, and repeated the maneuver.

The pigeons continued their cooing as if they alone were in The Baron's receiving chamber.

"I pay you how much to inform me of the royal court and all you can tell me is the Queen is off and away under heavy guard?"

"My apologies, my - "

Bassys stopped the arbalest bolt in mid swing and pointed the head at the spy. "I don't want your apologies, I want information. Where was she headed? Was she leaving the Royal Court because the King had no more use for her? Not bloody likely as she counsels the King better than all his lords together. Her children stayed with the King?"

"Aye, my Lord."

"But she took no carriage? She rode out with lancers and bowmen?"

"A full contingent of the Guard."

"Which direction?"

"The road north out of the capital."

"Bah. That road crosses too many others. She could be going to any of a dozen places. This isn't some royal expedition? Hunting party? She's not going to see the Sisters who raised her?"

"I do not know, my Lord."

Bassys rose from his throne. He threw the bolt with enough force it stuck into the wall. "What do you know, imbecile?"

"I know the King is also ignorant of her mission."

Bassys slowly sat back down and gawked. "Gaumand doesn't know where she travels?"

"No, my Lord. That much is open knowledge among those who serve him personally. He often mutters his displeasure in our presence."

"But he alone has the power to send that size a force. And not know it's purpose? Which Guards did he send? Who commands?"

"Adi, Commander of the King's First Lancers."

Bassys' eyes opened wide as he sat back on his throne. "King

Gaumand sends the Commander of His First Lancers to baby-sit his wife?" He shook his head. "This baffles belief."

"With a promise of title and lands if she returns safely."

"But the King doesn't know where the Queen goes?"

"Aye, my Lord."

The Baron tapped the pigeons' cage. They gathered as if crumbs would soon be offered.

"This may be an opportunity for me."

"My Lord?"

"Should the Queen return - moderately unharmed but returned none-the-less - and not in Adi's company, the King would be most displeased with the Commander of His First Lancers."

The spy nodded.

"But he would certainly reward whomever returns His Queen."

The spy nodded a second time.

"And with at least as much as he originally offered Adi."

Soka said nothing.

The Baron reached for a quill beside the pigeons' cage and a long but exceedingly narrow piece of parchment. He wrote a note on it and rolled it into a tight cylinder. He cooed and opened the pigeons' cage, took one out and held it upside down in his lap.

Using a small red thread, he attached the parchment to one of the pigeon's legs.

"Open that window for me."

Soka obeyed.

The Baron released the pigeon into the afternoon sky. "Go, bring my request to your master and return to me with his answer." He watched the pigeon wing away. "Hurry and there'll be good crumbs for you."

He pulled the window shut and turned back to his throne.

Soka stood to one side.

"Still here? Go back to the Royal court. Learn more. Bring me news I can work with. Go!"

~

Korol hurried through the town center and climbed into the back of the rearmost wagon. A scraping sound stopped him. Coming in from bright, midday sun, the tarp-covered interior seemed dark and his eyes didn't have time to adjust.

A deep voice chuckled. A scraping sound and a slurping sound followed the chuckle.

Korol blinked and saw the outline of the giant, Dobrogost, in the lessening darkness.

"Where is the tinker's cart?"

Dobrogost sat cross-legged on the wagon's floor; his left hand held a pail of thick red porridge in his lap. His right held a half-devoured loaf of rough grained bread. The bread reminded Korol of a breadstick, something he'd seen in his travels, in the giant's hand. Dobrogost dipped the bread into the pail and held it out, dripping, towards the jester.

Korol slapped it away. "I said, where is the tinker's cart?"

The giant's hand barely moved under the impact. He stared at Korol silently for a moment. "What do I know of tinkers carts?"

"It was behind the Bellman's office. Now it's gone. No one saw it being moved?"

Dobrogost looked back into his pail, dipped his bread, and shook his head slowly. "You travel with us because it is convenient to both of us you do so. We pay each other for that courtesy by helping each other achieve our different goals." He raised his head and offered Korol another taste. "But should our goals differ too greatly, will the courtesy remain?"

Korol stared the giant in the eye and was the first to glance away. He took the dripping bread, sniffed it, and handed it back. "What is it? It smells of ginger, cardamon, and garlic."

Dobrogost chuckled again. "Something for the townsfolk who attend our opening tonight. I will mix it with peppermint to sweeten the taste, yohimbe to increase its potency, and Devil's Breath so they might enjoy the ride."

"You sample it?"

The giant laughed. "I like the taste."

Korol pulled off his jester's hat and scratched his head. "Where is the boy?"

"At the ruins, in a cell in the tunnel under the altar. Until we need him."

"With the old witch and The Baron's sacrifice?"

"You should come with me next time if you're curious."

Korol shook his head.

"What has become of your brothers? I've not seen them since I directed them south. Perhaps they took the tinker's cart?"

"They've set up camp until they are called."

"I offered them the ruins for hermitage and not seen them there. They would not enjoy our hospitality?" He held up the bread again.

"Your ways are not our ways."

"Yes, but for now our ways travel together so we tolerate each other's excesses. Let's leave it so and when it comes time for our ways to part, we will part as friends."

A dark-haired woman, curls of thick hair covering breasts barely withheld in her blouse, poked her head in the wagon and inhaled deeply. She took the bread from Dobrogost's hand.

The giant smiled. "Are you ready for this evening, Circe?"

"I'm preparing the perfumes now. They'll be ready when the show begins." She looked up at Korol. "Will you be joining us tonight, Jester?"

Korol shook his head. "As clown on the stage, yes. For what you have planned afterward? No."

Dobrogost laughed. "We are of the same blood, you and I, Korol, yet you do not burn on occasion? Has your belief severed your manhood? Perhaps Circe or Diana could..."

The dark-haired, dark-skinned Circe ran a finger up Korol's blouse from belly to chest.

Dobrogost crouched over double, moved past Korol to the end of the wagon and stepped down. "Pity."

Korol jumped down and Dobrogost's huge hand gently patted his shoulder. "What troubled you about the tinker's cart?"

"The marks on the side."

"Notches where the metalsmith tested his work?"

Korol put his jester's hat back on. "I must prepare for our first performance."

"You will be our first offering while Diana offers them free wine. Then I will have the pony do some tricks while you play the drum." He paused and gazed down on Korol. "You do remember the rhythms of the drum, yes? Not the first you learned, but the second. You'll start with the first then, as our performance slows, you'll go into the second, yes?"

"I remember."

The giant patted the jester's shoulders a second time. "Good, good. Then Circe and Diana will work them into a froth and I will appear again." He laughed. "To lead fair Nant to the ruins, the Cloisters the ancients prepared for us, and to Nant's doom."

Korol shrugged off the giant's hand and went to his wagon while the giant's deep bellows echoed around him.

Nory fed the bear all the food he stored in the tunnels. Much of it was rotted but the bear didn't seem to mind. The bear kept pawing Nory's hands, not with his claws although the pads of his feet were quite rough enough. Each time the bear pawed Nory's hands, Nory chuckled and gave the bear more to eat. The bear grunted each time and Nory knew the bear meant "Thank you."

It was good to have a friend.

Now the bear slept. Nory hurried back and got a bucket of water from Dire's cellar.

Someone had been there.

Someone had taken Dire's walking stick.

Dire would not be happy.

Nory would make sure Dire knew he didn't take it.

The bucket sloshed as Nory walked. It took two hands to carry, and Nory waddled the entire time.

The bear heard Nory return and growled. Nory laughed and the growls turned to grunts. Nory took the bear's paw and put it in the water. The bear leaned over to it and drank deeply.

A moment later it slept again, which was good because Nory had no more food to give it.

Nory would let his friend sleep and go and get food.

There was no food in Dire's cellar. Nory had already been there.

Berries? Bears like Berries. Grandmother Dire told him so.

Honey! Bears like Honey. She told him that, too.

Nory would need help finding these...

Simon! Nory's friend Simon! Simon was very good and he already helped Nory once.

Simon would help Nory again.

Nory hurried towards Nant when he saw the bright, shiny thing on the path in the woods.

Nory picked it up. It was sharp and pointy just like a sword.

Nory didn't have his hammer but now he had a sword.

Nory played being a knight. Slash slash. Thrust thrust.

Bonk Bonk on the head?

No. Swords don't go *Bonk Bonk* on the head.

Nory knew that.

He wished he had his hammer, too. Perhaps he would get it later. He would ask the bear to help him get it because the bear was Nory's friend and the bear was big and strong, much stronger than Nory, and could lift the hammer easily.

Slash slash. Thrust thrust. Cut cut.

Nory tucked the bright shiny pointy swordy thing into the rope he used for a belt.

He would show it to Simon and Simon would help Nory be a knight!

CHAPTER 56

Thomas woke shivering in a slime of his own sweat. What happened to him? Where was he? He'd never seen a place so dark nor reeking so richly of deep earth.

Something scuttled across his chest on many legs. He snapped up into a sitting position, swiped the many-legged thing from his chest, and pushed himself back and away from it until he banged into a wall.

He whispered, "Hello?" and his throat cracked as if he'd swallowed sand. His tongue swelled and filled his mouth.

Water.

He desperately needed water.

He turned to raise himself on hands and knees and the movement forced him to stretch his hands out wide lest he fall flat on his face. Lying flat on his stomach, arms outstretched, he still felt himself moving, pitching, rolling, in all directions at once.

He closed his eyes against the dark and breathed slowly. It seemed his stomach wanted to escape his throat. Gurge prepared and he forced it down.

Again, what happened to him?

Someone dealt him a staggering blow. Eric took him home. He slept. There were women. One who danced before him and made his blood rush.

Had he?

No.

His mind cleared. Something he drank.

At the Red Fox?

No, in the wagon behind the circus.

His mind cleared. He rolled over and sat up. Where was he now, then? Prison? Tardiff's jail was never this dark.

He looked around and blinked. Over there, was that a slight release from the darkness?

He stood slowly and waited for another wave of nausea to sweep over him.

No, he was good. Weak, but good.

One step. Another. His footfalls grew more confident as he walked towards the increasing brightness. He stretched out his right hand. Nothing. His left. Something. A stone surface? A wall.

He slid his left hand along the wall towards his right. A doorway. He tested. Wide enough for someone twice his size to walk through.

He stepped through, one hand always on a wall for support.

More light. Coming through a grating in the ceiling and down a ways.

Panting behind him, towards the dark.

He turned.

Two eyes, animal eyes the height of his hips off the ground, glowed in the dark perhaps twenty steps away.

Behind them, he didn't know how far but definitely around a bend or curve in this hellish labyrinth, another light bobbed and grew.

He heard footsteps in the silence. Footsteps, the beast's pantings, and his own heartbeats, the latter pounding in his head.

He still held the wall, could find the doorway. Had there been a door? Could he hide himself inside whatever room he'd been in?

The eyes stepped closer.

The footsteps grew louder.

The light continued its bobbing approach.

He reached for his knife. Not there.

He patted himself. Did he carry anything he could use as a weapon?

Sweat burst out on him again. He reached into his pocket. Something. Anything.

The eyes rushed up to him.

Hot breath fell on his wrist.

Something nuzzled his hand in his pocket.

What?

The footsteps neared the bend in the tunnels. The light showed a stone and earthworks hallway.

"Buco? Where are you, damn dog."

Thomas belched a nervous laugh and collapsed to the ground, sitting and shaking as his nerves worked their last anxious moment through him. "Eric?"

Buco knocked Thomas down flat, nuzzled his pockets and licked his face.

Eric made the curve and stopped. "Thomas?" He held his torch well over his head and shaded his eyes to see better. "My god, man. What happened to you?"

Buco raised his head and growled low.

Eric and Thomas looked up simultaneously.

Thomas whispered, "Voices?"

Eric came up, grabbed the big dog's ruffled fur, doused his torch and whispered. "Quiet, Buco." He leaned into Thomas. "Shh."

Circe and Diana strolled the South Road out of Nant. Diana stretched her arms out to her sides and spun when the sunlight came through the trees. She took off a ruby colored scarf and let her thick, black hair fall. It curled down her back, over her shoulders, and down her chest and stopped just above her navel. When she spun, she turned as a dancer, her head pointing in the direction of travel, and her thick curls lifted and flew with her, barely stopping when she snapped her head around to return to point. Every quarter turn she stopped and partially lifted her hip scarf so her shapely and strong upper thighs showed as she rang the zills on her fingers. Circe chanted rhythmically to drive Diana's dance. She clapped in time to Diana's snapping hips. Diana's palms rested on her hips, her spinning slowed into a stirring gyration, her upper body unmoving but from her waist down a mocking invitation.

Circe's clapping increased and finally Diana's arms fell to her sides, her lower body rigid with knees bent, her upper body shaking and her breasts pulsing from side to side. She ran forward the length of the stage and groaned, deep and from her chest, when she stopped.

She turned, hands on hips, head cocked, and watched Circe walk up to her. "Well?"

Circe applauded. "Do that tonight and the fools won't wait to be led to the ruins."

Diana clapped her hands and laughed. "I had a good teacher."

Circe bowed.

"How old were you when you birthed me, mother?"

"Why ask me that now? You've known for years you're my child, neither orphan nor stray come into our Troupe."

"Because tonight is to be my night, my first, and I wish to be paid well for it."

"Dobrogost promises The Baron will pay you well. You did a

wonderful job tormenting that farm boy before Dobrogost carried him away."

"But I did not take him."

Circe shook her head. "Not then. Tonight, though. The first of many. To give them a little pleasure before they're sacrificed."

"Oh?"

"If done properly, strangled in the act. Or beheaded. Either way, a man's dying thrusts will drive you to ecstasy."

"Is that what you did? Is that how you had your first?"

Circe caught up to her daughter, who turned and continued south. They walked arm in arm. "No. I could not offer my first as you can. I was already taken when I joined the Troupe years ago. That's when I studied under Sullya. She taught me how to make people believe transformations had taken place."

"How old were you when you had me, when she taught you?"

"Younger than you are now answers the first, about your age answers the second."

"And you kept me. Why?"

Circe shrugged. "You are the last, best memory I have of your father."

"I have no memory of him. Do you remember him?"

"He came into my village wounded and seeking food and water. He had some silver and my mother, your grandmother, cared for him. They actually grew to love one another."

Diana shook her head, confused. "But I am your daughter?"

Circe snorted. "He grew feverish one night, the last onslaught of his wounds unwilling to heal. Mother went out for a physician. I had seen them together, seen the pleasure he gave her, and wondered. Before mother left she told me he had to sweat to break his fever if he was to live. I thought what better way to sweat than through a little thrusting."

Diana turned and looked at her mother.

"I did it to heal him."

"Of course."

"I thought the fever would make him weak, but it didn't. It made him strong. He entered me like a bull."

"He pleasured you?"

Circe laughed. "He entered me like a bull and lasted about as long. He didn't know what he was doing, even though he had me three times before mother returned. She saw him shivering with fever and dripping with sweat and might have thought it only his fever climaxing to its end, but the scent of sex was heavy and hung like a fog in our rooms. She turned to me and looked me up and down. 'Raise your skirt,' she said, and I hesitated. She reached out and tore it from me. I knew so little back then. Part of him flowed down my thighs to my knees and she knew. She kept him and cast me out."

"I didn't know. I'm so sorry, mother."

Circe shrugged. "A young girl willing to know men and learn from them? A young woman who learned skill with a knife in case some men wanted too much? A woman in full flower who didn't mind what a man did so long as he paid well for me to moan as if suffering from his thrusts? Don't be sorry, Diana. Be glad I am here to teach you."

"You never saw my father again?"

Circe laughed. "No. Not many days later he left. I heard it due to his shame at what he'd done. Little did he know how well he prepared me for life."

"Mother?" Diana hesitated. "Did my father have a name?"

"All we knew him by was Simon. A knight of some noble house, I think. Head to toe in black, his weapons strapped to his back and hidden by a cape. Only his white steel sword showed him a warrior. Everything else was hid."

Diana nodded.

Circe wrapped her arm through her daughter's. "Come. We have to prepare the altar for tonight's performance."

Galos pulled his cart along the path winding through the woods around his cottage. Oak, yew, pine and other branches and twigs - anything dried enough to be kindling - bounced topmost. Next came seasoned wood cut in various lengths for either burning or to form the cones of his heaps - oak, birch, maple and such - from stores he kept in the lands around his cottage, all within an easy walk from his pyres.

He caught himself.

Not pyres. Not anymore. Not now.

Long ago perhaps.

When the Mehtar released him to offer burial to his brothers of the Cross and he instead built a pyre to send their ashes up to heaven.

Many days that had been.

Many days.

And when he'd completed his service to his brothers, they let him go with food, water, a horse, and his weapons.

A great concession that: his weapons.

A sign of honor, or respect, of recognition.

At first he demurred. "I will not need them, ever again."

Akheb, who became his friend and one of his many tutors in more sciences and arts than Galos could count, shook his head and held them out to him. "It is true, my friend. You may never need them, but in case you do."

Galos remembered nodding, smiling, and taking them. "Because you are my friend."

"Because you are my friend."

But not pyres. Not anymore. Simple fires of a forest mason, a charcoal burner, making good of the horrors he learned and performed in the name of the church.

Hidden under the kindling and cut wood were aromatic herbs

- parsley, mints, basil, and oregano - and forest resins - pine, birch, maple - to make mixtures he learned before, during, and after his time in the Holy Land.

He came out to an open space, the easier to pull his cart.

Nory paced back and forth in front of his cottage. He moved like a pendulum caught in a whirlwind, a lot one way, a little another, changing direction, going in, coming out, stopping at a heap, moving over to another.

What's wrong with the lad? Did he sit on a nestful of hornets?

Galos quietly backed his cart into the tree line and lowered the handles.

Nory, coming towards Galos but not seeing him, abruptly stopped, turned, and waited.

Around the corner of Galos' cottage came a figure head-to-toe in black flowing robes. The figure carried a white steel sword. Even at this distance Galos recognized it for what it was: Damascus steel.

Galos' eyes went wide.

A Galatian Warrior-Priest and at his cottage?

Nory ran towards the Galatian then skidded to a stop. He looked right and left and shook his head, no, as he backed away from the Warrior-Priest.

The Galatian stopped his approach, knelt, and bowed.

To Nory?

He drew his sword and offered it hilt first to the boy.

Nory stopped his retreat.

The Galatian didn't move, remained on one knee, head bowed, sword offered in service.

Nory drew something from under his coat and held it out.

A Galatian pikehead?

Where did Nory get a Galatian pikehead?

The Warrior-Priest bowed and flipped his sword and caught it by the hilt.

Galos' heart sank. He reached into his cart for a formidable branch. No weapon against a Galatian sword but it might give Nory time.

Except the Galatian stood in mock battle and laughed a wholesome laugh. He waved his sword and Nory met it with the pike.

No, the Galatian made sure Nory could meet it with his pike.

The sword fell from the Galatian's hand. He bowed now as a defeated foe.

Nory couldn't lift the sword but dragged it to the Galatian, who took it, then embraced him.

What is going on in Nant?

The Galatian faced Galos and Galos heard him speak. A familiar voice.

But from where?

From when?

"Hello, Nory. I showed you there was food in the tinker's cart, remember?"

Nory raised a hand to his mouth, back and forth, as if shoving food in.

"That's right. Thank you for sparing my life just now."

Nory danced around The Galatian and swung his pike as if defending the Warrior-Knight from foes. He stopped, his eyes went wide, and he turned to face The Galatian.

"What is it, Nory?"

Nory glanced from side to side and waved his hands. Galos recognized the silent language Nory used with Grandmother Dire.

Someone was hurt? In trouble? Dire? Is that why Nory behaved so?

The Galatian watched Nory's hands dart about and shook his head.

Nory kept making eating motions.

"Are you hungry, lad?"

Nory shook his head, looked over his shoulder, past where Galos hid, to the south. He waved in that direction.

"You know someone is hungry? You want food for someone? For a friend?"

Nory nodded, took a step away, beckoned the Galatian to follow.

A lone pigeon flew overhead. Nory chased after the bird, his arms outstretched.

The Galatian reached behind him into his cape, withdrew an arbalest with a fitted bolt, aimed, fired.

The pigeon fell.

Nory raced and picked it up. He came back to the Galatian, kissed his hands, and ran towards the south.

"Nory, wait." The Galatian caught him in a few strides and held him back. "May I see the bird? Only for a moment, then it's yours to do with as you wish."

Nory handed the dead pigeon to him. The Galatian removed his bolt and left it on the ground beside him. Turning the bird over, he nodded. "Yes."

A red thread bound a tiny scroll to the pigeon's leg.

The Galatian took the thread and scroll, handed the bird back to Nory, lifted and cleaned his bolt.

Nory paid no attention at first. He faced northeast, his eyes closed, and shivered slightly.

The Galatian tapped his shoulder lightly. "Nory?"

Nory turned south again and grabbed The Galatian's sleeve.

"Want me to follow you, Nory? Want me to come with you?"

Nory nodded and attempted to drag The Galatian with him.

"I'll be right behind you, Nory. Go ahead. I'll follow."

Nory ran as if shot from an arbalest. The Galatian followed.

Galos came out of hiding. "Wait! Who are you?"

SECTION X
THE COUNCIL OF URS

CHAPTER 57

Her candle long gone out, Dire's fingers read the knots where two separate threads joined, her secret guides laid down long ago when she first explored.

The type of knot, its thickness, its distance from other knots, all part of a code she developed, told her which paths went where, where she was, how to get from here to there and back again. She smiled a secret smile and chuckled quietly to herself. She didn't need a torch to see where she was or where she went, she only needed to pick up the piece of thread where floor met walls on either side, impossible to see unless you knew where to look and indeed, that it was there. Nory might remember each passage - and glad she was he did. She told no one of them, not even beloved Nory - but she relied on her secret aids to find her way about, a gift from her studies in Crete of the Minotaur, the bull-headed man, the unholy offspring of Pasiphae, the goddess of witchcraft and sorcery. Dire lined the labyrinth's tunnels and chambers with a hidden thread and like Theseus, it kept her safe and true.

Except this time.

A rumbling came from the tunnels up ahead. Heavy footsteps. Grunting, laughing, singing. All in a voice so rich and resonant it shook the walls.

The darkness faded and the rumbling increased. The footsteps stopped for a moment. Hoofed clomps replaced them.

Dire shook her head, placed a hand over her heart. No, it wasn't possible.

Whatever approached on cloven feet walked like a man, not a beast. There were two footfalls to each stride, not four.

But she'd already learned two Galatians worked in Nant. What other creatures out of antiquity would be here? Especially in these caverns?

Perhaps she walked Daedalus' Labyrinth unawares all these years? She dabbled in unholy things. Had Mother Church called up ancient servants to claim her?

The dark hallway grew bright.

The Minotaur stopped upon seeing her. Its body filled the tunnel and it ducked as it walked lest its horns scrape dirt from the ceiling.

A bull's massive horned head, a huge, muscular body, and from the calf down back to being a bull; it walked on cloven feet.

It held a torch in its right and held it forward to get a good look at her.

"Hello, Ancient One. Mother told me there was a wisewoman in Nant but she could never find her. Are you she?" The Minotaur laughed and loomed over her with an outstretched hand coming down on her head.

Dire cowered, reached into her satchel, and pulled the threaded balls out. She held the loose ends between her fingers and threw the balls at the Minotaur's torch. They unraveled in flight, their contents sprayed as they flew.

Before they struck, Dire pulled her cowl over her head,

wrapped her cloak around her and fell to the ground in a tight, little ball.

The dust the balls carried caught the torch. The tunnel flared with light brighter than the sun. The torch's flames leapt over the Minotaur and it screamed.

With a human tongue.

Dire, huddled under her cloak, dared not look up until the alchemist's sun burnt itself out. Still she wondered, A man? A man dressed as a bull? The Cretan Minotaur never spoke, couldn't understand human words.

She felt the fire spread around her. Its heat engulfed her. The Minotaur's bellowing turned to coughing as its skin flared with the heat.

She heard it fall back against the wall, heard its hands slapping at the flames, and a moment later it grew dark.

She slowly drew back her cowl and rose.

In the dying embers, she saw the Minotaur, its head half off. It was a man. Giant enough, and still a man. Who groaned.

Dire touched the giant's face. It winced unconsciously with the pain. Its eyes were closed and she lifted one lid.

The giant's eyes had whitened, burned into blindness by Dire's Greek Fire.

She grabbed the giant's still burning torch and hurried on.

King Gaumand listened to visiting Prince Orel's request - safe passage for trade from the prince's Alan empire to the west and back - from his throne with several ministers in attendance. Nobles near and far came asking permission to cross his kingdom to establish trade routes with Europe. The Crusades made the West hungry for things of the East, and the further east the better.

Prince Orel's case was not well heard.

Until Orel brought forth a gold encrusted case and opened it before the King. Inside, in lush purple cloths, lay a strange device.

"My people call this a *Setāreyāb*. The Greeks know it as an *astrolabos* and the Arabs call it *al-Asturlāb*. It is a toy but a fascinating one. With it you can determine your position anywhere on the earth."

King Gaumand smiled. "Does the prince think I don't know where I am on the earth?"

The ministers and several in attendance chuckled.

The prince persisted. "See this?" He brought Gaumand's attention to a small gold cylinder attached to the Setāreyāb. "It is a magic-eye. It makes this *Setāreyāb* unique. It is a gift to you from my people for your indulgence."

Gaumand thanked Orel for the gift and left his ministers to gather more details - primarily the tariffs and taxes for travel across the kingdom - and studied his gift.

The device as a whole held little interest to the King, but the magic-eye...It brought distant objects up close! Things across a field came near enough to touch!

Now King Gaumand gazed out a throne room window onto his eastern lawn and used the sees-far element to laugh at his children's antics. The afternoon sun enlivened the verdancy of the grass and the separate gardens, each with a unique mix of rose, lavender, tulip, and other brightly colored and scented flowers. It sent heady fogs back and forth on the light winds, and the window stood open. He leaned over a gold and ivory surfaced table in front of the window, rested his hands on it, and inhaled deeply.

His eastern lawn brought him such delight. It was his family's private lawn. No guests to the royal household were allowed there. There King Gaumand and his family could be a simple family doing simple family things. Things such as he heard his subjects did.

And sometimes it was the simplest things which annoyed the most.

Case in point, his eldest daughter, Marianne.

Presently the sees-far showed him Princess Marianne flirting with every guard, every soldier, every servant, if it had two legs and could grow a beard or even a hint of one, she batted her eyes and ruffled her skirts and leaned over to tempt them to take a peek at places their eyes should not go.

A veteran of several campaigns, he worried about his eldest daughter. His father and grandfather were some of the few who kept the Mongols at bay but that had more to do with his kingdom's insulating geography than much else. If the Mongols attacked from the south or east, he would probably never have been born as his grandfather and father would have been pig food, the common last use of defeated foes of the Mongols.

They had lost some territory, far to the north, but what country doesn't?

Those lands were too distant to be of concern. He often hoped some other country would invade them and relieve him of any obligation to rule them. Holy Mother Church ruled them more than he, and should those lands need his protection, he would ask the church to fund the campaign.

But his daughter. As womanly as she was, she still played with the soldiers and harangued them to teach her battlefield maneuvers, made them hold her close so she could "overpower" them properly. She flirted and was typically unwise in the ways of men. And any of his people who thought to breach his kingdom through his eldest daughter?

Well, he'd been a veteran of many campaigns and knew what to do to such people. He'd learned from his father and grandfather: first crush them completely, next find a monastery or convent or church or cathedral or whatever other holy place lay along your route home so you could confess your sins and live with a free and guiltless conscious until the next campaign required your darkness.

His youngest daughter caught his eye and he smiled. Ouive saw her oldest sister getting all the attention and attempted to break her eldest sister's spell on the younger males in attendance. It wasn't enough she had her own people, her own ladies-in-waiting, her own maids and matrons, her own nurses, her own guards, all of whom happily played with her, no, it was the five or seven or ten younger court attendees circling like bees around her sister's budding flower on which Ouive set her sights.

The best amusements came when Marianne and Ouive fought over the same fool. Their weapons were different, as were their tactics. Ouive's escalation went quickly from talk to standing in front to tugging on a sleeve to screaming to kicking a shin. Marianne escalation was much more diplomatic. She used only words, but words accompanied by gestures, expressions, hints of kisses, and when all else failed?

Call the Nurses! She would say. Rid me of this child, this menace!

But always said with a smile and her eyes never leaving her target.

Which of them, when fully grown, would be the more formidable queen?

He lifted a bell from the table beside the window and gave it a gentle jangle. A steward came in and bowed.

"Where is my middle daughter, Solas?"

"She is off riding with a bowman, My Lord."

Gaumand leaned further over the table and scanned more of the lawn. His eyes roved its perimeter, the walls too high for any horse to jump. "Where and with what bowman?"

"I know not, My Lord."

The King's face reddened. He faced the steward and kept his voice calm. "Find me someone who does know, now."

One of Gaumand's secretaries entered as the steward hurried out.

"Yes?"

"Will the King review today's correspondence, my Lord?"

"Who writes me?"

The secretary shuffled through the envelopes, scrolls, and other material in his hands. He glanced at each and named a name. Some were lieges, some churchmen, some notables in other kingdoms, and then the secretary frowned at one envelope. "Princess Solas?"

"Bring that one here."

King Gaumand opened it. Few words, typical of his middle child. "Dear Father, my Lord and King, I fear for Mother's safety and have taken a bowman to help me find her. Your loving Daughter, Solas."

Gaumand nodded, refolded the note and put it back in its envelope. He glanced out the window as he tucked the envelope up a fold of his blouse above his wrist. "Call the Lords of My Guard to me. One of my archers is missing. They are to find out which one and have his name and rank ready when they enter this chamber."

The secretary bowed. "Yes, My Lord." He backed out of the room.

Before he got to the door, Gaumand added, "And have them order their troops ready to travel within the hour."

The secretary continued bowing and backing. "Yes, My Lord."

Baron Bassys rode his black courser stallion with his rich, red robes flanking the horse. They started at the courser's shoulder and ended at its hocks. Under his left arm The Baron carried a red plumed, silvered helmet. Under his robes he wore full armor. His right hand held the reins and guided the horse.

The stallion walked in an oval formed by fully one hundred of The Baron's guard made up of his best bowmen, lancers, and swordsmen, each on a white courser, each dressed in black armor. Many of the guard excelled in two martial disciplines, few in all three, and the Baron had his best lancers in front, his best swordsmen in his surround, and a mix of bowmen and swordsmen in the rear as they marched north towards Nant.

The entire parade appeared as some bizarre flower moving along the forest highway.

The Baron's Chief Lancer told him many times such a parade was dangerous. The Baron's courser and wardrobe caused him to stand out. Anyone could place him in their sights, and a skilled bowman could loose his arrow and be gone before it struck or they could give chase.

"Then best make sure there are none so skilled on the roads I travel."

Yezides, the Baron's sergeant-at-arms, rode close on his right and cleared his throat repeatedly.

The Baron inhaled deeply. "Have you ever read of Emperor Caligula? One of the Ceasars of Old Rome before the church?"

Yezides shook his head. "No, my lord Baron."

"There was someone, a nephew I think it was, in his court who had a nagging cough."

"Oh?"

"Caligula had him beheaded rather than continue being annoyed by his cough."

The sergeant-at-arms slowly held his courser back.

"No, come forward. You are more annoying than a gnat. Do you have something you want to say?"

"My Lord, we travel north and the only village on this road is Nant and then the border. It would settle the men to know what we're about."

"The men are unsettled, are they?"

"It does them no good to ride on edge, my Lord. It exhausts them before they engage and that's not good battle strategy."

"You think we're going into battle, good Sergeant?"

"I know not my Lord's mind."

The Baron laughed. "We go to rescue the Queen. She's been kidnapped by some of our Lord the King's Guard and no doubt will be held at ransom."

The sergeant-at-arms nodded. "How many of the King's Guard abducted our Lady the Queen?"

"Fully one hundred."

Yezides' horse missed a step. "There are but one-hundred of us, my Lord. It is good military strategy to bring superior forces when battle is presumed."

The Baron pulled a silk handkerchief from his sleeve and offered it to the man. "I did not know my Guard sweat so easily."

Yezides blanched.

"Be of strong heart, good Knight. I sent a message to a friend who is well connected and knowledgeable in the arts of war. He will meet us with many like him. They will arm with us. Don't fear."

"May I ask who this warrior-alchemist might be, My Lord?"

Bassys' head rolled back and he laughed deep in his belly. "Certainly. A Jannenite. He and several of his brothers will meet up with us at a certain place in the wood. There we shall marshal and rally."

Yezides kept his mount moving forward. "Thank you, my Lord. May I share this with the men to ease their concerns?"

The Baron nodded. "Do what suits you. Just see that your throat is soothed before we speak again."

"Aye, my Lord."

CHAPTER 58

Galos pulled his cart beside his piles, his head bowed and his eyes on the well-worn path he walked. Every few steps he mumbled to himself and shook his head in reply. "I've not seen a Galatian since the fall of Jerusalem. I thought..."

He looked up and let the handles of his cart slide from his hands. The cart rested on its front legs with a soft thud. Wrens and chickadees landed on the topmost twigs and branches searching for grubs and seeds and other morsels.

One chickadee chastised him for not having more.

"More for you later, little thing. Now I must see what Haasel has for me."

He sang, as always, as he approached her workshop. She neither called out nor sang in answer.

He checked the sun's position in the sky. She would not nap this time of day. Not that day or night meant much to her, light or dark she walked the same world regardless.

"Mistress Potter!" He stood outside her gate. "Haasel?"

He swung her gate open and closed violently, stamped his feet with each step, made as much noise as possible so not to startle her.

His fist banged on her door. Nothing.

"I'm coming in, Haasel."

It took effort to push her door open. Her toppled workbench wedged against it, her drying and setting shelves lay about in pieces. Pottery shards sharp as butchering knives gouged fabrics. Her kilns were open and cold.

Galos stepped over broken chairs and ill-formed clays to Haasel's private room.

Her wardrobe lay open and fallen like a soldier wounded and dead in battle. Some great force upended her bedding and threw it against a wall.

He pulled it forward, his arms shaking with fear of what might lie behind.

Nothing.

"Haasel," he screamed.

He followed the path of destruction through her cottage, through the rear door knocked off its hinges, and came upon her small garden. Few vegetables, mostly aromatic flowers she tended and gathered to place in her hair when she knew he would be by, now trampled.

He fell on his knees into her garden, lifted lavender and sage, and wept. "Haasel."

He stood and turned back into her cottage. Hanging like a garlic string on the wall by her shattered door he saw the little clay bulbs he asked her to make. Ten perfect little bulbs each with a tiny hole, slightly more than a small peg's width.

He lifted and held them tenderly up to his face, inhaled them to find the scent of her, kissed them, and placed the string around his neck.

Back at his own cottage, he stood naked out back and first

washed with fatted ash to mask his own smell, then wiped juniper, sage, parsley, and other forest scents over his body.

Satisfied, he went to his cart and pulled off the pile atop. The cart had a false bottom, carefully constructed to fit snugly and resonate as if solid if tapped.

He slid the false bottom forward.

A black robe. A cape the same. A black mask. A black silk scarf to hold it in place. Black boots.

And a white, Damascus steel sword and knife, both in belted scabbards the color of the night, with other weapons beneath them.

S lewe pushed his untouched mug of ale away from him. He rested his head in his left hand and turned pages with his right.

Tardiff sat across from him in the empty Red Fox. "Well?"

Slewe turned pages back and forth, forth and back, stopped at one page and pointed to the leftmost of four columns. "This is Latin. I know that much." His finger ran down the next column. "I think this is Greek." The next column. "Hebrew, but I'm not sure." The last column. "I have no idea."

"But can you read it? Any of it?"

"I'm an innkeeper, Tardiff, not a scholar. I read manifests and billing ladles, and keep my own books. But this is beyond me. Sorry." He kept turning pages, searching for something familiar.

The door opened. Zevke and Saida came in.

Slewe looked up. "Hello, friends. The ovens done for the day?"

Zevke pulled chairs over for Saida and himself. "We thought to see the circus' opening night. Doesn't look like much is happening." He pointed and laughed. "A book? Slewe, you can read?"

Tardiff sat back, arms across his chest. "A book, yes, but not one we can read."

Saida glanced at the page Slewe held open. Her eyes opened wide and she glared at Zevke. Catching his eye, she nodded towards the book.

Zevke sat forward, arms folded and resting on the table. "Why have a book you can't read?"

Slewe looked up at Tardiff. Tardiff raised his eyebrows. Slewe nodded.

"We think it's Sheriff Donam's book. Both he and his deputy are missing. I found it in his room. Slewe thinks it's written in several languages but can't figure them out and I can't read save my name on official orders." Tardiff hesitated. "Can either of you read?"

Saida kept wide eyes on Zevke. Tardiff and Slewe's eyes were on the book still in Slewe's hands.

Zevke met Saida's eyes and shrugged. "I have a few words. Probably like Slewe; who gave me what, what they want back, things most merchants know to do. I can take a look, if you like."

Slewe slid the book over. "Four columns. I think the left most is Latin, then comes Greek, the other two I guess at."

Zevke's fingers went to the third column. They started at the right and worked slowly left.

Slewe nodded. "I can't make that out, either."

"It's Hebrew." Zevke turned back to the book's opening page and his finger again moved right to left on the third column. "This first page explains what the book is, the languages used - you were correct, Slewe, the first two are Latin and Greek. The last column is Persian - and how to use the book."

Tardiff leaned over as if reading it himself. "So what is it?"

Zevke looked up at Saida and she nodded. "It's a grimoire. A book of magical incantations. A training manual for use by a magus, a master magician, to teach their disciples."

Slewe pulled his hands off the table. "It's devil's work."

"If you believe in such things."

Tardiff shook his head. "I can't see Sheriff Donam as a...what did you call it? Magus?"

Zevke flipped the book to the frontispiece and tapped it. "It's not Donam's book. He was the apprentice, one of the disciples, one of the ones being taught. The book belongs to Baron Bassys."

Tardiff leaned still closer but now focused on Zevke's finger moving down the page. "Why bring it here to Nant?"

The inn's door opened but their focus remained on the grimoire.

Zevke sat back. "According to this, they plan something called 'The Council of Urs', a series of sacrifices."

"Where? When?"

"It makes no note of where, only that the moon shouldn't be in the sky. That's the next three nights starting tonight."

Haasel's staff drew quick but careful arcs as she walked through the tunnels, the end of her makeshift cane touching, feeling, testing like the antennae of the night moths she so admired. Now and again she heard someone crying. Each time the voice grew louder the breeze brought the scent of an abattoir.

Disconcerting, yes, but she'd decided long ago fear would not help her navigate the world. She swallowed and walked on.

She catalogued her environment as she walked, and her voice served as pleasant comfort. A light, uniformly warm draft moved through the tunnels but only in one direction. "The air exits higher than it enters." She didn't remember a draft when she began so the air took alternate routes to reach the surface.

More often than not, the draft blew into her face. "I'm going down, not up. But the incline is slight. If this is a pathway to Hell, it is at least a gentle one." She chuckled at her wit. The echo of her breathing told her how far an opening went and whether it tracked down or up. So far it tracked fairly even. Interesting and not helpful to her escape.

She kept one hand on the walls as she walked. If not the walls, the ceiling. She felt the protruding roots, mostly unfamiliar. And the dirt. Sometimes she stopped to feel the loose grains of earth between her fingers, sometimes she brought them to her lips and tasted them with the tip of her tongue. "These walls. Mostly dirt but there's a natural clay running here. I shall remember this place should I ever have need." Sometimes her fingers brushed over stonework and she asked herself. "Masons built this place?"

Her fingers often came back damp and she heard occasional sounds of water moving. "This labyrinth passes near water now and again. If not a river, a stream with enough current for its water to work against its bottom." She pressed the end of her staff up into the ceiling and abruptly stopped. "Let's hope I'm above the swell. It would not serve to poke the ceiling and have some river bottom come down to greet me."

She continued her explorations confident she could find her way back to where Simon left her should there be a need. Like all blind from birth, she created a map of angles and occultations, of layers and textures, of echoes and silences, wherever she went, and held it foremost in her thoughts when she took known routes.

The sobbing that first drew her came and went as she traveled. That, too, had meaning; the labyrinthine system crossed itself many times, an underground highway system. Above ground she could rely on the feel of the sun on her face or the movement of the night creatures to tell her the direction she traveled. Down here she estimated distances and directions based on knowing where she was when Simon entered the first cave and knowing which way she traveled and the steps taken since then.

Which meant she was somewhere under Nant.

She stood at an intersection. Soft tears came from two of the intersecting tunnels. Whoever cried sobbed, the inhale louder in one tunnel than the other.

Haasel stood still, listened. A small person. Her size, slightly smaller. Smaller build, anyway. Not as much chest to resonate from. On the ground. Hurt? They didn't sound like painful tears. Not tears of the flesh. Tears of the spirit, these.

Tears of the lost.

And the smell of the abattoir strengthened as she neared the voice.

Haasel's blind eyes blinked. "Hello?"

The crying stopped.

"Hello? Can you hear me?"

The voice shrieked.

Haasel shook her head. Rage? Panic? Fear? "Hello. Are you hurt?"

More shrieking.

Haasel listened to its tone, its vibrance, did it come from the throat or the chest? Was it driven by the belly or the head?

She turned one ear then the next, listening to echoes to determine direction.

The shrieking weakened into sobs.

"Hello? I am Haasel of Nant. Who are you?"

The sobbing grew until Haasel ached with the feel of it.

Pain, now. Rage moved into pain.

"Are you hurt?"

Words in the middle of the sobs. "My child is dead." Dry tears now. Hoarse, rasping. Coming from a throat already strained and broken.

Keep them talking. You can find them if you keep them talking.

"Tell me about your child. Was it down here with you?"

The voice changed, became airy, wistful, as if telling tales of dreamt places and times, distanced itself from what it described.

"My child left me."

Haasel quickly inventoried: had she passed a child? Had she heard a child? Had she smelled...

The abattoir.

"Was it an animal? Did some beast get your child?"

"My tiny boy. A son. He floated away on a river of blood."

Listen. Echoes. Where is the voice coming from?

Haasel took a few steps into one tunnel running north from the intersection. "Tell me more." Her own voice moved more in one direction than another.

The voice screamed. "Don't leave me."

Back to the center. "I won't leave you. Keep talking. Why did your boy leave you?"

The voice calmed again, returned to the narrative voice of a moment before. "He couldn't live with me, with what I'd done. He didn't want me for his mother."

Listen. Echoes. Haasel moved towards the voice's origin. "How come he didn't want you for his mother? What did you do?"

"He wanted another. I held him for a while, but he wouldn't move and didn't cry."

Very close. One more turn. Haasel heard the breathing, steady, slow.

And weakening. The abattoir. Close.

"Are you hurt?"

"Finally no breath left his lips. He was done with me and I let him go."

Sobbing again. Sobbing mixed with peals of laughter. Hysterical laughter echoing all about her. She'd entered a room, the speaker on the floor before her.

"Be careful. He may still be around. Wouldn't do to step on him, poor little thing."

More laughter.

Haasel's staff slowed through a sticky puddle. Something popped, burst. The smell gagged her.

"You've found my son. Tell me, is he well?"

Haasel folded a sleeve and put it over her nose and mouth. If I'm walking into Hell, so be it. I'll go with my head high and my staff across the head and shoulders of any demon who challenges me.

"I must go. My mother and father will worry about me. My brother will be looking for me. I must tell them they were grandparents and uncle, albeit only for a moment."

Haasel's cane cut an arc and whacked a fleshy solid as she stepped around a corner. She quickly pulled back.

More laughter. "Come spirit, don't beat me now. It is too late for more damage to be done."

"How long have you been here?"

"I can see in the dark, do you know that?"

The voice directed away from her. Whoever spoke didn't face her.

"Where am I? What do I look like?"

The person retched. Amongst the bile, a different smell, familiar but vaguely so.

She inhaled and exhaled quickly, drawing the odor into her nostrils, clearing it, drawing it in again, clearing it until she placed it; she had been sick some years ago. A spider bite grown feverous. Galos brought Dire to her. Dire the WiseWoman. Dire made her drink a tea. A tea made from roots. These tunnels must be where Dire got her roots.

It was the only time in her life Haasel thought she could see.

And the retching. Dire later said the retching shook loose the spider's poison from her.

Haasel reached down and felt long, fine hair covered in dirt. "What have you eaten?"

Haasel heard a plucking sound. "These roots. I don't know their names or what flowers they serve."

A smallish hand, a woman's hand, took hold of Haasel's. "My vision is gone again. Can you see, spirit? Will you help me out of here?"

"I'm not a spirit. I'm Haasel of Nant. Who are you?"

"Haasel the Potter?"

"Who are you?"

"Julia. Idee and Byell's daughter, Thomas the Shepherd's sister."

"The girl courting Eric, Verduan's son? Half of Nant searches for you, girl."

Another peal of laughter. "Oh, Eric. He's such a boy."

Had the roots taken hold again? "What are you doing here?

"Nory led me through the underworld but I couldn't keep up. Then I got lost. Then my belly started quivering and there was pain, such ghastly pain, I wanted to die. But before I could, my child left me."

"The child, the son you talk of."

"Lost."

"Because of the roots you ate."

"Truly Sullya the Witch cursed me for taking her hand."

"I know nothing of that."

"How did you find me? You have no lamp."

"I need no lamp. Day and night are the same to me. Take my hand. I can get us back to where I started. Someone's workshop. In a cave, I think."

Julia stood on shaky legs and held Haasel's arm.

"Dire's cellar?"

Haasel shrugged in the darkness. "I don't know. Someone

named Simon left me there. He had a familiar voice but I don't remember where from."

Julia's voice lifted and steadied. "Yes. Simon! The Galatian Knight. He brought me there, too. He saved me."

"Yes. That seems to be what he does. Although I don't know why." She guided Julia's hand into hers and walked back along her map, listening, feeling, smelling. "Come. Tell me what you know of him."

CHAPTER 59

Verduan and Patreo heeded Baillot's warning and held back. "You may need weapons." He patted his sides and back, turned and looked along the path they came, and hissed. "By all the saints."

Verduan followed his gaze. "What?"

"I would afford you my pike but it's not here. I didn't hear it fall as we walked."

Patreo, his gaze ahead into the last vestige of light, shook his head. "You didn't have it on you when you met us in the cells."

Baillot chuckled. "You are far too observant to be a common priest, Father Patreo."

"What do you think is out there?"

"Have you ever heard of The Council of Urs?"

Verduan shook his head. Patreo frowned. "Urs? A celebration of some patron saint?"

"You know your languages, the words but not the use. It is a corruption used to signal a gathering, a celebratory mass, specifically to the Dēmiurgós, and is a mix of gnosticm, ophianism, catharism, - "

Verduan snorted. "It must be wonderful to be educated."

Patreo held up a hand. "Not in these things, Verduan. These are societies secret and dark."

"Yet you know of them?"

Baillot nodded slowly. "You are truly your father's son and uncle's nephew. This knowledge was in the books they left you?"

"Your pike, it's a four-sided blade?"

"Yes, a Galatian lancehead. It leaves a wound which will neither close nor heal and with a poisoned tip, nor will it easily fall out if broken from the lance."

"The flanged tip?"

Verduan face soured. "And the Galatians are the good ones?"

"Can either of you handle a crossbow?"

Patreo and Verduan shook their heads.

"A sword?"

Verduan reached for it. "I saw no sword in your wardrobe."

"Some weapons I hid where only I could find them should there be a need. Father Patreo, I'm sorry, I have no weapon for you."

Verduan smirked. "Oh, don't worry about him. He's got a magic sack with weapons galore."

Baillot nodded but kept his eyes in the direction they headed. "More learnings from your elder's books?"

Verduan glared. "I was kidding."

Patreo reached into his cassock and pulled out two small clay bulbs.

Verduan leaned against the tunnel wall. "My god, he's pulled his stones free of himself. What kind of witch are you?"

Baillot chuckled. "Aromatics?"

Patreo nodded. "And thrown together, explosive."

Verduan came off the wall and looked in Patreo's hands. "The Greek fire you showed me in Tomeka?"

"Exactly the same."

Forgeron pulled his cart down the south road and saw a campfire glow through the trees. A moment later he smelled the cooking nigella, cinnamon, and saffron. He called out in Old Arabic, "Hello the camp."

Two Jannenites emerged from the trees on either side of the road ahead of him, their scimitars in their hands.

Forgeron continued in the older tongue. "Hello, Brothers. A tinker am I, a metal worker by trade. Do your blades need sharpening? Cleaning? It would not benefit Allah to kill your enemies with the blood of another on your blade."

The left Jannenite stepped forward. "You know our language."

"I've travelled far in my youth to learn my trade from the best I could find and always, as I travelled, I endeavored to make friends."

"You carry no weapons?"

"Only what I work on for a day or two at most. I'll gladly go on my way if you have no need."

"Are you hungry, Tinker?"

"May I lower my cart?" He did so without waiting for a reply, freeing his hands and arms to gesture as he talked. "Oh, a man of the road am I." He patted his stomach. "My belly is always in need of a cup of *quwwa*." Forgeron waved the breeze toward his nose and sniffed. "Perhaps a bit of *Maqbous*?" He bowed. "And always the talk of good friends."

The Jannenites lowered their blades. The right one laughed and sheathed his sword. The left did the same and waved Forgeron forward. "Come then. Our blades can always be sharper and many need a cleaning. The stain of Christian blood weakens them."

Forgeron nodded, laughed, lifted his cart handles, and followed.

The camp held six strong men, a Jannenite each. Forgeron gave each a welcome and thanks as they offered him food and drink. He held up his hands in protest. "When I'm done. A good worker plies his trade first, is paid after."

Their leader nodded acceptance and offered him his scimitar. Forgeron took it respectfully, both hands forward, and tested the blade. "I have just the thing. Is there water nearby? I have a paste that both quickens and sharpens. Your blade will glisten like the sun." He placed the blade on the back of his cart and came out with two skins. "A little of each in a half cup of water makes the paste."

They gave him some water from their horses' buckets and he set to work, making sure he polished every man's blade several times and thoroughly. "Do you worthies carry knives? The paste works on all combat metals." And finally. "Your quarrels? Are their heads sharp and worthy?"

He worked long into the night. All but the leader and a lookout slept. "Will you dine now, Tinker?"

"If you find my work good and are willing, I will eat first then rest safe in the knowledge you good men surround me."

The leader filled a bowl and poured some *quwwa*. "You travel south. Do you know the village north of here, Nant?"

Forgeron kept his hands on his cup of *quwwa* and covered his mouth. "I travelled through it a while back plying my trade. I sharpened a few axes, some knives. Fixed some pots. A hoe or two. The usual for a metalsmith."

"How can you travel south and not have passed through it more recently?"

"There are some ruins in the woods between your camp and Nant. Cloisters, by their look, and from an ancient time." He smiled over his cup. "What I say embarrasses me, friend. I hope you'll pity me and hold me in your prayers. I left Nant with some wine I purchased hoping to trade in the next town I met. I stayed in the Cloisters because they offered protection from the creatures of the night. I fear the wine I hoped to trade stayed where I slept."

The Jannenite slapped Forgeron's back. "You are a man. A sinner, but a man, and men can be saved. Sleep and we'll talk more tomorrow."

"Your *quwwa* is delicious. May I place some sugar in it for you? It might liven the taste even more."

The Jannenite held out his cup. Forgeron reached into his pockets and came out with a pouch. He tapped a few brown grains into the leader's cup.

"What do you think?"

The warrior nodded vigorously. "Yes, it does enhance the flavor."

Forgeron offered him the pouch. "For your men for tomorrow's prayers. A gift for letting me eat and sleep safely."

The Jannenites breakfasted early, each sampling Forgeron's brown sugar greatly. They laughed until their speech slurred, then one by one they fell over asleep.

Forgeron opened his eyes, gathered his things into his cart, and travelled back north towards The Cloisters and Nant.

King Gaumand studied his marshalled troops like a mother hen counting her chicks. Some riders shuffled carefully to hide a bald spot in the formation. The King looked down, shook his head, and chuckled. "My middle daughter has taken Abruna with her?"

His Lance General rode beside him. "Yes, my King."

"Do you have children, General?"

"A son, yes, my King."

Gaumand nodded. "You are wiser than I."

"Doubtful, my King."

"Were any with Abruna when my daughter approached him?"

The general signaled and an arbalist came up beside him. "How may I serve my King?"

Gaumand smiled. He knew his children well. "You were with Abruna when Princess Solas sought him?"

"Yes, my King."

"Did you hear the conversation?"

"I, uh, I - "

King Gaumand held up an understanding hand. "You're a good soldier and you don't wish to get anyone in trouble."

The arbalest swallowed.

"I will tell you what I think happened and you will casually nod or shake your head. You won't even have to look at me. You can keep your eyes on the forest to protect your king from assassins. Agreed?"

The arbalest looked into the trees and nodded.

"She told him, what...she wished to hunt pheasants on the estate and learn how to handle a bow?"

A shrug and half a nod.

"And who better to teach her than the best archer in the kingdom?"

Definite nod.

"She knows he won't refuse her because all my guard are sworn to protect us, each and every one."

Solid nod.

Gaumand's gloved hand came to his face. His index finger tapped his lips. The finger tapping stopped, he lifted his whole hand to face height, and the same finger rose as if making a point. He nodded. "They didn't ride in our gardens or fields, therefore outside the castle walls. They rode north, so along the roads towards Tangeu Forest. And by the time Abruna realized he'd been tricked, it was too late to signal for help and he couldn't leave the princess to travel unguarded."

A wavering nod.

The King waved his hand. "In any case, he'll have to follow as he's the only one there to protect her."

The arbalest rode a bit in the general's shadow.

"I didn't quite see that last response."

The arbalest nudged his charger and nodded vigorously.

"Thank you."

The general dismissed the arbalest. "My Lord is wise."

Gaumand laughed. "Remind me to choose well a prince for her. My eldest daughter will hold a kingdom in bed, my youngest with her petulance. But my middle daughter. Beware of her. She'll be the dangerous one. It'll be tough to find her a worthy match."

"Yes, my King."

"Or even better, I could order Abruna to marry her. Do you think that would be punishment enough?"

The general moved a gloved hand over his mouth and coughed, cleared his throat and coughed again.

CHAPTER 60

Buco sat and wagged his tail while Eric and Thomas strained their ears. The voices passed quickly, never close enough to make out distinct words, and trailed down other tunnels in the labyrinth. Eric and Thomas waited until they heard nothing more and relaxed.

Eric kept one hand on Buco's massive head. "It sounded like women. More than one. Not a lot."

Thomas scratched his head. "I know those voices. They are witches."

"Sullya? No voice sounded like the Sullya Julia and I encountered in Ash Hollow."

Buco lifted his nose and took four-five-six quick sniffs, his muzzle turning slightly to best capture whatever scent teased him.

"No, not Sullya. These are witches from the circus come to Nant."

"The circus brings witches to Nant?"

Thomas absently rubbed his inner thigh. "Aye. The worst kind."

Eric relit his torch from his tinderbox.

"Which way do you think the voices travelled?"

"You know they're witches and wish to follow them?"

"I wish to know a way out of here and cherish daylight. Or nightlight. I have no idea how long I've been in here and my stomach is empty.

Buco took a step, sniffed, turned and trotted in the opposite direction.

"Buco, no."

"That dog only listens to your father or you when you have food for him. Otherwise he's his own beast."

Buco, a shadow in the dark, barked. A moment later a series of low grunts echoed back.

Thomas grabbed Eric's arm. "What was that?"

Buco broke into a run and barked as he went further into the tunnel system.

Eric moved to follow his dog. "You've never heard a bear before?"

Thomas grabbed his arm again. "A bear? Down here? In the dark? In a cave or knoll, perhaps, but in this labyrinth? I'd rather follow the witches than meet with a hungry bear."

Eric shrugged himself free of Thomas' hand. "And I won't leave my dog to face such a beast alone. Will you follow me or go your own way?"

Thomas reached out. Eric pulled away as Buco's barking grew fainter but came quicker. The bear's grunts remained the same distance away but also quickened. "Make up your mind now, Thomas. I won't leave my dog to do battle alone."

Thomas withdrew his hand.

Eric followed the trail of Buco's barks.

Thomas cupped his hands and called out. "You have no weapon. You plan on attacking a bear empty-handed?"

Eric continued until his footfalls faded into the dark.

Thomas shook his head and he spoke through clenched teeth. "You are a great, great fool, Eric. My sister is better off without you." He backed himself against the door of his prison cell. "You left me without light, without food or water. I curse you, Eric. I curse you, your dog, your father, and your lands." He slid down to the floor, crawled back into his cell, and pulled the door shut behind him.

~

King Gaumand watched a pigeon circle over his retinue. Two hundred of his Guard surrounded him and another two hundred of his First Lancers traveled with him as they moved north along the only highway broad enough to support so large a massing.

Except that one damned pigeon circling above them seemed to single him out.

An arbalist on the King's side followed his stare and readied a quarrel.

Gaumand reached into his coat, pulled forth his *Setāreyāba*, and brought the sees-far to his eye.

His hand knocked the arbalist's arm up as he fired. "No!"

The quarrel flew harmlessly into the trees on the far side of the highway.

"My King?"

King Gaumand took a whistle from his pocket and blew three short blasts. The pigeon flew to him and perched between his charger's ears. "This pigeon carries a message. Best we read it and let the poor thing live for the good service it provides, don't you think?"

"My King, I'm sorry, I - "

Gaumand shook his head. "No need. You couldn't know." He waved a minister to him and held up the *Setāreyāb*. "Give the Alan whatever he needs. Tax him well but not extravagantly. He's helped us without knowing it today. Let's reward him for that."

The minister nodded and let his horse fall back into place.

The King turned the pigeon over and removed the tiny scroll from one of its legs. The steady walk of his mount gently rocked him from side to side as he read. "If the Queen had borne me but one son, I could pass this cup on to him."

The arbalist replaced his crossbow on its saddle hitch. "My King?"

"Baron Bassys. He plans us poison."

The arbalist's eyes opened wide. "My King?"

"Call my ministers to me."

The Guard made way for five stately riders to pace the King. "The Alan. He visits our city with a host, doesn't he? Not an honor guard, real military men, aren't they?"

"Yes, my King, but there's no worry. He only wishes to open new markets and we have a battalion stationed there should - "

The King held up a hand for silence. "Take five fleet riders with you and go to him. Ask him if he'll do us a favor and bring his troops the south road traveling from Melia to Turo to Nant. Tell him we will be most grateful for this service. If you believe he hesitates, tell him an east-west passage will be his without tariffs for as many men as he can muster. But only if he hesitates, understand?"

"You are most generous, my King."

"I'm a strong believer in making sure I have the biggest hammer, nothing more."

Soka pulled his old mare to a stop at the castle foregate. His full wagon rattled a bit as the shafts pushed against the old horse's harness.

The gatekeeper glanced at the tied down covering and smiled up at Soka. "More swill for the serf's pigs?"

Soka returned the smile. "Aye, our Lord the King is most generous with what can't be used in his kitchens."

The gatekeeper patted Soka' horse. "How you doing, old girl? How many more trips you have in you before you're on the cart being pulled by another?"

"Oh, no. She'll never end up like that. Her meat's too precious and would make a fine stew."

"Stay ahead of him, old girl, and you'll not suffer the stench." The gatekeeper laughed and waved him on. Soka snapped the reins. "*Cht cht cht.* Come on, girl. We got deliveries to make."

He made several stops on the east road out of town. At each stop, he chatted with the swineherd and their family as he shoveled slop into their pens.

The swineherd at the last stop pointed at two barrels revealed when the last of the slop was shoveled away. A strong rope tied them to the driver's seat at the front of the wagon bed. "Soka, did you take some wine along with the swill when you left the castle?"

"Oh, if I did, you know I'd share it. I'd have to." He pulled a short utility knife from his belt. "I'd do a poor job of protecting it with this." He waved it like a sword and jabbed at imaginary attackers. "No, the barrels contain offal from diseased beasts the kitchen could not use. I'm to dispose of them in the forest where the carrion eaters can feast on them."

The swineherd waved Soka on his way.

Soka lit the torch at the front of the wagon. "*Cht cht cht.* Come on, girl. One final delivery and we're done."

His breath steamed when he stopped the wagon by a stream. He unhitched the mare to drink and pull up grass. "Go ahead, girl. Have your fill."

He dropped a flap on his pants and pissed a long, glorious stream by the side of the road. "Ahh."

A banging came from one of the barrels.

"Quiet!"

The banging continued. A tiny, muffled voice called out. "I must make water."

"Piss yourself where you are."

An older voice, also muffled, came from the other barrel. "Every hair out of place, every bruise upon our features, and whatever ransom or reward you hope for grows less."

Soka pulled his knife from his belt and pried open a barrel lid. Princess Marianne coughed and covered her eyes as the torchlight hit her.

"Stand up."

"I'm cramped. Give me your hand."

Soka put his hand around her throat and lifted.

She grabbed his forearm and slapped his face with her other hand as she stood.

He laughed. His knife flashed and her blouse, stained from when he drugged her in the larder and she fell, parted in front.

"Are these the buds which all the nobles quest after?" He spit on her breasts. "There, lass. Lather them up for me. Perhaps I'll take a taste later."

Princess Marianne gathered her cut blouse around her and pulled back from him.

An insistent pounding came from the other barrel. Ouive's demanding voice came from it. "I have to make water!"

Marianne stood as tall as she could and glared at Soka. "You harm that child and my father will hunt you down and kill you."

Soka laughed as he pried the other lid from its barrel. "Your father will be dead at the hands of a new king before you see him again. If not dead, defeated and offered for sport to his betters."

He lifted Ouive out of her barrel and put her on the ground beside the wagon. "Go, lift your skirts and squat wherever you'd like."

He turned back to the wagon as Marianne brought her barrel's lid down across his head and face.

Soka staggered back. Marianne followed and swung the lid as if she led a dance partner, the full weight of her young woman's body into the round, wooden lid, and heard Soka's skull crack with the blow.

He fell, took two breaths, shook, and stopped moving.

Marianne lifted the lid one more time and brought the edge down across his chest. More bones cracked and splintered, but Soka made no sound.

Ouive came over, lifted her skirts, and pissed on his face.

CHAPTER 61

Korol stood behind the seated Circe, her back to him, in the circus wagon supporting the back of the stage. A lamp threw shadows on the inside wall of the wagon's cover. Outside, night fell. Birds chattered less. Cows moaned in the distance, their udders full and wanting milking. The crossroads smell of trafficked dirt settled due to a heaviness in the air. Laughter and the scent of roast mutton came from The Red Fox across Nant's center.

He adjusted his jester's garb so no weapons showed. "Where is our leader? Has no one seen Dobrogost?"

Circe propped a silvered glass on a stand and applied black eyeliner. "I think he sampled his elixir too much. Or he's off looking for his bear and will return soon." Satisfied, she painted open, staring eyes on her eyelids.

"If Dobrogost doesn't return only you, I, and Diana will perform tonight?"

"Did the giant hire others I don't know about?" She adjusted her charcoaled corset so her reflection's breasts stood flush and firm in the glass.

Korol looked over her shoulder into the glass and applied clown makeup.

"Why do you travel with us, Jester?"

Her question made him stand back. "Why, I...to entertain, of course."

Circe laughed. "You're not an entertainer, Clown. Oh, you can do a few tricks, things to amuse the innocent and children, and a tale you tell well enough although you don't know many."

"Is there something wrong with the stories I tell?"

"Few clowns I know carry blades or have weapons hidden in their wagons."

Korol and Circe stared at each other's reflections. "You've gone through my wagon?"

She laughed again. "I have, Diana has, Dobrogost has, I wouldn't be surprised if the bear and pony have. Only those men on the wagon which sometimes travel with us kept clear." She looked up at him and blinked. The eyes painted on her lids looked through him. "That's another thing about you; you have no knowledge of circus ways. Few performers have personal things, maybe a bracelet or anklet or neck-lace. Maybe earrings. But nothing of value, nothing they'd leave unguarded for even a moment." She turned back to their reflections. "And if they do, they don't leave it where it can be so easily found."

Korol's eyes flashed towards his wagon.

"Oh, don't worry, Clown. You had nothing worth taking. Swords and bows and knives only invite the same or worse, and your clothing is finely made but not something to be worn this far north of Arab lands."

Korol's hand inched towards a knife hidden in his belt.

Circe shook her head. "You have no worries from us, Jester. So long as you do your job when the stage is set and the curtain rises, and you bring no harm to others in our troupe."

His hand continued its slow march.

"Your other garb. I've not seen its like since I was a child. You're a Gourdin by training or birth?"

His hand finished its transit and his eyes went wide.

Circe pulled his blade from between her breasts. "As I said, you don't know enough about circus ways to be trained or born to it." She offered it to him hilt first. "What is your story?"

His eyes narrowed on her face for a moment before they moved to his knife. He took it and slowly hid it back in his belt without taking his eyes from her. "Not a Gourdin, a Jannenite."

Circe closed one eye and raised both eyebrows. A human and an inhuman eye stared up at him. "The other wagon then, the one which sometimes travels with us?"

"My brothers."

"In belief or in blood?"

He snorted. "Jannenites know no difference. I travel with you to fulfill an oath. Long ago a Galatian-in-training, perhaps one day to wear the full mantle, escaped my blade. He was the last of the Galatians my people knew of and we'd vowed to end them all for their blasphemies to the Holy One."

The light flickered from a sudden wind. The cows moaned less. The birds grew quiet. Somewhere nearby a fox and its vixen cried to each other.

"The Galatians?"

"Warrior-Priests trained in ancient and modern ways. Formidable foes. In truth, they would have defeated us and Jerusalem would now be in Christian hands."

"What happened?"

Korol's head nodded gently from side to side and his lips puckered.

"Any secrets you have are safe with me. Who could I tell? The pony? The poor beasts who pull our wagons?"

"Their church - Rome - grew anxious of them. Their studies

showed them flaws in the church's own teachings. In the end, their own people betrayed them into our hands."

"If they were so learned, why didn't you take them in. Certainly the Mehtars or others would welcome them."

Korol snorted. "No. Their studies showed weaknesses in all beliefs. Even our own. I - "

"You didn't want to learn from them yourself? If they were so learned, why kill them? Why not use what they learned to help yourself and others?"

Korol placed his jester's three-lobed crown on his head. "Because their knowledge threatened even us. Some say knowledge is power, but that's not true. Knowledge is the enemy of power. The ignorant are far easier to control than those even slightly knowledgeable, and most people are happier stupid than wise. Make them think they're wise, that's enough. All beliefs do this. To think otherwise is a sign of your ignorance."

"You know this. Are you ignorant?"

Korol looked down at her. The bells at the ends of his hat's lobes jingled slightly. "I am alive. Isn't that the greatest wisdom of them all?"

"Tell me about these Galatians. You say one escaped? Perhaps I've seen him in my travels."

"One I know. Now I wonder if there's another, perhaps more. And you've seen the one I seek. You didn't know it and you've seen him, sure enough. In battle they dress head-to-toe in black: cowl, brace, blouse, pants, sash, and boots black as the deepest night and all fitted to them, nothing loose, nothing able to be grabbed save their capes, as black as the rest, and used to cover an array of weapons concealed on their backs. The only weapon they showed - and the clear sign of their order - a white, Damascus steel sword which couldn't be dulled and cut through hardened steel as easily as it cut through the finest silks. I've never encountered any other blade like them."

"You and your brothers killed most if not all of them and none of you saved a blade for study?"

Korol laughed in appreciation. "They carried powders. Oils and ointments. They knew metal, mineral, vapors, earths. There was a rumor they were witches and it could be believed. Before they died, they covered their weapons with some powder which dissolved the metals in a few days' time."

"A powder which dissolves metal?"

"I know. Can you imagine what other sciences are lost with them?"

"And you'll kill the one you found?"

"I have found him. I thought I killed him once but his belief saved him. Now I know there's at least one other. He left marks on my wagon. A sacred signature few can read, to both mark me and let his brothers know I am found."

Circe lifted a lid from a jar. Her fingers dug in and came out with a soft waxlike glob which she rubbed thoroughly into her hands, forearms, and what she exposed of her breasts. "He wouldn't leave marks unless he knew others would come to read them."

"No, he would leave marks to cause me fear there are many, not just one."

Circe opened a second jar and the wagon filled with a musk of patchouli, sandalwood, yohimbe, and others. She applied this on top of the first.

Korol coughed. "What is that? You've never worn its like before. The first, I know, is protection from fire. But what's the second. I don't remember it."

She smiled. "Something for the audience. To get them in the mood. Those who don't fall for the smell fall for the touch. The first keeps it from me." She looked at her hands and forearms, checked her bust in the glass. "The Galatian. What they wore. I knew a man like that when I was less than Diana's age." She turned and looked up at him. Only the painted eyes showed. She ran a finger over the back of his hand. "Will you kill me, then?"

Korol blinked, shook his head.

The circus pony neighed. Circe checked herself one more time in the glass. "Ah. Diana must be getting ready to perform." She stood and adjusted some of Korol's costume. "That tale you tell, of who you are and why you're here? That's a good tale to tell an audience. It would keep them enraptured and they'd remember it long after we moved on."

~

Abruna rode close beside Princess Solas. So close he sometimes took her reins when he thought the need, which was usually when she attempted to take the lead.

Solas kept her eyes forward, her hands on her own reins, her skirts fluttering about her because she refused both a proper saddle and to ride pinion. "You fear for my safety, Champion Archer?"

Abruna's eyes swept the road in front, the trees lining the road, and he regularly reversed his saddle to scan the road behind. "You said you wanted me to teach you the way of the arbalest and bow, My Lady."

"You doubt me?"

"No, only my own sanity at not questioning you further when we set out on this journey."

"You may leave me and return to my father's castle, if you wish."

"I may leave you and lose my head if I do so, my Lady."

Solas glanced over at him as he returned to riding face front, moving so he looked away from her while doing so. "Would you rather be teaching my royal sibling, Marianne, Champion Archer?"

"No, my Princess. I would rather be in your father's private garden with bullseyes a hundred paces hence."

"Abruna, I - "

Abruna grabbed Solas' reins. He wheeled his charger to block her and her mount from the road ahead.

She heard a *thwit* as Abruna raised his shield from his mount's side to protect both Solas and himself.

Something banged against it. Abruna raised his arbalest, let his shield slide back to its berth on the mare's side, and fired so quickly it seemed to Solas he fired without looking, wildly.

Fully fifty paces away a man dropped from a tree.

Abruna stood upon his horse and lifted another arbalest from his back, a bolt already fitted.

Solas heard two *thwits*. One she knew came from Abruna's weapon, the other from somewhere up ahead. Abruna fired first.

The assailant's bolt buried itself in the ground between his mare's legs, but she didn't move even though Abruna still stood upon her back.

Another man fell from a tree further on.

Abruna jumped down from his charger and pulled the arrow from the dirt. He inspected it while patting his horse's flanks. "There's some sugar in my pack for you, girl. Remind me."

His mare nickered and nodded.

Solas' eyes went from Abruna to the road ahead. "Your horse is well trained, Abruna."

"Thank you, my Lady."

"What does their arrow tell you?"

"It isn't an arrow, my Lady. You wish to learn the bow and arbalest, so here's a lesson for you. This is a bolt from an arbalest. By its weight and length, from one of the newer designs, what's called a crossbow. Less range, greater striking power." He held it up to her and pointed. "Notice the fletcher's markings?"

She took the bolt and crossed her eyes attempting to see.

"You read much, Princess Solas, and your education is a better weapon than any I carry. But it also means you'll never be worthy of your own bow, regardless of design."

Solas face hardened as she looked down on him and handed him the bolt. "You've been in my father's garden often as part of our guard. You've known I read all that I can whenever I can."

He bowed.

"So you knew my asking you to teach me was a fool's errand before we left the castle?"

He shrugged. "I also worry after our Queen."

Solas' face softened. "You knew?"

"I guessed."

She laughed. "You don't fear others on the road ahead?"

He shook his head and looked in the direction they headed. "No, these two came as a team, not really knowing what they hunted. Seeing our colors, they acted on instructions."

She leaned forward in her saddle. "Whose instructions?"

He tossed their assailant's bolt into the wood. "By the markings on the bolt, the Baron Bassys." He turned back to her. "Do you wish to return to your father's castle?"

She patted Abruna's mount's flanks. "What? And not see my father's Champion Archer in action? You'd deny me, Abruna?"

He mounted his horse and held Solas' reins. "As you wish, my Lady."

CHAPTER 62

Baillot took the lead. "Patreo, after me. Verduan, I doubt we'll be challenged from behind, still I'd like a strong man with a good sword at my back."

Verduan nodded. "Done."

Patreo placed a bulb in either hand. "You know quite a bit about these ruins, not-priest Baillot."

"I lived in Nant long enough to explore them. I saw similar constructions in the Order's books so discerned their purpose. One day I came on the new moon and saw an animal freshly topped and gutted on what I now realize is an altar."

"What brings you here now? And what were you doing the other times you came to us in our cell?"

Baillot lowered his head. "Not long back I took Julia to my bed and confessed my past to her. She devoted herself to me and I to her. We planned to flee Nant, to leave the kingdom and live south, by the sea. I could sell the last of my warrior tools and buy us some land, perhaps a few animals. We were to meet here when the time came."

Verduan let the tip of his sword rest on the ground. "And

when Idee came saying Julia was missing, you thought she'd be waiting here."

Baillot nodded. "But I would never tell her to come so close to council sacrifice."

The voices again.

Patreo stepped forward, his head bowed. He whispered, "So you came looking for her."

Baillot nodded and kept his voice low. "These celebrants had kept to animals but there was talk of their lord or some lord, some magistrate, coming. I feared a human sacrifice might be next. If Julia was here, she might fit their need and what better place to secret her than in these underground cells?"

Verduan's voice grew rough. "Why not free us when you first found us?"

"Because I didn't know you, Verduan, beyond the village, and Father Patreo I knew not at all. He knew things well beyond the priesthood, things I thought only a Galatian might know with some Jannenite knowledge mixed in. And when he knew the way of leaf and root, I couldn't know if he was a celebrant or not. The second time, your captors closed and I hadn't time to free you without risking us all."

Patreo leaned back. "The voices. They speak a mixture of Latin and Greek. There's another language, as well. Arabic? I can't be sure." He nodded at Baillot. "I would have wondered the same were the situation reversed. And been cautious. You were wise."

Baillot accepted the compliment. "I had good teachers. Douse the light. Our colors are dark. Let's get above ground and plan our next steps."

Verduan nodded vigorously. "Aye. Let's."

A few moments later they entered the archway leading to the Cloisters' main and stayed low behind the wall. Several people walked about purposefully. Some carried unlit torches on staves which they drove into the earth at regular intervals creating a path towards the altar. Others carried in pots from which whitish steam clouds rose in the dusk.

Verduan pointed behind the main altar stone. Baillot strained his eyes and whispered. "What is that?"

Verduan squinted to be sure. "Unless I'm mistaken, it is the tinker's cart."

Baillot rested on his knees. "The metalsmith who came through Nant? Do you think he was scouting, perhaps? Preparing for this?"

Patreo shook his head. "I don't believe it."

Verduan chided. "You said he wasn't a concern."

"And I still believe so."

Someone approached the wall with a vat. Another approached with logs and kindling.

Patreo, Verduan, and Baillot scrunched down and held their breaths.

Light grew as the fire crackled the kindling and the logs caught. Smoke climbed over the wall and stung their eyes. Their lungs ached for air but the smoke wound about them like a wispy serpent.

The celebrants moved back amongst the others.

Baillot, Verduan and Patreo waved the smoke away and inhaled slowly, quietly, and when they'd filled their lungs, they nodded to each other.

Baillot tapped Verduan and Patreo to crawl to the far end of the archway, then outside the ruins to freedom.

Verduan, his eyes on the ground, didn't move.

Patreo nudged his frozen friend. "What is it, Verduan?"

Verduan remained motionless. Patreo followed his gaze.

Cloven hoofprints. Patreo looked up and down, side to side. A two-legged walk. He shook his head and pulled Verduan forward.

Verduan held back, his voice a crack in his throat. "I told you this place was the coven of witches. Cloven prints. The Devil's own. We are cursed!"

Patreo pulled Verduan's head up by his beard. "You raise goats, sheep, and cattle. They have cloven hooves. Do they walk heel first?"

Baillot, his attention on the revelers, looked over at them. "What?"

Verduan refocused on the hoofprints for a moment and rocked back. "What does it mean?"

"It means we battle deceivers of the worst kind: human. Flesh and blood, nothing more. Those who use their knowledge and learnings to torment and torture others' minds, bodies, and spirits. But human. Nothing more." He started crawling towards their escape. "Come, we have work to do."

Marianne straddled Soka's body with the lid held over her head. "Ouive, into the wood. Not far, but off the road."

Soka neither breathed nor moved, but Marianne remained vigilant until her arms shook from the weight. She dropped the lid on his head and heard his blood seep into the earth.

Ouive came up beside her on tiptoe. "Is he dead?"

"As dead as I can make him."

"Why did he do this to us?"

Marianne rested against the wagon. "Because he's a fool. Come here." Marianne began tearing Ouive's sleeves from her bliaut. She lifted the bliaut and tore off a line of chemise from underneath. She lifted handfuls of dirt, weed, and vine and smeared them on Ouive's front, back, and sides. "Do you have any piss left?"

Ouive pulled back, shocked.

"Do you?"

Ouive nodded.

Marianne cupped her hands and put them under what remained of Ouive's chemise. "Piss here."

Ouive obeyed.

"Good." Marianne dribbled one hand's piss on Ouive's clothing, the other hand on her own, and dried her hands on both. She stood and began tearing her own bliaut, including two bright strands from her own chemise undergarment. "Give me your hands."

Ouive held them out.

Marianne rubbed them with pebbly dirt until Ouive pulled them back. "Ouch! Why are you hurting me?"

"Hold still."

She took more pebbly dirt and rubbed in over Ouive's face and hair.

Ouive spit out what fell into her mouth. "Mother will hear of this!"

Marianne turned her sister around and back, and looked her up and down a few times. "Good. Now you do me." She guided Ouive's unsure hands until she stood as filthy and rank as her little sister. "How do I look?"

"Why do you make us to look like peasants? Girls in the kitchen look better than me!"

Marianne nodded approval. "That's what I wanted. We need to get to a town, a village, somewhere where's there's someone in authority, someone who'll listen to us and get word to father."

Ouive shook her hair to get some dirt out and Marianne stopped her. "That dirt is our survival, sister. Didn't you hear what Soka said? Someone seeks father's throne, and he took us at the usurper's bidding. They may be waiting for him on this road. Two girls carrying offal will fare better with that kind than the two princesses they seek."

"Who seeks father's throne?"

Marianne hitched the mare and helped her little sister to the wagon's driver's seat. "I don't know. He died before he told."

"Then wherever we go, they could be waiting."

Marianne's head snapped towards Ouive. "What?"

"If we don't know who wishes us harm, it's best to assume all do until they prove otherwise, isn't it?"

Marianne raised her eyes to the moonless night. "Ah. Yes. Correct. You have some of your sister Solas in you." She gathered the reins and tapped the mare's back gently with them. The horse walked slowly forward.

"Shouldn't we go back the way we came?"

"I have no idea how many twists and turns Soka took to get us here, but from here the road goes only two ways. I choose the way the wagon faced and hope there's a town on the way." Marianne looked to Ouive for approval.

The little princess nodded.

"Good. Now remember, no matter what happens, I talk. You are silent, too meek to speak even when spoken to directly. And hold onto me at all times. Never leave my side, understand?"

Ouive tucked her head into her big sister's side and nodded.

"Say it."

"Yes, sister."

"Good."

The horse pulled them forward. Their torch lit eyes in the woods, to their front and behind, and all scattered as they continued on their way.

CHAPTER 63

Galos raced through the woods surrounding Nant, no longer worried if his robe caught on briar or stem, cautious of enemies but uncautious of any others, and slowed only as he approached Dire's cellar. Nory failed to bring his cold-smelting powders to him and he feared he would need them even sooner than imagined. He would determine the old wise woman's progress and finish the work if she hadn't, then so armed do what he could for Nant.

Sure he was not followed and not seeing anyone near, he parted the thorn bushes and vines hiding the entrance. No light came from the cellar as he entered, no one there.

Something shuffled. Not close, but close enough.

He took a tinderbox from the folds of his cape and a voice stopped him. "Stop! Make another move and I'll be upon you! Identify yourself!"

"Haasel?"

A loud, long inhale from deep in the dark. "Galos? Why don't you smell of wood fires and charcoal burning?"

He lit a torch. Across Dire's cellar, far in the back and emerging from the dark tunnel leading to the rest of the labyrinth, Haasel stood with one of Dire's canes held in front of her in opposing grips. Someone stood in shadow behind her. He drew his sword. "Who's with you? What harm has come to you?"

Julia stepped forward. "It's me, Galos. Julia. Byell and Idee's daughter."

"I'm fine, Master Charcoal Burner. No harm has come to me. Don't you remem - "

Galos rushed forward, lifted Haasel in his arms, and stopped her words with kisses. Haasel loosed the cane from her grip. It clattered to the ground beneath them.

Julia stood back. "But Galos, you are Simon?"

Haasel and Galos embraced a moment more. They separated only so each could catch their breath.

"We are all Simon. It is a sign among my warrior brothers." He went to Dire's workbench and shuffled things around.

Julia hesitated. "May I see your face to be sure?"

Haasel defended him. "It is Galos. I would know his touch and voice as surely as my own. And held close, his fires still burn." She heard him at the workbench. "What do you seek, Galos?"

"Dire was to make me some powders."

"But I thought you - "

"You thought I what?"

She reached out to him. "How many of your brothers are with you?"

"Here? None but I."

"No, in Nant."

"Why do you ask."

"Because someone wearing similar robes and moving as quietly as you but with a different voice told me to give you a message."

Galos removed his mask and one glove, lifted her hand, and kissed it. "What message, Mistress Potter?"

"The other dressed like you. He said you might come looking for something on Dire's workbench. When you did, I was to tell you you already had them."

Galos slowly refitted his mask and tied his scarf to hold it in place.

"What does all this mean, Master Charcoal Burner?"

"I have known for a while another of my kind moves in Nant, but not who. Until I do, I take no chances. With either of you."

Julia lifted a ladle from a pail of water. "But it was you who brought me here, Galos."

Haasel kept her hand on Galos' back. "And your brother brought me here. He must have thought Dire would be here because he expected to leave me in someone's care."

Galos took her hand and held it over his heart. "Then he does not know you to think you need another to care for you."

She gripped his hand and pulled it over her heart. "I need you to care for me, Master Charcoal Burner. Have your fires dulled your eyes so much you can't see my feelings for you?"

Julia brought the ladle close to her lips. "It was you came with Nory, though, wasn't it?"

Haasel turned to the briar covered opening to Dire's cellar.

Galos, knowing Haasel heard more than he, faced the vine strewn opening and drew his sword.

A second Galatian came through and loosed a bolt from his crossbow.

The ladle flew from Julia's hand.

Galos moved towards him.

The second Galatian held up his hands, empty and wide apart. "Hold, Brother. That pail holds poisoned water. Dire was testing for a cure or antidote. I noticed her studies when I read her notes."

Haasel turned her head slightly, letting each ear hear what it could. "Speak more. I know your voice."

Galos lowered his sword but kept it ready. "Who are you, then?"

The second Galatian removed his scarf and lifted his mask. "Has it been so long, Brother? You don't remember your own brother's voice?"

Haasel exclaimed, "Forgeron. You are Forgeron the Tinker."

Galos' sword fell. "Aldous?"

～

L ance Commander Adi rode beside Queen Danika through the forest. They rode at the head of Adi's lancers, bowmen, and swordsmen, and Adi voiced his concern over this arrangement at every twist, turn, and intersection in the road. The sound of their horses echoed through the dense green foliage. Each time Adi spied a thick-trunked tree he moved his charger closer to the queen's mount.

"You worry about your Queen, Lance Commander Adi?"

"I worry about my Queen, my men, and myself, m'Lady."

Several riders rode back and forth through the columns, from side to side, and periodically rode beside Adi to whisper in his ear.

Danika spoke kindly and patiently. "Is there anything we can do to assuage your worry, Lance Commander?"

"My Queen has an excellent command of the roads. She seems to know where we're going. Knowing our destination would do much to calm my heart, m'Lady."

"We head towards Nant."

Adi's charger snorted a reaction Adi could not. "Nant. I know of it. A simple village near the eastern border. By the River Vell, isn't it?"

"So I'm told."

"The Queen has not been there herself?"

"This is my first visit to that part of the kingdom."

A rider trotted up to Adi and whispered quickly. Adi raised a gloved, open hand above his head and closed his fist. The columns stopped with the next step. Even the horses held their breath.

Adi's hand whirled above his head. Riders Danika had not noticed before, riders in dull forest colored garb of browns and greens and grays, dismounted and moved silently into the surrounding trees.

Adi brought his hand down over his chest in a sweeping motion. His swordsmen surrounded the Queen and himself.

Queen Danika stayed tall and proud in her seat, but she spoke quietly. "Yes, Lance Commander?"

He held a finger up to her, his focus on slight movements in the brush, leaves fluttering on trees.

Danika sat patiently.

They stayed thus until the runners returned, each individually. Each looked at Adi and shook their head.

Danika leaned towards Adi, her voice still low and patient. "Lance Commander?"

He spoke in a whisper. "One man remains to report, my Queen. Please reserve your questions until then."

The sun moved into the later half of the sky and the man had not returned. Adi called the other forestmen back. "See to him."

They returned not long after carrying two bodies with them, one the forest runner, the other dark-skinned and wearing a white robe with a red girdle and cap.

Queen Danika crossed herself. "Lance Commander? Now can you tell me what goes on?"

Adi dismounted and inspected the dark-skinned man first, then the runner's body. He put his hand into a still flowing wound in the runner's chest and pulled out a broken knife. He whispered to his men and all shook their heads.

"Lance Commander?"

"Forgive my silence, my Queen. A forward rider saw signs of

recent travel on this road. As we'd seen none to this point, that meant someone coming our way, freshly ahead of us, or waiting. No one passed us in either direction, so someone waiting." Adi motioned his men to see to the bodies. "No camp was obvious, so waiting in stealth. I sent our scouts to learn more." He waved at the runner's body as it was carried away. "This fellow found out too much and not enough." He looked up at Danika. "Did anyone know where we traveled, my Queen? Did you share your desire to anyone, even in passing?"

Danika shook her head. "Neither my King nor my children."

Adi nodded. He continued his inspection of the remaining body.

"Wait. I planned our route on one of my husband's kingdom maps. A servant came in with some tea. He glanced at the map as my finger traced our route."

Adi nodded. "Thank you, my Queen. That answers much."

"Who is that other?"

"I've not seen his like but have heard tell of such. An Arab warrior from the last Crusade. No idea what he's doing this far north or why he troubles us."

"Are there others waiting?"

Adi shrugged. "That we do not know, so we shall travel cautiously."

"What intrigued you about the other's body?"

Adi held up the broken blade. "It is an exceedingly poor blade that breaks when it enters the body. This one did." He brushed blood off the broken end. "And this, where it broke, flakes and crumbles to the touch. No one carries a blade to be used only once."

"How did he die, then?"

"Our blades are better." He scanned the road ahead and behind. "I can't convince your Highness to return home, can I?"

Danika shook her head.

Adi shrugged again, gave instructions to his men, and mounted his charger. "I suspected not and had to ask."

"Memory tells me it is not much further to Nant."

"We'll be there around sunset, m'Lady, if we walk. Easily before if we trot. But I'd rather we move slowly and with caution than quickly and miss a serpent waiting to strike."

"You expect others?"

"I always expect others."

"Proceed as you wish, Lance Commander. I will do as you wish."

Adi raised his head to the heavens and rolled his eyes from one horizon to the next. "Then will my Queen for pity's sake ride in the center of her escort and not in front where every breeze causes my heart to become a stone in my chest?"

Danika laughed. "Yes, Lance Commander Adi, I will do as you wish."

Adi nodded and smiled broadly, happy to once again command all in his surround. "Thank you, my Queen. Thank you."

CHAPTER 64

Nory turned around but the good man wasn't there.

Where was he?

Nory moved slowly so he could keep up.

Nory thought the good man could move well through the wood.

He couldn't move as good as Nory, though.

Grandmother Dire taught Nory well.

Nory moved fast, very fast, when there was need.

Sometimes he played games with the people in Nant. He waved to them when they started down a road and went far past them and waved to them again when they caught up.

Nory laughed at them.

Ha Ha Ha!

Most people laughed with Nory. "Nory is good in the woods," they would say.

Some people didn't laugh with Nory. Some people threw things at him.

Not food, though.

Bad things. Thomas threw hurting things and encouraged others to do the same.

Grandmother Dire told Nory, "You have to be careful, child. People don't understand you, how special you are." And she would hug Nory to her. "You are blessed in ways beyond their ken, so they fear you because it is easier for them to fear than to learn." She would kiss his head then. "Do you understand me, Nory? Do you know what Grandmother Dire is saying?"

Nory kissed her hands and hugged her. If he had bread he would offer her some. She always pushed his hands away. "You keep that for yourself, lad. I have enough for now and what I have for now is enough."

One time Nory came to Dire's cellar with a gash on his face. "Who did this, Nory? Who did this to you?"

Nory signed a name.

"You stay here. I'll be back before sunset."

When she returned she carried a basket of eggs. "You'll not be bothered by that one again, lad." She gave him the basket. "Eat your fill and leave a few for me. That's a good lad." He took the basket. Dire turned to her workbench and chuckled under her breath. "You get this old and people fear you simply because you survived this long. Ha!"

Where was the good man?

It didn't matter. Nory had to get the food to his friend the bear.

Before he continued, Nory faced northeast, closed his eyes, and shivered slightly.

There would be cold soon. Not the cold of night. The cold of wind, the cold of rain.

Nory could always tell.

He would let Grandmother Dire know in case there was something she needed to lift off her cellar floor.

This rain had been coming for a while, Nory knew. It gathered in skies far north and east of Nant, waiting, as if something held it back until ready.

Nory knew.

He would feed his friend the bear and then tell Grandmother Dire to get her things off the floor.

And he would introduce her to his friend, the bear.

That would be nice.

Baron Bassys told his men to break up; some were to continue on to Nant, a few select individuals - some landholders, others lesser nobles in his surround - were to meet him at The Cloisters, others were to watch the roads to and from; he expected Soka to bring him a bargaining chip in case his quest for the Queen failed.

The Baron rode alone into the Jannenite camp and several swords greeted him, some appearing from behind trees as he passed, some meeting him before he got to the camp proper, some waiting at his arrival.

"Does anyone here speak my language?"

One Jannenite came forward. "What is your business here?" Some of the other Jannenites moved back into the forest, some surrounded the Baron.

"Do you know who I am?"

The Jannenite smiled strong white teeth through a thick black beard. "You are a heavily perfumed and garishly clothed infidel. Do I need to know more?"

"I am Baron Bassys. Is the one called Korol here?"

"Ah, yes. Baron Bassys. Korol has mentioned you. He plays games in Nant not far to the north." He spoke something in his own language. The men around Bassys chuckled.

"What has Korol told you?"

"We are to aid you in your schemes against your King. In exchange, your people will help us find the one we seek." Again he spoke in a foreign tongue to his men. "What of that? Have you found him? Do you have news for us of him?"

The Baron stayed on his mount, hands loosely on his reins, and looked down at those around him. He neither smiled nor frowned. "No news yet, but soon. It is rumored there's a priest in Nant who's not a priest at all. At least not the priest I sent to do my work in Nant. Perhaps he is your man."

The white teeth nodded in the thick black beard. "Yes. Korol knows of this man. You speak the truth so far. What do you want of us?"

Bassys looked around. "Is this all of you?"

"All save one. We also hear rumors. He is off to determine their truth."

"What rumors?"

The man spoke to the others surrounding Bassys. They debated, considered for a few minutes, then most nodded, the others shrugged noncommittal assent. "The Alan Prince Orel is about in your kingdom. The man who determines the rumors' truth comes to us from Prince Orel's land. If the Prince is here, he will ask him to join us. If he doesn't find him, he will make mischief and spread fear as he returns."

The Baron leaned on his pommel. "Prince Orel is in the kingdom? On what business?"

"The Alans seek trade with the West. Through King Gaumand's empire is the most direct route. Prince Orel seeks safe passage through your King's land."

Bassys sat back. "This is an interesting turn of events. But this man hasn't returned?"

The Jannenite shook his head.

"When is he expected."

"When Allah allows."

"Did Korol tell you to help me kidnap Queen Danika?"

The Jannenite frowned and shook his head.

"I sent a message some days ago. He said nothing?"

"No word came to us. You plan to kidnap your Queen to what end?"

"To ransom her, of course, but to ransom slyly, to gain favor and lands and prestige." The Baron's eyes glazed as he spoke. "Eventually to gain control of the empire and become king. Why else would anyone do such a thing?"

The Jannenite touched his forehead, his chest, and bowed. "Why else."

Bassys looked to the sky then back at the Jannenite. "We have had wonderfully clear nights for the entire summer. Today of all days there're clouds."

The Jannenite shrugged and ignored the sky, kept his eyes on Bassys. "They are a fascination to us. We seldom have clouds in our lands."

Bassys dismounted, took a ring from his left little finger, and held it out to the Jannenite. "Take this. Go south with your men and you'll meet my guard. Show them that ring and tell them you will help them find Queen Danika."

The Jannenite reached for the token.

Bassys pulled it back. "You will have to kill all those who escort her. They may be a formidable force."

The Jannenite's knife came out faster than Bassys could follow. The man swirled into Bassys and put the knife at his throat. "Not a concern."

Bassys laughed as the Jannenite put his blade away. "Another of my men, Soka, will arrive with the royal daughters. Insurance, shall we say."

The Jannenite nodded, turned, and spoke in his own tongue to his men. They took down their camp as Bassys headed north to The Cloisters.

SECTION XI
LAMP OF DARKNESS

CHAPTER 65

Taitano walked up to the table where Zevke, Saida, Slewe, and Tardiff sat and reached over them to Donam's grimoire. "May I see that?"

All sat back. Slewe stammered, "My Lord Deputy, we...I..."

Tardiff stood, whirled, and reached for his sword. "What evil have you brought to my village?"

Taitano lifted his hands, spread them wide, and stepped back. "Easy Undersheriff. I seek as many answers as you in these things."

Zevke glanced at Saida. She nodded. "Can you read Latin or Greek?"

"A little. Enough to get by."

Zevke handed him the book. "Then read what you can of the first two columns. Let's learn how well I read the Hebrew."

Taitano pulled over a chair. The five of them leaned forward. Their eyes went from Taitano's silently moving lips to his finger's movement on the page.

He turned pages, closed his eyes in concentration, mouthed

some words, shook his head, mouthed some other words, opened his eyes and continued until he hit the next difficult passage.

At the third passage, Slewe rose. Zevke looked up. "Not interested?"

"Thirsty."

Taitano kept his eyes on the book. "And some of that delicious rye and a dollop of mustard, if you have it."

Slewe went into the kitchen.

Saida leaned into her husband. "Slewe didn't ask who's paying?"

Zevke put a finger to his lips. "Shh."

An hour and more than a few cups later Taitano closed Donam's grimoire, sat back, and rubbed his tired eyes. "I had not thought such things possible. These are the tales used to frighten children. Worse. By all that is holy..."

Zevke stared into his half-empty cup. "This is Donam's book. Not something taken from another for evidence's sake?"

Taitano nodded.

Tardiff leaned back and rested his hand on the hilt of his sword. "And where do you stand on this? You're his deputy."

Taitano snorted. "Not any longer. In fact, I may be an accomplice in his murder."

Tardiff's eyes went wide. "Donam's dead?"

"Someone in dark robes, like a priest I thought, sent two arbalest bolts into him as he prepared to gut me."

"What crime had you committed?"

Taitano laughed. "I denied him and his lord a sacrifice."

Tardiff relaxed his grip. "Speak plainly, can you? Do you say the King has a hand in these things?"

Taitano shook his head and drained his cup before answering. "The woman you found dead and mutilated in the wood? She was my lover. She was to be sacrificed at the ceremony described in this book." He looked out the window at the fading light. "Tonight. Or tomorrow night, perhaps."

"You said his lord. Do you mean the King?"

Taitano shook his head again. "Baron Bassys."

Saida gently touched his arm. "You said she was your lover? I sorrow for your loss."

"Thank you. Because she and I shared a bed, she could no longer be a sacrifice. Because she could no longer serve as a sacrifice, she was to be killed anyway, quietly and where no one could see." Taitano chuckled, broke off a piece of rye, lifted it to his nose and inhaled the heady scent. "I was to be one of her murderers. No reason was given, only some vague statements about betraying the kingdom, which was impossible. What can a kitchen girl know of empires? When I heard the Baron's order, I told her and together we planned her escape."

Zevke had listened quietly to this point. "But why north of Melia? She could have traveled south or east and been out of the Empire or at least out of his provides in a day."

Taitano answered while he chewed. "She knew she had family here. She didn't know much, only some. She was kidnapped or abducted or sold to one of the Baron's agents, she wasn't sure of the details."

Tardiff took a deep breath. His face blanched. No one at the table noticed.

"We outfitted her with provisions, a horse, and a monk's hood and robe to hide her shape. We arranged to meet here. Donam asked all of us what became of her when her time had come, and believing Donam a good man, I told him a little of our story." He snorted and shoved a thick piece of rye into his mouth. "The next I know, we are riding here for reasons Donam wouldn't share." He pushed the grimoire away from him. "Now we know all too well."

Slewe gathered empty cups. "And now?"

"I don't know for you. For me, I avenge my woman's death."

Tardiff offered Taitano his hand. "We are old soldiers, you and I, but I am with you if you'll accept my sword at your side."

Slewe cleared the table. "What an innkeeper can do, I'll do."

Zevke reached across the table and took Saida's hand. "And a baker and his wife, also."

Taitano rose. "The circus holds a key to much of this."

And in the center of town, drumming began.

~

Aldous and Galos dropped their masks and embraced each other. Tears flowed from their eyes and turned their fine silk scarves into wet rags.

Aldous held him arm's length away and pulled him into an embrace again. "Brother. Beloved brother. I searched and searched, not knowing if you still lived. I all but gave up hope of finding any Galatians let alone my blood until I came to Nant some weeks back. I saw workings of Mehtar knowledge but no Arabs to be seen. It had to be a brother knight among the townsfolk."

Galos embraced his brother again. "You took the cold-smelting powders."

"Aye, and put them to good use in the Jannenite camp south of here."

Haasel and Julia held back until Haasel interrupted their reverie. "Why come as Forgeron, in disguise?"

"Ah, Lady Potter. Because disguise is one of the Galatian arts."

Galos continued. "To learn of the adversary. Or simply not be known."

"Why wouldn't you let me feel you when you first came to Nant?"

Aldous removed his hood and undid his scarf. "Your hand, Lady Potter?"

She held it out to him.

He took it gently and guided it to his missing ear. "For this reason, m'Lady. Forgeron's hat hid such a mark. Your hands would have felt it immediately and known me forever after. I couldn't have that. Not then, anyway." He placed Haasel's hand in Galos'.

Julia's eyes went from one's face to the other's. "You two are brothers, not just brother knights."

They nodded almost in unison. "Yes. We were called to the Crusades long ago."

"Why didn't you return home?"

Galos spoke first. "I had no reason to return and every reason not to. I became a prisoner of the Mehtars but they knew honor and treated me as a respected adversary. But the Jannenites lived and hunted us. The Mehtars let me go rather than make enemies of the Jannenites, which shows how feared they were. My last encounter with them left me the severely wounded victor, as did the one previous. For the first and if not for the kindness of a Mehtar woman, I would be dead long ago. For the second, Father Verrett found and brought me back to health." Galos closed his eyes and sighed, deep and from the belly. "I repaid the Mehtar woman with a child, a daughter, and would have stayed with them except the Jannenites found me again and I had to flee. For Father Verrett, I became Nant's charcoal burner and kept it as safe as I could." He looked at his brother. "Until now, it seems."

Haasel's canted her ears towards the cellar's briar-covered opening. Aldous listened quietly to his brother's tale and took up the story when his brother finished. "The church betrayed us into Jannenite hands and our last stronghold was overwhelmed. I returned that night wounded and before reaching the garrison saw them swarming like flies on the dead. I rode forward into a nest of Mehtars and realized there was no escape. I helped one rider escape. To warn our other garrisons of the attack. What became of him I don't know. But as Galos says, I could not return. I had a wife and child waiting, but would not put them at risk, so I wandered and offered my services where and when I could. I hoped to find other Galatians." He rested a hand on Galos' shoulder. "So far, just one."

Julia interrupted them. "But you two are not the last. Another survived. You know him, Galos. Father Baillot whose given name is Ioan."

Aldous exclaimed, "Ioan?"

"So he said, and at a time he would not lie, I think. He studied to be one such as you."

Galos and Aldous stared wide-eyed at each other.

Haasel moved towards the cellar's opening and canted her head first left then right.

Aldous went to Julia's side. "You are sure of this? How do you know? What is your - " He stopped. "The pike."

Galos nodded. "Yes, I wondered where Nory got it. But that would be where Baillot left it."

"Or dropped it."

Julia continued. "He..." She looked away.

Aldous rubbed her back. "Come, girl. There's no shame among us."

"He told me when we bedded each other. When he confessed his love and asked me to flee Nant with him, to make a life anew in some foreign land."

A few of Haasel's bulbs felt free of Galos' cowl. Aldous came over the lifted them. "Are these what I think, Brother?"

"A challenge to make, but Haasel's good hands did the trick."

"May I?"

Galos handed him the string. He'd painted a white stripe on five of them.

Aldous held them to the light. "Five by five, brother?"

Galos nodded. "Five by five."

Haasel, still at the vine covered opening, waved them forward.

Galos placed a hand on her sleeve. "Something?"

Aldous joined them. "Is it Nory? I expected him to be here before me. He led me a merry chase through the wood. I did my best to keep up, but his woodcraft left me far behind. He carried some roots and a pigeon I killed. Seemed he needed food for someone. I thought he'd bring them here."

Haasel shook her head quickly. "Shh."

Galos whispered, "No, he hasn't appeared since we gathered."

"I hope he is well. He's a good lad."

"Shh!" Haasel put an ear to the vines. "Listen. Thunder? No, too steady. There's a pattern."

Aldous listened. "Someone in The Cloisters proper?"

Galos shook his head. "We would hear it from the tunnel, not the wood."

Haasel straightened up. "It is a drum. From Nant. I've heard such before. It is from the circus."

CHAPTER 66

Eric trotted after Buco's barks. He knew the dog travelled faster than he but move any faster and his torch would go out. With each bark, an answering bear's grunt. Buco trotted with the scent of his packmate strong in his nostrils, his nose directing his steps. Eric wasn't so fortunate. He detected no scents, not even Buco, until one turn brought the heavy musk of bear scat to him.

"Buco! Come!"

A deep voice answered out of the darkness. "Who's that? Who are you?"

Eric stopped short. Could he have heard correctly? Buco still barked, a bear still grunted. These tunnels were haunted. Buco could not speak, what kind of creature could grunt like a bear and speak like a man?

The voice boomed at him again. "Answer me!"

Buco's barks stopped. He heard the dog yip and whine. The bear grunted and groaned.

"I said answer me!"

Eric stood still. "What manner of caves are these?"

"I hear you! Where are you?"

The voice echoed through the tunnel. Eric didn't know which direction it came from.

"Buco! Come!"

The big dog barked. The bear grunted.

Whoever spoke bellowed. The earthen walls shook. "I will find you!"

The voice echoed less. Whoever spoke, they approached, Eric still unsure of the direction.

Eric took a step towards the dog's barks. "Buco!"

A heavy hand lifted him by his shoulder. "Got you."

Eric looked over his shoulder and saw a gigantic monster staring back. "What are you? Let go of me." He brought his torch toward the creature. A bull's head, massive chest and arms, and hair covered legs ending in hoofed feet.

"Get me out of here first, then maybe after if I have no more need of you."

Eric raised his torch. The bull's eyes were white, no pupils showed. Nor did the creature follow the movement of Eric's torch. "Let me go before I - "

The creature gave a deep voiced laugh. "Ha. Small man. What are you, a boy? I have you and I will use you until I'm done with you. Understand?"

"Buco!"

"Call all you want, child. The more to lead me out, the better."

Eric touched the torch's flames to the creature's hand holding him.

The beast bellowed. It dropped him and clutched its hand in the other.

Buco's barks neared. The bear's grunts followed close behind.

The creature swung its arm in front of itself. His fist struck the tunnel wall with enough force to shake dirt from the foundation. "I will find you, bastard child, and I will end you!"

Eyes glowed in the darkness behind the creature.

Buco growled. His hackles rose in the dim light of Eric's torch. "Buco, stay back."

The creature turned, its arms reaching.

Buco snarled. A lumbering grunt came up behind him and turned into a roar. A bear appeared, raised itself up on its hind legs and came forward.

The creature stopped reaching. "Bron?"

Bron came forward on the creature's right. Buco came on the creature's left.

One of Bron's great paws slashed across the creature's bull head and knocked it clear.

Eric pulled back. "A man? You're a man wearing an animal's disguise?"

The man staggered into the tunnel wall from the impact. "Ah, foolish beast. You think you can hurt the mighty Dobrogost? Do you not remember how I blinded you as a cub? You think I can do less now?"

Buco lunged and bit deep into the big man's thigh.

The giant screamed and kicked.

Buco yelped and went back against a wall.

Bron bellowed and slashed at Dobrogost. Deep wounds opened on his chest and blood flowed freely.

Dobrogost got his arms around the bear and lifted.

The bear bellowed and sunk its teeth into the giant's neck.

Buco came forward again, this time taking a leg from behind. He bit through the giant's hamstring and pulled the twitching muscle free of its surrounding flesh.

The giant screamed. He clamped his jaws on the bear's nose.

The bear shrieked.

Eric jumped up and brought the end of his torch down square on the giant's skull.

The giant loosed Bron's nose and freed, Bron bit through the giant's throat.

The giant's hands let go of the bear. He dropped to his knees, his hands went to his throat. Blood spurted through his fingers. He fell forward, twitched, and then moved no more.

Buco limped over to Eric. "You okay, boy? You hurt?"

Buco whimpered and nuzzled Eric's hand.

Eric sat on the ground. "It's okay, Buco. I'm here. I've got you." The big dog lay down beside him and rolled onto its side. Its breathing came heavy and labored.

Eric inspected the dog for wounds. He ran his hands over Buco's fur, head, jaw, legs, sides, back and back to the big dog's side. Buco licked Eric's face. He smelt blood.

The bear lay down beside his denmate and cooed as if awaiting its mother's milk.

Eric hesitated, then patted the bear's head. "You are Bron?"

The bear raised its head.

Buco sighed and breathed his last.

Eric and Bron wailed their grief.

The drum thundered. The deep, booming voice of each strike vibrated townsfolk to their souls as they gathered under moonless, clouding skies.

Korol sat alone behind the main curtain on the stage. The single-headed drum filled his lap like a grinding wheel. Each beat sounded like a demon bellowing in the night.

Circe climbed the stairs behind him and he turned at the sound of her steps. He stared but kept the drum's driving rhythm steady. Circe spread her arms and paraded before him. He shook his head slightly and continued to stare.

Circe laughed. "You like?"

A thousand gleaming jewels covered her robe, woven of such fine gold and purple cloth it belonged more on a throne than a circus performer's frame. When she spread her arms the sleeves billowed revealing exquisitely stitched images of naked men and women in every kind of posture of desire and lust.

"Your mouth hangs open, Jester."

"I've not seen its like in all my travels."

"Thank you. The gift of a bey who favored me over his wife. Until she found out. She came in while I wore this for him. He gave me enough time to gather a few things - my daughter one of them - and flee."

"I didn't know you had a daughter."

Circe laughed at him. "Diana. In front of you all this time. You may be a Jannenite but you're not an observant one."

"I paid no attention."

"Such can get you killed."

"Where is our giant, Dobrogost? He's first to perform tonight, isn't he?"

Circe peered out of the curtain. "You drum well. People gather. I've not seen him since he went to see all was as it should be at the ruins. I expected him back well before this. Who will be our bull if he's not here?"

"I have neither the size nor the stomach for it. What shall we do?"

Circe held up a finger, went behind the stage for a moment, and returned. "Diana will offer the crowd some wine - "

"Your wine?"

Circe smiled. "Yes, our wine. A fine taste masking a touch of monkshood and belladona with some love parsley and wormwood for good measure. A few swallows and they'll believe they are flying. That's when we lead them to the ruins and into Dobrogost's arms. For those who need more," she lifted a small stoppered cup from the folds of her dress, "a chrism of oil and balsam. But those whom it touches will see it as witch's blood and know they are cursed by the First One,

Ahura Maternus, and beg us to fly them to safety, to his embrace."

"What if there's a problem?"

She took another cup from another fold, opened it, and swirled a long nailed finger in its contents. "Then this. One scrape of the nail is all that's needed. They'll fall and die soon after." She peered out the curtain again. "Do you know Dobrogost's opening? How he tells of strange places and things?"

Korol nodded.

"Then you lead our performance tonight. Keep them engaged until the wine takes hold. Tell that story you told me. Make it wondrous. Move about when you tell it. Look at people in the crowd. Individuals, but not always the same ones. Nod as you speak until you notice them nodding with you then smile graciously and move on to the next." She pulled the drum from him. "Go now. I'll drum until you're centered on the stage." She beat the drum as she walked offstage. "Diana!" she called. "The wine!"

Savage screams came from the tunnel. A roaring. A deep voice bellowed unintelligible words, more sounds of rage and pain. Another voice, young, hollering, moving quickly. A growling so fierce Haasel moved into Galos' arms.

A moment of silence then an unholy wailing, human and animal mixed and in pain, torment. Galos moved Haasel behind him and away from the tunnel entrance.

Aldous' eyes went from the tunnel to his brother and back. "Holy Mother, I've not heard suffering like that since our brothers fell in Jerusalem."

Julia, closest to the tunnel, turned to it. "It is my son.

Something comes to take his spirit, to burn him so he may never rest. She ran into the tunnel before Aldous could stop her.

"Quick. A torch. I'll follow."

Galos pulled the one lit on the wall. "How will she see? There's no torch light to guide her."

Haasel shook her head. "She still suffers from the roots she ate and believes she can see in the dark."

K orol parted the curtains, threw some smoke pellets on stage and tumbled into its center. The audience oohed and applauded as he rose up in the torchlights as if from nowhere. He snapped his head and his hat's bells jingled. He smiled at a little girl held in a man's arms. "Do you know how to juggle?"

She hid her face in the man's thick neck. The man and the woman beside him laughed. "Because I don't and can use some help."

Circe hissed from offstage, "Tell them to drink the wine."

Korol looked into the crowd and saw Diana with a pitcher in her arms and cups dangling from her belt. He blinked and looked at her again. She wore hideous makeup; her face the color of the night and a sunrise painted on her brow so its rays came down her cheeks and nose. Her eyes were red and it seemed snakes writhed in her hair. Her breasts were barely hidden by a necklace of small animal skulls, her lips were colored purple with beet juice and she sported fangs and tusks.

She laughed each time someone started at her appearance, offered them one of her cups, filled it, and carried on. Once she saw him looking and winked in approval. "Tell him to tell you a story. He tells good stories."

Korol made children laugh at his failed attempts to juggle

followed by amazing displays of skill and finesse. Adults called out, "A story! Tell us a story!"

Circe spoke from behind the curtain. "Start as Dobrogost does. He'll be here soon and do his part, I'm sure."

Korol noticed four men and a woman clustered together and off to the side of the audience. One he recognized as Tardiff the Bellman and the only local authority in Nant. Another was Taitano, the sheriff's deputy. The other three were new to him.

Korol gazed out over the audience. "Ladies and gentlemen. Nobles and Freemen, all you who are wise and wonderful enough to join us, listen now and listen well. I have traveled to lands where things are not as they seem, not as they are here in the noble but humble village of Nant. No, no, no. I have seen people with eyes in their shoulders!" He shaped his index fingers and thumbs into "O"s and moved them from his eyes to his shoulder blades.

The audience oohed and ahhed.

Diana continued moving through the crowd and made sure as many as were willing partook, suggested to those enjoying the wine to encourage their friends to sample a cup, and soon all but the group with Taitano and Tardiff swayed with Korol as he moved back and forth across the stage.

The short, fat one - the innkeeper? - leaned into Tardiff and said something.

Tardiff tapped Diana on her arm when she went to refill her pitcher. They spoke. Diana shrugged and shook her head. She went behind the wagons. Circe spoke through the curtains to him. "Korol, do you know if Dobrogost paid a tax for serving wine?"

"In Abarimon, the feet of people turn backwards so they must walk into their pasts continuously." He walked backwards until he got to the curtain. "I don't know."

"The Bellman threatens to close us down because we have not."

He heard Diana. "There are too many and they've already had too much. Stop us now and he'll have a mob to contend with. Finish your act, Jester."

She appeared a moment later with more cups and a fresh pitcher of drugged wine.

Korol walked towards the front of the stage. "Imagine being cursed to never know their future." He did a twisting handstand and landed on his feet but facing the curtain, not the audience. "Oh! Where did you all go?" He turned back to the audience and everyone except Saida, Zevke, Tardiff, Taitano, and Slewe laughed. "The Scyritae have no nostrils and the Astomi have no mouths! How cursed they are not to have listened and spoken on our own good behalf!" He covered his nose and mouth as he spoke.

Circe called from behind the curtain. "Now."

Korol bowed. "And now the beautiful Circe, yes, she who beguiled the ancients with her magic. One touch and you're hers forever. One kiss and you'll believe you're capable of flight! Follow her if you dare!"

Circe came out from around the wagons and embraced both men and women. Diana stood by Taitano and his group and poured them cups.

The woman with them sniffed hers and knocked the cups from the others' hands. "Poison! She uses poisons to entrance you!"

Circe raced through the crowd, passionately kissing anyone she neared. She grabbed their hands and rubbed her flesh. Men's heads she took between her breasts and pressed into their throats until their tongues came out and licked her. Women she pulled into her face and rubbed with her cheeks and hands.

And when she neared the woman who knocked cups from the others' hands, she stuck out her finger and scratched her face.

Saida's hand covered her scratch. Her eyes rolled back in her head. She fell.

Taitano and Tardiff reached for Circe.

Zevke hollered, "Don't touch her. Her skin is poisoned."

Circe yelled, "Korol, lead them to the ruins! Diana, prepare the firepots." She chased Taitano, Tardiff, Slewe, and Zevke through the crowd, a bizarre child playing an even more bizarre game of tag.

Taitano, Slewe, and Tardiff grabbed those already entranced and pushed them at her to block her. Zevke lifted Saida and carried her to the tavern. When they saw their friends safe, one by one they followed.

Korol danced through the crowd like a crazed dog flocking sheep. "Come, gentle souls! Come and have your dreams fulfilled, your wishes realized, your hopes made manifest! Come! Come!" The crowd, able to move but unable to resist, followed. Circe ran amongst them rubbing herself against any who showed signs of waking from her spell.

Diana came out of a wagon with several lantern-like devices hung from her arms. She ran from cottage to cottage and set one next to each.

CHAPTER 67

Prince Orel joked with his captains when a lead rider motioned for a stop and pointed far down the road ahead. Orel blinked and squinted. Just at the edge of his vision, how far away he couldn't guess, a faint light danced along the road, either a firefly gone mad or one of his grandfather's jinn sent to torment him.

He sent two riders ahead with orders to learn, not harm. They returned a few minutes later. "Two sisters, Prince, driving a poor man's wagon pulled by one sorry, old horse. They were to take offal from their father's farm to the next village and got lost, they claim, and now look for their way home."

Orel looked to his captains. "Lost and on a darkened road this time of night? Are they witches or fools?"

His captains chuckled.

"Let's see which they be." He kicked his horse and his men followed.

Still some distance from them he announced himself. "Hello, I am Prince Orel. May I present myself?"

Marianne pinched the dozing Ouive to wakefulness. "Remember, I do the talking."

Ouive nodded and fell back asleep.

Marianne waited until the prince was beside her. "We mean no harm, Lord Prince. We are lost and don't know our way home."

The prince's captains surrounded the wagon. He lifted a handkerchief from his sleeve, sneezed into it, and kept it there while he talked. "Who are you? What village do you come from?"

Marianne looked him straight in the eye. "I am Moria. This is my sister, Olive." She nudged Olive. Olive smiled without opening her eyes. "We left our father's farm in Bass not long ago, I thought, but the woods betrayed us and now I don't know where I'm going."

"Where were you heading?"

"Turo."

Orel sat back in his saddle. "I don't know of Bass and you are far from Turo. May I offer you travel with us until we can see you safely on your way?"

Marianne glanced sidelong at the prince's captains around their wagon but kept her face towards the prince. "That is most gracious, Good Prince. Where are you heading?"

"That I cannot say. Let us say I'm doing a favor in hopes of receiving a favor. But I can promise you no harm and safe arrival to either your father's land or Melia, whichever you choose."

"You are gracious to us and I thank you, good prince."

Orel snapped his fingers. A rider came up. "Give me your purse."

The rider handed over a jingling sack.

"How much are your goods worth? Name your price."

Marianne shrugged. "I don't know, Prince. Our father sets the price and we deliver where he wishes."

Orel nodded. He opened the sack and emptied ten gold pieces

into his other hand. "Will this cover the price of your goods and carriage?"

Marianne kept her eyes steady on him. "What do you propose, Prince."

Orel stared at her and laughed. "Did your father teach you to bargain so well? I propose to dispose of your goods because their stench weakens me and my men. I will have your wagon cleaned, if possible." He dropped two more coins into his palm. "And offer you and your sister baths and fresh clothes, if I may."

Marianne looked around at the dark-colored faces. Ouive's eyes opened. "A bath? Oh, sister, a bath."

Marianne pulled Ouive in close. "Quiet, sister." She looked at Orel. "And what else do you have planned for us?"

"On my honor as a Prince of the Alan Empire, nothing more." He held up a finger. "Except your horse is tired. Some good feed and water for her. And another horse to pull your wagon. She's old and done enough work in her lifetime."

Marianne kept her eyes on Orel as he spoke and said nothing.

Orel added. "No harm will come to her. She'll follow your wagon on a lead."

Marianne nodded. She held Ouive close and considered. "A bath and fresh clothing would be nice."

The horses shifted their weight. The riders' saddles creaked. The men whispered in strange tongues. Marianne sat in silence.

"Mistress Moria?"

She nodded.

Orel turned to one of his captains. "See what I've offered is done."

The captain leaned into him and spoke softly. "She does not behave like a peasant's daughter, O'Prince."

Orel nodded and answered in Alanian. "And until we know more, it is best she believes we think her so." He raised his voice and spoke so Marianne and Ouive could understand, "The first man to rest his eyes on them loses them."

Orel dismounted and offered his hand to help Marianne down. She accepted. He lifted Ouive from the wagon seat and set her on her feet. She mumbled and staggered into Marianne, who grabbed her and held her close.

Orel called back to his men. "We camp here, but not long. Let us see our guests fed and rested, then we continue at a double pace until our mission is done."

~

King Gaumand sent two forest runners into Nant while he and his men waited a short distance away on the North Road. They rode double-time quick and the king hoped Prince Orel had received his message and complied.

According to his counselors, the Prince had.

His runners returned with a strange report. "There is no one in the village, my Lord, and the air smells of strange oils, like the village is smoked but not burned."

Gaumand nodded. "Interesting villages on the borders of my kingdom." He prodded his charger and everyone followed.

They entered Nant at a walk, each rider held a comforting hand on his horse's mane so they rode in silence. A Lance Captain came up beside him and spoke softly. "My King, the night is overcast. We can mount torches on our lances to light our way."

"Tonight is a new moon and would be dark regardless."

Other horses approached, first known by their whinnies and the tromp of their hooves. They made no attempt to move quietly.

A general leaned towards the king. "My King?"

"Take a quarter and come up behind them. Do the same for their flanks. The rest, hold where we are. They make no attempt at stealth. Let us be kind but cautious. Perhaps they can tell us what's happened here."

Another rider pointed to the Red Fox. "A light, Sir."

Horses and riders appeared as a black mass as they turned the road to Nant's center. They spoke amongst themselves, not hiding their voices, and Gaumand heard laughter among them.

He turned his head to his men. "Hold."

The other riders entered the town center and Gaumand pulled the reins of his charger. The horse snorted and stomped a hoof.

The other riders and their horses stilled. Torches lit. A voice called out, "Who goes there?"

Gaumand motioned his charger forward and he felt his lancers and bowmen tense. "We are the King. I'll ask you the same."

The far horses grew restless. Hushed voices came across the center to him. A single rider stepped forward. "I am Yezides, sergeant-at-arms in Baron Bassys' service. May I approach the King?"

"Do so."

Yezides approached. The Baron's other men held back.

Gaumand spoke loudly enough to be heard across the town center. "Welcome, Yezides. What news do you bring me of my friend, the Baron?" As Yezides drew closer, the King spoke quietly. "I got your message, Yezides, but have not seen the Queen en route. What do you know of her? And what happened here? The town is empty save a lone light in a lone tavern?"

"The Baron seeks to capture the Queen and has sent mercenaries to take her and humiliate Commander Adi in the process with hopes of being granted Adi's lands." Yezides raised his voice. "The Baron sends greetings to your Highness and Queen Danika." The Baron's men heard and hurrahed approval.

Yezides lowered his voice again. "And if not the Queen, your royal daughters. As for the townsfolk, we passed them south towards some ruins. What the Baron plans there, I'm not sure, except he's in league with some assassins and seeks to control Nant to work some witchcraft, I believe."

King Gaumand nodded. "Pity he's not a right man. Such planners can prosper a kingdom much." He pointed to two forward commanders. "You and you, on either side. Yezides, with me." He nudged his horse and the four marched to the Baron's men. "Greetings, good men of Melia."

They replied almost as one, "Long Live King Gaumand."

Gaumand turned to Yezides. "Do any of them know of the Baron's plans?"

"I doubt it, my Lord. He told us we were on a rescue mission, that she had been kidnapped by Adi and we were to return her to you. I believe those faithful to his plans are with him at the ruins south of Nant."

"The Cloisters? An ancient place. What does he plan there?"

Taitano left the Red Fox by the side door. He stayed in the darkness of the night and moved silently to the town well where he listened to the last comments made. "I can answer that, my King."

Lancers and swordsmen advanced. Gaumand turned to the voice. "Wait. Who addresses me?"

"Taitano, my King."

"Taitano the Tracker? What are you doing here?" Gaumand's hand went to his sword. "Are you the Baron's man?"

Taitano held up empty hands. "Pray no, my King. Bassys didn't want me in his guard and passed me to Sheriff Donam as deputy. But I am still your man and have a tale to tell."

Gaumand looked back at Bassys' men. "Who here serves the King above all?"

Again the voices, almost in unison, "Hail King Gaumand."

He turned back to Yezides. "Can these men be trusted?"

"I've heard more questions of the Baron's mind than most would be comfortable asking, my King."

"Good." His gaze once again returned to Taitano. "Are there others with you?"

"There is one other who soldiered, but we are all old, my King, not fit for battle."

"Good, you can advise us, then. Get them horses. Yezides, lead us to the Cloisters."

Bassys entered The Cloisters under a lowering sky. Owls hooted and bats flapped in the darkness. Bassys smiled. His men had prepared well and set up an orange and black striped tent for him to use as a changing room outside the walls and near the main entrance. A single lamp lit the tent's interior. Not far away he heard drunken revelers approaching. Torches lit The Cloisters interior.

"That will be Nant. Dobrogost has done me well."

A naked man approached, his body tattooed with strange animal designs. Half-human-half-beast creatures frolicked on his stomach and back, up and down his legs and arms. Only his neck, hands, and face were free of colorings. He reached for The Baron's reins. "My Lord."

Bassys got down and handed him the reins. "Where is our first sacrifice?"

"Someone has left us a wonderful, fattened donkey. She'll burn nicely on Lord Ahura Maternus' altar."

"One beast? Dobrogost was to find the kitchen maid. She was to be tonight's offering, one of many to be sure, but our special guest."

The man shrugged. "No one's explored the cells yet, my Lord. The donkey is all we've found."

The Baron waved him away, entered his tent, and stood in front of a gold trimmed, blue chest. It rested in a burgundy-clothed cradle, itself supported by jeweled, polished silver legs, each leg shaped after a different animal: lion, bull, eagle, dog. The Baron ran his hand over the crown of the chest, breathed deeply, and opened it.

The villagers swarmed past the Baron's tent and into the Cloisters led by Circe. He parted the tent opening and called her to him. "Where is Dobrogost? Where is Korol?"

"Dobrogost we thought was here. He didn't appear for tonight's performance. Korol returned to Nant hoping to fulfill his mission."

"Good. Best be done with him and his brothers." Bassys watched the villagers stagger into the Cloisters, some falling over each other and coupling with whoever fell with them regardless of the pairing. "Dobrogost's potions work well. Better than I hoped. And you?"

Circe lifted her arms to him. "Would you like a taste?"

He laughed. "No, thank you. Where is Diana?"

"She'll be along soon. Do you have need of her?"

Bassys turned and placed a reflecting glass on the tent post behind the chest. "Dobrogost left me one fat donkey. If our virgin exists, she is hidden in The Cloister's cells. If I can't find her, I will need another one who's pure."

Circe canted her head. "Diana?"

Bassys nodded as he removed his clothing.

"She is my daughter."

Bassys answered dismissively, "And it will be her honor to serve Our Lord Ahura Maternus."

Circe looked down at her poisoned fingernail. Most of the poison came off when she scratched the woman in Nant.

But there was still some. Perhaps enough.

She raised her hand and leapt at Bassys.

He caught her reflection, spun, and met her with a knife hidden in his shirt. The knife penetrated her belly. Its point protruded from her back and dripped blood in the lamplight. Her hands went to the Baron's, still holding the knife in her stomach. She looked down at the knife then up to his face and shook her head.

Baron Bassys twisted the knife and played it back and forth, his free arm supporting her so she wouldn't fall.

Her head fell back and her eyes closed. He lay her down.

"Well. I suppose you'll do as a sacrifice if we remove your finery and move the torches back a ways. The villagers won't mind. Nor will the nobles and landholders, don't you think?"

CHAPTER 68

Nory ducked under pine boughs and stood behind the tree's thick trunk facing into the labyrinth.

He sniffed.

His friend Bear waited inside.

He worried Bear would not wait for Nory to return with food.

Nory looked at the pigeon in his left and tubers in his right.

He dug them out of Byell's field on his way back.

Nory was careful.

He chose roots from a part in the rear where Byell's ducts didn't feed, nor was there any of the whitish powder his friend Simon warned him of.

Nory entered the labyrinth and grunted to his friend Bear.

But Bear didn't answer.

Nory grew sad.

What had happened to his friend?

He went outside again and took deep breaths.

No, Bear hadn't come out this way.

Nory listened and looked. Simon hadn't kept up.

Silly Simon, can't keep up with Nory.

Nory is very good in the woods.

His back and shoulders shivered. He looked to the northeast and smiled.

Soon, he knew. Soon.

He remembered the pigeon and tubers in his hands again.

He had to feed his friend Bear.

He went back into the labyrinth and grunted along the way.

Julia walked with one hand along the tunnel wall. Somewhere ahead she heard angels weeping, shrieking in pain of loss, and the grunting of a demon wanting grace. Her fingers moved over packed earth, roots, and foundational brickwork. The scent of moist earth surrounded her like a miasmatic perfume. She waved her free hand in front of her face from time to time and caught the scent of rotted flesh. Her child, perhaps?

Someone called from far back in the tunnel system. "Julia! Are you alright? Say something, Julia, so I can find you."

She looked back once but no lights showed there.

She hurried on, always in the direction of the smell of strengthening decay. The wailing had ceased. She couldn't hear it.

Her child waited for her to find him?

Her hands passed over a break in the wall. Something different.

A door?

"Hello?"

No answer.

She felt for a handle, a way in. "Who's in there? Is my child with you?"

Something stirred. Shuffling movement. But not near where she stood. A voice croaked, "Hello?"

She didn't recognize it. Certainly not her child. He wouldn't be able to talk yet.

Her head snapped back and she cackled. Her child wouldn't be able to talk ever! She cackled again.

She felt a handle. She turned it. She gagged.

Her hand covered her mouth and nose but too late. What little was left in her stomach found its way out and added to the stench.

She convulsed once, fell to her knees, and her stomach released itself again. Her hands fell into the puddle of her own juices. She shakily stood and wiped her hands on first the door then her skirt.

She whispered into the darkness, "Child?"

More stirrings. More shufflings. "Julia?"

The voice. More recognizable. But not here. Not with her child. Not near her bile.

She stepped out into the tunnel. "Thomas?"

She heard hinges creak. "Yes, yes. Sister Julia? You've come for me. To help me out of this prison. Where are you? You sound near. Where is your torch? What food did you bring me?"

Eric's sobs weakened. The bear gently placed a huge paw on his head and patted as if to tell Eric it was alright, it was better this way, they both lost a friend, time to move on.

Eric patted the bear's head in return. "I will not leave my friend here. Even in death, he is still my friend." He looked around but nothing came to mind.

The bear turned its head and grunted.

"Have an idea, do you?" Eric laughed at his own joke.

The bear, its head still turned away from him, grunted.

"Is that the way out?"

The bear nuzzled Buco's body, its nose going into the earth under the dead dog.

Tears filled Eric's eyes again. "You will carry my friend? I thank you."

The bear waited.

Eric rested his torch against the wall and dragged the huge dog onto the bear's back, resting it so it rocked but didn't fall as the bear moved. He tore straps from the giant's dress and tied Buco to the bear.

"Let us see if we can find our way out of here, friend Bear." He looked at the blood covered giant. "He can stay and rot with the devils for all I care."

The bear grunted.

"I agree. He can rot with all the devils he knew and those he didn't."

Eric lifted his torch high.

Dire covered her eyes and blinked in front of him.

"Your friend is blind. Poor thing."

"Grandmother Dire! What are you doing here? Can you help us find a way out?"

"Eric, Verduan's boy, yes? Is Julia down here with you? Nory? Anyone else close by?"

"Yes, Grandmother. Verduan's son. Only me and my new friend, Bear, I'm afraid. How did you find us?"

"It was I who blinded the giant. I fled from him at first, then sought to follow him and do him in." Her eyes adjusted to the torchlight, she looked at the giant's body on the ground between them. "You've done my work for me. Thank you."

"Did you know him?"

"I know he meant to kill me. I don't give people with such intent a second chance. What is your friend carrying?"

"My dog. Dead. From when the three of us battled this crea-ture." He pointed at the body. "Do you know a way out of here?"

"I sorrow for your loss. Beasts are better friends than men in most cases." She turned, one hand found and gathered up her hidden thread. "Come. Follow me."

Eric fell in behind her. "Come, Bear."

Bron grunted and shuffled after them.

CHAPTER 69

Queen Danika felt suffocated in a surround of soldiers and covered by a lowering sky. "Lance Commander Adi, how long until we reach Nant?"

"Not long, my Queen."

She kicked her horse and it trotted up beside his. "You have said 'Not long, my Queen,' for each of the five times I've asked, Lance Commander."

"And each time I answer, rest assured, my Queen, we are closer and I speak the truth, not long, my Queen."

She sat stiffly in her saddle. "You are enjoying this, Lance Commander."

A sharp crack came from the front of the column. A lead rider fell from his charger.

Adi circled his mount in front of Queen Danika. "Bowmen, find your marks. Lancers, forward. Swordsmen, protect the Queen."

Another lead rider jumped off his charger and looked to his comrade, he rose shakily and pushed his friend away. "I'm well, Commander."

Adi peered through the gloom. "Is he dead and doesn't know it? Bring him to me."

The second rider helped the first to his charger, handed him something from the ground, and the two trotted back to Adi's position with the Queen.

The fallen rider's armor had a dent, nothing more.

The second rider took something from his friend's shaking hand. "This felled him, Commander."

"A bolt without a head? What foolishness is this?"

The fallen rider brushed the dent in his armor and looked at his hand. "May we light a torch, Commander?"

Adi signaled a man. "Hold it low and covered. Let's not give them a clear target." Four men took a horse blanket and framed a low tent around the flame.

The rider took his glove off and handed it to Adi. "My Lord, isn't that the same powder as the assassin's blade?"

Adi sniffed, tasted, pulled back and spit. "It is." He peered back into the enveloping trees. "What game is this? Attacking with weapons that shatter and break before damage is done?"

The second rider turned his horse to retake his spot at the lead of the column. "Aye, but it is proof there are more of them, and how many we know not."

"Agreed." Adi handed the glove back to its owner. "Can you ride, man? Are you hurt?"

The man took the shaft from Adi's hand. "I owe this one's owner a favor." He turned to follow his partner. "I doubt I'll repay it properly, though."

Adi laughed. "Good man." He addressed his troops. "Swordsmen, bowmen. We know their weapons can't hurt us. They'll sting but nothing more. Be careful what you strike. They wear red and white. Find them. Flush them out. Bring at least one living to me, if he speaks our language. Otherwise do to him as he would do to us."

~

Bron followed with his nose to the ground, directed by smell and sound. Now and again he grunted and Eric patted the giant bear's head.

He raised his head and stopped, his nose up in the air, his mouth open, his cheeks puffing as he huffed air in and out.

Eric rubbed Bron's ears. "What is it, Bear?"

Dire whispered, "Shh. Put out your torch. Someone's approaching."

Eric dropped his torch to the ground and rolled it in the dirt. Its light died.

Bron grunted.

Dire hissed, "Quiet the bear."

A light filled an intersection ahead of them. Footsteps. Someone approached from a side. A black boot stepped around the corner. Black pants and cape came next followed by a torch held in a black glove at the end of a black sleeve. "No need to silence the bear, Grandmother."

Dire relaxed. "Simon. Who else is down here? Are you alone?" She looked at his right and left ears but his cowl covered both. "Which Simon are you?"

Simon removed his scarf and mask. "Aldous, the one-eared one, although never introduced as such, but I suspect you know me."

"You know there's another Galatian Knight in Nant?"

"Recently found. My brother, Galos."

Eric patted Bron's head. The bear continued huffing. "Galos my father's friend? The charcoal burner?"

"The very same."

Dire shook her head. "Two knights from an Order long gone and both in Nant. Pity no others survived."

The bear huffed again and walked past Aldous. Aldous moved

to let the beast pass. "I hear one other remains. I saw him once but didn't recognize him as such. Father Baillot."

Eric called after the bear. Bron paid no attention and continued on. "Father Baillot? He teaches Julia and me the wedding rites."

Dire and Aldous glanced at each other but said nothing. Aldous pointed after Bron. "Where is your friend going?"

Dire squinted as the bear faded into the dark. "That way, he's going out."

"To your workshop, Dire?"

She shook her head. "To The Cloisters proper."

Bassys looked around at the various things in his tent. "If Dobrogost will not attend, we will make a Dobrogost for them." He stuck his head out of the tent and called to a painted man hurrying past. "The giant's chests, bring them to me."

A moment later two more chests sat beside the first. Bassys opened each, shuffled around a bit, and *hmm*ed as he lifted out a headdress similar to the minotaur Dobrogost wore. He rummaged further and took out stoppered cups. He opened them, checked himself in the reflecting glass, and went to work.

Someone ruffled his tent flap. "Stay out! Don't enter! Are the villagers in The Cloisters proper?"

A weak voice. "Yes, Lord Baron."

"And my followers, in their places and ready?"

"Yes, Lord Baron."

"Let them drink, then. Bang the drum! Prepare for me!"

The weak voice left. A moment later the air shook with a steady throbbing. Bassys finished his preparations and looked out the tent flap. Corners of The Cloisters' main area glowed and crackled as fires were stoked. Sparks crept up into the sky, the clouds so heavy and thick the rising flames caressed their bellies. It seemed the very flames pulsed with the beating of the drum.

Bassys looked around. No one waited. Everyone was inside the main gate. He strapped on boots that drove his heels up and bent his knees. The boots themselves were unshorn, blackened bull hide ending in hooves.

He stepped out and donned the headdress. Two mouthpieces neared his lips as he tied it in place. He tested his walk. Good.

Baillot, Patreo, and Verduan stopped at the far end of the archway. They stayed behind the wall but the next ten or twelve steps to freedom would be in the open.

Bassys stood in the gate, put his lips to one mouthpiece, and blew. The headdress bellowed through a horn. Everyone turned.

Verduan froze. "What is that?"

Patreo and Baillot hazarded a look. All eyes inside The Cloisters' main were on Bassys.

He walked in, a ram's head covered his own, its horns rising over his head and curling back to his ears. Red coloring covered his body. The ram's hair hung to his waist. Tassels of different colors hung from his arms. A ram's head tattoo adorned his loins and belly so that his penis became the swaying tongue of the beast. Otherwise he was naked.

He paraded up the center aisle to the altar. His mouth took the other mouthpiece. "I am here to lead the Council."

Baillot came back down. "It is our opportunity for escape. Hurry."

Verduan peered over the wall. Naked bodies, men and women, all with animal masks. Two lesser horned beings handed them out to villagers, people Verduan knew, as they removed their clothing and tied the masks to their faces.

Verduan moaned. "We are doomed."

Patreo pulled him forward. "We are men and so are they. You saw them handing out and putting on masks. Do demons need masks to do evil? No, only men do. And many of those don't need masks to do evil at all."

Bassys turned to face the crowd when he reached the altar. "All must drink from the vats around you. Drink and you will be able to fly!" He clapped his hands with the rhythm of the drum. "Bring. Me. The. Sacrifice!"

A braying.

Patreo, crouched with the others behind the wall so not to be seen, stopped. "Geselda?" He peered over the wall. Geselda, a halo of thorns about her ears, fought a naked, masked reveler tugging on her lead. Two others pushed her from behind. A woman writhed on Geselda's back.

Patreo stood without hesitation. "Stay away from my Geselda!"

Geselda brayed louder at the sound of his voice.

Verduan and Baillot stood and pulled him down but too late.

Everyone turned towards the vats against the wall.

The fires' flickering light showed their faces.

Bassys bellowed, "Take them, Children! Take them as offerings to the Great Ahura Maternus!"

CHAPTER 70

Gaumand quietly ordered his generals to make sure every Baron's man rode beside one of the King's own until their loyalty proved such precautions unnecessary. Taitano and Tardiff rode on either side of the King.

Gaumand rode silently halfway to The Cloisters. "Are the skies always so dark here?"

Tardiff kept his eyes on the road ahead. "We've not had rain for most of the summer, my King. Many of Nant's people fear we are cursed by a witch, Sullya by name. Our crops and our livestock wither. If these clouds last through the day it would be welcome relief to us."

"Nant has a witch? Sullya? My mother told me stories of Sullya the Witch when I was a child."

A general peered through the night and pulled his sword. "Her fame is known in many lands, my King."

Gaumand glanced at the man. "Do you fear her?"

"Not fear, my King. Caution. I am cautious around the unknown, the unexplained. They say knowledge is power. I've never found that so. Understanding is power. Knowing something only allows you to decide if you should go towards or away from it. Understanding, though. Understand something and you can use it to your own advantage, your enemy's disadvantage."

Gaumand chuckled. "Tardiff, can you explain Sullya to my good general?"

"I know nothing of magic or witches, my Lord. A lad in our village, Eric, took her hand with his axe. She cursed him and the girl with him. She disappeared and I've not seen him in a day. A girl's body was found, though, and the two so alike you'd think them born of the same mother. All this since he chopped off the witch's hand." Tardiff looked away.

Gaumand measured him before speaking. "Is there more to this story, Undersheriff?"

Tardiff sniffed the air. "I am nothing more than Nant's bell-man, my Lord. Your flattery is best spent elsewhere."

"I think your tale is left untold."

"The two girls. They were born of the same mother. Twins. The Baron regularly chooses hags from among his servants to bring him young children. I believe his hag bartered one child for her father's good fortune. It was a common deceit on the ignorant."

"Did the child's father prosper?"

"No, my King."

"What did Bassys want young children for? To work in his kitchens?"

Tardiff took his knife from his belt and handed it hilt first to the king. "For a while, then to either serve him in bed or as offerings to some foul god he worships."

Gaumand looked at the knife then back into Tardiff's face.

"And I've known it since I served in his house guard and overheard him talking with some nobles in his court. He bought my silence with a pension to serve Nant as Undersheriff but a bellman is what I be."

Gaumand took Tardiff's knife. "Do you follow Bassys' foul god?"

"No, my King."

"Have you confessed your sin to Mother Church?"

"I held its weight as long as I could, my Lord. But what's happened over the past fortnight made it too great to bear. I confessed my sins before the Cross to Christ."

Gaumand tested the weight of the blade in his hand. "And tell me, has our Lord forgiven you your silence?"

Tardiff nodded.

"We cannot easily see silence in the dark, Undersheriff."

"I believe Our Lord has forgiven me, yes. My faith tells me so. But I am prepared to pay for my silence. You hold my judgement in your hand, and I will not back away from it."

Owls hooted in the distance. A wolf howled and another answered. Nightjars chirped, nightingales sang, and curlews hunted. The riders around Tardiff and King Gaumand made no sounds and kept their mounts' pace a good quiet.

Gaumand raised the blade to make an easy thrust at Tardiff.

Tardiff met the King's gaze. His face showed no fear, only peace.

"It is a brave man or a fool who stares face first at his King."

"Or one who knows his forgiveness is sure."

Gaumand flipped the knife and caught it by the blade, its hilt towards Tardiff. "Then I would be a fool to not honor that forgiveness, wouldn't I, Undersheriff." He held the blade out to Tardiff.

Tardiff took it and put his eyes back on the road ahead. "Thank you, my King."

Gaumand turned to Taitano. "Now, Deputy, what can you tell me of the Baron's doings I don't already know?"

H aasel reached out to Galos' arm. "We are alone, Master Charcoal Burner."

He took her hand and kissed it. "There is still much for me to do, Mistress Potter."

Haasel sniffed the air. "Take me outside, Galos."

"Galos? You call me Galos?" He parted the briarwork. "Is all well?"

Outside she raised her nose and took a series of quick sniffs of the air. "Something is burning."

He demurred. "I am so use to the smell of things smoldering, Haasel, I - "

"No, taste the air. This is not the smell of a charcoal burner's fire. Nor a cooking fire. Nor my kilns nor Zevke's ovens. I've not smelled its like before."

He closed his eyes and inhaled slowly so the night scents could be brought to consciousness, first facing east, then south, then west, and finally north. His eyes opened and he shook his head. "I smell no - "

"What is it?"

Galos faced north, towards Nant. Plumes of orange and black danced among the clouds above the town. "Nant. Someone's set fire to Nant." He held Haasel tight against him. "Promise me you'll stay here and be safe."

"I can make no such promise. I have as much to lose if Nant's gone up in flames as anyone. Take me with you if you go there. If you won't take me with you, I'll find my way on my own. If you'll not go to save our home, then out of my way and never seek me again."

Galos took her hand, laughed, and guided her towards the village. "As I learned long ago, if I cannot stop you I might as well use you."

~

Solas and Abruna rode off the roads for the entire day, their only respite a few moments to relieve themselves and eat. Further, Abruna removed all metal adornments from their saddles and reins. His last act, and one for which he asked forgiveness, was to cut Solas' fine clothing from her and tie what remained into cuffless pants. "We stay off the roads because it is tougher to be seen walking through a forest, and what is difficult to see is difficult to hit," he explained. "Your clothing is fine for your father's court, not for moving quickly and silently in the wild."

Earlier he called her to silence and held their horses still. She looked where he looked but saw nothing. When they moved again, she questioned him.

"It is nothing, my Princess. I am perhaps too cautious."

She nodded as they rode side-by-side. "You carry two crossbows."

"An arbalest this." He lovingly raised the one always near his hand. Returning it, he shifted one from his back to his other hand. "This a crossbow."

"You have bolts fitted to each, Champion Archer."

"You are observant, Princess Solas."

"Wouldn't it be more cautious if you taught me their use? That is why we travel, isn't it?"

Abruna faced her and smiled.

Two riders approached Adi at a gallop and slowed only when it appeared they'd crash his front line.

Queen Danika tightened her grip on her reins. "What is it, Lance Commander?"

"Scouts, my Queen. Sent ahead to fathom the road for us. Stay here until I find out what word they bring us."

Adi raced forward while his troops continued a fast walk. Adi and the riders parlayed but Danika couldn't hear what was said.

Adi returned, the riders turned about and galloped back the way they came.

Danika rose in her saddle and didn't give Adi time to turn his horse about. "Well?"

"It is Nant, my Queen. The village is a'blaze and deserted except for a few wagons gathered in the town's center and the few souls battling the fire."

Danika kicked her horse and took off through Adi's troops. Adi wheeled about, momentarily stunned. "Quick, you fools! After her! Protect the Queen!"

Orel kept Marianne and Ouive close beside him as they rode a quick trot. Ouive fell asleep more than once as they journeyed, and Orel more than once lifted her onto his saddle and rode with her tucked against him. He smiled more than once watching Marianne. "You hold your seat well, Mistress Moria."

Marianne smiled over at him. "I had - " She stopped and quickly turned her head forward.

Color rose in her face and Orel smiled anew. "Yes, Mistress Moria? You had...?"

"Our father made sure we could handle the animals in our care."

Orel turned to observe the mare which had pulled their wagon. It now trotted behind it and whinnied to other horses nearby. "Wise father, he."

Marianne fixed her eyes forward. "Yes, he is. Thank you."

Two men, white robed, black booted, with red sashes and caps, their robes blood stained, staggered out of the woods into the column's path.

Orel called a halt.

The men came forward and spoke. Orel shook his head, not understanding. They spoke again. Orel shook his head. The third time they spoke Persian. Orel nodded, understanding. "Please, Bey, we are all who survive."

A captain leaned in and whispered to Orel in Alanian, "He believes us Mohammedans, my Lord."

Orel whispered back in the same tongue, "Let us humor him at present. He may talk more freely if he thinks us friends."

One of the men drew his sword and held it up. Only the hilt, guard, and finger's length of metal remained. "The Jinn have stolen our weapons through magic."

"You are Jannenites. I thought you invincible."

"We are men like you. Nothing more."

The second man nudged the first and nodded towards Marianne.

"Forgive me, Bey. The woman, she is an infidel?"

"She is not a follower of Mohammed, if that's what you mean."

"Did she travel with a man named Soka?"

Marianne tensed hearing the one word she knew. Ouive's eyes fluttered open. "Are we there yet?"

Orel stroked Ouive's hair. "Shh, Olive. Not yet. I'll wake you when we arrive."

The second man spoke. "They are sisters, those two?"

"So they tell me. What is it to you?"

"Where are they from?"

"We found them lost on a forest road. Where they're from before that, I know not."

The two men stood straighter. "Then by our shared faith, we claim them."

Orel's men came forward. He raised a hand to stand them down. "To what purpose?"

"To meet an oath to Baron Bassys, and to come into this kingdom once he is king."

Marianne leaned into Orel. "What are they saying about Baron Bassys and Soka? I know those names."

Orel kept his eyes on the men and turned his head slightly to address Marianne. "Pray do not speak, Princess. You and your sister are safe with me."

Marianne gasped and her face flushed.

Orel turned back to the Jannenites and smiled slightly. "I did not know Bassys had plans to rule this kingdom. Does King Gaumand know? He may argue with such a claim."

"By our shared faith, Bey, we ask you help us fulfill our oath." The two men stood with their hands on their sword hilts as if prepared for battle.

"You are brave for weaponless warriors."

Their hands fell. "Have mercy on us, Bey, so we may rejoice in heaven."

"I did not know the Jannenites were active this far from home. Are there any others in these lands?"

The first shook his head. "We were in two bands but we joined to expedite our purpose. There are no others this far north."

"No others? Not even passing through?"

"We would know and we know not."

"So you are of the band that assaulted the caravan traveling south of the kingdom on a trade mission? No one survived, nor were any prepared for heaven. We didn't know what became of them until a second trade mission found their bodies rotting on the road, their animals and valuables taken, their clothing stripped from them or left in tatters. Crows and vultures, fox, wolf, and badger feasted before we found them. Only some shreds of their attackers' dress remained to tell the tale."

The Jannenites glanced at each other.

"My cousin led that mission. If not for the marks of honor given him at birth, we would not have recognized his body."

"Bey - "

"If not for the fine silks Jannenites and Jannenites alone wear, we would not know who committed those crimes."

"Bey, we - "

"I will show you the same mercy you and your brothers showed my cousin and those with him." He turned to his men. "Take them into the woods, off the road. Wait 'till we pass. Cover their mouths so they can't scream, then kill them. Do it silently. I would not want our Princesses alarmed."

His soldiers nodded. They covered the Jannenites mouths and carried them into the woods.

Prince Orel, Princesses Marianne and Ouive, and Orel's men quickened their trot towards what lie ahead.

SECTION XII
THE QUEEN

CHAPTER 71

Sweat streamed from Saida's brow. Her body quaked and her clothes stuck to her as she shivered from the poison in her system. Zevke dried her one moment and placed wet towels over her to cool her the next. She babbled about their breads and people's orders, her words making no sense from one moment to the next.

Her eyes opened wide but focused on nothing, unaware of being in the Red Fox or who was around her. "Fire, Zevke. They've found us. They've come for us. They're burning our house again."

Slewe kept Zevke in towels and a ready bucket of water. When not fetching and filling he stayed at Saida's side making sure her convulsions didn't throw her from the table on which they'd placed her.

Zevke dabbed her brow and whispered. "No, my love. No, no, no. No one's come for us. We are all friends here."

He looked up and saw Slewe staring out the Inn's main window. "No, Zevke. Saida knows more than we do. Look."

Across the town square and up the north and east roads,

cottages caught fire. The dry season had turned cottages, roofs, barns, backhouses, sheds, gardens, everything into kindling.

Zevke stood and looked out the window. His eyes went to his wife and back. Saida grabbed his arm, her eyes rolled up in her head. "They know about us, husband. Save us. Save our daughter."

"Help me move her to the floor."

Zevke picked up a bucket of water and emptied it on her. He handed the bucket to Slewe. "Once again, hurry man."

Slewe knocked over chairs in his haste and came back with a second and third bucket filled with water.

"Pour them on her. Saturate her."

"What are we going to do?"

"Save the town."

"Zevke, Malkah! Don't let them take Malkah!"

Slewe frowned from Saida to Zevke. "Who is Malkah?"

"A child we lost. I lost. When we fled a town which did not want us."

"A town not wanting a baker?"

"A town not wanting Jews."

Slewe lifted the empty buckets. "We can't save what's already burning. We'll have to save what's not yet aflame."

They ran out. Zevke, outside, looked through the window. Saida struggled as if gripped by a monster then lay still. "Know I love you, wife."

They ran to the town well, filled their buckets, and threw the water on the buildings just starting to smoke.

Slewe pointed to two figures rushing up the South Road. "Zevke, help is coming."

Galos and Haasel caught them at the well. Haasel stood with her hand on the well. "What can I do?"

Zevke put her hands on the three buckets. "You can keep these full. I will get more."

Slewe stood frozen looking at Galos' Galatian robes. "Are you a demon come to thwart us?"

"What? Oh." Galos removed his mask. "I am a Galatian Knight. Father Verrett asked me to serve Nant in return for his bringing me back to health. What started the fire?" He took part of his scarf and ran it inside his mask, then secured both on his face.

A third figure, female, barely dressed and heavily painted, ran down a lane with firepots banging on her arms and a torch held in one hand.

Galos spoke through his mask and scarf. "Haasel, you can do this? Zevke, Slewe, you will see to her?"

Haasel had already filled two buckets. "I need no one to see for me, Master Charcoal Burner."

Galos ran after the woman and came up behind her as she placed another firepot at a cottage's door. His sword knocked the pot from her hand before she could light it.

She turned, her eyes widened. "You! My mother told me of one such as you. Tell me your name. Tell me what you are."

Galos gave the Galatian sign name without thinking. "Simon."

"It is you!"

Galos held his sword at the ready.

"You don't recognize your own daughter, Simon Knight?"

He lowered his sword slightly. "My daughter? I have no daughter."

"You escaped the fall of Jerusalem wounded. My grandmother took you in, nursed you to health. You slept with her daughter in your fever. Or have you forgotten the sweetness of her meat?"

Galos stepped back. He lowered his sword. "I remember, in my fever, I..."

"Your fevered passion caused my birth, and that sweet child you had, my mother, her mother refused her, kicked her out, would have nothing to do with her when she realized her daughter carried your child."

"I didn't know."

Diana's head rocked back and she laughed. "Didn't know? You ran from her house once the truth was told! Gallant and brave Simon Knight could not bear the cries of the child who carried his child, the screams of the woman now beating her daughter because she rode you 'till she was full!"

"I didn't...I'm sorry. I - "

"My mother and I have wandered the earth ever since. She only told me the full story a night back. But even knowing only a quarter, then a half, I hated you. Hated you!"

"Child, I - "

Diana threw a pot at him. It opened in midflight, its oils soaked his clothing as it flew harmlessly past. She lifted her torch to him. "I am your daughter! I am your end!"

She threw the torch.

He pivoted out of its path. Old instincts and training moved him without thought, his sword arced to ward off the killer blow that often came next. But no such blow came. His sword instead found her heart.

She fell. Her pots fell with her and opened. Their oil moved across the ground like a living thing. It turned first one way then another like a horrid, fluid worm on a quest. The crest of the oil found the torch.

A moment later her body blazed.

Galos removed his Galatian robes and tossed them on the flames. His underclothes were untouched but his robes stank of the firepot mixture. He watched while they caught and burned steadily. Their flames crackled with an almost human voice and rose before him, a fire spirit freed. It waved and rippled whip-like arms.

The fire spirit looked over Galos' shoulder. He tucked himself into a ball and rolled to his left.

~

Where was Bear?

His scent stayed strong but went too many ways.

There was another scent with him.

Buco?

But not Buco any longer.

Nory wiped tears from his eyes. Buco was his friend. He often brought Buco scraps and shared what food he had with him.

And Buco always shared with Nory.

They often ran in the woods and played.

Nobody bothered Nory when he was with Buco.

Sometimes Buco did bad things and Nory took the blame.

He wouldn't let Buco get punished because Buco was Nory's friend.

But not Buco anymore.

And where was Bear?

No matter.

Nory headed back out of the labyrinth. He stopped outside, in the dark, listening to the toads come out of the ground.

The toads. They knew.

Nory shivered.

Nant. It glowed.

A taste of smoke in the air.

But not a cooking fire.

Who blazes so bright a fire without cooking?

Nory left the pigeon and roots for his friend, Bear.

Nory would go see the fire in Nant.

Maybe someone was going to cook something and share a bit with Nory?

Nory would go to Nant.

~

Geselda braced her hooves against the revelers' pushing and pulling. She brayed so loudly it could be heard over the drum. One reveler put his arm around her head and she bit his hand so fiercely he screamed and pulled it back. The Council's bonfires blazed and showed their shadows as some bizarre, multi-headed, multi-armed, throbbing beast.

Baillot and Verduan raised their weapons as naked, masked men and women climbed over the wall, their arms grasping, threatening.

Baillot yelled, "Patreo, behind us."

Verduan swung his sword and opened the nearest. The man's belly fell forward and blood spurted from him, but he still stood and reached for them.

Verduan swung again and took the man's head. As the man's head fell, so did his mask. Underneath, a contorted grin but in a human enough face. The eyes looked up at Verduan for a second then grew blank.

Verduan stepped back. "They are human." A woman, naked and masked as the other, jumped over the wall and reached for him.

Verduan sliced through the woman's arms. She reached for him with her stumps.

Verduan's sword went through her heart. "Men. Men and women, all."

Baillot, his bolts near useless at such short range, swung his arbalist like a hammer. "Then kill them like men and women, for God's sake!"

Two soldiers came up behind them and grabbed Patreo. "Hold or your man dies."

Verduan and Baillot turned to the new threat.

Patreo lifted his hands and smashed a bulb in each man's face. They screamed in unison and released the Tomekan. Their hands went to their faces and came down with smoldering flesh. Patreo picked up one of the soldiers' swords. "I have no further tricks, Brothers. It is fight or die."

They stood with their backs to each other, a triangle of space between them. Two more soldiers came over the wall. The second landed behind the first.

The second bumped into the first, so close it appeared he wished to enter his comrade's body.

Baillot raised his arbalist to do battle. His eyes opened wide as the two men fell. "What?"

A single bolt entered the second man's head, its tip protruding slightly from the first's. "This place may be haunted but at least the ghosts show us good favor."

A second bolt took out two others who jumped the wall together.

Korol moved after Galos, his sword in one hand and his knife in the other. "I have found you, Galatian."

Galos rose, stepped back, and undulated his body and sword but not in Korol's direction. It seemed he battled an invisible foe.

Korol hesitated but kept his sword and knife ready.

Galos spun, his white Damascus steel blade bleeding air with each pass.

Korol caught Galos' face at each turn. The Galatian's eyes remained closed throughout.

Galos ended his movements on one knee in front of Korol, his sword held tip down to the earth. He passed a hand over his forehead, palm inwards, and bowed.

Korol's arms relaxed. He lay his weapons down and performed the countersign; he held his right ear with his fingers and supported his elbow cupped in his other hand.

Galos bowed again and stood.

Korol spoke in his own tongue. "The Sword Dance? Are you a brother masquerading all these years? Is that what you signaled me when you scored my wagon? Tell me you name?"

Galos bowed a third time and spoke in Korol's tongue. "You made the witch's glove? It is how I knew you walked among us. A specific schooling that."

Korol spread his arms to embrace Galos. "Yes. At Baron Bassys' request. That and poisoned both river and wells to make people flee this village so the Baron could make it a haven for his black dealings. If I knew you were here, I would have warned you. But quick, what is your name?"

Galos raised his sword and ran Korol through. "My name is Galos. I am a Galatian Knight who was taught your ways by Mehtar brothers who knew you corrupted Allah's teaching as much as Rome corrupted Christ's." He twisted the blade, pulled it out and thrust it in again. "And while I thank you for your courtesy had you known me here, if I could butcher you for each one of my brethren - Mehtar and Galatian alike - I would."

Abruna whispered to Solas but kept his eyes on the revelers. "Can you move along the branches to that far tree?" He pointed without looking.

"I believe so, yes."

"Good. Two bowmen together are too easy a mark." He handed her a full quiver. "Remember, when you hunt a moving target, the bolt takes time to hit the mark. Aim where they will be when the bolt reaches them, not where they are when you let it loose."

She nodded and determined her path through the upper limbs, which would support her weight and which would not.

He turned her to face him, this time meeting her eye. "And we have few bolts compared to the number we must fell. If you can hold your shot until two enemies are in line, do so, as I did."

"I understand." She prepared her first leap.

He held her back. "And one more thing. We may die before we're done. Your father will not think well of me."

She smiled. "Nor of me for taking his champion archer from him."

"So if I am to be damned by the king, I may as well be damned for all." He pulled her forward, kissed her deeply, then released the startled princess. "Now go. If you're alive after you've spent all your arrows, run. Go back to the horses. Don't worry about me."

She said nothing, only moved off to the tree he indicated.

CHAPTER 72

The Queen's forces entered Nant at a gallop. Zevke and Slewe ran back and forth, their breaths hoarse and ragged, their clothing soaked with sweat as they threw pails and buckets of water on burning buildings.

Adi dismounted and ordered his men. "Bring more water. Help them. Fill your helmets if you have to.

Two swordsmen came up beside Haasel. She held a bucket before her as a staff as they approached. "Easy, good woman. We are with the King's Lancers and here to serve."

She reached out to them.

One stood back and raised his hands as if to ward off an attack. "What gives here?"

The other pulled him forward. "She is blind. Let her feel your standard so she knows your purpose."

Haasel put a hand to each's mantle and tested. "Thank you. We've all the buckets and pails we could find. Do you have more? And the well runs dry. The church has its own well. Can you fill buckets from there?"

Soldiers formed lines between the wells and burning cottages. Others opened doors and grabbed whatever they found which could carry water.

Queen Danika looked about. "If you have no buckets, piss on it!" She dropped her reins, raised her skirts, and ran to help.

Adi intercepted her. "My Queen, the horses' blankets. See if there's enough water to soak them. We can use them to dampen the fires."

Danika hurried to the supply wagons. As she ran past Slewe and Zevke she slowed and looked into their sweat- and soot-streaked faces. "You are men of Nant?"

Slewe and Zevke seemed grateful for a moment not filled with smoke, cinders, and dust. "Aye, Queen Danika."

She stared first at one then the other. "Take yourselves a moment's rest, then direct my men the best you may." She pointed to Adi. "He is Lance Commander Adi. Tell him what must be done." She hurried off to get blankets.

What are all these people doing in Nant?

Is this why there's so many fires?

Grandmother Dire always tells Nory to be careful around fire.

Zevke the Baker and Saida his wife make sure Nory doesn't put his hands in the ovens.

He could get burned.

Haasel the Potter won't let Nory touch her glazings until they're cooled.

Nory sniffed the air.

It doesn't smell like cooking.

Foo!

Everyone's wearing shiny clothing.

Nory's never seen anything like it.

It's pretty.

It reminds Nory of his hammer.

Where is his hammer?

Nory remembers.

Nory will get his hammer and show these people he has shiny things, too.

But right now Nory is hungry.

But Nory can't go where there is fire.

The Red Fox.

It has no fire.

Nory will go there and see if any of these rushing people have food or drink for him.

~

Aldous, Eric, Dire, and Bron stopped where the labyrinth opened to the archway. "Put out your light. Stay back."

He took his arbalest from under his cloak, bent low, approached and peered over the wall.

The bonfires lit the main as if a risen sun.

Five men and a woman, naked and masked, dragged a fighting donkey into The Cloisters' main. A painted and tattooed man wearing a ram's head stood at the altar, his arms lifted as if calling down heaven. A group of people surged over the far end of the archway wall and wrestled three men with limited success. The man at the altar barked an order. "Bring them to the vats! Make them drink! Drown them if they won't!" Everywhere people howled to the sky or writhed on the ground. Many attempted to mate each other, some with success, others without.

A single arbalest bolt dropped the two revelers to the right of Geselda. Another dropped the two on the left, its flight so soon after the other it seemed both loosed at the same moment in time.

The man holding her lead dropped it and backed away from

her. She bucked the woman from her back, kicked out and knocked those behind her down.

A head emerged from the group at the archway's far end. Fists struck him down as he shouted, "Run, Geselda. Run!"

The donkey turned and ran out of The Cloisters and into the forest. The crowd lifted the three over the wall and dragged them to the nearest vat.

Aldous came back to Eric, Dire, and Bron. "Eric, is your friend able to battle?"

"I've not seen it so. He's a gentle soul, and blind, unable to really hurt anyone, except by accident"

Dire snorted. "But his size in the night and carrying another beast's head and legs on his back? He'll scare the soul out of anyone."

"Let him have an accident. Make him groan, grunt, bellow, anything. Get to those three before the vat and set them free. One is your father, I think. Set them free and tell them to get outside The Cloisters. Hurry."

Eric nudged Bron. The great bear stood on his hind legs, his front legs swinging, and he waddled to an archway opening nearest the vat.

"Dire, can you make your way through this crowd unscathed?"

"I'm old. I can act as crazy as anybody. Why?"

"We're about to save Nant and end this farce once and for all. Go, woman, go!"

Another bolt took down a man holding Patreo. A second dropped two men holding Verduan.

Aldous looked into the trees. Where had the bolts come from?

The bonfires' blaze left the wood dark, its fires glistening off already too dry leaves. He reached over the wall and lifted a burning log in a gloved hand. He stood and waved it face height in front of him, his face to the trees.

Bron bellowed and revelers backed away.

A single bolt, a white cloth attached to it, buried itself in the wall beside him.

Aldous nodded and leapt over the wall, arbalest in hand.

Bolts drew down what seemed like half-human, half-beast creatures on all sides of him.

Eric called out, "Father. Baillot. Patreo. Outside, quickly."

Dire turned in circles, each step bringing her nearer The Cloisters' gate.

Eric called out again. "Bear! Come!" Bron followed his voice and raked his talons on any who got in his way.

Aldous took Galos' bulbs from around his neck and strapped them to five bolts' shafts. More revelers fell, sometimes singly, sometimes in twos and threes, as he made his way to within sight of his tinker's cart.

He fired his first bolt. It *thwanged* in the cart's side. A naked man came at him with a sword. A bolt from the trees spun him around and he fell on his own blade.

Aldous fired his second, third, and fourth bolts. Each stuck fast in his tinker's cart.

The ram-headed man ran out the main gate.

More revelers came towards Aldous, their hands outstretched. He used his arbalest like a club and made his way to the bonfire beside the main gate. His last bolt carried the last of his brother's bulbs. He stuck the bolt's head into the fire until the strapping burned.

Weapon to his shoulder, he aimed at his cart, loosed the bolt, and ran. Outside the gate he braced himself against the great stone wall.

A new sun flared inside The Cloisters. Thunder like god's hammer flattened the earth as night turned to day. Leaves blew off trees. Their trunks rocked. Birds took to the air. Deer ran. Fox cried, gathered their young and fled. Boar raced in retreat. Human eyes fell blind, ears deaf.

A lamp of darkness fell and the world went quiet.

The explosion blew the door to the cells off its hinges and down the stairs. Thomas held Julia back. "What was that?"

The light made the hallway bright and showed them the way out. Julia pulled Thomas after her. "Come. It is a sign. My son has ascended to heaven."

They came out of the underground passage to a scene worse than any imagined hell. Bodies, some still burning, others blown apart, lay around them. Fires caught and blazed here and there, then just a quickly went out.

Thomas refused to leave the top of the stairs. "No one has ascended to heaven. This is hell."

Something moved outside the gate. Julia ran.

"Wait, Julia! Stop!"

Prince Orel's men pulled up their horses as the blast lit up the forest and rocked the trees. Orel handed Ouive to one of his men and galloped his horse through those stopped ahead of him. "First rank! Protect the Mistresses! Do it with your lives! The rest, with me."

Two-thirds of his men followed at a gallop. A man riding beside Orel wheeled his horse and pointed. "Prince! A demon!"

A creature, half-man-half-ram, ran out of the woods, crossed their path some lengths ahead, and into the woods on the other side.

Orel raised his sword. "That is no demon. That is a fool wanting to be one." He turned his horse into the wood and followed.

Riders followed.

Those still on the road heard a scream.

~

Gaumand and his men shielded their eyes. Gaumand yelled, "Taitano, is the Baron capable of that?"

Taitano's ears rang but he heard. "No, Sire. Not that I know of."

"I asked you to advise me. What do you advise?"

Taitano looked back over the pale faced men listening on all sides, then back at the King. "A small force. Perhaps five men, ten at most, to scout and report."

"And where will we get five or ten willing men?"

Tardiff nudged his horse forward. "I will go."

Taitano nodded. "As will I."

Gaumand looked at his troops. "Any others willing to let us know what unfolds ahead?"

Yezides came forward.

"No, Yezides. Best you stay with your men. Keep them together. Do you have two you know can be trusted above all?"

Yezides pointed. "Will you men serve the king?"

They came forward.

Gaumand nodded. "Thank you, Yezides. We need at least one more." He lifted his shield from its hook on his saddle. "And now we have one. Let's go."

Taitano blocked his horse. "No, Lord. You are King. This is not your place to be."

"It is exactly my place to be. If such power is in Baron Bassys' hands, I will yield my throne to him and hope to give my daughters and queen time to escape. If it is another's, I hope to make him my friend." He pointed at a rider. "You. If we don't return before sunup, ride to the castle. See my children and wife safe. Understand?"

The man saluted.

CHAPTER 73

Queen Danika carried two armfuls of horse blankets to the town well and stood beside Haasel. "May I wet these, Good Lady?"

Haasel, her face stained and reddened by the heat, cocked her head at the voice. "Who speaks? I don't recognize your voice."

Danika saw Haasel's cataract covered eyes and hesitated. "I am Danika. I serve the King in his castle and travel as aid to these men."

"You've come a long way to help." Haasel reached out to Danika. Danika held the blankets up between them, not letting Haasel feel the fine clothes she wore.

Haasel took the blankets and soaked them in waiting buckets. "It would be good to have a strong woman beside me."

Slewe and Zevke came up. Zevke took the blankets from her. "We can do that. Haasel, rest for god's sake. You'll do no good dying from this inferno."

The sky lit to the south and thunder came through the skies over Nant.

Haasel put a hand to her chest. "What was that?"

Zevke looked at Slewe. "Something far, far away, I hope."

Slewe pointed to the Red Fox. "Queen, if you are willing, there are towels and rags in my kitchen, plus more buckets and pails."

She tore her skirts above the knee and handed the bottom to Haasel. "Wet this and cool yourself, Mistress." She glanced at Slewe to see where he pointed. "Done."

She opened the Red Fox's door and stopped. A misshapen boy, dirt covered and dressed in rags, knelt beside a still woman, his nose to her mouth, and breathed deeply. He moved to her legs, parted them, and repeated the exercise at her anus. She looked around for something to throw at him.

The boy licked the woman's face twice.

"Who are you? What are you doing?"

The boy stood, smiled, waved his hands at her, then ran out the back.

Danika ran back out empty handed. "There is a boy, a creature of some kind, in there with a dead woman. He waved his hands at me then ran out the back."

Zevke lifted soaked blankets from Haasel's hands. "A boy? In rags? Hunchbacked and a misshapen head?"

She nodded at each statement.

Slewe grabbed what blankets Zevke couldn't manage. "That's Nory. He's mute and simple, strange but harmless. He doesn't understand fire, though. He won't hurt you, regardless of what he does. Best bring him to us."

"And the dead woman?"

Zevke hurried off. "My wife, poisoned. Dead."

Queen Danika went back to the inn. She pulled a small crucifix from inside her blouse, kissed it, and placed it in the dead woman's hand.

The hand clasped hers. The woman's eyes opened, rolled about, settled on her and rolled about again. "Malkah? Where is my Malkah?"

~

Nory knew.

Grandmother Dire taught him.

He knew these tastes and smells.

He helped Grandmother Dire when people were sick.

She asked him to hurry and he did.

She asked him to fetch roots and herbs and he did.

She told him he was good and he was.

Nory watched.

He knew what this was.

Grandmother Dire helped another who had these smells and taste before.

Nory watched.

Grandmother Dire would tell Nory what flasks and what pots on what shelf and where in her cellar to bring her.

A woman came in as Nory licked Saida's wound to be sure what the trouble was.

He signed that the woman was Saida, the Baker's wife. Grandmother Dire taught Nory what to do. He would help her.

The woman yelled something at him.

She didn't understand.

Didn't matter.

Nory knew what to do.

He ran out the back of the inn across Byell's field to Dire's cellar.

The pots and flasks were there.

Nory knew how to mix them. He grabbed a bowl and did as Dire did, exactly as she did.

He poured the mixture into a skin. He dribbled some of the flask's contents into another bowl and poured oil on top, stirred for a moment, then grabbed a rag and smeared the greasy mixture on it.

He ran back to the Inn with both in his hands.

Grandmother Dire would be proud.

Nory knew what to do.

The Baker's wife still lay on the floor when he entered. The other woman wasn't there.

Nory knelt beside her, opened her mouth and poured the mixture in. He remembered Grandmother Dire doing so. "Slowly, slowly," she would say so that's what Nory did.

He took the greasy mixture on the rag, opened her wound, and smeared the mixture in until Saida's face bubbled with green pus.

He gave her more to drink and waited.

Saida vomited. Nory rolled her onto her side so her vomit wouldn't enter the wound.

Saida's eyes opened, closed, and she vomited again. Her hand went to her face. "So hot," she whispered. "So hot."

Nory stood and smiled.

He did what Grandmother Dire taught him to do.

Saida would be safe.

Nory smiled.

Zevke the Baker would give Nory a whole loaf of bread for this!

Gaumand, Taitano, and Tardiff together rode down the south road. The two soldiers with them rode one ahead, one behind. The lead man spoke quietly over his shoulder, "My Lord, there is movement in the forest. In the trees. Someone forest trained."

Gaumand nodded. "Keep moving forward. Slow and steady. Tardiff, are there any other villages or people around here? I've not seen a recent census."

"Only The Cloisters, now on our left, and they are normally deserted."

Taitano stared into the trees, into the rustling of the branches in the darkness. "Not tonight or the next two, though. These are the nights Baron Bassys planned his Council to meet."

Gaumand tightened his grip on his reins. "A council now, is it? Well, I shall not give up my kingdom so lightly." He kicked his charger to a trot. The others followed suit.

Two people dropped from the overhead branches on the road ahead. The gloom of night showed only their forms, not who they were. One held an arbalest at his shoulder.

The King's lead man lit a torch.

One of those ahead called out, "Halt, who goes there?"

Gaumand motioned his horse forward. "Who is it orders the King to halt?"

One of the two broke from the other and ran towards him.

The lead man raised his sword. Taitano and Tardiff got beside the king.

"Father!"

Gaumand leaned forward. He grabbed the torch from the lead man. "What? Solas?"

Abruna lowered his weapon and trotted forward. "My Lord the King?"

"Abruna?"

Solas ran around the horses and jumped up into her father's arms.

"Daughter!" King Gaumand held her close, pulled her head to his breast, and wetted her hair with tears. "You disobedient child."

Abruna stopped and knelt before the King. "I have returned your daughter safe, my Lord, but I know I have erred. I accept what is your will."

Gaumand held Solas beside him on his horse. "My will comes later. Report. What happened?"

Abruna explained the best he could, and quickly, from falling for Solas' deception - without placing any guilt on her - to seeing the black robed figure to Bassys fleeing to the explosion itself.

Gaumand listened quietly. He stroked his daughter's hair. Her eyes slowly closed. He kissed her head. "Rest, daughter." His eyes fell again to Abruna. "The black-robed figure, did you see their face?"

"All in the ruins wore masks, my Lord."

"But his mask, it was simply a blackened face, was it not? The others wore animal skins and such?"

"Aye."

"I've heard of such warriors but never seen one. Tell me, did he make it?"

"I believe so but can't be sure."

Gaumand waved up the rear man. "Take my daughter. Abruna, stay here with her. There are troops not far up towards Nant. If we do not return, I ask you see my daughter safe and out of the kingdom, if necessary."

Abruna stood firm and reached for the sleeping Solas. "I will take her, my King." He gave two sharp whistles. Two saddled horses broke from cover and trotted up to him.

Gaumand looked down at his champion archer for a moment, his arms still out and waiting. "Very well." He let Solas slide into the archer's arms.

Julia did not wait for Thomas. She left The Cloisters' main gate and headed through the wood towards Nant. A wheezing to her side stopped her. "Child?"

The wheezing turned into a bray. She followed the sound and

found a donkey lying down, its head caught in some briarwood as it sought to rise. In her mind's eye, a weeping child fell from the sky and merged with the donkey, becoming one.

The donkey whined.

"Poor thing. Mother's here. I'll get you home." She pulled the briars free of the donkey's hair. Her hands bloodied in the process, she wiped them on the animal's side. "There. You're mine now. Come along."

She continued through the woods towards Nant, the donkey by her side.

Nory would show the bright, shiny men he was just like them.

He ran to get his hammer from the tree where it hid.

Had anyone taken it?

No!

The bright, shiny hammer was still his!

He lifted it from the tree and it fell to the ground.

Nory stood. He faced northeast. He shivered.

Not long now, he knew.

Nory would hurry to show the bright, shiny men his hammer.

It glowed as he reached for it again. Nory was so excited the hair on his arms and head lifted.

Oh, this special hammer, it was his!

Nory lifted it with two hands between his legs. He waddled as fast as he could back to Nant.

His magic hammer glowed and shined and was bright!

The bright, shiny men would be so happy to see it!

Aldous stood and shook himself off. His ears rang and bright spots blurred his eyes. Others would suffer the same, as well. He called out, "Verduan? Dire? Eric? Can anyone hear me?"

Voices answered from different parts of the wood. "Here." "Here." "What was that?" "I am blind!"

"Your eyes will clear in a moment. Move east. To the road. It will be quicker."

He arrived first and counted as they staggered through the trees to him. Dire felt her way, Patreo, Verduan, and Baillot helped each other along. Eric and Bron came last.

Dire shook her head to clear it. "Greek Fire, Galatian? I've not seen it's like and would learn its ways."

"Chinese powders. Like Greek Fire except its effect is instantaneous. It doesn't last as the Fire would." He looked to the others. "Are we all well?"

Eric patted Bron's head. "Bear?"

Bron lifted his muzzle and licked Eric's hand. Eric blinked and ran his hand over Bron's back. "We've lost our friend, Bear."

Dire looked to the others, then to Bron. "Your dog?"

"I tied him to Bear's back. He must have fallen when night became day."

Verduan blinked to clear his eyes. "Buco?"

"I'm sorry, father. He helped guide me to you when I thought you lost."

"Was it a good death?"

Bron moaned. Eric wiped a tear from his eye. "He died saving Bear and I."

Verduan rubbed Eric's back. "Then he died well if not easy. We'll come back for him if we survive the night. Lay him to rest as a good lad should be."

Aldous looked into each's face and said nothing as Verduan and Eric shared their loss. His eyes quickly took in the others, stopping only to look hard at Baillot. "Ioan?"

Baillot looked away. "Yes."

Aldous removed his scarf and lifted his mask. "Don't you recognize me, your tutor in the ways of warriorhood?"

Ioan came forward and kneeled before him. "I recognized you from the first, but in my shame, hoped to remain hidden and run again lest you see me shamed."

Aldous raised him up. "If you are all well, I must head back to Nant. I have unfinished business there. I could use a good man by my side."

Ioan's face brightened. "I am yours."

Aldous and Ioan took off at a trot. The rest followed at a walk.

CHAPTER 74

Orel let go the reins, lifted his bow, and fitted an arrow. The ram-headed man ran through the forest along a clear path.

Orel called out, "Let no man be in front of me."

He loosed the arrow.

The ram-headed man spun and fell.

"Bring him to me."

His men gathered the ram-headed man and followed Orel back to the road.

"Bring me a torch. Let's see a demon who bleeds." Orel's arrow went through the man's shoulder. He pulled the mask from the man's face.

The man stood tall and groaned. "Release me. I am Baron Bassys and am under the protection of the King."

Orel raised his eyebrows and nodded. "Oh? I did not know I was in the presence of one so worthy." He drew his sword, skewered the ram's head mask, and lifted it. "Do all the King's barons dress so formidably?"

Bassys eyed Orel's men. "Hear me. Do you want lands? Power? Your own place in a new kingdom by my side?"

Orel and a few others laughed. "A grand offer, except only I and a few others speak your language. To prevent any from straying. You understand."

Bassys focused on Orel. "I will give you half my kingdom to set me free."

Marianne and Ouive moved their horses up behind Orel. "Mistresses Moria and Olive, do you know this man? I think he means to take your father's - I mean King Gaumand's - kingdom. What do commoners think of such a thing?"

Marianne whispered, "Kill him."

Ouive spoke loudly. "He had us kidnapped! Kill him."

Orel looked up at Marianne and smiled. "Odd a baron in the kingdom would kidnap a serf's children." He looked back to Bassys. "But no matter. We bring him to the King. If all is right, he should be ahead of us, perhaps a day or two's march, and we will meet him." He kept his eyes on Bassys but spoke to his men. "Find any who treated with him. Kill them all." His eyes went back to Marianne and Ouive. "I don't think the King will mind, do you, Mistress Moria, Mistress Olive?"

They shook their heads in unison.

Bassys stood tall. "If we are to travel, give me a horse."

Orel laughed. "Put him in chains and let him walk."

Saida's fever broke as quickly as it came. Her eyes fluttered open and stung as sweat entered them. Blinking, she looked about. "The Red Fox?" The sounds of the inferno, the cracking of timbers, voices yelling, the smell of smoke, all swam around her.

Her hand fell into her own vomit as she pushed herself up.

"What filth is this?" She rose, staggered, and fell into a chair. "I am weak."

Danika came back for more rags. She stopped when she saw Saida sitting at a table. "You live? We thought you dead. Or is this place haunted."

Saida stared at the Queen.

"Do you have speech, woman? Do you need something?"

"Who are you?"

"A simple woman, nothing more."

Saida blinked at Danika's finery. "No simple woman wears clothes such as those."

Danika moved past her. "I have no time right now."

Saida reached out and took her hand. "Tell me your name."

Danika pulled her hand free. "I have work to do."

Saida took it a second time but held it gently. "I thought it a dream. Malkah? You are Malkah?"

A memory came unbidden to the Queen. The woman's voice. The feel of the hand on hers. The eyes, so like the Queen's own when she peered into a reflecting glass. "Do I know you?"

Saida's eyes flooded. She whispered, "Malkah."

The Queen's chin quivered and her lips tightened. Her eyes closed as one memory led to another. When they opened, tears flowed like heavy rain. She knelt before Saida and rested her head in the old woman's lap. "Mother." Danika sobbed so deeply her body shook. "Mother. I have searched so long for you."

Adi ordered his men, "Remove your armor. It collects the heat. You'll die from it faster than any sword strike." He pointed to the far side of the village center. "Pile them there, away from the fire, away from the homes, but waste no water on them, save that for the flames."

Galos, already wearing nothing but his underclothes, joined in without anyone noticing.

Zevke threw his bucket down and sat down roughly beside it. His fingers clawed through the blowing dirt. "There is no more water. The wells have run dry."

Adi called forth again. "Do your last, then back with the Queen. We leave Nant now."

Slewe came up beside the Baker. He frowned over Zevke's head. "Nory?"

Zevke turned.

Nory waddled into the village. Something reflected the blazing light as it swayed between his legs.

Zevke rose. "He doesn't understand. Save him."

Nory waddled as fast as he could into the village.

The men!

They weren't bright and shiny anymore.

All their bright, shininess lay in a pile on the far side of Nant's center. They ran about. All the cottages were covered in pretty fire.

Everything, so bright and shiny.

Nory would show them his bright, shiny hammer.

He climbed the pile of armor. His hammer glowed brighter. The hair on his arms stood tall like trees in the forest. The hair on his head crackled and sparked like Nory's friends the fireflies in the night.

Nory got to the top.

He stood tall and proud.

He would show them his hammer.

It glowed so brightly.

He struggled but he lifted it high over his head.

A bolt of lightning cleared the sky over Nant's center as it arced its way down. Thunder pealed like a thousand church bells and knocked all standing to the ground. The horses, away from the heat, away from the flames, tied to trees in the dark, snorted, their eyes wide, their heads thrown back, pulled on their reins to escape the beast rolling before them.

The hammer's handle smoked where Nory stood.

Before anyone rose, a wind like leviathan shrieking blew the flames from what burned. Soldiers tumbled over each other. Rain came in sheets so thick it seemed dark cloth snapped about. A second lightning bolt struck the circus wagons and stage. They exploded from the oils and camphors Circe and Diana spread before their performance.

Adi rose first and crossed himself. It seemed the Elementals of Earth, Air, Fire, and Water battled in the town of Nant.

"Take shelter! Everyone, take shelter. Get the horses under cover. See to the Queen."

~

Zevke rose to all fours, shook his head, and looked about. It seemed bodies lay everywhere. Some rose slowly and staggered about. Slewe lay with his body surrounding Haasel as if a mother protected her young.

Zevke got to his feet. He leaned against the well. "Saida!" He ran to the Red Fox.

He gazed through the inn's window and slowed. Saida sat in a chair, not dead. She stroked Queen Danika's hair. The Queen's head rested in Saida's lap and the Queen herself sat on the floor, her arms around Saida's knees.

He entered, afraid to disrupt what he saw before him. He whispered, "Saida?"

"Zevke, our Malkah. Our little Malkah." She stroked the Queen's hair and kissed it again and again.

Danika looked up. "You are my father?"

Zevke stumbled over to them and knelt beside the Queen. "Malkah?"

"Yes, father?"

"How can this be?"

Saida looked up at him as tears streaked her face. "What does it matter now? Our little Malkah is returned to us."

Danika took her arms from Saida and pulled Zevke to her. "Yes. What does it matter? I have found you both."

Zevke held back no longer. "Malkah." He blubbered like a child lost and suddenly found, only able to repeat her name. "Malkah. Malkah."

Orel's men pushed Bassys ahead of them, now all rain-soaked, their clothes on them like second skins. Orel rode with a careful eye on his prisoner. He let his horse fall back to where Marianne and Ouive rode. "I hope to meet the King soon. I have much to tell him. More to offer him, perhaps."

Marianne kept her eyes forward. "Do you plan to ask for a reward?"

"Will I ask? No. Will I accept if one is offered? I would be a fool not to, don't you think?"

A forward rider motioned for a stop. "People in the road, Prince."

"I did not know these roads so busy. Let us see who we may entertain."

They continued until five figures could be made out. "Four travelers and a beast, Prince."

"Announce us. See what they do."

Another rider yelled in first one language then another, "Hail, Travelers. Will you join us or will we pass?"

Another flash of lightning revealed faces.

Bassys ran forward until his chains tripped him and he fell. He stared up at Dire. "Sullya! Work a spell on these fools! Free me!"

Patreo turned to Verduan. "She's Sullya the Witch?"

Dire waited until Bassys rose. She kicked him in the groin so hard his breath left him. He fell and rolled, knees tucked up, on the ground.

Verduan watched. "I didn't think so, but I didn't think she could deliver such a blow."

Dire kicked Bassys in the side. "Your grandfather took my older sister. What did he offer her that she gave up the healing ways?"

The arrow still protruded from Bassys' shoulder. It snapped in half, each half still buried in him, as he fought to get away.

Dire held part of the arrow and moved it about. Bassys wailed. "What did he offer her?"

Bassys' nostrils flared as he fought back the pain. "To be his mistress, to rule in his castle."

Dire twisted the arrow and Bassys screamed. "How did she become Sullya the witch?"

"He tired of her and gave her to some Mohammedan traders on their way home. After that I do not know."

Dire kicked him in the face. "Your grandfather's betraying blood runs true, I see."

Orel came among them. "Please, dear woman, Grandmother, I need him for King Gaumand. Perhaps, if there's anything left when the Good King is done, you can have him."

Dire spit on Bassys.

"Are you traveling to Nant, good people? If so, may I offer our wagon? It will be faster and we may journey together."

Tardiff spoke over the wind-driven rain. "Runners approaching, Lord."

Gaumand shook his head. "I never knew I had such lands in my kingdom. The sky lights and rocks the earth over ruins long unused, the Thunderer wakens behind us in what I always thought a quiet village, now I can't travel with friends without interruptions." He addressed the forward rider. "See what they're about."

The rider escorted Aldous and Ioan to the king.

Gaumand's eyes took in the Galatian and he chuckled. "I've heard of your kind, never thought to meet one. Tell me, Good Knight, do you serve the king?"

Aldous shook his head. "No, my King. I serve the Queen."

"That is good to hear. My journey started questing to find her. What do you know of her?"

"The Queen is in Nant."

"What is my Queen doing in Nant?"

"I sent her there, my Lord."

"We just came from Nant. She wasn't there."

"I suspect you came with many and had to take a warrior's route. She had fewer men. If you chose her escort wisely, he would have taken a more wooded route."

Gaumand smiled. "It's good to know what I've heard of the Galatians is true. Tell me, what was her purpose in Nant?"

"To find her mother and father."

Ioan turned back the way they came. "Riders, Aldous. Many. At a trot."

Gaumand looked to his men. The lead man nodded.

Taitano drew his sword. "I suggest we take to the woods, Sire."

Gaumand shook his head. Riders already appeared, their shapes masked and unmasked by the rain. "It is too late for that. If we can see them, they can see us. Perhaps they'll let us dry ourselves before we die."

A single rider galloped to them. He wiped his eyes, dismounted, and held his sword up to Gaumand as he shouted over his shoulder.

A second rider galloped forward. "King Gaumand? It is Prince Orel. I've brought you gifts." He called his troops forward.

"Tell me, Alan Prince, was it you who turned night into day?"

Orel laughed. "Well, my King, if it was, certainly I wouldn't tell you."

Gaumand laughed in return. "You serve your father well. What gifts do you bring me? It was your last, the *Setāreyāb*, that brought you here and may have saved my kingdom. What better gifts can you bring?"

Orel signaled his men. A rider came forward. Bassys, chained and bloodied, his face swelling, staggered behind him.

Gaumand frowned and cocked his head. "What manner of creature is this? Certainly it is no one of royal blood, not in my kingdom."

Bassys fell to his knees. "I beg mercy of the Church, my King. Mercy of God Our Father, please."

Orel laughed. "You beg the Christian mercy but you did not ask for Allah's? You demean us both, Baron."

Two more riders came forward. Blankets covered them and dripped rain to the ground. Two voices called out. The first said simply, "Father!" The second, "I'm hungry. I want to go home."

"Marianne? Ouive? Why do you ride with the Prince?"

Orel's hand lightly slapped his cheek. "The Princesses Marianne and Ouive? I'm shocked! Shocked, I tell you."

Ouive kicked her horse to her father. "It was Soka. You remember Soka? He was mother's houseman. He kidnapped us, Father. He put us in barrels filled with pig's offal."

Gaumand lifted his youngest daughter to his own saddle. "Oh, my. How frightening that must have been."

"I wasn't frightened, Father. I helped Marianne kill him, then I pissed on his head."

Gaumand laughed. The others showed various signs of amusement and amazement. "Marianne, you know I believe every word your sister says."

"It is true, Father. All of it. Except we'd been in barrels and when opened, I didn't know where we were so kept to the road in the hope of finding shelter."

The King nodded at Orel. "And it seems you have." His eyes fell full on the Alanian. "You traveled well and safe, then?"

Marianne motioned her horse beside Prince Orel. "As if under your own guard."

Orel shrugged and smiled.

Gaumand looked at Tardiff. "Whether bewitched or no, it seems Nant has much magic about it."

Ouive tugged on her father's beard. "When are we going home, Father?"

"Soon, child. First we must head north a bit to gather your mother. Is that acceptable to you?"

"I would like that, Father."

Orel motioned to Bassys. "What of him, my King?"

Gaumand considered. "Galatian, would you see this child safely to the Queen?"

Aldous mounted Ouive's horse and gathered the child. "Do you have a mount for my Brother-Knight, Ioan?"

Orel spoke up. "He can have mine. Perhaps Princess Marianne will let me share hers."

Gaumand muttered, "Magic," as horses took new riders, then more loudly. "Daughter, someday you'll be queen. Observe and learn."

Gaumand dismounted and drew his sword. Lightning cracked overhead and thunder shook rain from the trees.

"Stand, Baron. I do not fear the man who stands before me with a sword, I fear the man who swears his allegiance and comes at me with a dagger from behind." He looked at his daughter. "Show mercy to those who show mercy, to those who benefit one who can't benefit them. They should walk the earth. All others should burn. Do not let your heart alone decide these things. Add a heavy helping of your head."

Bassys' head turned heavenward. "Ahura Maternus take you all!"

Gaumand swung his sword. Bassys' head rolled on the ground. The mouth opened, closed, opened again, and quickly filled with mud.

CHAPTER 75

The King and all with him rode into Nant at a trot. Adi saluted and Gaumand drew him near. "Where is Queen Danika?"

Adi, soaked, bloodied, his hands and face blistered, sighed. "In truth, my Lord, I do not know, but not far."

Gaumand tossed Adi his reins and leapt from his horse. "Danika! My Queen!"

Marianne and Ouive joined him. "Mother!" "Momma!" "Mother!"

Solas alone saw movement through the Red Fox's window and ran to it. "Here, Father. Here."

Gaumand moved through the door as if it had no hinges and reached to free her from Zevke and Saida arms. "Danika. Are you alright?"

She looked up with tear filled eyes. "I've found them, Husband. My mother and father. I found them."

Aldous came in behind him. "Have I fulfilled my mission, my Queen?"

She stood and embraced Aldous. "Yes, my faithful knight. For all the years you watched over me, rest."

Gaumand looked at Aldous. "What does she mean, for all the years you watched over her?" He took Danika to him. "What secrets have you kept from me, Queen?"

She wiped tears from her eyes. "Worry not, Husband. You are my first and forever my only. This knight saved me when I was a child."

Zevke rose and stood beside Saida, still in her chair. "What?"

Aldous removed his scarf and mask. "I chanced through a village long ago, drawn by the sounds of a riot. I saw you packing as villagers approached, torches burning. They closed on the child and would have trampled her, so I took her into my arms and ran to keep her safe." He removed and threw down his robe and cowl. "Many broke away and came after me claiming the girl I carried was a devil child. I took her to a convent where I knew the Sisters would care for her and came by when I could to see her well. The only one I told was the convent's confessor. He knew the girl's story."

Danika nodded to Saida and Zevke. "Father Verrett. He told me my history but did not know your names."

Aldous removed his weapons and lay them on his robe. "And when a new Baker and his wife came to Nant, he got word to me."

King Gaumand sat alone at a table. "And when I passed the convent returning from battle with my surviving men, weary and hungered, to confess what had transpired in battle." He reached out to Danika. "You took care of me. I fell in love the moment you came through my door with food and wine. I couldn't even ask you after my men, my heart beat so strongly for you I could not bear for you to leave." The King, as Danika came to him, also wept.

Solas came up to Zevke and Saida. "Grandmother? Grandfather? I am your daughter's daughter, Solas."

~

Galos put an ear to Haasel's nose and lips, and a hand over her heart. "It still beats. You still live."

Her eyes fluttered open. "I must see to my pots."

Galos kissed her hands, face, and finally her lips. "Not now, my love. Not now."

She nudged his hand away from her breast. "Galos? Galos! Master Charcoal Burner! You take liberties."

"I pray I do not."

She guided his hand back and he lifted her to her feet.

King Gaumand came out of the Red Fox with Danika at his side. "Daughters! Marianne, Ouive! Come, you have grandparents to meet."

Marianne stayed in the saddle with Orel a moment longer. Ouive pouted. "I'm hungry. I want to go home."

Aldous exited the inn next, saw his brother with Haasel, and signaled Ioan to join them.

Patreo came over as well. "You were knights in the Holy Land?"

Galos looked at his brother and nodded. "Yes. Galatians. Warrior-Priests, Knights of the Old Order," he answered.

"Did you know many men in the Crusades?"

"Many, yes. Certainly not all."

"Perhaps you knew my father, and what became of him? He joined on a march with my uncle. I never knew them. They left before I was born."

"What were their names?"

"My mother never told me their names. I only know them from her stories and their books."

"They were scholars?"

"*Apothēkē*, along the order of Melchizedek. They knew the old ways as well as the new. I studied their books to learn more of them."

Galos looked at Aldous again but was silent.

Aldous' hands reached for the well wall. "Your uncle and father studied these books together? They were from the same village?"

"Yes. My mother always hoped one or both would return and she would know their fate."

"What was your mother's name? What village saw your birth?"

"Catrina was my mother's name. She passed shortly after she saw me installed in my Order. I pray the Lord to keep her. As for my home, I doubt you'd know the village of my birth."

Aldous' hands quivered on the well wall. "Meya? Were you born in Meya?"

Patreo searched the Galatian's face. "Yes. Do you know it?"

Aldous slid down the well's side until he sat on the ground. "I have found two sons in one day. One by blood, the other by honor."

Gaumand saw his wife's savior and protector weeping and dried his own eyes. "Magic, yes. Magic." He waved to Adi. "Are there rooms here where the men can be quartered and the horses cared for? We have had much for one day. We would see all rested before our talks continue."

Nant returned to life late in the afternoon. The sun opened the skies, and the clouds became wisps pushed by the winds. The wells, once barren, now topped off and dripped down their sides. By twos and threes those who remained ventured from borrowed homes and cottages.

Eric, Bron, Aldous, Ioan, Verduan, and Patreo woke and stretched as they rose from Verduan's floor.

Verduan tapped Eric's shoulder. "We must tend to our animals, Eric. Come. The bear must come with you."

"You will not hurt him, will you, Father?"

"That depends greatly on the bear."

They entered the barn and Geselda stuck her head out of her stall. She brayed them welcome. Verduan stroked the donkey's head. "Ah, Patreo will be glad of you, girl."

Hay stirred in the stall. He raised a shovel. Julia stood. "Julia? We thought you dead!"

She brushed hair and dirt from her soiled clothes and hair. "How did I come here?"

Patreo came at the sound of Geselda's voice. He put his arms around her neck. "Oh, my girl. I worried for you so."

Verduan called back to his cottage. "Another straggler is found."

Aldous called from inside. "Who now?"

"Julia. Byell and Idee's daughter."

Ioan pushed his mentor aside and ran to the barn, past Eric who stood mute by Geselda's stall as Ioan took Julia in his arms and she didn't resist.

She cried into his shoulder as he gathered her to him.

"Julia, why sorrow. We are together again."

"Our child," she sputtered. "Our child has not survived."

He lifted her head and looked into her eyes. "What child?"

"A son. A tiny thing. When I thought all was lost and I wandered alone in the dark. The child knew he was conceived in sin and left me."

Eric quietly left. He patted Bron's massive head. The two walked off into the fields.

SECTION XIII
DIRE

CHAPTER 76

Dire sat in her cellar, torches lit on the walls around her, making entries in her books. Now and again she stirred a pot filled with carrots, celery, and a freshly killed and cleaned rabbit.

A grunt sounded outside her briar covered entry. A moment later she heard a voice. "Bear, where are you going? Bear, stop."

A massive head poked through the briar.

"Bear, what trouble have you gotten into?"

Dire cleared the vines away. "Eric and his friend. Come in. Are you hungry?"

"The bear eats what he will. I have not eaten since yesterday. Perhaps the day before. I don't know anymore."

Bron waddled directly to her cooking pot. "Hold your friend back. He will burn himself."

Eric pushed the great bear aside. Dire spooned a thin layer from the pot into a pan, fanned it cool, and put it down in front of the bear. "Let him eat."

Bron slobbered and rasped his tongue around the pan.

"I am hungry, too, Grandmother."

"Did you know Nory is gone. He carried the tinker's hammer, I'm told, and the skies took him."

"I did not know."

"I have no one to help me."

"I have hands and am willing to work."

She turned back to her books. "I have no bread and all my spoons are used for things your tongue shouldn't touch."

"At least Bear is fed."

"I have no one to learn from me, to keep my knowledge once I go."

"I will learn, Grandmother."

She turned back to him.

"There is a crazy man living in the labyrinth - the tunnels under The Cloisters and much of Nant - now. He used to be Julia's brother, Thomas."

"Perhaps we can restore his mind to him."

She once again turned to her books.

"Yes. Perhaps."

CHAPTER 77

King Gaumand rose to his saddle. Queen Danika and his daughters sat their horses beside him. "Father Patreo, it seems Nant needs a new priest."

"I will have to ask Mother Church for a transfer."

"To Hell with Mother Church. There are many faiths to choose from. Whichever one you go with, keep it holy."

"Yes, my King."

"And non-threatening save those who would take what is mine from me."

Patreo chuckled. "Yes, my King."

"What of the Galatians?"

"Aldous learns to be a charcoal burner from his brother, Galos. Galos is learning a new trade, pottery. Ioan and Julia...Ioan and Julia will be my first service if not my second."

Gaumand ordered Yezides and his men to rebuild Nant and, if they wished, prosper there.

The rest of his forces, along with Orel's, headed for his castle. "Let's keep it at a walk, shall we?"

No one argued.

It took six days at the walk.

His first order was to make chambers available for Zevke and Saida. He summoned his counselors to him. "And find me a rebbe for them. Someone good with children. I'll have him teach Ouive, as well."

His second order was for a reception in his great hall the following night.

In the midst of the celebration, seated on his throne with Queen Danika beside him, he held up his hand for silence. The musicians stilled their instruments, the kitchen staff stopped their replenishings.

"Lance Commander Adi."

Adi, his wife with him, came forward. "Yes, my King?"

Gaumand took Danika's hand. "You have served me well, Lance Commander. What reward can I offer you?"

"A quiet retirement, my King?"

Gaumand shook his head. "No, that I cannot do. I'm sorry." He raised his hand again and Prince Orel stepped out from the crowd. "Prince Orel, will the Emperor's court accept Lance Commander Adi as ambassador in the hopes that all remains well between our kingdoms?"

Orel smiled. "Surely, the Emperor will, my King."

Adi sighed, smiled, and introduced his wife to Prince Orel.

King Gaumand gazed through his gathered nobles and staff. "Where is my Champion Archer?"

Abruna, who'd been by himself all evening, eaten little and danced less, approached King Gaumand and knelt before him.

"You have brought my daughter to me safe."

"But - "

Gaumand stared him into quick silence. "I have a barony in need of a baron."

Abruna looked around. All eyes moved from him to the King to others standing in the great hall. Whispers rose and fell like breaths on wings.

King Gaumand nodded to a counselor carrying a scroll on a red and gold pillow. Gaumand lifted his ceremonial sword from its scabbard by his throne. "Come forward."

"My King?"

"Come forward, man. I'm not going to take your head."

The Queen hid a smile. Laughter chittered through the hall.

"In the name of Saint Peter, Saint Michael, and Saint John, rise Abruna Nole, Baron of the eastern province from the southern borders to the eastern lands and along the River Vell to Nant."

Abruna rose, startled by the applause around him.

"Now, Baron Nole. My daughter tells me you took liberties with her beyond teaching her the ways of the bow."

Abruna stepped back. "My King, I - "

"And you were not wise enough to see her plan before you were lost to it."

Abruna hung his head. "Yes, Sire. All that you say is true."

"Daughter Solas. He has wronged you and us as well. What punishment befits him?"

"I will marry him, my King."

Abruna raised his head. His eyes were wide, his face was flushed.

"I suspected that would be your punishment for him. It's a good thing he's nobility now." He looked at Abruna. "My wedding gift to you shall be a thousand barrels of ale and a thousand barrels of wine. I suspect you'll need them."

Solas put her arm through Abruna's and guided him back into the crowd followed by well wishes and cheers.

"Taitano and Tardiff. To me."

They rose.

"Taitano, we need a new sheriff, but not one for each part of our kingdom. We wish a single sheriff, a High Sheriff, to watch over all to make sure justice is done evenly throughout. Will you be my Lord High Sheriff?"

Taitano bowed. "Thank you, my Lord."

"Tardiff, such a sheriff will need a strong deputy by his side to advise him. We ask you to be that man."

"With honor, my King."

Gaumand sat back in his throne and turned to Queen Danika. "Good. All is done. Let the merriments continue."

Prince Orel stood out from the crowd. "King Gaumand?"

Gaumand rolled his eyes. "A problem with the ambassador already? Can the King have a moment's peace?"

"I have a request, my King?"

"You wish another ambassador?"

"I wish the Princess Marianne to wife."

Gaumand turned again to Danika. "Thank goodness Ouive is too young to wed."

Ouive's nurse wiped confections from around the princess' mouth. "I will have you and mother all to myself then, Father, won't I?"

King Gaumand nodded and smiled. He whispered to the Queen, "I'm so glad you found her grandparents, my love. So glad."

CHAPTER 78

Eric visited Dire's grave daily. Bron, whose name he learned from the Circus people's ledgers, slept beside her and he dribbled honey on the great bear's grave each day, as well.

He'd gathered all the learnings from Aldous and Galos, what Ioan could remember, and grew to love Julia more even though he knew she would never be his.

Before Patreo received his official orders making Nant his own bishopric - provided he never approach Rome again - he and his father made one last trip to Tomeka and gathered all of his things to bring them to Nant. From Patreo, he learned what he could.

He learned to read the strange, old writings on The Cloisters' walls and the purpose of the underground labyrinth. In the Old Ways, people went to The Lower World to discover themselves, to find themselves, to learn their gifts and return to help others. Thomas, he could never help, and Eric's once-friend haunted the labyrinth the rest of his days.

In the books he gathered, he learned many priests mixed old and new beliefs, rituals and ceremonies, often worshipping the Old Faith and the new simultaneously.

But not anymore.

He did what he could to keep the Old Ways alive. It was easier in the woodlands, along the old paths, in the hidden villages.

And he learned the difference between religion, true religion, and magic, or what some called magic; religions demonstrate worship. Magic seeks to control. He noted in his journals, "Gods only have the power people allow them. Doesn't matter if they're light or dark, old or new."

He counted Patreo only next to Dire as his greatest teacher, and together they periodically tested for any white lead remnants and found none.

He remembered always Patreo's last teaching. "Holy Mother Church, any church, remember always they aren't gods, they are men, men who want to be gods but know they can't achieve it. It is the frustration between desire and reality that makes some act as they do."

-end-

LEAVE A REVIEW!

COMING SOON

The Book of the Wounded Healers

Ben Matthews and his son, Jiminy, are enjoying some bonding time together at New York City's South Street Seaport watching jugglers and other buskers on a warm late summer day, eating fried dough covered in brown sugar and cinnamon, and getting to know each other.

Suddenly the East River and beyond because a vast desert. A warm wind blows sand in people's faces. In the distance, three creatures walk towards the City.

Havoc ensues. People run, carts are overturned, mounted police work at crowd control to no avail, and Ben loses Jiminy in the chaos.

Ben grabs the leg of a mounted officer asking for help and is knocked down as the horse turns.

The three creatures walk up to him, stop, and peer down. The one in front says, "We are Healers from the Land of Barass." It points to the one on his right. "He is Cetaf, who cries for his own pain." It turns to the one on his left. "This is Jenreel, who tends to his own needs. I am Beriah. I will tell you how I feel. We are Healers from the Land of Barass."

About Northern Lights Publishing

Northern Lights Publishing/Press is an association of five professionals (one graphic artist, one marketer, one editor/book designer, one copyeditor, one editor/educator/author) and a rotating group of ten published authors and poets all of whom are passionate readers. Financial backing is provided by a small group of investors led by Susan and Joseph Carrabis through the NextStage Evolution Corporation. Everyone receives remuneration and owns an equal share of the company with the exception of Susan and Joseph Carrabis.

We're developing our publishing/marketing model so we're not accepting submissions at present.

We'll open our doors to submissions (and announce it through various social networks) once we're sure we can break even and preferably turn a profit. Until then, wish us well.

It's an exciting journey and one we'd love to share, but only after we're sure we can successfully navigate the publishing seas.

Join Northern Lights Publishing's Journey
http://nlb.pub/JoinNorthernLights

About the Author

Joseph Carrabis told stories to anyone who would listen starting in childhood, wrote his first stories in gradeschool, and started getting paid for his writing in 1978. His work history includes periods as a long-haul trucker, apprentice butcher, apprentice coffee buyer/broker, lumberjack, Cold Regions researcher, mathematician, semanticist, semioticist, physicist, educator, Chief Data Scientist, Chief Research Scientist, and Chief Research Officer. He was an original member of the NYAS/UN's Scientists Without Borders program and held patents covering mathematics, anthropology, neuroscience, and linguistics. After patenting a technology he created in his basement and creating an international company, he retired from corporate life. Now he spends his time writing fiction based on his experiences. His work appears regularly in anthologies and his own novels. You can often find him playing with his dog, Boo, and snuggling with his wife, Susan.

You can follow Joseph on BookBub, Facebook, Goodreads, Instagram, LinkedIn, Pinterest, or Twitter.

Become a member of Joseph's blog - http://nlb.pub/JoinJoseph

9 798987 804889